VANTAGE
POINT

VANTAGE POINT

A MacNEICE MYSTERY

SCOTT THORNLEY

SPIDERLINE

Published in Canada in 2018 and the USA in 2018 by House of Anansi Press Inc.
www.houseofanansi.com

House of Anansi Press is committed to protecting our natural environment.
As part of our efforts, the interior of this book is printed on paper that contains
100% post-consumer recycled fibres, is acid-free, and is processed chlorine-free.

22 21 20 19 18   1 2 3 4 5

Library and Archives Canada Cataloguing in Publication
Thornley, Scott, author
Vantage point / Scott Thornley.

A MacNeice mystery
Issued in print and electronic formats.
ISBN 978-1-4870-0332-6 (softcover). —ISBN 978-1-4870-0333-3 (EPUB). —
ISBN 978-1-4870-0334-0 (Kindle)

I. Title.

PS8639.H66V36 2018   C813'.6   C2018-900495-9
                                               C2018-900496-7

Library of Congress Control Number: 2018931767

Book design: Alysia Shewchuk

 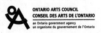

*We acknowledge for their financial support of our publishing program the Canada
Council for the Arts, the Ontario Arts Council, and the Government of Canada.*

Printed and bound in Canada

MIX
Paper from
responsible sources
FSC® C004071

For SBT
The fire in your heart
contintues to reveal
the light within.

When you turn the corner
And you run into yourself
Then you know that you have turned
All the corners that are left

— Langston Hughes, "Final Curve"

[PROLOGUE]

FATHER HOWARD TERRY WAS JUST BEGINNING TO NOD OFF WHEN A rapid burst of amber shards raced along the living room ceiling and slashed across the bookcase. Irritated, he closed his dog-eared copy of *King Solomon's Mines* and waited for it to stop.

A minute later he heard the heavy thump of a truck door closing, followed by footsteps on the stairs and three sharp raps of the door knocker. He placed the book on a side table and checked his watch — 9:48 p.m., an odd time to be making calls. His body was tucked deep into the armchair, and Terry struggled to hoist himself to his feet. He walked on stiff legs to the door.

His son called from upstairs. "You got that, Dad?"

Looking through the bevelled glass of the window, Terry saw the reflective X glowing brightly on the back of a man

1

in an orange traffic vest. Splinters of light ricocheted off the side of his hard hat. Hearing the *clunk* of a deadbolt, the man swung around and peered through yellow-tinted wraparound safety glasses.

Howard Terry opened the door. "Can I help you, young man?"

"Dundurn Hydro, sir. Is this . . ." He paused, withdrawing a notebook from his side pocket. ". . . the Matthew Terry residence?"

His son, halfway down the stairs, called out, "I'm Matthew Terry. This is my dad, Father Terry. Is there a problem?"

The man informed him that power surges were being experienced in the area because of the recent rainfall. If it was okay with them, he was there to check their electrical panel. The Duke Street relay station was indicating that their house was the source of the surges.

"At best, sir, it's a reset. Worst, we'll have to replace your meter." He hoisted a large orange nylon bag over his shoulder and picked up a metal toolbox before stepping inside.

Father Terry closed the door behind him and, out of habit, turned the latch. "Looks like serious work, son."

Stepping past him, the man said, "This stuff? Naw, it's all for show." He sat down on the bench near the door, opened the bag, and retrieved two clear plastic bags. He put them over his boots before standing again. "Don't want to mess up your floor."

Father Terry appreciated the care he was taking. "You're working overtime, then?"

"No, just my shift."

"Can I offer you coffee or tea, perhaps, when you're finished?"

Matthew Terry was impatient and didn't mind showing it. "Dad, he's probably got a lot —"

The man interrupted him. "You're right, I do have a lot to do. But I'd be grateful for a coffee." He picked up his gear and followed Matthew to the basement door. Looking back, he added, "Black, with a spoonful of sugar." He smiled at the old man and disappeared down the stairs.

Father Terry went through to the kitchen and turned on the coffeemaker and then the kettle for tea. He took three cups from the cupboard, though he was certain his son would decline. Matthew never had empathy for those he referred to sneeringly as "common people." He'd likely excuse himself the moment they emerged from the basement.

As the coffee brewed, Terry wondered what had made his son such a bitter man. He smiled sadly at his own grey reflection in the window above the sink, certain that he was staring at the reason. How it had happened, and when, was lost on him. Matthew had seemed a sour soul from the beginning. He shared his mother's temperament, along with her assessment that his father was a weakling and a failure. Terry found that hard to dispute. He dropped a chamomile teabag into his mug and reached for the kettle.

Suddenly the kitchen went dark. Moments later, Terry heard two muffled pops from the basement — faulty fuses, he guessed. Apart from the strobe effect of intermittent orange shards, Terry was in total darkness. He turned to feel his way to the door and was halfway there, hands out-stretched, when the power was restored and light once again filled the kitchen.

[1]

"DO YOU KNOW WHY YOU'RE HERE?"
MacNeice smiled and took a deep breath. The sheer curtains covering the open windows behind Dr. Audrey Sumner billowed casually, sending pale grey shadows of the mullions dancing across the fabric. He would have been happy to spend the hour watching them move, ideally with something mellow from Miles for a soundtrack. Though Sumner exuded patience, she was waiting for a response. He wondered if she might wait through the entire session.

MacNeice took another breath. "The last two cases were very hard on my team . . . hard on me." A blue jay called from the garden, so loud and sharp it might have been inside the room. He looked at her and smiled. It was a good omen, he thought, as he searched the shadows for a flash of wing between the sun and the sheers. "Beyond the physical trauma, I think it's reasonable for Wallace to question what psychological damage might have occurred during my time in Homicide."

She didn't miss a beat. "And do you have an opinion on that?"

Of course he did. MacNeice knew that his dreams weren't normal. Flying beside a talking bird wasn't normal. And he was also having conversations with Kate, who'd been dead for years. He wasn't speaking out loud, but in his mind he'd speak to her and she'd respond. He also suspected that his consumption of grappa as a sleep aid had increased to the point where the distinction between want and need was blurring.

"Leaving aside that I'm unqualified to answer that, I can say that I'm developing a theory. It goes something like this . . ."

Sumner put down her pen, folded her hands, and looked over her glasses at him. He couldn't tell if she was amused, intrigued, or both. He told her about cops he'd known who dealt with homicide fatigue by putting in time at the firing range, hammering round after round into paper targets. Others turned to drink, punched holes in walls, or fought constantly with their wives or husbands. Few ever volunteered to go into therapy.

"I haven't done any of those things — a few glasses of grappa being the exception."

"True," Sumner said softly. "But you moved on to the next case very quickly." Referring to her notes, she added, "Two bodies pulled from the bay. Another explodes in Gage

Park, and that one led to the discovery of his young wife. He'd tortured and buried her in a basement. Following that, you nearly drowned trying to save her son." She smiled briefly and again waited patiently.

He returned the smile but didn't take the bait. "Here's my theory. I talk to my wife, who died ten years ago. For a long time I'd dream that she was somewhere near but just out of reach. Those were cold-sweat nightmares." MacNeice put his right hand to his temple, as if shading his eyes from a bright light. "Now I'm having quiet conversations with Kate in my head."

He looked over to see if Sumner's eyes had widened, if she was smiling or appeared concerned, and was greeted only by the gaze of a committed listener. "I believe on some level that she's there and that I'm not talking to myself. In those conversations, I shed or siphon off the violence and bloodshed of my job so that I can work another day." He wanted to stop talking about it before he convinced himself he was crazy. "That's it. That's my theory. My conclusion? I don't have PTSD because I've got someone I can talk to at any time. And I can say anything to her."

He was expecting Sumner to lecture him on the dangers of magical thinking, but she didn't. She smiled and picked up her pen, then waited, sensing that he wasn't done.

As a detective, MacNeice understood the power of dead air — the vacuum that begs to be filled by speaking. Throwing caution to the wind, he continued. "It's not just with Kate. It's worse. I can look at a bird, or a coyote, and if they look back at me, as they often do, I can imagine a conversation with them. Meaningful stuff, where I actually feel

I'm being coached by a higher being." An uncharacteristic grin crept across his face as he heard his own words.

"Do you have these conversations in the heat of the moment?" Sumner asked.

"No. In that moment I'm focused on what's in front of me. I see things — a tic, a worn sleeve, a torn carpet, a tightening of the jaw, a flicker of nerves around the eyes or mouth."

The list could have gone on. It could have included how Sumner picked up her pen with the index fingers and thumbs of both hands to lay it slowly on the desk. He suspected that the tiny ritual served as a pause, like engaging the clutch before selecting a gear. He also noticed that she was too disciplined to be caught glancing at her cellphone when it lit up with a message. And he spotted traces of hand cream shining on the windowsill behind her chair, suggesting that she stood there to enjoy her garden or to unravel a tangled thought.

When she laid her hands palms down on the desk, he studied her fingers. They were straight and elegant, but sturdy like a gardener's. Her fingernails were trimmed close and free of nail polish. She raised the fingers of both hands slightly. He assumed the gesture was meant either to suggest that he refocus his attention or to make a point.

"While Deputy Chief Wallace holds you in the highest regard, Detective Superintendent MacNeice, he is nonetheless concerned about your health. Therefore these sessions are indeed mandatory, but he wanted me to assure you that they are compassionate and not punitive in intent."

MacNeice's eyebrows snapped upward and his attention returned to Sumner's face. Her words weren't remotely like

Wallace's, but he smiled and accepted that it was her interpretation of what he had said. "I understand. Thank you."

"Are you currently in a relationship, Detective MacNeice?"

"No."

[2]

THE NEXT MORNING, AS THE SUN CRESTED THE MOUNTAIN, MACNEICE left his stone cottage. Originally the gatehouse for an estate long since gone, it was nestled among the trees below the escarpment, the only destination on a lonely road. He climbed into the Chevy and headed for the hill Kate had referred to as "a pretty woman's bottom." The trip was long overdue. Before she died, MacNeice had made a solemn vow to visit her grave every month, but he hadn't been there since December, more than four months ago. That broken promise filled him with guilt. Kate might have known it would happen; she had chosen the site because it would force MacNeice to leave both Dundurn and the Homicide Division to be with her.

Driving north to choose the plot, Kate had been reclining

in the passenger seat, propped up with pillows. MacNeice remembered how she had whispered through the pain that it would be okay if he eventually stopped coming to see her. She'd meant it. He had recoiled at the idea but said nothing. Instead, he'd reached over and held her hand until she drifted back to sleep.

As he turned onto the narrow road, MacNeice caught the reflection of the fresh spring canopy on the car's hood and the sparkle of sunlight through the leaves. He had to drive slowly where the road had heaved up during the winter, and he welcomed the distraction of sunlight and the riot of a new season. He was happy to stop thinking about Kate's final days.

At the intersection with the highway, MacNeice reached over to the glovebox to retrieve a CD from his collection. Sonny Criss's *Saturday Morning*. He'd never heard a better soundtrack for the beginning of a long drive, and it was Saturday. He slid the disc into the player and waited for it to begin, before joining the northbound traffic.

He had yet to turn on his cell, but MacNeice decided to check in with Division before leaving town. It had been quiet in Homicide for several weeks, giving his team a much-needed break. But that might be too much of a good thing. Swetsky had summed it up best: "Folks round here better start killing each other soon, or we're gonna have homicide cops doing traffic control."

THE CLEANING LADY called it in just after eight a.m. She'd opened the door to silence — no morning talk radio from the kitchen, no "Good morning, Luisa" from Father Terry.

Keys in hand, she stood on the threshold listening for the sound of the shower or the creaking of floorboards upstairs. "Hello. It's Luisa," she called. It had been three days since her last visit, and she hadn't been told that the Terrys were going away. Concerned that she may have misunderstood or forgotten, she stepped inside and eased the door shut behind her.

With her next breath, Luisa was caught short by a terrible smell. Had something gotten inside and died? As her eyes adjusted to the dim light of the foyer, she noticed the bloody tracks on the hardwood floor leading from the basement door to the kitchen, and from there upstairs to the second floor. Luisa covered her mouth and nose with her scarf and quickly moved outside, quietly closing the door.

Within minutes two patrol cars had arrived at the scene, parking on the street on either side of the driveway. Two uniforms circled the house, checking for signs of a break-in, while the others tried to calm a very distraught cleaning lady.

Homicide detectives Michael Vertesi and Fiza Aziz arrived shortly afterwards. As they walked up the driveway, Vertesi took in the black Mercedes. "Nice wheels." Aziz led Luisa to their car while Vertesi spoke with the uniforms and organized a perimeter to protect the fresh tire tracks in the driveway.

MACNEICE STOOD AT the Terrys' door, putting on gloves and a mask and plastic covers over his shoes. Aziz was in the doorway to the kitchen, feet astride a large bloody footprint, taking photographs of a folded cloth on the table. "Just in time, Mac. We've got two dead by gunshots in the master bedroom — Father Howard Terry and his son Matthew — but it's not as simple as you'd think. It looks like the son was shot in the basement and then moved upstairs." She pointed to the blood trail. "From the dried blood and the smell, it's been at least a couple of days."

Vertesi appeared on the second-floor landing, lifting his mask. "So far, boss, it doesn't look like anything was taken. Wallet, cash, keys to the Mercedes — all here. But like Fiza says, it's pretty strange. The footprints come up from the basement, where there's a big puddle of blood near the electrical panel. Looks like the killer carried the body from there."

MacNeice stepped over the footprint and made his way into the kitchen. He smiled wearily at Aziz, but his attention was drawn to a large bloody handprint on the doorframe.

Aziz was looking at something in the kitchen. "That cloth — it's not a tea towel or a facecloth — was left neatly folded on the table. The killer used it to mop up the blood. Though from the look of things, he wasn't very thorough."

"Maybe he knew the cleaning lady was coming," Vertesi said.

"Not now, Michael," said MacNeice, studying the hand-print. He opened his own hand next to it, noting that the bloodied one was larger. The fingers were spread wide, like those he'd seen in the prehistoric caves of France, though they'd been tiny compared to this one.

"He likely worked alone. There's no sign of other foot or handprints." Aziz took her pen and pointed to a crease line in the handprint. "He was wearing gloves."

The carafe from the coffeemaker was on the stove, a

teabag in a saucer, and two empty mugs in the sink. Another mug, clean, sat on the counter. Two glasses were on the table. Both contained water, one almost empty.

From the cleaning lady, they'd learned that Howard Terry was a retired priest and his son, Michael, a successful businessman. For six years Luisa had come to the house twice a week. "She calls it beautiful," said Fiza, "but all I see is a depressing pile of grey stone, with every room sinking in dark oak wainscoting."

A century ago the Terry home would have been considered luxurious and elegant, but now it was just a remnant of another time, a fading reminder of old-money Dundurn. Whatever lustre its interior had once held was dulled with age, and the exterior offered little hope of relief.

"Those tall cedar hedges and evergreens outside don't help. They make it what the Scots would call dour." Fiza turned to face MacNeice. "I thought you were headed up north today."

"I was. I'll go up later, possibly in a few days. Show me what you've got here."

ON THE HARDWOOD of the second-floor landing, a well-defined bloody boot print stood out. Studying it, MacNeice could see fold lines in the print that suggested the killer had worn plastic bags over his feet. He wondered why, since they didn't obscure the sharp definition of the sole's tread.

Vertesi was watching. "New work boots, size eleven or twelve. The killer doesn't care if we identify them; he just doesn't want to clean them."

Stepping around pools of congealed blood, MacNeice

stood by the bedroom window to survey the scene. His eyes landed on Matthew Terry's body. "Interesting," he said quietly to himself. If he was murdered in the basement, he hadn't just fallen out of bed on the second floor. And yet, it looked as if Matthew Terry had slid off the bed, like a drunk startled awake in the night, taking with it the grey duvet now stretched taut under his butt. His head, turned slightly to the right, had dropped awkwardly to his sternum in a position that would have made breathing difficult — had he been breathing. A nightcap had slid back from his forehead and was held in place by the duvet. An overturned armchair lay wedged between the bed and his left shoulder. His legs splayed outward past the hem of his blood-soaked nightshirt.

Vertesi pointed to the young man's bloodied chest. "There aren't any bullet holes through the son's nightshirt, but Father Terry took two through his. Guessing from the blood near the doorway, he was shot there and then dragged over here."

Father Terry lay on his back in a blood-and-urine-stained nightshirt, near the overturned chair. His eyes were wide open and his mouth agape, as if he were about to say something.

Aziz joined MacNeice at the window. "The old man must have put on that nightshirt before he was killed — or he was forced to." She shook her head, adding, "I can't believe either of them actually owned these things. They're very heavy, rough cotton; you'd suffocate in them."

Protruding from under Matthew's body was a doll in a tiny white T-shirt. Its soft plastic head had been split open to reveal blood-red cotton wadding spilling over its blonde curls onto the plush white broadloom, where it merged with the real blood from Matthew's chest. One of the doll's glassy blue eyes gleamed above its puckered smile. It appeared blissfully unaware of the gaping wound in its head.

In the shadows to the left, a female mannequin lay on its back, wearing a nightshirt that matched those worn by the Terrys. Its streamlined, featureless feet were mere inches away from Matthew. Like the doll, its pouty face appeared unperturbed by the knots of red cotton gore gushing from the twin holes in its chest.

The bed's blue-striped pillow sagged like a bloated sausage over the edge of the mattress. The same bloody boot prints they'd found elsewhere were scuffed about on the white carpet, suggesting that the killer had worked hard to arrange the bodies. Something about that didn't make sense to MacNeice. Matthew Terry, a man of medium height, perhaps 160 pounds, had been carried from the basement, not dragged up the stairs. It was clear to MacNeice that his weight hadn't been an issue. The killer had carefully arranged the bodies, but for what purpose?

"Who wears a nightshirt and a nightcap in the twenty-first century?" asked Aziz, tugging her latex gloves on tighter.

"These two guys." Vertesi glanced down at the younger man. "And that mannequin. It's like a religious order. Everyone's in sackcloth."

Aziz turned her attention to the bed. "And this bedding also looks out of time, like something you'd use if you didn't have central heating and it wasn't spring."

ON THE CARPET, a few feet away from the bodies, was a small brass letter V. It looked new. There weren't any other letters, or anything from which a brass V could have been removed. In fact, nothing about the room — the paintings, the furnishings, the Inuit soapstone carving perched on a stately dresser — suggested that the Terrys were interested in one-inch brass letters.

MacNeice was squatting over the letter, trying to get a closer look, when Vertesi asked, "What's with that V, you think? Is the killer trying to send us a message? Victims, vengeance, Volvo . . ."

"Venality, violation, vanquished . . ." Aziz was looking at the doll. "And then there's the baby doll and that shop mannequin." She gestured to the figure in the shadows.

"Maybe V's for a name."

"A name? Perhaps, but not theirs. I think the doll and mannequin complete a tableau — like theatre." MacNeice scanned the scene. "They're all actors playing parts. We're supposed to name the play."

MacNeice took out his digital camera and began photographing the V on the floor. He asked Aziz and Vertesi to step aside so he could take horizontal and vertical shots of the bodies and the room. Looking at the images on playback, MacNeice became even more convinced that the letter's placement was intentional. "I think the killer is telling us the best place to stand to view the murder scene. Like tourist vantage points at Niagara Falls or the Grand Canyon."

Looking through the images on the small screen, MacNeice had a vague sense that he'd encountered the scene before. It was like a shadow passing by on the periphery of one's sight, so quickly that it leaves you wondering if it was there at all. Not enough of a thought to seize and hold, but too much to let go.

Vertesi straddled Father Terry's body and lifted the open collar of the nightshirt with his pen to examine the entry wounds. With a sucking sound, the cloth surrendered and gave way. "Nine millimetre, I'd guess. Small burn circumference — the muzzle of the weapon must have been close. He was probably using a silencer." He stood up and turned. "But why not leave him over there in the doorway? Why move him here?"

"Exactitude. He was put there for effect. He'd be out of place over there," MacNeice said, pointing to the door.

"Like this is a scene of a crime scene? He's matching this to something he's seen or done before?" Vertesi's tone was respectful but incredulous.

"Possibly."

[3]

AT EIGHTY-THREE, WITH ALL HIS ACHES AND PAINS AND A MALIGNANT tumour growing at the base of his skull, Father Howard Terry would have prayed for an end to his suffering, had he still believed in the power of prayer. He wasn't a priest any longer; if anything, "Father" was just a ceremonial title now. The members of his flock had long since died — leaving him standing over their gravesites — or had quietly abandoned his fledgling breakaway church.

Father Terry's New Catholic Congregation was positioned to the left of the Church of England and to the extreme left of Roman Catholicism. Terry called it "God's home for liberal-minded Catholics." What that meant in practice was a complete absence of Latin liturgy, statuary, grand Gothic arches, a high altar, stained-glass windows, a building fund, great fonts for holy water, a choir loft, and an imported organ. There wasn't a need for the last two because Father Terry felt the only instrument required was "God's choir" — his congregation. At a time when every penny was being counted, the elimination of these Vatican trappings had also reduced his costs. This frugality might have left the impression that Father Howard Terry had a strong grasp of the financial realities of religion. He did not. In fact, he didn't have a clue. However, his wife, Harriet, who didn't give a fig about God but was nonetheless happy to accept the status that came with being a priest's wife, did care a great deal about money, and she guided Terry in all aspects of its deployment.

Although he was ordained as an Anglican priest, Terry's faith had been slowly eroding for years. Even after he broke with the Church of England and established his New Catholic Congregation, he had found it harder and harder to summon the fire to convince anyone of his mission, least of all himself. Terry had never renounced his faith. It was much simpler than that — it had just evaporated.

He'd kept the doors open for thirty-one years, slowly burning through the inheritance his father had left him. In his last decade, the only joy he took from his duties was the summer camp he ran for inner-city boys out on Long Point, Lake Erie — two groups of twelve, each at camp for a month. Leaving the smoke and smells of Dundurn behind and seeing the boys live free had made it all seem worthwhile.

More than once he'd wondered, as men do in old age, what path he would have followed if he could do life all over again. When he was his campers' age, Terry had wanted to be an explorer. His father, an Anglican bishop, had persuaded him to follow another path, one he said would offer more certainty and spiritual reward. However, Terry wasn't willing to forgo completely his dreams of adventure. They were fuelled and sustained by two books that he returned to time and time again: *Arabian Sands* and *Desert, Marsh, and Mountain: The World of a Nomad*, both by Wilfred Thesiger.

Terry longed to follow in Thesiger's footsteps to the "Empty Quarter" — an enormous swath of desert in south-eastern Saudi Arabia. Had he done the research, he would have discovered that much of what Thesiger described no longer existed. On some level Terry had suspected as much, but he preferred to keep faith with Thesiger until the end. That dreams are untethered from the cold, dark stare of reality is surely their true value.

TWO DAYS AFTER his sixty-third birthday, Father Terry took off his clerical collar, folded his cassock, vestments, and ceremonial robes, and dropped them into a large cardboard box. He placed his black Canterbury cap on top gently, with some reverence, like a man returning a baby robin to its nest. He surveyed the few things he wanted to keep: the heavy Bible he'd been given by his father following his ordination, and the silver Communion chalice, which he put in a white plastic bag. The Communion wafer box, two silverplate collection bowls, two ornate gold candlesticks, and a cross bearing Jesus, rendered in alabaster, he placed in their own box. Someone from St. Thomas Anglican Church would come by to collect them. Then he nodded half-heartedly towards the altar and left, closing the painted plywood doors for the last time.

Once outside, as if the weight of the chalice was too much for him, he placed it on the curbside and walked to his car. As he drove away, it sat like a tiny trophy of failure, glittering in the sun as the plastic bag sagged shamelessly down its silver stem.

Eight months later, Terry sold the church building and property for development; he never inquired about what became of the pews, altar, chairs, or his heavy oak desk. A year after that, giving in to his wife's demands, he sold the thirty-acre beachfront camp property on Lake Erie. That was the cruellest cut.

The Terrys moved to Mount Hope and never went to church again. He made several attempts at writing a memoir, but each found its way into the trash. Though life continued to unfold in glorious ways, it did so only in his head, a part of his anatomy he quietly referred to as his own Empty Quarter.

Years later, Terry's son Matthew was a successful lawyer and investor and engaged to be married. As he and his bride were both agnostic, they could have had a civil wedding, but they chose to be married in a Unitarian church. Matthew did so not because he gave a damn about faith; he was clever enough to spot that hypocrisy in his father. For Matthew, it was a business decision — a conclusion borne out by the guest list and the number of luxury cars in the parking lot.

They didn't see much of their son after that, as Matthew's law practice and investments seemed to consume all of his time. On the few occasions when the younger couple came to the house, it wasn't for Harriet's home cooking or affection; it was out of obligation. Even before he pulled into the driveway, it seemed that Matthew regretted the impulse to visit. Those awkward get-togethers ended when, six months later, Harriet sat up in her bed and then fell back, dead of a heart attack.

As far as Howard Terry could tell, Matthew's marriage mirrored his own, never rising to the level of love and affection. It ended in divorce after just four years. Following that, months would go by without so much as a phone call. So it had come as a surprise when Matthew invited Terry to move back to Dundurn. "It's a big house and I've got a cleaning lady," he'd said. "You and I will have our own spaces. I don't want to worry about you keeling over up there, left for dead on the mountain."

Who could resist such an invitation?

[4]

VERTESI LOOKED OUT OF THE MASTER BEDROOM WINDOW TO SEE
the orange-clad haz-mat team walking along the narrow
passage between the driveway and a towering cedar hedge.
Each was carrying a backpack and a black metal case.
"Forensics is here, boss."

MacNeice scanned the scene one last time. "Fiza, I'd like
you to lead the interview with Luisa. We'll do it back at
Division."

"With no forced entry, do you think the killer might have
been known to the family?" Vertesi asked.

"Possibly, but it could just as easily have been someone
with a delivery," Fiza said.

"Someone with a lot of gear. The nightshirts, pillows
and duvet, the mannequin and doll . . ." MacNeice stepped

over the bloody threshold to the landing. "And wearing size-twelve boots." He picked up a silver-framed photograph of Matthew Terry from a table on the landing and passed it to Vertesi. "See if you can find one of Father Terry as well. We'll release them at the news conference."

Three members of the forensics team were making their way up the stairs. MacNeice stepped aside. "Michael, take two of the uniforms and start a thorough house-to-house. Let's see what the neighbours know."

As he left the house, Mary Richardson, Dundurn's chief coroner, was approaching, running a hand lightly along the yellow tape. "Hello to you, Mac. Two males, dead of gunshots — correct?"

"Correct. Though, as you'll see, it's complicated."

"It was ever thus, Detective. Good to see you. Tio Pepe awaits." A breeze caught her silver hair as she passed by, obscuring the smile he knew was there, before she disappeared inside.

MacNeice knew that Tio Pepe would take the edge off viewing what Richardson's assistant, Junior, referred to as an M&M, or "meat on metal." Though he preferred grappa to sherry, it was mostly tea and digestive biscuits with Mary. A somewhat austere woman in her sixties, the chief coroner carried herself like a British aristocrat — if that aristocrat had a sharp, black sense of humour that often led to brilliant insights. For so many reasons, MacNeice was always on his toes with Richardson.

The black Mercedes beeped. MacNeice swung around to see a young woman in a haz-mat suit emerge, holding the keys and a metal case.

Two more units had arrived to block off Amelia Street

and redirect traffic. As he made his way around them, MacNeice's cellphone rang. Before answering, he turned back to the forensics team member. "These tracks in the driveway look wider than a sedan. Get all you can from them."

He looked at the call display. "MacNeice."

"Wallace. You up north, Mac?"

"No, I'm on Amelia. Double homicide." It seemed as if everyone in the division knew he was going to visit Kate's grave. "I'm just heading in to interview the cleaning lady who was first on the scene. We'll also announce a press conference."

"Good. Let's get ahead of this one. I don't know Matthew Terry, but I'm told he's fairly wealthy and his father's a minister."

"A retired priest."

"Yeah, okay. It's a double homicide in a neighbourhood full of doctors and lawyers. This kind of thing makes them very nervous." Wallace didn't need to say more.

MacNeice put the cell back in his pocket and looked around as Aziz came down the front steps. "Mac, I was wondering what had happened to the clothes those men were wearing. They weren't in the bedroom with the bodies, so I went looking for them. I found them in the old man's bedroom closet, neatly stacked as if the cleaning lady had been. The men's pant pockets hadn't been emptied; folding money, coins, and tissues were still in them. The rest of the clothes were crisply folded and in more or less the same order: Matthew's pants, socks, T-shirt, and sweater — all bloody, of course — and pants, socks, undershirt, shirt, and cardigan for Father Terry."

"What do you make of that?" MacNeice asked.

"Honestly, my first thought was that our man must work in clothing retail, hospitality, or a laundry."

"Unlikely."

"Maybe he's just neat." She smiled. "Give me the keys. I'll get Luisa settled in your car."

MacNeice stopped on the sidewalk to study a dusty tire track. There were slashes and small chunks out of the tire's well-worn surface. They were as unique as a thumbprint and suggested a utility vehicle or something you'd find in the construction and renovation trades. He snapped a photo.

WEEKS BEFORE, WHEN THE RAIN FINALLY STOPPED, IT WAS AS IF every living thing in Dundurn had been forgiven a dreadful sin. Each morning, steam rose from waterlogged lawns, pavement, and sidewalks. After a week had passed, teens in T-shirts and tank tops were strutting stuff not seen since the previous fall. And no one could find a plumber. They had been dealing with all the flooding, clogged drains, and sewage-filled basements, making their money the hard way. Within days of it being over, people assumed they'd all gone on vacation to someplace where it never rains.

Next in the line of exhausted services were the funeral parlours. There were several funerals a day now — three-month-old bodies taken out of refrigeration, eased into their coffins, and sent off to the cemetery, where the water table had at last receded enough to lower them safely into the ground. While many of the families had been frustrated by the delay, the story of Wally Ecclestone was enough to keep them quiet.

Walter "Wally" Ecclestone, a retired insurance salesman from Dundurn, had been buried in mid-March, when the rains were still falling. His family gathered under black funeral-home umbrellas as Wally's coffin was slowly lowered. Bright green Astroturf surrounded the graveside, hiding the soil that would cover Wally for eternity. Despite the rain, it was a dignified and solemn end befitting the gold-star salesman, husband, father, and grandfather.

As the family said their final farewells, dropping roses or small handfuls of earth into the grave, the coffin moved slightly. Those who noticed thought it was just settling onto the bottom. But, slowly and unsteadily, it began to rise. Wally's widow collapsed in horror and would have dropped on top of the casket but for a steadying hand. Wally's grandchildren began screaming and crying. Wally's son turned away and vomited, sending several of Wally's arthritic colleagues staggering into one another. A pimply-faced sixteen-year-old pointed at the coffin — now ascending quickly — and hollered, "Holy shit! Granddad's a zombie!"

The cemetery attendants were stunned. The priest was speechless. And Wally kept rising, the space between his coffin and the mud walls filling with gurgling brown water. "It appeared," a relative said later, "that the priest and the family suddenly realized they were about to be swept away by whatever was gushing out of the grave."

The water rose over the edge of the grave, washing away the Astroturf and forcing anyone who hadn't already retreated to hop awkwardly through the surf until they reached the road. With the funeral's mood and solemnity unambiguously dashed, Wally's friends and family scattered to their cars. The gushing eventually subsided, but the water in the grave did not. The attendants stood, jaws dropped, as the coffin tipped like a torpedoed freighter and sank head first beneath the surface with a loud extended belch. One of the attendants, a veteran, stood to attention and saluted.

It didn't take long for the story to spread. Wally's golfing buddies made cracks about whether Wally had had the foresight to insure against having to be buried twice. But all agreed that being stripped, rewashed, recoiffed, resuited, and stored in an industrial cooler until the weather changed was no laughing matter.

[6]

SHE APPEARED UPSET, BUT FIFTY-NINE-YEAR-OLD LUISA ROCA nonetheless sat erect in her neutral-toned blouse, sweater, and slacks. On the way to Division, she had described this as the worst morning of her life, barely able to get out a sentence without sobbing. But once they were settled in the interview room, she calmed down after MacNeice brought her a glass of water. She thanked him and sipped from it several times.

Aziz waited for another minute or so before pushing the button on the recorder. "Tell us about the Terrys."

Luisa shook her head slowly. "I knew Father Terry was dying. He told me last year about the brain tumour." She swallowed hard, looking down at her glass. "But he didn't let it get him down."

Twice a week, after she'd put the laundry in the machine, Luisa would sit with Father Terry to enjoy a cup of tea in the kitchen. They'd talk about her children, who were both married, and how excited she was at the thought of becoming a grandmother. "Father Terry seemed excited for me, even though he'd never met my kids."

As a devout Catholic, Luisa would occasionally ask him about his faith, and even invited him once to Mass at her church. "He smiled, but he never came. I asked him if he still believed. I remember he said, 'I still believe in dreams.'"

Concerning Matthew, she was less sanguine. Her relationship with him was strictly business. He never asked about her or her family. He wanted a cleaning lady, not a friend. She understood that and it wasn't an issue.

"Can you tell us anything about his friends?" Aziz asked.

"No." She looked from Aziz to MacNeice. "I never saw anyone at the house and he never spoke of friends."

"What about female friends?"

"No, though Father Terry once told me Matthew was dating someone. I don't think it worked out."

"And she never visited the house?"

"Not when I was there. Father Terry said he'd seen them together at the Starbucks near the library. Matthew was with a young woman and he said it didn't look like business."

She'd never seen Father Terry and Matthew talking together. Nor had she seen a photo of the old man anywhere in the house. She'd asked Father Terry why that was, but he just smiled and shrugged his shoulders.

Most days, Matthew was gone before she arrived. He left her cheque on the radiator in the front hall, usually with specific requests and clothes folded on the nearby chair: iron this shirt, take this suit to the dry cleaner, store these golf clubs in the basement.

Luisa knew nothing about Matthew's business but assumed from things his father had said over tea that he was no longer practising law. He was managing his investments. "I didn't know what that meant, so I asked, 'Is that work?' Father Terry laughed and said, 'Well, my dear, he manages money to make more money.'"

"Did you sort the mail when it arrived, Luisa?" asked Aziz.

"Yes."

"Letters for Father Terry and Matthew, bills, and so on — you'd separate those?"

"Yes, though Father Terry didn't get much mail. Just a few Christmas cards from his congregation. Matthew wanted the bills in one pile and his letters in another."

Aziz nodded. "So you'd read the senders' names."

"Yes."

"Try, if you can, to recall some of those names. For example, there'd be services like telephone and gas, or heating oil, electricity, tax bills. Were there any business or personal letters that stood out?"

Luisa was uncomfortable with the question. "I don't snoop, Detective."

"I don't doubt that. But just as you'd notice a vase out of place or something that wasn't on a table the last time you cleaned, the same is true of an envelope. A company's name or logo, someone's handwriting, something you'd never seen before . . . can you think of anything?"

"I'll try." She lowered her head, gazing at her hands, which lay flat on the table. A minute or so passed before she looked up. "There was one letter. I remember it because of the name on the envelope: Nancy Pretty. I thought that was funny because the envelope was such a pretty cream colour. It was addressed to Matthew in fancy handwriting."

MacNeice glanced at the clock; he had eight minutes before his briefing in Wallace's office. "I apologize, Luisa, but I need to leave for another meeting. Detective Inspector Aziz will continue with you. If there's anything else you recall . . ." He shook her hand, picked up his notebook, and stepped outside.

[7]

WITH A WIDE GRIN, THE WORKMAN SLAPPED THE KITCHEN DOOR-frame. "Now, how about that coffee?" His voice was upbeat, cheerful. He removed his helmet and safety glasses, pulled off his latex gloves, and put them on the table. "Mind if I sit down, Father Terry?"

"Of course not, son. I'll be right there." He was pouring water over his teabag. "What do I call you, young man?"

"You can call me William, sir." He sat down at the table and began using a work cloth to wipe the blood from his face and the reflective tape of his vest. He was casual about it, neither rushed nor particularly thorough. As Terry approached with the mugs, William folded the cloth and set it next to his helmet. He took a sip of coffee and nodded his approval to Father Terry before putting the mug down. "Can I tell you a story?"

Father Terry realized that he hadn't really studied the young man's face. The sheen of his bald head made it look like pink alabaster. Under his dominant forehead, both cheek and jawbones were well defined; they conspired to compress his mouth into a wide slit held in place by laugh lines that looked like inverted commas. His eyes, focused on Terry, were hooded with softer flesh, a gentle relief from the hard surfaces. Though he wasn't smiling, he had the lightness of someone who'd found God. For a moment, Terry was jealous.

"I'm afraid I've made a mess of my uniform." He drew Terry's eyes to the smeared bloodstain on his chest and picked up the cloth to wipe it again.

Terry was suddenly aware of the van's orange light fragments zipping past his head. "I don't understand." He pulled his hand abruptly from the mug, spilling tea across the table.

"I know, but you will." William wiped up the puddle of tea, leaving a flourish of blood from the cloth. "You see how easy it is to make a mess of things?" He refolded the cloth and drew slow circles over the blood. "Then, just like that, they're gone."

Terry could feel the colour draining from his face at the sight of the blood. His lips quivered and he felt like he was freezing. "I don't feel —"

William spoke. "It's fear, Father. It'll pass." He sipped his coffee as his eyes remained focused on the old man. "Matthew's dead. I can't tell you whether it was painless or not, but it was quick."

Tears filled Terry's eyes. "Why?"

"Ah." William smiled, returning to his coffee. "Because a psychopath can always spot another psychopath." He finished and wiped his mug with the bloody rag.

Terry's hands were shaking. Self-consciously, he dropped them into his lap.

William undid the front of his jacket and sat back against the wall. When he spoke, his voice was warm and compassionate. The first thing he told Father Terry was that he too would be dead within the hour. He wanted him to want death — or, failing that, to accept it.

"Your son was a manipulative, arrogant, uncaring man. But I suspect you already knew that."

"How do you know my son?"

"I don't know him, but I've observed him. We frequented the same coffee shop." William raised his hands. "Confession time, Father. I'm not with Dundurn Hydro."

Terry listened as best he could, through waves of panic that were overtaken by disbelief, sadness, and remorse. For the previous three months, William said, every Tuesday and Thursday at ten a.m., Matthew had been meeting an attractive young woman at a local Starbucks. The coffee shop offered both an informal sit-down section and high stools at a bar along the window. "I was always able to get a seat and overhear their conversations, no matter how crowded or noisy it was."

Seeing the confusion on Terry's face, he explained. "Ever since I was a kid I've been able to follow conversations across a room. And because I also have an amazing memory, it became a party trick. People would say, 'Okay, Willy, what were we talking about across the room just then?' And off I'd go, recounting what they'd been saying, while jaws dropped around me. Would you like another tea, Father?"

Terry shook his head and answered in a whisper, "No."

"I'll pour us some water then. We should stay hydrated." He put the two mugs in the sink, opened cupboards until he found two glasses, and filled them from the tap. He set one down in front of Terry before retaking his seat. "Matthew was working her; her name is Nancy and she's a financial analyst. And because I'm a story collector, I was there every Tuesday and Thursday to listen. Everything seemed to be going well, though there was no outward sign that it was an intimate relationship. Your son was making a serious investment in her, and that piqued my interest. Anyway, about two weeks ago, after the usual small talk, she said, 'Tell me about your folks.'"

Father Terry could feel his throat tighten. He felt faint. Instinctively he pressed his thumbs into his ropey thighs until they hurt.

William sipped some water and wiped the corners of his mouth with the back of his forefinger. "Your son's answer won't come as a surprise, Father. He said, 'That's a boring story. There's not much to say about them.'"

Terry picked up his glass and took a deep swallow, then lowered it shakily to the table. "No, I'm not surprised."

"Well, I was," William said. "So was Nancy. She said he'd been asking all about her parents at dinner the night before and she hadn't held back. That was a quid pro quo moment — I should mention that Nancy's father is an extremely wealthy investor. Anyway, your son was stuck. He went to the counter for another latte, but I think he really wanted to gather his thoughts. When he returned, he spoke to her in bullet points."

Father Terry felt as if he were sinking. His head nodded slightly as he looked into the eyes of Matthew's killer and listened as he softly, slowly, recited the list.

- Mom was bitter and angry. The only time she wasn't was in the summer, when my father was away.
- I think she hated him.
- My father was a priest. He created a sect of Catholicism that went nowhere.
- Selling the church and the summer camp on Long Point was the only time he made any money.
- I became a good student to avoid going to church and the camp.
- Father wanted to be an explorer like Wilfred Thesiger, but other than going to Lake Erie, he never left Dundurn.
- He was a failure as both a priest and a father.

"I didn't know the name Wilfred Thesiger. But thanks to that conversation, I've read two of his books, and through him I got to know you." William finished his water. "Anyway, Matthew recited that list like he was reading it off a menu. He was determined to discourage any further discussion about his family, and it worked. Nancy never returned to Starbucks."

Terry couldn't help but feel that Matthew's assessment, though cold and unforgiving, was unquestionably honest.

It more or less mirrored his own. But it was surprising to him that Matthew knew anything about the hold Thesiger had on him. He thought the seventy years of questions and observations scratched into the margins of Thesiger's books had never been seen by anyone, even though they'd been hidden in plain sight on his desk.

Terry's thoughts turned to his options. Could he get to a phone or push his way, screaming, to the front door and hopefully to freedom? William had yet to produce the weapon that would end his life, but Terry felt certain the young man's amiability would end quickly if he was given a reason. Already reeling from his sense of guilt and failure, Terry added cowardice to his list of faults. But what weighed even more heavily on him now was his inability to think of a reason why his death shouldn't happen.

[8]

MacNEICE RETURNED TO THE STONE COTTAGE JUST BEFORE
nightfall. He took a single serving of lasagna from the
freezer and put it in the microwave to thaw. The meal was
part of a care package that Marcello had delivered when
MacNeice was recovering from his near drowning in the
sewer. Marcello's wife, Chris, his chef and partner in the
restaurant, had prepared a range of delicious meals, each
labelled and signed with a large, curling C. With the lasagna
thawed, MacNeice slipped it into the oven, poured a glass of
red wine, and walked outside to breathe in the forest.

A cool breeze was raking along the escarpment. Sparrows
and chickadees were chatting in the trees, no doubt comforted by the last warm rays of the sun. Come dusk, they'd
find their way home to nest. One particular sparrow had

taken to nesting in the hubcap-sized outdoor light MacNeice had installed under the overhanging eaves, so he and Kate could enjoy dinners for two in the garden.

He recalled how hushed those conversations had been; even when they weren't being romantic, their voices rarely rose above a whisper. It had become a sacred place, but one not without its surprises. On one occasion a skunk had waddled by casually, less than six feet from their table, without even glancing their way. They froze and held their breath, looking at each other wide-eyed. When the skunk had disappeared up the hill, Kate whispered something that meant there was nothing left to say: "Well, peeing in your shoe won't keep you warm for long." They broke into rolling laughter that continued until their glasses were empty and tears were streaming down their faces. He was convinced that the crickets had stopped chirping and hundreds of unseen eyes in the brush and trees were blinking back at them. When they finally retreated inside, both of them were light-headed and ready for bed.

Now, as MacNeice turned to look up at the light, the sparrow looked back, its head poking over the white glass lens. They'd gotten used to each other, but their coexistence meant there was a little pile of sparrow droppings on the stone terrace and, judging by the shadow on the glass, there was another pile inside.

"You'd like this sparrow, Kate. She's so unafraid."

I'm sure I would. Maybe I sent her to watch over you.

"Did you?"

No. At least, not knowingly.

MacNeice could hear his cellphone ringing in the kitchen. He swallowed his wine and went inside. It was Aziz.

"Mac, I want to give you an update on the interview with Luisa. Is this a good time?"

"It is, though I'm just about to burn my supper. Give me a second."

He took the lasagna out of the oven and placed the steaming container on a plate. He poured another glass of wine and sat down. "I'm back."

"There's an epilogue to the story about the letter from Nancy Pretty." On her next cleaning day, Luisa had found it in the garbage. It had been torn to bits — not just crumpled up and tossed away, not just torn in half, but in her words, "ripped almost to confetti." She noticed it because, when she emptied the wastebasket in Matthew's room, cream-coloured paper had fluttered onto the carpet and she had to vacuum it up. She felt certain it was the Pretty letter.

"After I sent Luisa home, I looked up Pretty's name. There's no home phone registered, but I got her office number. It's closed for the weekend, but I'll call Monday morning. How was your meeting with Wallace?"

"Well, now he knows what we know — which isn't much. The press conference is scheduled for Monday morning at eleven o'clock."

"Do you think this was a one-off?"

"Seems like a lot of effort for a one-off."

Aziz apologized for interrupting his dinner, then said, "Mac, why don't you go up north tomorrow? It might help to clear your head."

"Thanks, Fiz, but I think I'd better stay here."

"DID YOU ASK GOD TO SAVE YOU?"
MacNeice glanced up at her. Sumner's eyes were fixed on his. "No, I didn't." He cleared his throat unnecessarily. "I was running out of breath. The boy was no longer fighting to save himself; he was dead weight. We were underwater. I was failing. It wasn't heroic. I couldn't let go at that point, even to save myself."

"Tell me more about that."

MacNeice envied her stillness. There was no evidence of the internal twitches he was certain she could see flickering behind his eyes or pulling at the corners of his mouth. Without realizing it, he began rubbing the heel of his right thumb. She noticed. Of course she'd notice.

"I remember two bodies from a decade or so ago." He

looked down at his hands. "I never forget the bodies." He continued massaging his thumb. "Two men dead in an industrial lot out in the east end, one from knife wounds, the other from strangulation. We weren't able to tell if the one with the knife had acted in self-defence against an attacker who was strangling him, or if it was the other way around. It took two of us to pry the dead man's hands off the other's neck." He cleared his throat again. "Though I'd heard about it, that was the first time I'd actually seen a death grip." He sat up straight and took a deep breath. "Underwater, I was holding on so tightly to that boy. If it had ended differently, that's how they would have found us."

Sumner's face softened, but she was still waiting.

"The next thing I knew, I was opening my eyes, surprised to see the paramedics and firefighters standing over me. The boy was alive too, on the ground not far away. I remember the smell of wet grass. I closed my eyes. After a while, I sensed someone directly above me and I looked up to see Aziz. That was when I prayed."

"Prayed to whom?"

MacNeice swallowed hard. This was a question he'd avoided asking himself since Kate died. Throughout her illness he had quietly prayed for miracles. If there was a line between praying and begging, he'd crossed it the day she was diagnosed with cancer. After each prayer he would kiss her cheeks and whisper softly, "My love is like a red, red rose," though he didn't know why. She'd smile briefly, and that was reason enough to continue saying it. In the last few weeks she was either too weak to respond or comatose from the morphine, but he kept on saying it.

The last time he prayed for a miracle, he was returning

to the bedroom after a shower. Sensing a terrible quiet, he stepped inside quickly to find that she was gone. A tear had pooled in the hollow beneath her right eye — the last living thing of her. He dipped his ring finger into the hollow and touched the tear to his lips. Lying beside her, he begged her spirit to send him a signal, though of what, he didn't know.

"I prayed to the great unknown — a god I can neither define nor defend, a being I'd never have invented but for Kate's illness."

"It must have been difficult to realize that your prayers didn't make any difference."

The remark stung. MacNeice was overtaken by an involuntary headshaking, as if he were dodging a careening fly. When it stopped, a weak smile drifted across his face. "I wanted to be granted a miracle on credit, with no deposit other than the unsupportable claim that I'd be a better man. When it was all over and she was carried out of the cottage, I whispered, 'My love is like a red, red rose' for the last time."

MacNeice thought losing her might have been different if he had attended church every Sunday, singing hymns with conviction, reciting words of salvation. Kate would still be gone, but he'd be comforted by knowing she was in heaven. Except she had been cremated, put in the ground to more or less become soil, and he was left with only a shred of a romantic poem he didn't know and a god he'd invented who hadn't come through.

"And when you were lying on that wet grass, who were you praying for?" Though her pen was poised, Sumner hadn't used it.

"It was a prayer of gratitude. First, just for seeing the boy breathing beside me. And then for Fiza — DI Aziz. She was . . ." His voice softened to a whisper. "Heroic. When I opened my eyes" — he cleared his throat — "I thought for a moment she was an angel." As if to manage the impact of that sentence, he added, "It was the play of light, with the mist curling all around her. Her eyes were shining and she was smiling."

"A mirage."

"In a way, yes."

"Except Aziz is very real."

"Of course."

[10]

"IS YOUR NAME REALLY WILLIAM?" The man said nothing as he lifted himself slightly and produced a handgun from behind his back. Howard Terry's eyes widened at the sight of it. His mouth opened, but he said nothing. He thought he'd have more time to get ready, to say something, to forgive the young man sitting so casually before him. He looked down at the weapon. It was unlike anything he'd ever seen.

Seeing the reaction on Terry's face, William laid a hand flat on the pistol and swung the barrel towards the wall. "Sorry, it was getting uncomfortable under my butt."

Terry managed a weak smile but continued to study the gun. "What is it?"

"Ah, that's a grey polymer cz p-09. Czech, originally."

He patted it the way Terry imagined a salesman might. "Nine millimetre, with a twenty-one-round double-stacked extended magazine. Well, nineteen rounds now," he said, gesturing towards the basement door. "This long append-age is a suppressor — a silencer. I use it for two reasons: one, because it's quiet, and two, because I think a loud noise is unnecessarily cruel and inhumane."

"My —" Terry looked into his eyes, expecting to see some sign of hate or derangement. He found neither; if anything, the man's gaze was compassionate.

William reached down and took a bundle of cloth from his bag. He stood up, put the bundle under his arm, and lifted the weapon. "It's time, Father Terry."

Climbing the stairs, Terry's legs felt like lead. Behind him, weapon in hand, William ensured there'd be no escape.

"Leave your underwear on, Father Terry, but remove the rest of your clothes, please." William placed one of the pieces of fabric on the railing and unfolded the other. "You'll be wearing this nightgown." He held it up. "It's one-size-fits-all."

Terry's eyes widened and he shook his head. It was an involuntary act; he was aware that he had no choice. William raised the barrel slightly to emphasize his point.

Terry stood before him as bravely as he could manage. There was a brief moment when he wondered if old-age pee stains were evident on his white underwear, but then he understood that worrying about incontinence was a trivial concern at this point. With as much dignity as he could muster, Father Terry took the nightgown and pulled it over his head. It had a magical effect. The fabric was less than friendly, but somehow he uncurled his spine and stood erect. He imagined Thesiger's silver-handled crescent sword hanging from a twilight blue waistband, and a white headscarf wrapped loosely across his face so that only his weathered eyes could be seen. He was ready to wander the Empty Quarter under heaven's eternal blanket, following its stars to the next oasis where he and his camel would sleep.

William's face lit up and he smiled. He seemed to know what Terry was thinking. "Don't worry about your clothes, Father. I'll put them away." He stepped forward, put his hands on Terry's shoulders, and moved him into position on the threshold of Matthew's bedroom.

Fear tremors rippled through Terry's body. *This is the moment*, he thought. *This is going to happen and I can't do anything to stop it.* He ignored his shaking knees and straightened his back. It wasn't that he was determined to be manly at this moment — he'd never had the urge to be, and wouldn't know how anyway — he simply wanted the death Thesiger might have had, had he not withered away from Parkinson's in a Surrey retirement home.

William levelled the P-09 at Terry's chest.

"One last question. No one will —"

The pistol spat twice. Terry's chest imploded and he was thrown backwards, desperately reaching out for the doorframe to keep from falling. He looked down to see two red plumes blossom through the holes in the cotton. The pain, sharp and intense, was strangely brief. He struggled to keep his footing and struggled harder to breathe. But his legs gave way and then he was falling, floating.

William caught him and, like a father laying a child down to sleep, he eased Terry gently to the floor. "Only a few moments more, Father. Thank you for your courage. May

God bless you and keep you." He gently stroked Terry's silver hair back into place. "My name's not William."

Terry blinked. He could taste blood in his mouth. His breathing was ragged as he slowly accepted the dying rhythms of his heart. Looking up, he mouthed the words *Thank you.*

With his final breath, a bubble of blood broke through Terry's lips and splattered over his face. His executioner took out a clean work cloth and tenderly wiped the old man's face until it was clean.

Now he moved quickly. At 4:15 a.m. he placed a brass V on the carpet, packed away all his gear, and quietly left the house on Amelia Street.

[11]

"HOW DID YOU TWO MEET?" SUMNER ASKED.
Hours later, MacNeice couldn't recall what he'd said to her, but whatever it was, it had been brief. He didn't know why he wanted to keep that part of his life to himself, given what he'd already told her. But, as with a treasure or a secret, when you're alone and you open that box, you've got no choice but to look inside.

It was her shadow that had captivated him. She had appeared on a street in Paris when he was in his early thirties. He had gone to France in early October to understand why so many of his heroes had gone there — a few writers, but mostly jazz musicians like Sidney Bechet, who'd spent a year in a Parisian jail for a gunfight in the street, Duke and the Count, Holiday and Simone, Bird and Miles, Monk and Billy Strayhorn.

Until then, the only life MacNeice had known was Dundurn. In Paris he wanted to walk quietly — to be the stranger, the wanderer — but mostly he wanted to get murder out of his head. It seemed odd for a homicide cop to admit, but thinking about it now, MacNeice realized he had gone there to find himself. He'd follow clues, pursue leads, look for tiny things that might expose who he was. He knew the trip was a romantic idea, but he didn't care. He wanted to hear the musicians, to see how Parisians had responded to them. He wanted to breathe in Paris the way they had, to be grabbed and attached by the same magnet to something that wasn't going anywhere.

One afternoon before the clubs opened, he left his hotel on the rue de Buci and started walking. The sun hung low in the sky, spilling a golden haze over everything and everyone. He was studying people, the cars and scooters, the buildings — but most of all the couples sitting outside cafés. He was inhaling more deeply than he had in a long time and he could feel his shoulders returning softly to their bone-weary cradles. The stiffness in his legs was melting away and his rangy optimistic stride was returning. As he turned onto a narrow street, he noticed the liquid shadow of a pair of legs ahead. A swing tune he'd heard the night before had been running through his mind, to the extent that he didn't know exactly where he was. Paris was working its magic. He'd finally left Dundurn behind and was as lost as he imagined Strayhorn and Bechet had been. He watched the long grey shadows stretching towards him on the cobblestones. Resisting the urge to look at their source, he smiled at the elegance and certainty of the stride. The gap between them, opening and closing as they crossed boulevards and turned down lanes barely wide enough for a compact car, grew longer as the sun sank lower. He was determined to follow those legs for as long as there was sun, and after that for as long as there was moonlight. He wasn't stalking — not really — or if he was, he was stalking shadows. He smiled, impressed that he could trail someone for half an hour without being discovered.

She hopped a curb. The shadow folded slightly before lengthening again; the end of it reeled him in and flowed past him. He was too close to the shadow's source. He stepped onto the cobblestone road, intending to fall behind before once more matching its pace.

Too late. The shadow stopped and its owner turned. MacNeice stumbled on the curb. The woman looked at him suspiciously, angrily, and said in English, "You've been following me, haven't you."

It wasn't a question. Her eyes fixed on him before glancing up the street to see if there was someone she could call on if necessary. There wasn't. He swallowed hard and felt his face getting warmer, redder. "Not exactly. Yes . . . but not exactly."

She had her hand on the courtyard door next to her. Why didn't she step through and slam it in his face? She crossed her arms, dropped her chin, and waited for a coherent response. Her posture suggested that he should be quick about it. He started to explain that he was just following her shadow, but, realizing how ridiculous that sounded, he leaned against the opposite stone doorframe and told her everything. Dundurn, jazz — all those heroes; he spoke about the light, how like butterscotch it seemed at that time of day in Paris, about her stride and how fearless it seemed, about how beautiful her shadow was on the cobblestones, and how he meant no harm. He added that he would have followed her shadow for as long as there was light, simply because it was so beautiful. But that didn't mean he was crazy or a predator; he'd simply come down with a bad case of Parisitis. He had gone there to get lost, and this was proof that it was working. He looked up and down the street and added, "I honestly don't know where I am."

"I see." She had softened considerably. Nonetheless, she again reached for the door. "Where are you from in America?"

"Dundurn, Ontario, actually. In Canada." That sounded so provincial that he shook his head, searching for better words.

She dropped her hand, leaned against the stone wall, and waited. He told her about the clubs he'd been to and how the music and the place and all that he'd read and heard had come together in the shadows of her legs.

"What is it you need to get lost from?"

There was nothing specific — no lost love, no desperate need to flee, nothing at home that he was escaping. He finally said, somewhat apologetically, "I'm a homicide detective."

The door opened suddenly and a man in a dark blue suit stepped over the bottom frame into the street. He nodded to both of them — "*Bonsoir, monsieur, dame*" — as if he wasn't surprised to see a man and a woman standing on opposite sides of his carriage door.

"I love murder mysteries. Do you?"

He was going to say no but was suddenly concerned that would put a swift end to their conversation. He thought she was beautiful, especially now that the anger had melted away. Her face was softer and brighter, even in the twilight, and her smile when she said *mysteries* disarmed him.

She was waiting for an answer. Her eyes were lively; she was taking in the details of his face, enjoying his discomfort. Eye contact. It was so unlike his work, where people mostly looked away, at tables, walls, floors — or at their hands. She was wearing an ochre dress under a dark khaki raincoat. Her legs, initially braced for a confrontation, were relaxed as she leaned against the wall; they were clad in calf-length dark brown boots, one ankle casually crossing the other. A brilliant cerulean scarf hung loosely around her neck. Her shadow was already a memory. He wished he'd been more prepared, more polished.

She smiled and let him off the hook. "Of course you don't read them. One doesn't fill an evening with the work of the day."

"No, I don't. But you seem to understand that from experience. May I ask what you do?"

"Ah, yes, well, I'm a violinist. And before you ask, when I go to a restaurant, I much prefer a quiet table."

He would say later that he had no idea what he was going to say next. He didn't know where the words sprang from; they came out on their own, like shadows. "Let me take you to dinner. I promise you, it'll be a quiet table."

[12]

SITTING IN DURAND PARK OFF CHARLTON, THE STRANGER STUDIED a young woman walking her miniature black terrier. The two seemed like kindred spirits. If she stopped to look at flowers or a hedge, the dog stopped to sniff or pee on them. Each time they walked away, it was like Fred and Ginger — light on their feet, moving together. He smiled.

From the corner of his eye he noticed a young man approaching warily. Dishevelled and nervous-looking, he increased his pace towards the woman. With his faulty-wiring gait, he wasn't difficult to read; his legs moved like sticks. He appeared to be in his early twenties, with ratty hair and clothes that looked dirty even from a distance. He glanced around anxiously to see if anyone was watching. Six women were seated at a table near the playground, talking, while several more were with the toddlers attempting to climb the Big Toy monkey bars. A couple sat nearby on a bench. When the young man turned his way, he saw only a stranger immersed in a book.

Before the young man arrived, the stranger had been discreetly sketching the women at the table, but when he saw the young man approach, he turned over the page and wrote down MID-20S / 5'-10" / 140–50 LBS / LONG BROWN UNKEMPT HAIR / BEARD / CHEEK RASH / CLOSE-SET EYES / TORN GREEN AND BLUE LUMBERJACK SHIRT / FADED DESERT STORM CARGO PANTS, A FEW SIZES TOO LARGE / BLACK SNEAKERS, MOSTLY HIDDEN BY THE PANTS. If his instincts were correct, he'd soon be giving that description to the woman to hand over to the police.

She hadn't been aware of the stickman careering her way, but when he coughed just behind her, she and the dog froze. Instinctively she moved her bag to her shoulder and prepared to stand her ground. The terrier lowered its head, squared off its skinny little shoulders, and put on its game face.

The young man lunged for the purse but missed. The dog barked and snapped at the air. The woman clutched the purse to her chest.

The man sitting on the bench with his wife yelled, "Hey! I'm calling the cops!" That got the stickman's attention. He made another attempt, this time knocking the woman to the ground on top of her purse.

Frustrated, he realized his moment had passed. He was about to run away when he decided to exact revenge on the dog. He stomped down hard and missed. But the dog was tangled up in the woman's legs; it was an easy target. Its attacker stomped again, harder, cracking the animal's back. With a yelp it was down, its spine broken.

The young man pointed his finger in the dog's direction, screaming, "You asked for it! You asked for it!" Then, like a drug-addled Olympian, he sprinted over the grass berm and through the ornamental gates to Charlton Street, where he disappeared.

The couple from the bench were standing over the younger woman when the stranger approached. The woman insisted she was unhurt as she carefully untangled the leash and made her way to her knees. Then, looking down at her dog, she cried, "Oh my god, no! What's he done to Freddy?"

"I've called 911. They'll send help," the man said.

"They'll be here soon. They'll find him," said his wife, resting a hand on the woman's shoulder.

The stranger was certain the dog was finished. Its legs were trembling, its breathing was shallow, and its eyes were frozen black orbs. He handed the woman the page from his sketchpad. "Give this to the police. Don't try to move Freddy."

A young mother pushing a stroller arrived on the scene. Without saying a word, she took a comforter from the stroller and placed it gently over the dog.

The stranger turned to the couple. "Make sure the police get that description." He glanced at Freddy once more before walking off towards the Charlton gate.

[13]

THE STRANGER HAD BEEN FOLLOWING FROM A DISTANCE, BUT HE closed in on the young man at the intersection of James and Bond. For two blocks he'd studied his walk. It was interrupted by face scratching, nervous tics, and leg spasms. A few times he'd turn around quickly to see if anyone was pursuing him, after which he continued to speed-walk for half a block. Drawing closer, the stranger noticed the stickman short-stepping and staring downward, as if he could see through the knees of oncoming pedestrians. Avoiding faces. He was an addict, and something speedier than his brain was driving him downtown for a fix.

OxyContin, the stranger thought. Before the young man had seen the woman in Durand Park, it was likely he'd already been turned away from St. Joseph's, which was only a couple of blocks away. After that he was a hyped-up water spider, circling, darting this way and that, every step more desperate than the last. The stranger was far too healthy-looking to assume the role of drugged-out fellow traveller, but there was a part he could play. He rolled his shoulders forward and gave himself an easy, loping stride. Head down, hands deep in his pockets, he began chewing imaginary gum.

When the young man stopped at the red light, the stranger stepped past him, forcing a driver to hit the horn and slam on the brakes. He turned back to the young man on the curb. "Follow me." He lifted his middle finger to the driver and swaggered through the intersection. On the opposite side, he turned around, opened his arms, and exaggerated his gum chewing.

The young man looked nervous. Crocodiles were waiting for him the moment he stepped off the curb — it was going to take courage to do it. He darted out suddenly, running in a zigzag between several cars, causing more braking and honking. Relieved to make it to the other sidewalk, he was suddenly hit with the giggles.

The stranger smiled. "That wasn't so hard, was it."

"No . . . no. Not hard, not hard." He was out of breath from fear and giggling.

The stranger turned and walked west on Bond. Behind him, the young man was coughing and muttering. Like a stray dog, he had fallen into line. Without turning, the stranger said, "Cotton?"

"Wha — what? Yeah . . . Oxy. Yeah." He laughed nervously and skipped to catch up. "When I can. Yeah. Apache too . . . now. I mean today. Yeah."

"Ever try China White?"

"Wait . . . that fentanyl heroin shit? Not for a while. No, man."

"Yeah, it's something crazy. New and improved — you'll see God."

A nervous chuckle. "Man, I don't know if that's a good thing."

"Follow me. My van's just down the block."

The young man was so desperate for a hit that he nodded nervously and quickstepped, trying to keep up with the bigger man.

"What's your name, chief?"

"Lenny . . . Yeah, Lenny."

They settled into the front seats of the van. The stranger reached behind to a cooler. "Wanna Coke, Lenny?"

"Coke? Naw, I don't do coke no more. I get real bad nosebleeds."

The stranger pulled out two tins and handed him one. "Coke."

Lenny slapped his hand on the dash and fell into hysterical laughter. "Shit, man . . . busted. So busted."

"Common mistake." He opened the glove compartment and took out a zip bag containing several pale yellow capsules. "Two will fix you up." He put them in Lenny's open palm.

Lenny grinned, cavalierly popped them into his mouth, and swallowed them quickly with the Coke. The man started the engine and pulled away from the curb. "I'll take you up the mountain so you can see the city. Dundurn opens up like in *Close Encounters*, when that mothership arrives."

"What's close . . . close end counters?" Lenny asked, as

he slid back comfortably against the seat and the door, nursing his soft drink.

HE PULLED INTO a layby overlooking the city and turned off the engine. Lenny mumbled something before closing his eyes.

"How you feeling?" He took Lenny's Coke and put it into the console holder, next to his own. The young man didn't appear to notice that the tin was gone; his left hand still curved around the space it had occupied.

"Huh? Oh . . . high, man . . . high."

"You're missing the view." When Lenny didn't respond, the stranger smacked his face. "Wake up."

Lenny didn't open his eyes but mumbled something about what an awesome view it was. Leaning over, the older man shook Lenny's shoulders. His eyelids opened slightly and he managed, "Okay . . . Yeah, so cool," before they closed again.

He shook him harder until Lenny's eyes opened wide. "Lenny, listen. Pay attention. You shouldn't have killed that dog. That wasn't right. Can you hear me, Lenny?"

"Huh? Yeah, no . . . What?"

"Killing that woman's dog was wrong. That was a very bad deed. For you, a fatal one."

"The black devil, man. I seen it . . ." Lenny waved his hand. "He was the devil. Hey, wait — you saw that?" His eyes opened, but with their pupils the size of pinheads, they wouldn't focus. Try as he might, he was looking through the wrong end of the telescope. A few seconds later, his eyelids fell like lead shutters.

"Yes, I saw it. Lenny, twenty minutes ago you swallowed heroin, but sixty percent of each capsule was fentanyl. One's probably enough to kill you, but two . . . Well, you can imagine . . ."

"Who are you?" Lenny couldn't decipher what was happening. He struggled to sit up but, abandoned by his strength, he flopped back into the seat.

The stranger looked out at Dundurn. Beyond the silhouettes of the steel mills, the light danced across the bay, leaving its surface shivering in the breeze. It reminded him of daybreak and the gossamer light on a spider's web. "There's only beauty. That's all there is."

Lenny's head moved in a slow-motion circle before coming to a stop on the headrest. His jaw fell slackly and the tensions and tics that had gripped and twisted his face softened. It was a study in battered grace. Lenny was a boy again, at peace.

Wanting to capture Lenny's last breath, he reached for his pocket camera. But the moment was gone. The final sigh left Lenny's body without notice, the way an infant on the breast slides quietly into a gentle sleep.

[14]

"MAC, IT'S SWETS. YOU UP NORTH?"
MacNeice shook his head. "No. I'm on my way to Wallace's for the Amelia Street press conference."

"Okay, we've got one male, took two in the chest. I'm looking at him now. You gotta see it — this one's nuts."

"Where are you?"

"Devil's Punchbowl. I'll meet you in the parking lot off Ridge Road. Bring your boots, Mac. The scene's slippier 'n shit."

MacNeice turned onto Main and punched in Wallace's cell number.

"You're on your way?"

"No, sir. DS Swetsky has another body, out at the Devil's Punchbowl. There's a possibility it's related to Amelia Street. I'm on my way there now."

"Shit. Okay, no problem. I can handle this." Wallace covered the mouthpiece and spoke to someone in the room before coming back to him. "You got anything new on Amelia?"

"Not yet, sir."

"I'll go with the Matthew Terry photo. Keep me posted."

Five minutes later, as MacNeice was passing Gage Park, Vertesi called to report on the "two-block knock" around the Terry house Saturday and Sunday. "Father Terry — only a couple of people knew he'd been a priest, but everyone said he was friendly when they'd meet on the street. He'd pet dogs, tousle kids' hair, say 'nice day' before going on his way. One neighbour said she saw him occasionally at the library."

Matthew Terry, on the other hand, was aloof. "He never walked in the area, and even when he pulled out of his driveway, the tinted windows of his Mercedes meant you couldn't see him. One woman said, 'I swear if he passed me on the sidewalk, I wouldn't recognize the man.'"

Some had seen the cleaning lady come and go, along with a guy in a pickup truck who shovelled the snow every winter, but otherwise the house was quiet. "Apparently the kids didn't even go there on Halloween, and not just because there weren't any pumpkins outside. That's a sure sign you're not fitting in."

No one had seen anything unusual around the time of the killings. No one had heard any loud noises or the squealing tires of a getaway car. "Mind you, one old lady said, 'The neighbourhood has changed so much. People don't know each other like they used to.'"

"Not much there."

"Sorry, boss. We dug hard and came up empty-handed."

DRIVING THROUGH DUNDURN, MacNeice kept pace with the green light changes; it was the most efficient way to cut the city in half. Inevitably his mind would wander back to her. And when it did, the familiar streetscape of low-rise office buildings and apartments, detached houses, intersections, and weaving traffic lost its definition. Together they became objects to negotiate, more landscape than flowers and weeds. No need to notice the church they were married in, that she had been buried from. And the passing beige mass of the oncologist's clinic could be avoided altogether with a simple glance into the rear-view mirror, moving steadily forward while looking backwards.

"I wanted to be the tears in your eyes, the joy in your smile."

You were, Mac.

"I wanted those things because that's who you are for me."

I recall there were times when you'd look at me and your eyes filled with tears.

"That's just the Celtic lunatic fringe, to quote your father."

No, Mac, it wasn't.

"The first time you played the violin for me, I felt like I'd been freed from some terrible task."

I don't understand.

"Once I saw a horse tethered to a long rod attached to a pump. The horse wore blinders. Its task was to walk in a circle all day, providing power to the pump. Its path was so worn down that at night when he was released, he had to climb out. He was led to a pen, fed, and blanketed. And in the morning he went back to work. I never dreamed you,

Kate. I couldn't have invented you any more than that horse could invent being free to roll about in the fields, drink water from a stream, or eat apples fallen from trees."

My, oh my. If I'd known I played that well, I might have stuck around.

"It's still hard, is all . . ."

Have you ever thought that at some point you willingly walked back to that pump and tethered yourself to the rod?

"No, I haven't."

Recidivism.

[15]

IN ADDITION TO SWETSKY'S CAR, THERE WERE THREE CRUISERS, A DOZEN or so civilian vehicles, and two police-commandeered school buses in the Punchbowl parking area. A uniformed officer opened the barricade and allowed MacNeice to ease his car alongside Swetsky's.

He popped the trunk and retrieved a pair of rubber boots. As he sat on the bumper taking off his shoes, Swetsky came lurching in his direction with his suit pants rolled up to his calves and his boots covered in what looked like dry cement. Still limping from a hip wound, he stopped, looked up briefly, and waved.

"Williams on the bus?" MacNeice asked, giving the big man a chance to catch his breath.

"Yeah," Swetsky said, glancing in their direction. "There

are fifteen of them to interview. Five are kids: two boys, three girls. The rest are adults, all ages. He's got two female cops to assist."

MacNeice stood up and tucked his pant legs into the boots. Swetsky smiled. "I was over at the viewing platform under that big metal cross with the lightbulbs." He looked back over his shoulder. "You'll be happy to hear that our guy isn't in the Punchbowl. He's down at the Lower Falls. We got two ways to get there."

The first was to walk up the road past the country market to a trail leading down the escarpment. "It's a nice walk in the country," said Swetsky. The other was to get in the car, drive down and across Secord, and walk up to the scene. "Time's a wash. About twenty-five minutes either way." Looking back at the cross again, Swetsky added, "I know you've got an issue with heights, Mac, but if you come over to the cross, there's a viewing platform. You can look down and see where we're going. If you lean over that rail you can just see the body."

"No, I'll wait to see it." The thought of leaning over the abyss was already making him queasy. MacNeice closed the trunk and locked the car.

Swetsky was still favouring his hip, but before MacNeice could say anything, the big man said, "I'm fine walking. I just limp a bit."

"Let's walk, then. You can give me the topline on the way."

"Escarpment cleanup volunteers found him." The sound of the falls increased as they passed the edge of the bowl. It was frighteningly close to the road. "It's louder than normal here. Usually there's just a trickle going over, but the land's still wringing itself out from the rain. The volunteer cleanup team was climbing down to pick up a winter's load of dumped trash and debris. One of them spotted the body. At first he thought it was someone being a smartass, or maybe a nature-loving homeless guy — until they smelled it."

Above the Punchbowl they were buffeted by such strong winds that MacNeice's jacket flapped wildly behind him. He pulled it in and buttoned it up.

"Apparently it's windy up here all the time. Woman in the shop — great butter tarts, by the way — tells me this is nothing." Swetsky looked around. "There's a history of suicides and lovers leaping here, but that's not our guy."

Swetsky turned down the path. "We've got four cops to secure the area and two units on the roads below to keep folks away. We're waiting for the coroner and a forensics team." He turned to MacNeice and grinned. "I was told they're busy."

"Has the site been disturbed?"

"Team leader of the volunteers said they never went near it. They were here at first light. Once they realized this guy was dead, they called 911 and told everyone to return to their vehicles."

Swetsky stopped walking.

"You okay?" MacNeice was concerned.

"What? Yeah, I'm okay. There's something else I gotta tell you about. It's unrelated to this."

MacNeice picked out the sound of crows calling down the sides of the ravine. Call, response; call, response. He braced himself for bad news.

"I heard from Deputy Chief Wallace just before you

arrived. He wanted to talk to you. I thought you were headed up to Kate's grave, so I told him that. Wallace seemed relieved to hear it. Anyway, the bastard proceeded to give me the news instead." Swetsky spread his arms wide as if he were calling a penalty in a football game.

MacNeice began to tense up. What news? It was odd that Wallace hadn't mentioned anything during their call. The sound of the wind and the falls faded and he struggled to take a deep breath.

"DI Palmer's coming back to us, Mac." Swetsky gave that a moment to sink in. He found something to look at in the trees and waited for MacNeice to respond. When he realized that might not happen, he added, "Apparently the guy was up to his old tricks, though this time it was a woman in the precinct, a civilian on contract. No one knew about it, but last Tuesday her husband came in screaming that he was going tear Palmer apart."

"Palmer should have been fired long ago." MacNeice exhaled. "He's going to get someone killed."

"Well, not if he keeps picking women whose husbands are built like Brahman bulls, no-fear guys with short fuses. Last one was that firefighting Charles Atlas, the guy from the DFD beefcake calendar. I think Palmer's got some kinda death wish."

"My point exactly." MacNeice looked around, trying to focus on the sleek black flashes slicing through the air above the trees. But their calls were distant now; they were off somewhere riding the thermals. "Okay. Thanks for telling me. We'll deal with it."

Most of the options he'd have for Palmer — desk duty, cold-case research, liaising with national and international law enforcement — might be considered "constructive dismissal" for a line DI with seniority. It was complicated, but he didn't want to think about it now. "Show me your dead man."

THEY STEPPED INTO a quiet and immense world on a leaf-and-needle carpet where scale tricked the eye and ear. MacNeice found it majestic, reverent. He felt compelled to speak in a hushed voice — in part because if he spoke normally, it could be heard a hundred yards away. Everywhere, tall trees reached skyward. But towering above them all was the metal cross and its platform, cantilevered outward like the bowsprit on a ship.

Looking beyond Swetsky, MacNeice could see that the rock face was made up of a series of plates, some projecting far enough into space that they could provide shelter from a storm. Others, however, reached so far out that it would be tempting fate to stand beneath them. There was no telling when they'd decide to let go.

Swetsky took two respirator masks out of his pocket. "Put this on when we get up there. He's been here overnight."

[16]

"I WAS EXPECTING A CALL, DETECTIVE. I JUST SAW THE MEDIA briefing about Matthew Terry and his father," the female voice said. No hello, no introduction.

"Ms. Pretty, my name is Detective Inspector Aziz. The purpose of this call is to establish a time for an interview, either at your office or home or here at Division One."

"I'm okay doing it downtown, but if possible, I'd prefer to do it now. I mean, over the phone."

Aziz's eyes widened. "Yes, we can do that, with the understanding that a face-to-face interview may still be necessary. For the record, this call is being recorded." She pressed the Record button. "Ms. Pretty, can I assume that you know the reason for my call?"

"Because I knew Matthew Terry?"

"Start by describing to me, if you will, Ms. Pretty, the nature of your relationship with Matthew Terry."

"Please, call me Nancy. Matthew and I started dating about a year ago. We saw each other until a couple of weeks ago. It was intensely romantic — until it wasn't."

"Who ended the relationship?"

"I did."

When Nancy didn't continue, Aziz took a page out of MacNeice's notebook and waited. She could hear breathing and what sounded like a ring or bracelet tapping on a table.

"Well, Matt could be — He could be charming. He was very smart, and to be honest, I was swept away."

"Go on."

"I guess I began thinking of us as a couple." She chuckled briefly, and sadly. "I put aside or didn't notice the tiny signals — some not so tiny — that Matthew wasn't being entirely honest with me."

"In what way?"

"I'm an analyst, Detective. Matthew had a Type-A personality. I am always analyzing, but with him I let that side of me slide." Aziz could hear a chair squeak; Pretty was shifting her posture. "My father introduced us. He thought Matt was a brilliant investor. I suppose, in Dad's eyes, he was also a good catch." A bitter laugh this time. "Look, nothing I say can overlook how tragic this situation is, and I do feel terrible about it. But to be honest, my sympathy is for his father, a man I never met."

"What were the signals, Nancy?"

She sighed heavily. "Do you know the poem 'The Hollow Men'?"

"T.S. Eliot? Yes."

Pretty cleared her throat and there were more chair squeaks. "Matt would send flowers to my office, he'd open the car door for me, in restaurants he'd pull my chair out, he put my coat on . . . He had his role down pat. He was an extremely attentive lover."

"Go on."

"It was all rote. He knows — he knew — exactly what to do. He probably studied me; he certainly out-analyzed me. And he delivered — overdelivered — on the details that would win my heart."

"And then?"

"He slipped." She breathed in deeply and exhaled slowly. "He lost it. He couldn't keep it up. That's when the analyst in me kicked in. I ran like hell — not literally but mentally, romantically." She stopped speaking.

"The hollow man . . ."

"Oh, yeah. Matthew was a hollow man. There was no core there, no *there* there, and there's no cure for that." She cleared her throat. "He'd been so incredibly interested in me, in my family, my history, in my mind . . ." She laughed, and this time it sounded like self-ridicule. "Christ. It's so seductive to have someone be so interested, so focused on you. Extraordinary." She sighed. "Though I guess I would have tired of that eventually."

"Then something happened?"

"Well, I realized one day that I knew very little about him — only what he wanted me to know to fit the part — and I knew even less about his family." She sounded exasperated with herself. "I could suddenly see through it, through him. I pressed him about his family. The things he said about them were so fucking cruel. He was smirking, and speaking in such a blithe, casual tone. I felt like I was looking at a ghost. Matthew was cold to the core — no soul, zilch. I sent him a letter afterwards, saying as much."

"You're convinced he was playing you? For what reason?"

"I'm a very good financial analyst, Detective, but Matt could have hired any analyst, so it wasn't about that. I think he wanted to cement his relationship with my father through me. It would have been an effective strategy. In the movie version, Dad would become his father-in-law and most likely his business partner. My father would do that for me — all he wants is grandkids — and when Dad retired, Matthew would be in control."

"But wasn't Matthew already wealthy?"

"Yes, but my father is considerably wealthier. And more important, he's much more connected, not just here but throughout North America."

"Did you know anything about Matthew's business dealings?"

"Not really, at least not then. Dad told me he'd made a considerable amount of money when he cashed in some shares, enough that he could stop practising law — where he probably also made a small fortune. It may sound disingenuous to you, Detective, but I'm not impressed by wealth. I've never taken money from my father or used his name to my advantage." She laughed; this time it sounded genuine. "Admittedly, with a name as ludicrous as Pretty it's hard for me to say we're not related. And yeah, if I'm being entirely honest, the thought of being Nancy Terry wasn't lost on me."

"And later, what did you learn about his business?"

"When it was over, I spoke to Dad. He said Matthew was the chairman and principal investor in a tech company. The moment it was doing well, he resigned as chairman, cashed in his stock, and doubled his money. Of course, it almost bankrupted the firm. As I said, no soul. They're doing well now and they're better off without him, so at least that was good."

"Can you think of anyone who would want to harm Matthew Terry?"

"Only his father, if Matt ever told him what he told me."

[17]

MAcNEICE SPOTTED TWO UNIFORMS WEARING MASKS ON EITHER side of the ravine, each pair standing as far from the body as possible while still adhering to Swetsky's orders to secure the perimeter. He felt that if he drew an X connecting the four men, the corpse would be found dead centre.

No longer sublime, the ancient rock face loomed over the men, rendering them insignificant. High above, from the viewing platform, the city spread out like a picnic table in the distance. Beyond it was Burlington, and to the right the seemingly endless blue of Lake Ontario. MacNeice felt like he was entering the domain of a vengeful mountain king. The ground beneath him changed from soft and dry to slick, wet grey rock. The water flowing over the Lower Falls had found a path around fallen stone slabs, creating rivulets everywhere. And after 450 million years of falling and grinding sandstone, that muck had the appearance of liquid lead.

Any trees, if they had ever existed here, had long ago been crushed to dust. In spite of its name, he couldn't think of anything lighthearted about the Devil's Punchbowl, even less for the Lower Falls. This place had nothing in common with the gentle pine-and-leaf-hushed world below. Even coyotes steered clear of it. They knew nothing good would come from getting closer. MacNeice could imagine them passing silently by in the safety of the forest floor, with only furtive glances upward.

"Over here, Mac." Swetsky pointed to an enormous sandstone slab positioned directly across the water's path. "We've called it everything from 'the Subzero' to a 'VW minibus,' but my personal favourite, from the Mick on the hill over there" — he nodded his head towards the cop standing high on the right — "is the 'cathedral's altar.'"

Not bad. Though the Lower Falls were still forty or fifty feet farther on, there was something undeniably sacred about the setting. The slab was its own island, resting on a dry rock plate, around which the water bubbled and spat its way downward. At first MacNeice couldn't see what Swetsky was pointing at, but as he climbed higher, he saw an outstretched pair of legs. They were relaxed, the way they'd be if their owner had fallen asleep on the grass after a summer picnic. As he continued upward, the rock and the body appeared to rotate in his direction. He could make out a cotton nightshirt, then the shoulders . . . and then the head.

"What's that on his head?" MacNeice asked, louder than he'd intended. Cop laughter rippled around the gorge.

"Yeah, I don't think this guy's day was planned on a desk

calendar," Swetsky said. "But right about now's a good time to slide that thing over your nose."

High on the other side of the ravine, a cop said, "Pinch it tight, sir." Sure enough, a few feet on, MacNeice made contact with a smell so intense it had a colour — yellow — and it grew worse with every step. At first it suggested sweetness, but another step farther it quickly turned sour. It wasn't a stench; those often clung to the ground. This one floated upward, carried on the slightest breeze. It had a taste as well, but its description had always eluded Mac. Once in the mouth, it was never forgotten.

"It's a bit pancaked up here and the mud's bad around the edges, even though it may look solid on the surface. Follow my footsteps." Swetsky made a short hop over a stream snaking downhill. "I'll stand back a bit. Tell me what you make of it."

MacNeice was looking down, carefully stepping from rock to rock. There were several boot prints in the mud. When he was a dozen yards away, he squared himself on a larger rock and looked up at the corpse. A grey donkey's head swallowed the shoulders to within inches of the two dark holes in the chest. The animal's head looked like papier mâché, while the enormous and comical ears were made of grey and white velour. If it weren't for the chest holes and the blood, it would have been an amusing costume. Nothing about it made MacNeice smile.

"Weird, right?" Swetsky said.

The body was slumped against the slab the way Matthew Terry's had been against the bed. Arms relaxed at the sides, his hands were lying open on the gravel and mud skim. Knowing how sound carried in this strange place, MacNeice kept quiet but started cataloguing his observations: The body was clean. No scrapes or bruises on the knees, shins, or hands. No mud or abrasions on the feet. The blood flow, heavy around the entry wounds, dropped out of sight and reappeared in the folds of cotton over his lap. Curiously, there was no blood on the legs. MacNeice assumed that the body had been carried here clean and then shot sitting like that. That was going to a lot of trouble. A burp of blood, feces, and urine suddenly escaped the body to merge with the muck, swirling like oil dropped in a rain puddle.

"He was dead before he got here, but dead from what?" MacNeice said quietly. He looked closely at the ground around him. Stepping off to the right, onto another rock, he squatted to study the terrain in every direction, each time casting an eye back to the corpse. Then he leapt to another, looked down, and squatted.

A sharp whistle pierced the air from the other side of gorge. Swetsky looked over at the cop who was lifting his shoulders and throwing his hands out to the sides in a silent *What's up?* Swetsky returned the gesture and turned back to MacNeice, who had jumped to another rock to study the ground.

MacNeice took a photograph of a boot print in the mud. Tucking the camera away, he surveyed the path those boots had taken. He moved twice more before reversing his steps, jumping quickly and deftly from rock to rock till he was circling the body in the opposite direction. Each time he stopped, he looked down and then back to the body. Several stops later, he turned to Swetsky with a smile.

"You want me over there, Mac?"

"No," he said, taking out his camera.

Swetsky watched him point the camera straight down before taking a shot. Then he took several shots of the body, framing them vertically and horizontally. After a few minutes, he tucked the camera away and stepped from rock to rock until he was next to Swetsky. MacNeice launched the image display. A brass V, the one found at Amelia Street, popped up.

"What's that?" asked Swetsky.

"It's a brass letter V found at the other murder scene. Look." MacNeice scrolled through the images from Matthew Terry's bedroom. "Now this . . ." An identical V appeared in the mud and gravel. "Right over there."

"No shit. So our scenes are linked. But what's he getting at with the V?"

MacNeice scrolled to the next image: the body in repose against the massive rock, the Lower Falls, a rock wall rising to the sky with the cross standing watch above. "Makes quite an image, eh?"

"You mean a dead guy in a canyon?" Swetsky swatted away a fly.

"Gorge. I think these V's are telling us where to stand so we can best appreciate the view."

"I don't follow."

"You and your wife drove through the Rockies to Vancouver last year, right? How many times did you pull off to take a picture?"

Swetsky nodded. "Plenty."

"Right. And some of those places would have had a sign saying 'Take a picture here.' I think our killer is telling us where to stand for the best picture."

"Okay, but why here? There's a goddamn viewing

platform up top, with the whole city spread out in front of you and the lake and shit." They both took the time to look up. "But he had to climb down here — or up from below — carrying a guy in a dress wearing a donkey's head?" Disbelief spread across Swetsky's face.

MacNeice listened to a crow calling somewhere in the canopy. He marvelled at the volume of it, the sound amplified by the shape and size of the gorge. He smiled and turned back to Swetsky. "It's a nightshirt."

"What the fuck's a nightshirt?"

"It's what people wore to bed over a century ago."

Swetsky was truly lost. "I understand paybacks, biker-on-biker killings, mob hits, crimes of passion . . . but killing a guy in an old-fashioned dress for a photo op?" He snorted and looked back at the body. "So, we gonna take his head out of his ass?" Ripples of laughter from the cops.

"Brilliant, and beautifully timed, John. But no, we'll wait for the coroner and Forensics." MacNeice turned to leave. "Aziz had a hunch at Amelia Street. She went looking for the original clothes worn by the two victims. She found them stacked neatly in one of the closets. Have these men search the area."

"Looks like we're back in business, Mac. I'll also call dispatch and get some more uniforms. We'll send 'em up to that market shop and to the houses above and below." Swetsky pulled out his cellphone.

MacNeice was already making his way carefully across the stream to the soft, dry land. "I agree. Let's start by asking questions."

Swetsky watched him descend, impressed by his agility. He called after him, "You mean like 'Have you seen a guy carrying a guy in a muumuu wearing a donkey head' kinda questions?"

MacNeice removed the surgical mask from his face. "Precisely."

[18]

MAcNEICE ARRIVED FOR HIS TUESDAY-MORNING APPOINTMENT early. With his cellphone tucked away in the Chevy and no one but Wallace aware of his Sumner sessions, he would use this time to think. Avoiding the magazines, he stood by the window looking out to the front lawn, waiting for something to fly by or land. However, minutes later, when a blue jay began hopping down the massive evergreen, he didn't notice. He was lost in thought about the crime scenes at Amelia Street and the Lower Falls. He was convinced the bodies were set pieces, actors in a play. But which play, and why? More importantly, why these particular actors?

The door opened and Dr. Sumner stepped forward. "Come in, Detective MacNeice." Her greeting voice was always cheerful. He wondered how she managed that when her day was full of people's anger, sorrow, grief, and guilt. "You know, Detective," she said as she closed the door behind them, "if I were asked to make a graph of how many clients arrive early or late, they'd be fairly even, male to female. If I eliminated all but Dundurn's finest, that graph would tilt sharply towards those who are consistently late. Except for you."

"Is that a compliment, Doctor?"

"Merely an observation, though you may take it as you wish." She smiled warmly and sat down at her desk. "Though it raises the question, why are you always early?"

The Celtic brain is quick to see the other side of any compliment, and MacNeice's was no exception. His had already swung into action, digging out all the times he'd been late. His serial lateness included police budget meetings, the dentist, most of his schooling, and cocktails with strangers; he was fifty-fifty with arriving on time for meetings with Wallace. Still, here he was. "I recognize the value of these sessions. How's that?"

Before she could answer, her desk telephone rang. "I apologize." Her brow furrowed as she reached for the receiver. She looked at the call display, then turned to MacNeice. "I was going to ignore this call, but I suspect it's for you and may be important." She put the telephone to her ear and listened. "Yes, we were just beginning. Yes, it is inconvenient . . . Right . . . Very well, here he is." She handed the phone to MacNeice and stood up. "I'll give you some privacy."

He waited for her to leave the room before speaking. "MacNeice."

Wallace cleared his throat. "I won't ask how it's going with the good doctor; I'll just assume that since you're there it's going well." Wallace wasn't interested in a reply, so MacNeice didn't offer one. "Mac, I know you're leading two different homicide investigations right now, and I don't want to add to your work —"

"What's happened?"

"David Palmer's happened. Now, I know Swetsky spoke to you, but there's a new wrinkle. Palmer missed his shift this morning and isn't answering his cell or the landline at his house. McMillan had sent a patrol car to check on him and another to the house of the woman he'd been screwing. Everything seemed fine; the husband quickly apologized for the scene he'd made, and neither knew of Palmer's whereabouts. Palmer didn't answer the door at his place, so the cop looked in through the windows. It looked trashed. His car's in the driveway and there's no sign of him."

"Is the woman he was involved with still working at the precinct?"

"She is." Wallace cleared his throat again. "Mac, we've got several problems here, first being that Palmer's an embarrassment to the force. He's lazy and no one on his team trusts him — and I'm getting that from McMillan, the head of their division. God knows what they say among themselves. Second, and this one's on me, Palmer has a history of screwing other men's wives, yet he remains a DPD detective. Third, we don't know if he had more women on the hook, and maybe one of their husbands found out."

"Why is he still on the force?"

"When I overlooked his behaviour the first time, I set a

precedent. And the Police Union would come out swinging if I dumped him now. They'd connect his dismissal with Dundurn's budget crunch."

"What's the status at his house now?"

"I'm trying to pry loose a small team from Forensics to go through the place. The DI who went in said it was a mess but there weren't any signs of a struggle or blood. So maybe we can add 'slob' to Palmer's list of achievements."

"Leave it with me." MacNeice put down the phone.

Moments later, Sumner returned. She could see he was distracted. "Mac, I think it's best that we reschedule this session." She opened the door to her reception area before MacNeice could say anything.

Back in the car, MacNeice slipped Tom Waits's *Foreign Affairs* into the CD player and turned on his cellphone. The deep purr of the Chevy's engine connected with the gravel-voiced Waits. There were four messages from Wallace and one missed call from Richardson with no message. Punching in the number, he called dispatch on the radio-telephone. Lucy of the smoker's voice answered. "What can I do for you, Detective Superintendent?"

"Give me DI Palmer's home address, please. I'll wait." MacNeice watched a cat rolling around on Sumner's lawn, scratching its back. "Ready, yes . . . 678 Upper Paradise Road. Perfect. Thanks, Luce."

DO YOU REMEMBER *how much I hated Tom Waits's voice?*

"Yes, but I expected it. That's why I focused on his choices, his taste, his strength as a storyteller. And anyway, I was so far gone on you, I couldn't be offended. I just kept looking to see how Tom and I could turn you around."

Ha! You and Tom won me over with "Foreign Affair." That song was written for the me I was before I met you. Remember when I asked you to play it at my memorial?

"I do. And I kept that promise. I can't listen to it now — I mean, really listen to it — without weeping."

I know . . .

WITH TWO CRUISERS blocking the driveway and orange traffic cones diverting traffic to the next lane, the split-level on Upper Paradise was easy to find. Tucked into the driveway, an unmarked blue Chevy was parked next to what MacNeice assumed was Palmer's beat-up beige Corolla.

MacNeice stepped out of the car and scanned the street. With one exception they were modest, well-kept homes with wide, trimmed lawns bisected by the city's sidewalk. Palmer's was the missing tooth in that pleasant but uninteresting smile. The paint on his house was blistered and cracked. The roof needed attention where several shingles had given up and slid down to the eavestrough. The grass in front was a foot tall and giddy with dandelions. Palmer was the neighbour others loved to hate.

"When travelling abroad in the continental style / It's my belief one must attempt to be discreet . . ."

"You do a passable imitation of Tom's voice. Is 'travelling abroad' a reference to my visit to Paris?"

I'm dead, you sweet man. I don't have a voice, but for the one you give me. And now I have the ability to sing. Thank you. And yes, though it could also have been a reference to my time in Paris.

"I'm tired, Kate. Or maybe *weary* is a better word."

I'm not surprised, Mac. You've been holding it together for so long. "And subsequently bear in mind your transient position / Allows you a perspective that's unique . . ."

"I never imagined you'd be singing 'Foreign Affair' to me."

Oh, I love this part. "Most vagabonds I knowed don't ever want to find the culprit / That remains the object of their long relentless quest / The obsession's in the chasing and not the apprehending / The pursuit, you see, and never the arrest."

"I won't take that personally."

I wish you would.

"I knowed."

A YOUNG DETECTIVE wearing a light grey suit greeted MacNeice at the door. He looked football-tackle fit and introduced himself as Charlie Maracle. Backing into the living room, he stepped aside and said, "Welcome to paradise, sir."

MacNeice studied the high cheekbones, wide-set eyes, and ready smile. "You're from the Six Nations, Detective?"

"Yes, sir, born and raised."

MacNeice smiled. "I believe I know your father. You walk in very large shoes."

"Thank you. He also speaks highly of you, sir."

"What do we have here, Charlie?"

Maracle looked into the living room and shook his head. "Other than this place being tipped over, there are no signs of a struggle. No broken windows or shattered doorframes. We don't know if this is foul play or just Palmer going for a different kind of casual."

"How well do you know him?"

Maracle paused, then stepped back through the door-way and outside. MacNeice joined him. They stood together facing the street. "No need for the guys inside to hear us, sir." Maracle picked up an unopened copy of the *Standard* and tossed it inside. "Thing is, Palmer's a brother, and I owe him."

"In which case consider the question as coming from another member of the family."

"Yes, sir." He squinted against the sun and looked up at the taller man. "We're a tight unit, sir, smaller than yours. We rely on each other. I'm not bothered because Palmer's a bigot; I can deal with that." Maracle put on his aviators to cut the glare. "Straight up, sir, Palmer's a fuck-up. When he's next to me, I go into the field knowing I'm on my own. And sloppy doesn't come close to it; I don't think the man has a clue when it comes to police work. His thing for women . . . since I've been in Homicide I know of three, and two of those were married."

"That's a blunt assessment."

"I'm told he came from your division, so I figure anything I have to say isn't coming as a surprise . . . sir."

"Correct." MacNeice changed the subject. "Which branch of the service were you in?"

The question surprised Maracle. "RDLI, 31 Brigade Group — three tours in Afghanistan." Maracle paused as a Harley rumbled down Upper Paradise Road. "Trust over there cuts cold through the bullshit, sir."

They went back inside, where two uniformed officers were combing through the shelving above and beside a huge television screen. They were wearing gloves but noth-ing over their boots. Seeing MacNeice look down at their footwear, Maracle said quietly, "We don't know that this is a crime scene, sir. Palmer could come walking in any minute, wondering what the hell is going on."

MacNeice looked at the overflowing ashtray and the three empty beer bottles on the coffee table. They hadn't found his cellphone or computer, nor anything that would suggest Palmer had packed up his things and left. There were a significant number of adult videos in the bedroom, and a television screen even larger than the one in the living room. The refrigerator and cupboards were bare, except for beer, a jug of milk, cereal, canned soup, crackers, and cheese.

"He was hoarding *Standard*s; there's a stack of them next to the back door. And — this is interesting — the real estate sections were in a separate pile, with properties circled in all of them. Cottages and houses on the Great Lakes, up north, and all the way to the Quebec border."

"A second career in real estate?"

Maracle laughed. "Yeah, well, this place is definitely a renter."

"And those four impressions in the carpet?" MacNeice asked.

"A heavy chair, we figure, but where it is or why it's gone? No idea."

MacNeice thanked Maracle and requested that he not put up police tape. "For now," he said, "ask the neighbours if they noticed or heard anything unusual, but don't refer to Palmer as a missing person. He may just have gone to Vegas for the weekend."

"You believe that, sir?"

"No, but I do know the Mountain has only two squad cars, and both of them are sitting outside. If we put down tape, we're obliged to leave one of them here. Lock up when you're done, Detective. After forty-eight hours we'll reassess." MacNeice shook Maracle's hand and turned to the door. "And Charlie, give my regards to your father."

AS HE WAS walking back to the car, MacNeice's cellphone rang. It was Mary Richardson.

"Amelia Street's fairly straightforward, Mac, and the bodies have already arrived at Barton Street. Dead three days, perhaps a little less." Judging from the background noise, Richardson was standing in front of the Punchbowl corpse. "Thank you for leaving the donkey mask on. There were fluids trapped inside from the deceased's mouth, and I suspect from the colour that they're toxic. Based on speculation as I stand here, the cause of death was a drug overdose, and that occurred several hours before he was shot. I'll know about the toxins once we get him on the table. However, those two holes in his chest were absolutely unnecessary." She paused to let MacNeice consider the news. "Are you surprised?"

"No. I think all three men were murdered as set pieces, like theatre. They were wearing the same nightshirts . . ."

"Ah, yes. On that subject, I wear nightshirts and I also dabble in oil painting. These nightshirts are made of duck cloth — artist's canvas. Good for painting but unbearable in the sack."

MᴀᴄNEICE WALKED INTO THE CUBICLE EARLY WEDNESDAY morning and handed Ryan his point-and-shoot camera. Though it was sunny and warm outside, there was every reason for the mood in the cubicle to be dark, but it wasn't. Dundurn had had its vacation from murder; killers were back at work.

John Swetsky's barrel laugh interrupted MacNeice's thoughts; the big man was in the canteen with Vertesi, making coffee. Fiza noticed the stitch in MacNeice's step when Swets laughed. She smiled her "boys will be boys" smile. "I think John's sharing his line about getting the dead man's head out of his ass."

Aziz took a red marker and wrote AMELIA STREET — HOWARD / MATTHEW TERRY at the top of the whiteboard, and next to it DEVIL'S PUNCHBOWL — JOHN DOE. Turning to MacNeice, she asked, "Is there anything else?"

Before he could answer, Swetsky and Vertesi appeared carrying mugs of coffee, tea for Aziz, and a double espresso for MacNeice. Swetsky glanced up at the whiteboard before handing a cup to DI Montile Williams.

"Does this mean we'll be recruiting, boss?" Vertesi asked. "I mean, I've heard we're getting Palmer back, but anyone else — like someone who actually does cop work?"

MacNeice raised an eyebrow in Swetsky's direction, "David Palmer will be returning, but he's currently out of communication and didn't report for duty yesterday at Dundurn East." He turned to Aziz. "Leave room on the board. If Palmer doesn't show up here tomorrow morning, we'll assume he's come to some harm."

"Wouldn't that be a Missing Persons job?" asked Williams.

"Yes, and they may be called in. The distinction here is that Palmer's a homicide detective, not a senior suffering from dementia or a runaway teen. That and he was threatened by the husband of a woman he was seeing romantically." MacNeice thought for a moment before adding, "His house has been trashed but there's no indication of a break-in, or that it wasn't done by Palmer, for reasons unknown."

"Jesus." Vertesi leaned back in his chair with his hands behind his head. "So it's possible that the prodigal fuck-up may never return?"

"Let's just hope he does," Swetsky said, with a tone of correction.

MacNeice stood looking at the Amelia Street photograph on the whiteboard. He couldn't decide whether he'd seen something like it before or he'd been looking at the crime scene photos for so long he'd memorized the details. Turning away from the board, he sat at his desk to write down everything he could remember about the scene. When he'd finished, he turned the page over and did it again.

After a third attempt, he stood up abruptly and went to make another coffee. Lost in thought, he didn't notice the cup overflowing. When the espresso machine shut down, he came back to reality. In that moment, a fragment of memory surfaced. Leaving his coffee behind, MacNeice went back to the cubicle, as if unaware that sound travels in an open office.

Aziz turned when he walked in. "What is it, Mac?"

He was staring at the whiteboard. "I've seen it. I don't know where or when, or whether it was television or something else, but I'm certain it's a reproduction of something." He tapped the image. "Amelia Street . . . I know I've seen it."

Aziz smiled, waiting for him to piece together the puzzle.

"You mean, like this is a copycat case, boss?" Vertesi asked.

MacNeice shook his head. "In a way, but not in the sense that you mean. I've never seen or heard of anything like it." He pointed to the photo of the V on the carpet. "I'm certain he's telling us where to stand for a reason." He looked across at the Devil's Punchbowl photo. "And here as well." He pointed to the donkey-head man. "Though I have no idea at all about this one."

"So it's like these are real crime scenes," Williams said. "The scene of the crime . . . A restaging or retelling?"

"But couldn't that V have been anywhere in the room?" Vertesi still wasn't convinced.

"No." MacNeice pointed to the brass letter on the carpet.

"Had it been anywhere else, it wouldn't have been in the right place."

If intense concentration on a single point in space had the power of revelation, it should have happened right then. Aziz, Vertesi, Williams, Swets, and MacNeice were all staring at the Amelia Street photos on the whiteboard. It was like they were willing his memory to come to the surface.

The telephone rang and the moment was gone. Ryan swung around. "It's for you, sir. Dr. Richardson."

The large ceramic-tiled morgue produced an echo that made Richardson's voice seem almost godlike. "MacNeice, Junior and I are midway through the Amelia autopsies. You might be interested to know that in addition to the tumour in Father Terry's brain, he had another on his lung. It's the size of a walnut and may not have been detected."

MacNeice could hear the sound of an electric saw. He decided to sit down and wait for the next shoe to drop.

"However, I'm ringing to let you know I can confirm that the cause of death for your Punchbowl chap was a mix of fentanyl and heroin, which he'd coughed up into that lovely donkey head. The toxicology report for his stomach contents will come later, but he had several needle-mark sites, some recent but most several months old. He'd injected into his arms, abdomen, and ankles and between the toes. I hope that's helpful."

"Before you go, Mary, I'll send someone down to take a photograph of that man's face. Please don't cut into it just yet."

"Quick as you can, Mac." As she was hanging up, he heard her shout, "Tools down, Junior."

He put the phone in its cradle and turned to Vertesi.

"Michael, go down to Richardson's lab and take some head-shots of the body from the Punchbowl. Ryan will clean them up for publication. Go quickly, though — Junior's revving up his saw." MacNeice picked up a marker and wrote: *Cause of death: drug overdose (fentanyl/heroin)* below the Punchbowl photo.

A few minutes after Vertesi had bolted for the door, MacNeice grabbed his notebook. "I'm going over to Amelia Street. I won't be long."

"Do you want company, Mac?" asked Aziz.

"No." He smiled. "I just need to clear my head. And I want to see that bedroom again. But, you can lend me your camera."

[20]

OUTSIDE AND HEADING FOR HIS CAR, MacNEICE HESITATED AND retraced his steps, walking through Division and across the plaza to the street. As he started walking west on Main, he slipped his notebook into the pocket of his jacket. He turned south on Queen and increased his pace to a Rover Scout march: run for a block, walk for a block, and so on.

As he ran, MacNeice's spirits lifted and his head cleared. He began to notice things — a grey squirrel pausing on the trunk of a maple to look his way, a cat curled up on the steps of a porch, a toddler waddling happily towards the arms of its mother . . . and, of course, the birds. Mostly sparrows, but he saw two robins and a male cardinal. He heard the calls of crows banking high above, riding the thermals, looking for opportunities along the way. As he neared the police cruiser and the windowless forensics van, he caught sight of a Baltimore oriole touching down on a dogwood.

When the uniform in the patrol car saw him coming, he quickly got out of the vehicle. "Sir —"

"Give me an update, Constable."

"Just a small team in there now, sir. Forensics going for prints, fluids, hair samples."

"Thanks" — MacNeice looked down at his nameplate — "Officer Muti. Any relation to Riccardo Muti?"

"The maestro from Napoli? Naw — don't I wish."

"Time's a circle, Muti. Somewhere along that circle, your families met." He shook his hand and walked towards the house. "Keep an eye out."

"For who, sir?"

"A Baltimore oriole. There's one close by."

A younger cop approached with coffees. Handing one to Muti, he nodded towards the tall man going into the house. "Who's that guy?"

"That guy?" Muti shook his head. "Detective Superintendent MacNeice — the Homicide Gretzky. He speaks in tongues, talks to birds . . ." He took a sip of his coffee. "One guy told me he was in his unit up on Wentworth — same detail, securing the scene. It was pissin' buckets, an Old Testament kinda rain. Outta nowhere, the DS walks by his cruiser all casual-like. He heads onto the road, cars screaming by, assholes calling him an asshole, the whole bit. He stands in the rain talkin' to a crow. Guy swore it was true. I believe him." As if for evidence, Muti added, "He just told me to watch out for a bird . . . shit, that baseball bird."

"The Blue Jays?"

"Naw, the other one."

"Cardinals?"

"Shit, no. Gimme another one."

"Orioles?"

"That's the one. Anyway, this is his crime scene."

The young constable looked up and down the street. "So where's his car?"

"Dunno. He musta walked here."

THERE'S NO SOUND hollower than the closing of a door when the bodies are gone. MacNeice thought that peculiar emptiness should be studied and given an official name. He could feel it now. Every room in the Terry house was lifeless. People often called it haunting, but it was simply and sadly the complete absence of life and spirit. The house knew what had happened and it wasn't about to forget. It didn't matter that there were three or four people from Forensics inside. The place was hollow. He was reminded that *hollow* was how Nancy Pretty had described Matthew Terry.

MacNeice could see someone in haz-mat gear working in the kitchen. Whoever it was didn't respond when he closed the heavy door behind him. The stench of death had lessened but it hadn't disappeared. It had seeped into the carpets, wood, and wallpaper, the books and chairs. MacNeice slipped baggies over his shoes, pulled on his latex gloves, and walked slowly up the stairs, avoiding the patches of dried blood.

The boot tracks had all been marked. There were flag markers on the landing next to two shell casings, and on the opposite side of the bedroom, two paper markers — "3" and "4" — taped near black holes in the wall where the bullets had

lodged after tearing through Father Terry's chest. The enormous stain where he had fallen was crisp and dry. Similarly,
where Matthew had been placed was a large, dark stain, but
this one had been scuffed, likely by the killer adjusting the
body for effect. A strand of bloody wadding from the doll's
head was still on the carpet, stuck to a stain of the real thing.
The overturned chair had been removed. So too the bedding and mattress; the bed's wooden frame seemed to be
waiting for something.

MacNeice stood where the V had been. The little brass
letter had been replaced by a cryptic square of pink paper
marked "8." He took Fiza's point-and-shoot and squatted to
frame the same image without the set and actors.

Sitting on the windowsill, he studied the image. He put
away the camera, stuck his hands in his jacket pockets, and
waited.

Ten minutes later, a figure wearing an orange haz-mat
suit appeared in the doorway. "Sir, you okay?"

"I am. Thank you."

"Sorry. We got a bit spooked when the floor up here
stopped creaking."

"Just waiting for the room to speak to me. I won't be
long."

The man nodded and made his way downstairs.
MacNeice could hear him telling his partner in the kitchen,
after which there were some muffled giggles.

When it was quiet again, he stood up and looked past
Father Terry's blood and urine stains to the doorway where
his blood was splattered on the wall. He looked from there
to the carpet stain and back again. Blood-red, almost black.
He walked over to the pink 8 and squatted again, glancing

at the mahogany headboard. Sunlight streamed onto the walls; it defined objects large and small.

"It's too sharp, too bright. This stage was supposed to be seen at night, just before dawn. The effect doesn't work in daylight." MacNeice jumped up so quickly he felt light-headed, and had to reach for the windowsill to maintain his balance.

He went downstairs and called out, "Thanks. I'm gone." He slammed the door behind him and never heard the haz-mat man in the kitchen say, "Oh, you're gone all right."

Outside, he tore off the baggies and gloves and shoved them into his jacket pockets. This time MacNeice didn't consider the Rover Scout march. He hit the gravel running and didn't slow down to wave when he passed Muti's cruiser.

[21]

WELL BEFORE HE REACHED MAIN STREET, MacNEICE HAD SLOWED to a jog. A block farther, he was so out of breath that he felt as if his chest were going to explode. He stopped running altogether and walked normally the rest of way. His thighs were burning when he climbed the stairs to Division, and when he entered the cubicle, Aziz looked alarmed.

"Everything okay, Mac?"

The others swung around in their chairs. MacNeice's face, already flushed from the run, grew redder with embarrassment. He smiled and took a deep breath. "I'm fine, thanks. I've been jogging — well, running and jogging." He took his jacket off and threw it over the back of his chair, hoping that the casual gesture would distract them. Then he exhaled and settled his breathing. "I've got something. I still don't know what it is" — he turned to the Amelia Street photo — "but I know this image. I mean the original. This scene is a copy."

No one said anything. They were waited for something to follow. "I'm not entirely sure, but I think the original's a print or a photograph, maybe an illustration, but it's very dark. I've definitely seen it before."

"You mean, like art?" Vertesi asked. "Like a painting?"

"Maybe a painting. But yes, art."

"And donkey-head man?" Swetsky asked. Next to the crime scene photo was Vertesi's headshot from the morgue.

"No, I've never seen that before." MacNeice turned to Ryan. "Can you make this photo look like he's alive?"

"Already on it, sir."

MacNeice turned back to his team. Williams had thrown his hands behind his head and sat rocking on his chair, a wide grin on his face. The right side of Swetsky's mouth was tucked firmly into his cheek in disbelief. Vertesi was looking out the corridor window. Aziz smiled her da Vinci smile.

"You ready to bank on that?" Swetsky had to express his disbelief. He lived in a Dundurn where killing and art were as separate as apples and spaceships.

"Absolutely."

Vertesi shifted his gaze to the whiteboard. "How would we research that?"

Ryan swivelled around. "I could do a search for 'Art: four bodies shot dead in a bedroom.'" By the sound of his voice, he thought it was unlikely.

"Hang on," said Aziz. "A friend of mine from the gym is an associate curator at the DAG. She's five minutes away."

"Call her. Better still, if she's there, we'll walk over

together." MacNeice took a marker and wrote below the photo *Art!* before glancing back to Swetsky with a smile.

"Vertesi, send the cleaned-up photo of donkey-head man to the media and post it on the DPD site. Let's see if someone knows him."

IT WOULD BE an hour before the Dundurn Art Gallery opened, but the DAG café was serving coffee and tea, mostly to docents and security staff. A young family of four was seated in the corner, likely coming from the hotel across the street. The coffee was strong and smooth, but the real draw was the homemade muffins and cinnamon buns.

A slender woman with short white-blonde hair, wearing a turquoise blouse with black collar and cuffs, slim-cut trousers, and black shoes, stood up as they came in the door.

"*Bonjour,* Fiza," she greeted Aziz, with air kisses to both cheeks, then offered her hand to MacNeice. "You and I have not met, Detective MacNeice, but I feel I know you. I am Nicole Clement." She held his hand slightly longer than was necessary and said something in French to Aziz. "Please, sit down. What can I do for you?"

They made small talk until the waiter came to take their orders: three coffees, and a cinnamon bun for Aziz. Then MacNeice put an envelope on the table. "Inside are photographs from two homicide scenes. If the thought of seeing them is too upsetting for you, please tell me now."

"No, endless evenings of American television have desensitized me, I think."

He laid the photographs from Amelia Street on the table and sat back. Nicole reached over to her bag and took out a pair of red-framed glasses. A minute went by before she pushed the glasses back into her hair and smiled at MacNeice. "It is quite horrible. *C'est un hommage, non?*" She looked at MacNeice. "The details are not quite right."

MacNeice and Aziz exchanged glances and sat forward.

Nicole pointed to the photo. "The room, that furniture . . . of course, the doll and the mannequin — which are quite funny, no? It is, of course, Honoré Daumier's lithograph *Rue Transnonain, 15 April 1834*." She put the print down. "It depicts the slaughter of an innocent Parisian family. It's very famous in France. It was incendiary, explosive, when it appeared in a newspaper. The government shut down the paper and confiscated the edition, but not all the copies." Clement smiled ruefully. *"Alors"* — she retrieved a cellphone from her bag and in a few seconds placed the phone next to the photo — *"c'est ça."*

And there it was, a broodingly dark and evocatively real black-and-white lithograph. And while MacNeice's snapshot was lit by the light of day, there was no mistaking the similarity.

"V for vantage point," Aziz said under her breath.

"Where could you see that print today?" asked MacNeice.

"Ah, oui. I believe the Metropolitan in New York has one. And of course there's one on display at the Musée d'Orsay in Paris."

MacNeice felt the back of his neck shiver as the memory suddenly came back. Days after he'd met Kate, they had wandered through that vast former train station, looking at but not seeing the art. She had her arm in his and they spoke in whispers about many things, occasionally stopping to study something on the wall.

He didn't recall stopping at the Daumier, but now he remembered passing it by. Seeing only what he'd come to Paris to escape — homicide was something he preferred not to discuss with Kate — he had turned away. For her part, Kate had been intrigued by a sculpture and missed it entirely.

Nicole pointed to the envelope. "Another test?"

MacNeice smiled and took out the image. "This occurred at the Devil's Punchbowl."

Nicole picked up the photo and slid her glasses back into place. Several times over the course of the next minute, she gazed over her spectacles at MacNeice to see if he was serious. "This one I don't know. Perhaps it is the context, that muscular landscape."

The waiter arrived with the coffees. "I really don't know this one. It is satire, no?" Nicole put two spoonfuls of sugar in her coffee before looking back to MacNeice. "I'm sorry, this is outside my area of interest — assuming that it makes a reference to art. I will introduce you to the DAG's contemporary curator, Dr. Ridout." She turned her eyes away from the photo. "Now, unless you have more photos, Detective, please let's enjoy our coffee and watch Fiza eat her sugar bun."

ON THE WAY back to Division, Aziz noticed the lift in MacNeice's step. "He's giving us the clues he wants us to find." MacNeice crossed Main in long strides that had Aziz running to keep up. "We'll take them, but I want the ones he doesn't want us to have."

"Do you have any idea what those might be?"

"Not precisely. But think this through: he goes to all this trouble so that we or the police photographer can take a picture?" He looked at her, shaking his head. "He wants to show us the images he's taking — making. He's proud of them."

"I can't imagine what he could do with them."

"Neither can I." MacNeice was troubled by the question. Why choose Daumier? He recalled the work depicted the state-authorized slaughter of its own citizens. Whether the family on rue Transnonain had been chosen by mistake or by design, their murders had sent a chilling message to anyone who might talk of rebellion. "It was ruthless. By design, like the original. I think our man is sending a message."

"Do you remember now where you saw that print?"

"I do."

"When you were there with Kate."

He nodded. "She wanted to show me a part of Paris that wasn't a jazz bar filled with smoke."

He opened the division door for Aziz and they made their way slowly across the lobby to the stairwell.

"Mac, would you like me to join you on your visit to Kate's grave?"

He stopped short of the stairs and looked down at her. "You'd be willing to do that?"

"A day in the country, a breather from this . . . Yes, I would." That wasn't the reason, but it would suffice. "But I'll understand if you want to go up alone."

He smiled. Noticing a tiny fleck of pastry at the corner of her mouth, he took a tissue from his pocket and wiped it away. "No, I'd like that. I don't know when we can go, now that we're back in business, but yes, come with me. On the way back I'll take you for a bite at my favourite truck stop."

"Mmm, yum. Trucker food."

"Race me up the stairs?" Before she could answer, MacNeice tore off, two stairs at a time, up to Homicide Division.

[22]

WITHIN MINUTES, A PRINTOUT OF DAUMIER'S LITHOGRAPH WAS mounted below MacNeice's snapshot of the Amelia Street scene. Swetsky was staring at the two images. "Jesus H. Just when you think you've seen it all . . ." He slapped MacNeice on the back. "You know, I remember shit too, but it's mostly basketball facts and stats. I'm impressed, Mac."

MacNeice studied Vertesi's photograph of the man in the donkey head. Ryan's retouching was deft; though the man's eyes were closed, he looked peaceful rather than dead. You might think he was meditating.

"It's already up on the *Standard*'s website and ours. Local radio and television are driving people to their websites to see the image." Vertesi added, "Everyone wants to know what happened to this guy. I tell them, 'He's a person of interest.'"

"That'll buy us a day or two, but sure as hell, word'll leak out," Swetsky said. "I'll get that donkey-head pic off to costume rental houses here and in Toronto."

"Check with theatre companies too." MacNeice didn't want to overlook anything, but he doubted that the head had been rented, bought, or stolen. Like the nightgowns, which had no labels, he thought it was probably custom-made.

"I'll check the art supply shops to see if anyone has been buying large amounts of artist's canvas or duck cloth," Williams said. "Though the amount of canvas it would take to make four nightshirts probably isn't a jaw-dropper, it's worth a try."

"Mister V might not be done making nightshirts just yet," Swetsky said in a grim whisper.

BY 5:42 P.M., six costume rental shops from Buffalo to Toronto; four theatre companies, in Niagara, Stratford, and Toronto; and the ballet and opera companies had all failed to recognize the donkey head. Where the duck cloth was concerned, five artists' supply shops claimed that sales of canvas hadn't changed in any significant way. If anything, Williams was told, sales had been in a slow and steady decline for two or three decades.

For his part, Vertesi spent the afternoon researching Matthew and Howard Terry. "Forensics said the Mercedes was undisturbed; the only fresh prints were the son's. Matthew Terry had a few speeding tickets over the past three years that cost him some points. No drunk-driving charges, no interactions with the courts other than his divorce." Vertesi turned over his notes. "But there were two investigations initiated by the Securities Commission concerning a sell-off of shares. Both cases were dropped before the hearings began; there's no record of why."

"Anything else?"

"Not much on Father Terry," Vertesi said. "He closed his church years ago and gave up the religious habit." He paused for the groans and a withering glance from MacNeice. "Sorry, boss. He retired from the Church and moved in with Matthew after his wife died. I also checked with the cable companies, Dundurn Hydro, water, and gas. None of them were called or sent to the Terry residence."

MacNeice was about to call it a day when the phone rang. Ryan called out, "Detective Aziz, it's for you. Someone from the gallery."

She looked MacNeice's way. "I sent the Punchbowl photo to Ridout, the curator Nicole recommended."

They all turned in her direction. She was listening, writing furiously on her notepad. After a moment she threw a thumbs-up into the air. It was a gesture so culturally out of character for Aziz that MacNeice smiled.

"Yes . . . You've been very helpful. Goodbye." She was still transcribing the conversation. "That was Jeffery Ridout, the DAG's contemporary curator. He recognized the image straightaway."

"Jesus, Joseph, and Mary," Swetsky barked.

"Quite." She looked in the direction of the whiteboard photo. "It's by two brothers named Chapman — they're alive, working in the U.K. But it's really about their defacing of a work by Goya."

"Goya?" Swetsky asked. "Is he a local guy?"

"Spanish. Not local." Aziz smiled and turned to Ryan.

"Ry, search for 'Goya's *Disasters of War* — victims wearing animal heads.'"

In less than a minute Ryan swung around on his stool and clapped his hands on his knees. "I'm printing out some images." Turning back to the "Millennium Falcon," his homemade supercomputer, he read, "'Francisco de Goya completed *Disasters of War* in 1820.' It's gruesome, but he wasn't into animal heads." Then he looked over his shoulder and smiled. "But Dinos and Jake Chapman are."

The printer slowly began spitting out images. MacNeice, functionally illiterate with any technology beyond a CD player, occasionally worried that Ryan's customization and recycling of parts from the division's obsolete-computer trash heap might one day set Division ablaze.

Ryan continued. "Two brothers, born in the U.K. in the 1960s. They painted over a rare set of Goya's original etchings with" — Ryan lifted the prints from the machine — "clown faces, dog and rodent heads, and a horse's head." Ryan handed the images to MacNeice, and the printer shut down with a descending mechanical whine.

MacNeice began taping the printouts to the whiteboard but said nothing.

"So what've we got here, boss?" Vertesi asked as they gathered around him. "The Chapmans, as Fiza would say, are taking the piss out of Goya, and our guy's taking the piss out of the Chapman brothers?"

"Accurate," MacNeice said, standing back to study the board.

"It's pretty esoteric," said Fiza.

"Meaning?" Swetsky asked.

"Obscure." Fiza felt embarrassed for sounding too posh.

"Well, esoteric or obscure, it's seriously sick shit." Swetsky had seen enough. He turned away, shaking his head.

"The eye of the beholder, I guess." Williams shrugged.

"What's V's point, though? And what did that guy in the Punchbowl do to deserve this?" Vertesi was examining the clown face pasted over Goya's etching of a naked man jammed onto the trunk of a tree.

"A coincidence of circumstances, perhaps?" MacNeice said as he compared the images. "Wrong place and worse timing — he and the Terrys somehow fitted a profile?" He shoved his hands into his pockets. "It appears to confirm that our man is an artist and that his subjects are chosen to play dead stand-ins."

Aziz offered, "I think he's walking a fine line between fiction and reality." When Swetsky swung around with his eyebrows close to his hairline, she qualified her comment. "In these photographs," she said, pointing to the Amelia Street and Punchbowl bodies, "the viewer naturally assumes that it's beet juice or ketchup and not blood. Most people would think they're just models posing as corpses —"

"Meaning no gallery knowingly exhibits snuff art," Williams said.

"Exactly. And because we think it's theatre, the artist will have the satisfaction of duping us, or at the very least leading us to the critical point of his work." She shrugged her shoulders before adding, "I'm making huge leaps here."

The telephone rang. Ryan picked it up, listened for a moment, and put the receiver down. He turned to MacNeice. "Sir, that was Dr. Richardson calling. She would" — he closed his eyes to recall her exact words — "enjoy the pleasure of your company. Now, please. Then she hung up."

Aziz was looking at her cellphone. "Mac, Ridout's email-ing me. 'Anything I can do to help, just let me know.' Now that he's found the Chapmans, do you want me to keep him available?"

"Yes." MacNeice turned away from the board. "He might know some of the artists working in Dundurn. It's a long shot, but one of them may be our man, or someone that might know him or his work."

Looking at the snapshot of the brass V, MacNeice glanced at Williams. "First thing tomorrow, get on to signage com-panies in the area. See if you can identify where the V's are coming from." Williams nodded. "And anyone who's come in lately to buy two V's . . . or maybe a dozen."

The room fell silent. Once again it was clear that every-one thought this was just the beginning. MacNeice felt that if the perpetrator was going to exhibit the images somewhere in some form, two were probably not enough.

As if she were reading his mind, Aziz asked, "Is it too soon to consider where these images could be exhibited?"

"No, it isn't. I would think not in Canada or the States."

"Maybe," Williams said. "But if they're redone as paint-ings, like Fiza said, no one will think they're really dead. What kind of market is there for that stuff?"

"Collectors of social commentary. European and Asian tastes tend to be edgier than those in North America," Aziz suggested.

"Let's find out about newly arrived artists from Toronto and elsewhere." MacNeice picked up a notebook and pen. "I'm off to Barton Street."

[23]

A CORPSE ON A TABLE UNDER PAINFULLY BRIGHT LIGHTS IS A forlorn sight. But three bodies lined up side by side took MacNeice's breath away. As he struggled to gain his composure, he searched for a neutral site to park his attention.

"MacNeice, you are prompt. Thank you." From her office, Richardson's crisp and cheerful voice was exactly what he needed.

He turned away from the tables and stepped out of the punishingly lit room and into the soft incandescent lighting of her office, though not before catching a sly smile from Richardson's assistant. In MacNeice's opinion, Junior found too much pleasure in the discomfort of others.

"Do take a seat, Mac. We can do what I've called you here for in the relative comfort of my office. Tea or Tio Pepe?"

"If I'd stayed out there much longer, sherry would have been as essential as oxygen." He sat down, trying to hide the first deep breath he'd taken since leaving the Chevy. "But no thank you, Mary."

"To the Terrys, then." She opened her file folder, the corners and the fold still crisp, though he'd seen enough of her bloated and dog-eared case files to know that wouldn't last. "Matthew, the son — nothing unusual. He had spaghetti carbonara, several glasses of red wine, bread, and what looks like vanilla gelato earlier in the evening. The father had eaten very little: toast and marmalade, tea — several cups." She eased the turquoise glasses down her nose and peered over them at MacNeice. "Both men died at roughly the same time, two nights before they were discovered, Matthew between nine and ten and his father between ten and eleven.

"The weapon was a nine-millimetre pistol, judging by the entry and exit wounds. No doubt that will be confirmed by the slugs that Forensics retrieved from the wall. But here's what I find particularly interesting." She arranged four slides on the illuminated X-ray screen. "They're cross-sections of the blood vessels in the upper-left heart muscle. These two" — she pointed to the images on the left — "are from Matthew. The others are from Howard Terry." MacNeice rose from his chair. "Notice any distinctions between them?" She stood back so he could get a closer look.

He looked from one set to the other several times. Moving a large circular magnifying glass along the shelf, MacNeice stopped where he could frame Matthew's and his father's slides at the same time. After studying them, he turned to Richardson. She stood with her arms crossed, smiling with anticipation.

"I don't know how to describe it beyond this: the son's slide looks dense and Father Terry's looks open — the difference between salami and capicolla. Does that make sense?"

"Perfect sense. Yes, splendid. I won't bore you with the medical terminology; I'll just speculate about why they're different." She moved the magnifying glass out of the way. "Discounting the ravages of time, diet, lifestyle, and so on, I think you're seeing two responses to the situation they found themselves in." She paused. "Do you have any idea why Matthew was in the basement?"

"None. He was shot near the electrical panel, but why he was there isn't clear. We checked with Dundurn Hydro and they hadn't dispatched anyone, because there wasn't a problem."

Richardson nodded, then began a lucid and, happily for MacNeice, understandable analysis of the slides. Matthew Terry, she said, may have been under extreme stress. "Possibly just being down there with a stranger was enough, but certainly once the weapon was revealed, that would have instilled immediate terror. I believe the constricted blood vessels are his response to terror, as occurs when livestock enter an abattoir." She glanced at MacNeice. "A reaction, it's speculated, that can explain tough meat."

"And you think his father wasn't under the same stress?"

"We'll likely never know what transpired in that house, but it's clear from this image" — she tapped the slide with her pencil — "that he didn't react to the situation the way his son did." Richardson then talked about Jesuit monks who had been burned at the stake or stripped of their flesh on their way to sainthood. "First-hand accounts of their torture consistently report a calm, almost serene, beatific demeanour. In other words," Richardson said, "a priest, even one who's renounced his faith, might find the deity within and be able to accept and possibly even embrace his own death."

"Do you believe that?"

"Of course not — it's rubbish. Though it's conceivable that Father Terry did. And there's more." She opened the folder again and flipped through two pages of commentary digitally transferred from the autopsy voice recording. "Howard Terry had a Stage Four brain tumour and a cancerous mass in his lung. You already know about those. We also found a cancerous lymph node in his neck and another in his left armpit." She pointed to the right side of her own neck and more generally to her upper left arm. "I suspect the brain is the source, but without dissecting all his organs, we're not ready to declare that the primary site — what Junior refers to as 'the mothership.' It's likely that his health records would tell us, though for our purposes it's not important, because he didn't die of cancer. He died — again as Junior puts it — from 'lead poisoning.'" She shook her head. "He's very good, Mac, but he can be such a tiresome boy."

"He's not a boy."

"Touché." Turning back to the slides, she concluded. "I think this man knew his time on earth was limited — very limited."

"And so his killer just talked him out of life?"

She shrugged, nodded slowly, and closed the file. "Going strictly by his blood vessels, I'm confident enough in my theory to suggest that he wasn't terrified at the time of death."

"I'll take that sherry now, if you don't mind."

Richardson took two small, delicately engraved glasses from a silver tray and poured two measures from a heavy crystal decanter. "My grandfather gave me this set. It was something he acquired in India before the war." She handed MacNeice a glass and lifted hers. "Chin-chin, Detective."

While he was tempted to throw it back in one go, MacNeice sipped the sherry as he imagined a gentleman would. It warmed his throat, not with the spirited heat of grappa but with a dry/sweet overtone that made him reach for a chair. "Can we do the next one sitting down?"

"Of course. I won't be needing the screen." She turned off the viewing light and sat across from him at her desk. "I apologize, Mac, for not inquiring as to your health. Can I assume that you're fully recovered from the last case?"

"I am, more or less. A bit fatigued at times, but that's all." He was now regretting his earlier run.

"This next one won't take long. It's pretty much as I said earlier." She opened another virgin file. "A user, twenty-five or so. I'll spare you the details of his stomach contents, other than to say there were traces of a variety of pharmacological substances, from codeine to cough syrup. They didn't kill him, nor did the chest wounds. This fellow died from a dose of fentanyl and heroin, a lethal mixture that would have killed an Olympic shot putter within a half-hour of ingestion. There are two things I can say now that I couldn't earlier. One is speculative and the other concerns timing, and is factual."

"How long after he died was he shot?"

"Five or six hours." Her certainty was delivered quickly. She turned a page in her file. "As to the other, given what we found in his system — and this is a leap, Mac — his addiction had progressed to the point where all but a few of his injection sites were months old. However, the cough syrup and codeine were fresh, within several hours of the overdose." Richardson could see that MacNeice was waiting for more. "I'm in your territory suggesting this, but given the street value and purity of the drugs that killed him, I find it hard to believe that he came into a windfall to obtain them."

"His killer murders him with the drugs and then, five or six hours later, fires two rounds into his chest?" MacNeice wanted Richardson to confirm what he and his team already suspected.

"I know it beggars belief, but yes."

"Good. Then we're on the same page." He drank the last of the sherry and smiled. "I'd better get back to it, then."

Leaving Richardson's lab in the bowels of DGH, MacNeice gazed up at a fundraising poster for the hospital's cancer wing. He was struck by the language and reminded how it hadn't changed. It was, and seemed always to have been, the language of conflict and war: fighting, defeating, winning or losing battles against cancer. His heart sank as he remembered how brutally Kate had lost, even with his help. He turned and walked slowly towards the Chevy.

Do you recall that first examination room? How it was caught somewhere between clinical cold and warm domesticity?

"It's etched in my mind, Kate."

The sink, the cleansing solutions, the paper-towel dispenser, and that odd kitchen cabinet that didn't appear to serve a purpose.

"I remember the stillness as we waited. Even together, our shallow breathing wouldn't have fogged a window."

If there'd been a window.

"The fear of what we might hear."

I was already becoming more of a condition than a person. What was that awful yellow plastic box on the wall for?

"Used syringes and soiled bandages, darling. Not for you."

Small mercy.

[24]

MAcNEICE'S DESK TELEPHONE RANG AT 8:35 P.M., STARTLING BOTH him and Aziz. They were the only ones still on the floor. The phone's ringing echoed insistently through the empty office.

"It's DI Maracle, sir."

"What have you got, Charlie?"

Maracle had knocked on the door of Palmer's neighbour. During the interview he was told that the missing detective was building a motorcycle in a rental unit nearby, to replace the one that had burned up years before. Maracle went back through the house and, after an hour or so, found a garage-door opener. "Palmer's garage doesn't have an automatic door. Stamped into the back of the fob is 'USI' and a seven-digit number."

"USI?"

"Yeah, I didn't know either. Turns out it's a new chain of storage units called U-Stor-It. The closest one is a half-mile south of Palmer's house. USI gives out two fobs per customer, so it's possible he's got the other one on him." Maracle had gone back to Division to write it up, and then, pursuing a hunch, he'd called one of the fleet mechanics responsible for maintaining the force's motorcycles. Palmer was a regular visitor, asking all kinds of questions about parts and performance. "Apparently he's been building that bike for at least six years."

"Why doesn't that surprise me?"

"Agreed. Sir, I know we want this on low heat, so I was thinking I'd drive up to USI now, just to rule it out." Maracle added, "Couldn't hurt, right?"

"Aziz and I will meet you at Palmer's house. We'll go on from there in my car. Be there in thirty minutes."

Aziz looked up from her desk. "Where are we going?"

"I'll tell you on the way. Do you have your weapon?"

"Yes."

IT WAS 9:40 P.M. when MacNeice eased the Chevy off Upper Paradise into the USI driveway. Two rows of back-to-back storage units stretched a hundred yards into the lot, with three paved lanes for easy access. The centre lane was the widest. Tungsten lights washed over the bright orange of the unit doors, but the lighting didn't cover the entire facility, so many of the units faded into the night.

MacNeice parked the car so that it partially blocked the entrance. They spread out and walked slowly down the middle lane, with Maracle squeezing the opener at every unit on the right. When they reached the end, they switched sides and started walking back. Moths dive-bombed the light fixtures above them and the night birds were darting about, screeching warnings.

As they approached the third unit closest to the entrance, Maracle pointed the fob as he kept walking. *Click-click-click.* They heard a door respond, but it was on the outside row.

"Do it again," MacNeice said, as they stood silent. The distinct hum of machinery and the rattle of a garage-door chain. "Stop it, then start again to let it open fully."

They walked swiftly around the corner. The orange door of the third unit had given way to a black void. Maracle took out his side arm, released the safety, and held it close to his thigh. Aziz and MacNeice drew theirs as well.

A late-model silver minivan sat collecting dew on the grass that edged the asphalt. Maracle circled the vehicle and signalled that it was empty. The nearest tungsten lamp was shattered, leaving the unit to the ink-black gloom inside.

MacNeice was reaching for his Maglite when they heard a vehicle swerve off Upper Paradise and bounce over the curb. It swerved again to avoid hitting the Chevy.

"Behind the minivan," MacNeice said. Huddled below its windows, MacNeice and Aziz released the safeties on their weapons.

"Dodge Ram 3500," Maracle whispered.

Aziz looked at him, puzzled.

"Sound of the engine, and the suspension." Maracle smiled.

Slowly the truck appeared, and more slowly still it turned towards them before stopping. Its high beams raked the driveway, broadsiding the minivan and merging their legs with its shadows. "Don't move. Not a muscle," said MacNeice.

After what seemed like minutes, the truck inched forward. "Wait for it. When I give the signal, Charlie, you go around to the other side. I'll give the driver an order to surrender. Aziz, stay low and take out the wheels if he tries to make a run for it." MacNeice took out his Maglite and squared it along the barrel of his weapon.

As the truck drew closer to the unit, its headlights pushed aside the dark of the opening like a curtain. MacNeice's eyes widened as what appeared to be two human feet emerged from the darkness.

The truck eased forward again and stopped. MacNeice nodded to Maracle and switched on his Maglite. He stood up, leaning on the van's hood and training the Maglite and the weapon on the driver. "Police! Shut down that vehicle. Get out and lie face down on the ground."

Maracle's flashlight hit the driver's face from the side. Startled, he raised a hand to shield his eyes and then began revving the engine, at the same time talking to someone in the passenger seat and someone else behind.

MacNeice repeated the command and received more revving in return. Seconds later, the engine dropped to a rumbling hot-metal idle, after which the driver's and rear passenger windows slid down.

MacNeice was about to give them a final warning when a shotgun blast from the front passenger seat tore into the storage unit, driving the feet into darkness. The engine roared to life and the driver opened up with a semi-automatic. He fired at Maracle and then dropped the truck into gear. The wheels shuddered and screamed. As he accelerated past them, the driver sprayed the minivan's windshield with several rounds before howling down the lane and disappearing behind the units.

Maracle didn't hesitate. He sprinted for the entrance and the cover of the Chevy.

MacNeice looked down. Aziz was frantically tearing at the bottom of her blouse, which was covered in blood. MacNeice pulled it up to reveal a hole above her left hip oozing blood. He felt her lower back and then pulled his hand away; it was also bloody.

"It went through. Put pressure on it as best you can, Fiz. I'll be right back." Running up the driveway, he could hear the truck accelerating on the other side, the roar of its engine echoing off the metal units.

MacNeice squared himself into a firing position and opened up the moment the front bumper came into view. He had no idea how many rounds he fired, but when asked later by siu, he said, "As many as you can fire in two and a half seconds. I emptied the clip."

For his part, Maracle was firing into the truck's windshield and engine block as it sped directly towards him. The Ram slammed into the rear of the Chevy, tossing it sideways into Maracle, who disappeared from view. The truck skidded onto Upper Paradise and careened south, leaving a cloud of blue smoke behind it as it tore away.

Running over to the Chevy, MacNeice saw that Maracle was on his back. He pulled out his cellphone and punched in some numbers. "Officers down! Officers down! Paradise Road U-Stor-It facility — that's Uniform. Sierra. Tango. Oscar. Romeo. India. Tango."

"Roger that, sir. 2900 Upper Paradise Road. Assistance is on its way."

"Patch me through to all DPD radios." MacNeice waited until he heard the hoarse beep. "All units, all units to the mountain. Pursue a black Dodge Ram heavily damaged by gunfire. Last seen heading south from 2900 Upper Paradise Road. Three suspects, considered armed and dangerous."

Maracle lifted his head as MacNeice approached. "I'm okay, sir. Maybe a broken ankle. I got smacked pretty good by your car. Was Aziz hit?"

"She was. Help will be here soon, though. Stay where you are."

AZIZ HAD REMOVED her jacket and blouse and was using the jacket to slow the bleeding. MacNeice knelt beside her and eased her hands away from the wound. Shining his Maglite on her lower back, he said, "It's a clean exit, Fiza."

"So now you're a homicide cop *and* a doctor?"

MacNeice removed his jacket and placed it over her for both warmth and modesty. He sat down, pulled her up between his legs, and leaned against the wheel of the van. "Think of this as a bicycle built for two, or our first sleigh ride together. Use the warmth from my body." Wrapping his right arm around her, he pressed his hand over the entry wound. With her blouse in his left hand, he tried to plug the torn and bleeding exit wound. Aziz arched her back from the pain.

"I'm going to increase the pressure, Fiza. Tell me about where you go when you want to escape."

Aziz felt faint and slightly nauseated. She was shivering

and taking slow, deep breaths. Leaning into him, she looked up at his face. "I don't have a place to go to, Mac."

He could see the fear in her eyes. "A beach, or maybe a forest? A city. London, New York, Paris?"

Her head rolled slowly back and forth across his chest as she closed her eyes. "Paris, only once . . . when I was twelve . . . a school trip."

"Fiza, stay with me. The ambulance will be here soon. Stay awake now. Open your eyes."

"Mmm. I can feel your heart beating, Mac." Aziz didn't open her eyes, but she smiled again briefly before passing out.

TEN MINUTES LATER, Aziz was on her way to St. Joe's. Maracle refused to go to the hospital but allowed the paramedics to tape up his foot and ankle and leave him a pair of crutches. MacNeice was picking up Fiza's jacket and blouse as the detective approached.

"How's Aziz?" Maracle asked, glancing at MacNeice's bloodstained shirt and the dark red pool at his feet.

"She lost a fair amount of blood, but she'll make it."

MacNeice was using his jacket to wipe Fiza's blood from his hands when he realized he still hadn't looked into the storage unit. He dropped the clothes near the soiled wound packs by the paramedics and turned towards the open door. A crowd of uniformed men and women stood there, many of them talking softly, while others wisecracked and some just shook their heads. He turned to Maracle. "That is not a good sign, Charlie."

They crossed the driveway and the emergency personnel

began stepping aside. The cops among them addressed the detectives with "Sir, sir" and the firefighters and paramedics nodded or did nothing. It wasn't a sign of disrespect. MacNeice assumed that it was more an acknowledgement that what had happened to Aziz might have been a mistake — his mistake.

[25]

OTHER THAN LUMPY UPHOLSTERY AND THE PAIR OF HUMAN LEGS relaxing on the cantilevered footrest, it appeared to be a classic La-Z-Boy recliner.

"Christ, the body's inside that thing," said Maracle.

MacNeice sighed. "Now we know what happened to the chair in Palmer's living room."

The reupholstered vinyl of the chairback had been blown apart, leaving an angry blackened hole the size of a large cantaloupe. That and the legs would have been reason enough to draw a crowd, but the blast had shattered the flesh and bone and muscle within, mixing them up with the chair's foam.

Standing nearby were four officers and three firefighters, one with his Leatherman knife at the ready. As MacNeice and Maracle approached, a sergeant turned to meet them and the others stepped back towards the door. "It's a lousy upholstery job, sir. Should we cut him out of there?"

Too weary for humour, MacNeice told the sergeant to clear everyone from the unit and install a tarp across the entrance.

"Will do, sir." The sergeant turned to the cops and waited until they'd left before adding, "Speaking for everyone here, sir, we're sorry about your partner. We're pulling for her." He wasn't expecting an answer and didn't get one. The blood that covered MacNeice's clothes and hands was answer enough.

What the sergeant didn't ask, but likely thought, was why there hadn't been more backup. MacNeice was way ahead of him. That two of his detectives had been injured — one seriously — was taking its silent toll. Maracle's statement that it couldn't hurt to check out the unit had been prophetic in its way, but he didn't fault the man. It had been MacNeice's call to go, and it was his call to include Aziz.

Twenty or thirty rounds had been fired into the Dodge and it had still managed to escape. MacNeice's Chevy, on the other hand, was bullet-ridden and bent, twisted sideways like a dog with a broken hip. And it was bleeding gasoline. Firefighters were busy spreading bags of kitty litter to contain the spill from its ruptured fuel tank.

When the storage unit was cleared of people, Maracle leaned up against a workbench.

"Looks like that scatter gun ended it for him." He looked over to MacNeice. "Gotta be Palmer, you think?"

MacNeice shrugged. "Likely." He looked around the unit. There was a workbench running along the back wall, covered in power tools, pliers, wrenches, and a myriad of small tools. On another table sat a pair of cutting shears, a heavy rubber mallet, an industrial staple gun, a roll of three-inch white webbing, and a box cutter. Strips of brown vinyl lay rolled up under the bench next to the chair's discarded original leather skin.

The motorcycle, Palmer's six-year project, was twisted and destroyed. Its tires and seat were slashed, the spokes mangled, and the gas tank hammered from a teardrop into something resembling a crumpled soda can. In the corner of the unit was a pile of bloodied clothes, a pair of sneakers, and some sweat socks.

"You gotta be seriously pissed off to do this to a man," said Maracle. Looking away from the chair to three vodka bottles — two empty, one almost done — he added, "Though I guess this stuff made it more bearable."

On the floor were the remains of two family-sized buckets of fried chicken, and rags soiled with a mixture of oil and blood. A large Rubbermaid bin nearby was brimming with vinyl trimmings and beer cans. With his cellphone MacNeice took several shots of the chair, the feet and lower legs, the gory hole in the seatback. The body had been upholstered into the geometry of the chair. The arms emerged from inside to rest on the chair's arms; the head and body were buried, closely matching the contour of the original chair.

MacNeice put on his latex gloves, picked up a long screwdriver, and rummaged around in the Rubbermaid bin. In seconds he was scooping out clouds of white foam. "They removed this so he'd sit more or less flush with the surface." He took out several springs and saw that there were more at the bottom.

"He would have suffocated in there. May've been dead before we even got here."

"I hear some wishful thinking, Detective," MacNeice said with a brief, rueful smile. "Okay, hand me that box cutter."

He was about to cut into the chair when Williams and Vertesi appeared. "Jeezus, boss, you look like the sole survivor in a slasher film," said Vertesi.

Williams cleared his throat. "Swets is down at St. Joe's. Aziz is in surgery now. He'll call us as soon as —" He looked at the chair. "Man, this is ugly."

"Upholstery gone wrong," Vertesi suggested.

"Way wrong." Montile leaned over to study the massive blackened hole. "I assume that's not for ventilation."

Everyone but MacNeice laughed. "We believe this is DI Palmer." In a heartbeat, the levity left the room. "Michael, use your cell to record what I'm about to do."

MacNeice drew the blade deep across the top of the chair and down the length of the seatback on either side. Feeling for the man's limbs within, he made an incision around each arm and another to free the legs.

"Right." MacNeice took a deep breath. Holding the top of the covering in both hands, he pulled it away with an unintended flourish, like a magician lifting the cloth from a top hat to reveal a rabbit. A sickly gust of sweat, blood, and urine blew by the men.

Palmer, naked but for his underwear, had been set into the workings of the chair. The recliner's springs and foam stuffing were all around him, as if he were dough in a cookie cutter. His weight was resting on the wooden seat frame. His eyes were black and swollen shut. A stiff webbing gag pulled grotesquely at his mouth. The same webbing had been used to tether his body, legs, and arms to the chair's frame. Judging by the amount of blood on his boxer shorts and the massive bruising on his upper thighs, his genitals had sustained blunt-force trauma.

The shotgun blast had removed Palmer's left shoulder, leaving shreds of flesh, vinyl, foam, and bone. Down his torso, large staples had been fired randomly into the flesh; from each of the staple sites, blood had flowed freely. Given the devastation of the shoulder wound, however, there was very little blood loss. Though he said nothing, MacNeice assumed Palmer had been dead before the shotgun was fired.

"Boss, any chance this is related to Amelia Street and the Punchbowl? I mean, Donkeyman — and now the Chairman?"

"I'd say no." MacNeice nodded towards the far corner. "Palmer's clothes are tossed against the wall; there's nothing neat about this scene. And there's no V that I can see. This looks like payback, revenge. Worse, the inhumanity of this suggests that the killer was trying to reclaim the manhood stripped away when Palmer seduced his wife."

Maracle shifted his weight in an attempt to ease the pain in his ankle. "I guess the men in that truck were here to pick up their gear and leave town."

"You mean the guy who came into your division raising hell?"

"Yeah, him — or his sons or brothers. Start there. Find out who owns that black Ram. It's fulla holes, maybe even a body or two." Maracle let out a groan and leaned back against the bench.

"Give me your keys, Michael. I'll take Maracle to St. Joe's and check on Aziz."

[26]

THEY WERE APPROACHING STONE CHURCH ROAD WHEN A CALL CAME in over the radio. "DFD called to a vehicle fire south of 127 Glencaster Road. Believed to be a pickup truck."

"Can you stand the pain a little longer, Charlie?"

"Hell, yes." Maracle sat up in his seat.

MacNeice switched on the blue grille flashers and powered the car into a tire-screaming U-turn through the intersection. In seconds the speedometer climbed to 110 miles per hour. Maracle tightened his seatbelt and smiled.

"Put a fresh clip in your weapon, Detective, and another one in mine." MacNeice tore past the U-Stor-It facility. In his rear-view mirror he saw cops running out to the entrance to see what was going on.

In a hard right on Rymal Road, the Chevy clawed for

traction. Skidding across the lanes, it dropped onto the gravel shoulder before launching back onto the pavement. MacNeice powered the car through a left turn on Glencaster. Its rear end swung around, threatening to send machine and men rolling into the ditch. At the last second he twisted the wheel, driving the Chevy's rear end in the opposite direction. The tires shuddered and spun, filling the car with the smell of burnt rubber. The Chevy slalomed, then straightened; when it did, MacNeice buried the accelerator in the floor. In seconds they saw a plume of black smoke rising behind the trees and shrubs in the distance. There were no other emergency vehicles in sight.

MacNeice turned off the flashers and pulled to a stop as quietly he could. Getting out of the car, he looked across to see Maracle hoisting himself onto his crutches and making his way towards the lane. MacNeice caught up to him. "You might want to sit this one out."

"Not gonna happen, sir. I learned how to run on crutches when I was a kid, so trust me, I'll keep up."

The lane was barely wide enough for a truck as large as the Ram. There were shrubs and blooming forsythia on either side. As it curved away from the road, they could hear the popping hiss of a burning vehicle.

When the Ram came into view, it was engulfed in flames. The smell of burning paint and plastic was mixed with something more organic. There was no sign of anyone. The wind-whipped flames drowned out the whine of any approaching sirens. MacNeice considered pulling back to wait for support, but, working on the assumption that the men weren't injured and might make a run for it, he kept going.

Several steps later, the Ram's fuel tank exploded, sending metal panels and debris into the air and significantly increasing the height of the flames. MacNeice and Maracle waited for the high-flying metal to land. It wasn't hard to track; the fire illuminated everything.

MacNeice was moving forward when he heard a high-pitched whistle. He looked over at Maracle, who was holding up his index finger, making a slashing motion downward with his hand. *There's one man ahead on the left.*

MacNeice nodded and waited. Maracle made walking movements with his fingers and signalled three times with his open hand. *He's fifteen feet ahead.*

With that, Maracle dropped his crutches, got down on the ground, and began crawling forward. When they had moved another six feet or so, he whistled again. MacNeice crouched down and looked over at him. Maracle put two fingers towards his eyes and quickly pointed beyond the clump of forsythia directly ahead of MacNeice. He extended two fingers to suggest a gun and nodded. *He's armed.*

Maracle was on his belly. With his arms extended, he took aim, then nodded to MacNeice. MacNeice signalled for Maracle to hold fire. Stepping into the open, he could see a middle-aged man sitting upright against a tree, his head leaning back against the trunk. MacNeice took aim, then called, "Stay down. It's over. Throw away your weapon."

The man was wounded and bleeding from both legs. He managed to square himself on the trunk to face MacNeice, but he kept his semi-automatic resting on his thigh.

"Drop the weapon."

The man's face was blackened from the smoke, but his lips parted slowly to reveal a mouthful of bright white teeth.

He was grinning. He raised the weapon and wildly fired three quick bursts.

It was hard to tell who was first to return fire, but he was struck several times. The shots sent him into a forsythia bush, where dozens of yellow blossoms fell and settled on his face, some not far from the entry wound above his left eye.

MacNeice kicked away the weapon and squatted over the dead man. He checked the man's pockets and found a wallet with several credit cards, a driver's licence, vehicle registration and insurance, a health card, and two thousand dollars in hundred-dollar bills. Kyros Galanis, fifty-four years old, 269 Parkdale Avenue North, Dundurn. The Ram was registered to Galanis and Sons Upholstery, 1646 Main Street East.

As MacNeice walked over to Maracle, five members of the Tactical Unit came running towards them with assault rifles. After a quick assessment of the scene, they helped Maracle to his feet, handing him the crutches. They left the two detectives alone and went to check the body.

"Kyros Galanis. Is he the one who came for Palmer?" MacNeice was looking back at the burning vehicle.

Maracle was studying a scorched piece of metal. "I never saw him, but yeah, that's his name. I was planning to make a house call to his place tomorrow morning."

Minutes later, firefighters had transformed the Ram into a foamy white hulk. The flames that had ignited the nearby shrubs were extinguished and the lane returned to darkness. MacNeice stepped forward to examine the Ram. It was riddled with bullet holes and its interior appeared gutted. Between the darkness and the steam, it was impossible to see anything inside.

The tactical team produced two enormous floodlights

and directed them through the side windows. Fire-retardant foam covered everything and dripped in glops from the roof. The door panels and seats had burned down to their metal frames and the dashboard had melted. But MacNeice wasn't interested in the truck; he was looking for something else. When he found it, he called Maracle over. There were two bodies, one in the passenger seat and the other stretched awkwardly over the driveshaft in the rear. Covered in foam, they looked like ash-encased citizens of Pompeii.

The head of the tactical team came over to see inside the truck. He didn't say anything at first, but once he'd seen what was in the front and back seats, he asked, "Is there anything you need, sir?"

"No, I've seen enough for now, Commander. I shouldn't ask it of you, but we'll need a positive ID for that man over there. Please call DS McMillan to organize a viewing for Mrs. Galanis. Make sure she goes to the morgue with two female officers — preferably tonight."

"Will do, sir. It's not exactly in our job description, but I realize you're tapped out."

MacNeice shook his hand. "We'll let you get to it."

They began to make their way back down the lane. Maracle kept his eyes on the ground, dodging ruts in the dark with his crutches. He glanced up at MacNeice. "I've got an awful feeling that Mrs. Galanis didn't escape that guy's rage, sir."

"We'll know soon enough, Charlie."

MacNeice checked the registration again: Galanis and Sons Upholstery. A wave of fatigue swept over him as he understood the name's implication. "It's also possible that the two bodies inside the truck are his sons."

MACNEICE TOOK VERTESI'S car through an unhurried U-turn, weaving through the police vehicles, fire trucks, ambulances, and emergency personnel heading towards the narrow lane or standing in clusters discussing what had happened. Many of their eyes fell on the dark blue Chevy as it slowly headed north.

They didn't talk; both men were exhausted. Each preferred to focus on the night and the passing cars and pools of light sweeping over the hood, guiding them to the edge of the mountain and down into the embrace of the city. As he turned into Emergency at St. Joe's, MacNeice said, "That was an impressive shot from that distance, Charlie."

[27]

IT WAS 11:45 P.M. AND JOHN SWETSKY WAS BORED. HE SAT HUNCHED over his knees in the hospital corridor, twirling a paper cup between his fingers, as he kept vigil for Aziz. He didn't notice when MacNeice stepped out of the elevator. Others did, and gave the tall detective covered in dried blood a wide berth.

Seen from a distance, Swetsky dwarfed the chair. He looked like a lineman about to snap the football. His suit jacket was straining to overcome the muscles and meat that buttressed his chest, arms, and lower legs. MacNeice picked up another chair and sat down next to him. Swetsky glanced over at him "Christ, brother, you're a mess." When MacNeice didn't respond, he said, "She'll be fine, Mac. They brought her back a while ago. It went through clean. No contact with bones or organs, and no shell fragments."

MacNeice inhaled sharply and leaned forward. He looked back towards the elevators, and Swetsky understood why. "Surgeon said they did a good job closing up her exit wound. Said Aziz will be in a bikini by summer." Swetsky walked over and dumped his cup in the bin. When he sat down again, he looked at his colleague. "Never occurred to me that Aziz would even own a bikini, her being a Muslim and all."

"Can I go in, John?"

"She's still doped up. It'll be another hour or so." He turned to MacNeice. "You eaten anything?"

"No. It's been a day."

"There's a decent all-nighter on King Street. I'll get something good for both of us, but I'll take mine home." Swetsky didn't wait for a response. He was about to leave when he turned back. "Donkey-head's got a name, Mac. Leonard James Tundell, twenty-six. No fixed address. Cops found his wallet and clothes stacked high up on a rock shelf east of where he was found. There's a rap sheet on him. Drug-related, mostly petty stuff, nothing violent. Since we didn't hear anything from the dead shot, the photo ID from his health card is going in the paper tomorrow. I've already seen it on the waiting room TV."

SWETS HANDED HIM the comfort food in a grease-stained brown paper bag. MacNeice watched him lumber off to the elevators, where he turned, nodded, and waved his big paw in the air before disappearing inside.

MacNeice was aware that the bag's aroma was drifting along the corridor. He opened it to find a toasted Western sandwich in wax paper, a sliced pickle in tinfoil, and a can of

Italian lemonade to wash it down. MacNeice ate as the shifts were changing, avoiding the shocked eyes that passed by.

It was 1:35 a.m. when a nurse emerged and told MacNeice he could see Aziz. "For ten minutes only, Detective. She's asleep. If she wakes up at all, she'll be very groggy." Holding the door open with her foot, she whispered as he passed, "Ten minutes."

The light in the room was directed at the ceiling from the valance above the bed. MacNeice stood inside and listened as the door closed behind him with a soft *whoosh*. The hallway sounds fell away, replaced by the electronic beeps of monitors. Asleep, Aziz looked like a gift-wrapped package. The sheets had been tucked crisply across her chest; a baby-blue blanket lay reassuringly over her legs and feet. Someone had smoothed the shiny black hair away from her forehead. Even in the dim room she was striking.

As he approached the bed, he noticed how free of tension her hands were, even though two drips, one clear and the other deep red, disappeared into her right arm and wrist. Her chest rose and fell as a calm sea rises and falls — gently. MacNeice put his hand on her shoulder but pulled it away moments later, feeling selfish. He'd wanted reassurance on so many levels, but he decided to let her sleep. He backed silently out of the room.

Outside he found her nurse and asked, "Can you give me an idea of when Detective Aziz might be discharged?"

"You'll have to speak to the surgeon or his resident tomorrow, but I'd guess a few days to a week. She lost a lot of blood. But by the look of your clothes, you know that." She smiled warmly. "She'll be fine, Detective. Talk to the surgical team in the morning."

AT 2:30 A.M. MacNeice was standing at the window of the stone cottage, a double grappa in hand. He wasn't searching for the night-stalking coyote that often passed by. He was studying the tiny ripples on the surface of the grappa in his glass. It reminded him of movies where the ripples in a glass foreshadow a coming earthquake. He changed hands but the ripples remained. MacNeice made a mental note to rebook his appointment with Dr. Sumner. Not trusting his memory, he wrote it down and left the piece of paper propped up against his service weapon.

By now you're thinking you are the reason people around you get hurt.

"Maybe. Though this isn't self-pity."

No. You're at war with your decisions, your intuition.

"I've run tonight over and over in my head, Kate. I failed to keep my team safe."

Isn't that like carpal tunnel syndrome for a violinist?

"You mean an occupational hazard? I hunt people who kill people. And yet I believe in reason, that no matter how committed to killing they are, there's a moment — not big, not for long — when they can be talked down from killing again."

And does that work?

"Not tonight. Not this time."

Is that approach based on self-confidence?

"At this hour, I fear it's based on my ego."

And had it worked tonight, would you still think that?

"No. I'd say, 'It's time for a grappa.'"

As I recall, anytime you came home was time for a grappa.

[28]

HIS TELEPHONE RANG AT 5:45 A.M. MACNEICE HAD NO IDEA HOW many times it had rung, but it finally punched through the brain fog to wake him up. He fumbled for it and looked at the caller ID before answering. "Give me a minute." He put it down and went to the bathroom.

Standing over the toilet, he peered out the window into the darkness for signs of life. Seeing nothing, he flushed the toilet.

"Did I wake you up?" Deputy Chief Wallace asked, insincerely enough to suggest that he wasn't looking for an answer. MacNeice opened the curtain and sat on the edge of the bed, looking up the road to the yellow spill of the lamp. Wallace got to his point, or at least one of them. "I'm calling about last night. We're holding a press conference this morning at ten a.m." He could hear Wallace flipping the pages of a notebook. "I need to get it straight from you." He paused. "Given how it turned out, Mac, did you make the right decision to go up there?"

"Next question." MacNeice went into the kitchen and turned on the espresso machine.

"Okay. The tactical team discovered a small arsenal of weapons in that truck. Given that two officers were wounded, the tactical team leader was curious to know why they weren't called in to deal with the situation."

"That's an elaboration of the first question."

"You're stretching my patience, Detective." Wallace cleared his throat. "Last question: we don't have an autopsy report on Palmer, so how certain are you that he was dead before the shotgun blast?"

"Give me a minute." He put down the phone and made his coffee — short, strong, and black. For good measure he poured in a shot of grappa, then picked up the phone. "There was no reason to call in the cavalry. We were investigating Palmer's storage unit, just as we'd searched his house."

"Until the suspects arrived."

"Yes, though they weren't suspects until they opened fire." MacNiece downed the coffee.

"Tactical counted twenty-eight shell casings from police service weapons at the storage depot."

"I would have guessed more." He rinsed the cup and turned off the machine. "I'm fairly certain Richardson's autopsy will reveal that Palmer died of suffocation before he was shot."

"From being upholstered into the La-Z-Boy?"

"That and a gag applied so tightly that he couldn't swallow, plus the blood loss from his groin, which had been pounded by what I think was a heavy rubber mallet. This was a vengeful husband who was not the least bit interested in hiding his identity. Actually, he was so proud of the family business that he may have taken his sons along." MacNeice listened for Wallace's response but could hear only breathing.

"We'll include an update on the Punchbowl killing, with the victim's name. You got anything to add to that?"

"We're pursuing a very interesting theory but it's too soon to mention it."

It was a measure of the pressure Wallace was under that he didn't ask to hear more. He coughed, cleared his throat, and said, "Okay, good. Let me know," before hanging up.

The day slipped by in Homicide. Everyone was doing research or connecting dots. It looked like progress. But to MacNeice, it felt as though the momentum had shifted in favour of the killer. And no one had any idea what he might do next.

ST. JOE'S, EAST WING, fourth floor, 8:05 p.m. The dinner trolley was parked outside Aziz's room when MacNeice arrived carrying a paper bag from Ola Bakery. He went to the nursing station, looking for the surgeon or his resident, and was told they were on rounds.

"Detective Aziz is doing well, sir," the day nurse said, adding that the surgeon had been there when her dressings were changed. "She's just having dinner now, if you'd like to go in."

The blind was up, the mountain looked purple in the distance, and the monitors were beeping like robot sparrows. One of the intravenous tubes had been removed and Aziz was sitting up, sipping orange juice through a straw. Seeing MacNeice, she put down the container and uncharacteristically swept the hair from her face, then looked embarrassed at being caught trying to make herself presentable. In sweet betrayal, several strands fell back over her eye. MacNeice reached over and smoothed them away, tucking them gently behind her ear. "I brought you a treat." He set the bag down on the tray. "Have you eaten anything?"

"The smell of the white fish sauce put me off. And while I'm tempted, that crimson Jell-O has yet to win me over. But the coffee smells good." She lifted a paper doily off the plastic cup and fanned the steam towards him.

"In that case . . ." He put the coffee cup on the table and took the fish and Jell-O tray to the radiator. From the bag he produced two Portuguese custard tarts on top of a napkin. "Pastéis de nata." Not minding that he'd slaughtered the pronunciation, he reached for a chair and pulled it close to the bed.

When he sat down, Aziz was in tears. He gave her a tissue and waited quietly at her side, holding her hand. *It's complicated*, he thought. He studied her hand, the long fingers falling loosely over his. They looked lovely together, though he thought her darker skin made his appear vaguely pale and sickly. She withdrew hers to better focus on a tart.

"Thank you for these, Mac." She broke off a piece of the tart. "And for last night." Her eyes welled up again. "I was scared and in shock, I guess."

OVER THE COURSE of the next half-hour, Aziz finished one of the tarts and MacNeice refilled her coffee. They spoke about the case, how the night had ended, and what still lay ahead. He was going to apologize, but she seemed to anticipate it. "I know you probably blame yourself for what happened, but please don't. You made the right call by going up there."

When he got up to leave, MacNeice wanted to lean over and kiss her forehead, but he didn't. He held her hand and told her to rest and get well — then he kicked himself all the way to the elevator for not saying something more thoughtful. He pressed the button, but when the doors opened, he stood for a moment before turning back down the corridor.

She was just finishing the last of the second tart when he swept in. "I want you to know, Fiza, that I don't know what I'd do if . . . Well, if this was worse." He took her hand, felt the sticky custard on her fingers, and smiled. "I just wanted you to know." With that he said, "Rest," and left.

He went back to the nursing station, where he met the surgeon. He was told that Aziz could go home the next day, but she'd need bed rest for at least a week before being cleared for active duty. "Normally I would recommend a patient lay low for four to six weeks, but I know that's not going to happen. Detective Aziz can be on her feet in a few days. It will be painful, but she can do it. Her only risk at this point is the possibility of infection, which," said the surgeon, "could present fairly quickly. She'll be taking antibiotics and iron for the next ten days, but that alone isn't enough. I've ordered a wound specialist to see her once a day for the week. When she said that she lives alone, I suggested getting in someone from homecare to bathe her. The key is to keep those sites clean and dry."

"Other than that," he added, "she's a very healthy woman."

[29]

AT NOON THE NEXT DAY, THE CHECKOUT LINES AT THE GOLDEN GOOSE Family Market tracked between stacks of cereal on one side and potato chips and nachos on the other. Ahead of him, a kid maybe four years old was eyeing Miss Vickie's BBQ chips while his mother flipped through a Hollywood tabloid with a pregnant beauty on the cover.

For his part, he was content to study the shoppers from under his hoodie. He believed that standing in line revealed a lot about one's character. Not just being frustrated — no one would choose to wait in line at the Goose — but about an individual's approach to life. You could see it all in a queue: the resigned, those with low self-esteem, the nervous and anxious, the optimistic and energetic. Body language wasn't the only betrayal; it was also the mouth, the eyes and hair, the clothes and shoes.

Take the woman to the left. Dyed black hair with silver roots growing from the crown like a fraying skullcap. A pilling grey sweater over worn beige pants, the cuffs still showing salt stains from a winter several months gone. Those hadn't been chosen to show off her figure; they were just what she'd reached for this morning. Her back hunched forward in response to a sunken chest; her legs, while thin, looked as if they carried the weight of her world. Her mouth had given up to gravity and curled down at the corners; he wondered if she ever laughed. Her eyes appeared to be focused on the magazine rack, as if she was studying the covers and reading the pitch copy. She wasn't. She was killing time — or perhaps it was the other way around. Often there'd be something, maybe a spectacular hairdo, a gorgeous pair of shoes, something that would holler, *Don't look at me, look at my shoes. I am my shoes!* Not her. She wore scuffed-up, worn-out tan walking shoes.

In front of her was a young man, tall and slim, carrying a deli wrap and a diet Coke. He wore a royal blue suit, a white shirt with slim pink tie, and stylishly pointy brown shoes. His blond hair, with close-shaved sides and back, sported a stiff top that fell like a bird's wing over his ear. He was definitely shouting, *I am my hair!*

The kid suddenly caved. He grabbed the Miss Vickie's bag and tugged at his mother's leg. Without looking down, she swatted him across the face with the magazine, accidentally dropping her wallet on the floor. The boy let go of the bag and fell bawling to his knees. As she squatted to pick up her credit cards, his mother said something under her breath that reduced his wailing to breathless sobs. She didn't notice that a black business card had slipped from her wallet and was under the heel of her boot. Still angry, she stood up and raised a hand above the kid's head; he closed his eyes, cowering as he waited for the blow. Instead she took his bony shoulder and shook him hard. His sobs reduced to a whimper and he stood up.

The young man with the birdwing hair reacted without thinking. "Hey, you can't do that!" Undeterred, the woman smacked the kid's head and, with a slender finger inches from his eyes, told him to quit whining. She picked up the chips and slammed them back on the shelf. Wiping the snot from his nose, the boy was doing his best to stop crying. His posture suggested that he knew the real punishment would begin when they got home. At four he was already defeated.

The man in the hoodie watched as the woman emptied her buggy of tinned soups; frozen pizzas, peas, and fries; milk and soft drinks. She looked like someone from Central Casting who'd been hired to play a party girl. All dressed up in black: shiny tights below, feathery and fetching above. Long black hair with purple highlights — she could be a Goth rock star who specialized in a bad attitude. Her cleavage, spiked heels, and studded purse made a strange sight in daylight. The boy's clothes were worn and stained and one of his running shoes was torn at the toe; he clearly wasn't part of the act.

The man behind him reached for a Kit Kat, tousled the boy's hair, and put the treat in his hand. "Don't touch my kid. Who the hell do you think you are?" She wrestled the Kit Kat away from him. "Gimme that." The kid was down and crying again. "See what you've done? What are you, a perv, in that cheap sweat-hoodie?" She threw the Kit Kat at him and he caught it without effort. That only seemed to make her angrier.

The young man piped up again. "Jesus, lady, you are so twisted. People like you —" He didn't get to finish his thought.

"Shut your fucking mouth, you pussy in your first suit!"

"Oh my, what a potty mouth," said the woman in the grey sweater, lifting the corners of her mouth for a moment.

"Fuck you, you old hag!"

"Well, someone's having a bad day." The woman pursed her lips, looking up to the young man for agreement. That comment was apparently too pathetic to respond to verbally; the young mother simply sneered and raised her middle finger in their direction.

The checkout girl kept her head down, happy to be punching in purchases, and the faster the better. It was about getting the angry lady on her way so she could hear the easy-listening music again and say "Have a nice day" with some degree of sincerity. If there was a manager, he or she had found something urgent to do somewhere out of sight and sound.

"Do you have bags, ma'am?"

"Do I look like I've got bags?"

The woman in grey and the young man in blue were watching the man in the hoodie. He seemed to be studying the mother as if she were the most interesting thing in the world. While her payment was processing, she glared back at him. Retrieving her credit card, she said, "What the fuck are you looking at?"

He put his basket down on the conveyor belt, smiled, and

walked slowly towards her. Though his eyes were gentle, the wide, thin-lipped smile was unnerving. Still, she was game and responded with a sneer. "You don't scare me."

Towering over her, his smile widened. He pulled his hoodie further over his head and leaned into her, whispering, "When your boy is thirteen, he's going to slit your throat as you sleep." Standing upright, he motioned with his finger. "From here to here." Then he winked.

The colour drained from her face. She picked up her bags, grabbed her kid by the shoulder, and shoved him through the sliding doors. She never looked back.

"That's if someone doesn't do it sooner," he said to himself as he unloaded his basket. After he'd paid, he picked up the black card and put it in the pouch of his hoodie.

[30]

AS HE STEPPED OUT OF THE STAIRWELL, MacNEICE COULD HEAR Williams and Vertesi talking, the whirring of Ryan's printer, and Swetsky on the telephone in his cubicle. While that wasn't much, it had the instant effect of energizing him. At the same time, he realized that he was physically and emotionally depleted. He was still reeling from his role in the deaths of three men. As for Palmer, MacNeice couldn't rise above anger and pity. The man had been an alcoholic and the department had stood by him through detox and treatment, yet the DPD had continually turned a blind eye to his sexual misadventures. "And here we are," he whispered to himself.

MacNeice went to make a coffee. Swetsky didn't look up; he was listening and making notes, the phone locked between his head and shoulder. As the espresso poured, MacNeice sent a high-priority text message to Dr. Sumner requesting an appointment. In less than a minute he had her reply: "You're lucky. Had cancellation. Come at 3 pm today."

MacNeice gave his team an update on Aziz's condition and her expected recovery time. Then he provided a top-line summary of his conversation with Wallace and the likely fallout in the media.

Williams spoke first. "Are we groomin' the goat now, sir?"

"The scapegoat?"

"Yeah. Where's this one headed?"

"The DC's taking responsibility." MacNeice changed the topic slightly. "Any reports from McMillan on the interview with Mrs. Galanis?"

Vertesi nodded. "He called. He and a uniformed female were at the apartment by 2:30 a.m. Mrs. Galanis appeared at the door with a black eye, bruised cheek, and split lip. She said her husband had left the previous morning to take their twenty-four-year-old twin sons to the airport. The young men were going to Greece for a month to stay with their grandparents. When McMillan pressed her about the black eye, she admitted that her husband had beaten her. The boys were present at the time, and they knew the reason for the beating. When the boys left, each was carrying a duffel bag.

"Mrs. Galanis accompanied them to the morgue to identify her husband. When the attendant rolled back the sheet, McMillan said she looked shocked and took hold of the constable's arm, but she confirmed that it was him. When she had regained her composure, she asked about the other two bodies. McMillan said he was waiting for DNA confirmation, at which point she lost it and had to be led out of the building."

MacNeice dropped his chin to his chest. "She's afraid her boys didn't leave for Greece after all. Is someone with her today?"

"Yeah, a cousin from St. Catharines came to stay. McMillan left the uniform and a grief counsellor, but they're probably gone by now. Galanis has been calling Greece, but her sons haven't arrived yet—and their cellphones aren't working."

"Any word on Maracle?"

"Broken ankle," Vertesi said. "Should be out for a few weeks. But get this: he asked McMillan if he can be seconded to D-1 till Fiza gets back."

"McMillan says it's your call, sir," Williams added.

By the looks on their faces, MacNeice didn't need to ask their opinion. "Okay, I'll call him. What else?"

The conversation stopped as Swetsky heavy-footed towards the cubicle. He swung in smiling, waving his notes. "That was a young woman named Wendy Allen. She saw the photograph we posted in the *Standard* and recognized Tundell as the man who attacked her and killed her dog in Durand Park."

All eyes went to the whiteboard photograph of the donkey-head man. Someone had already printed his name on the image. They wondered why this news had Swetsky so charged up.

"Turns out, four or five people came to her aid. She has all the names and contact information — all except for one." Swetsky went over to the board. "Apparently he was sketching in the park when Wendy was attacked and was one of the first to reach her. He gave her a complete description of her attacker before heading off in the same direction as Tundell." Spreading his arms, Swetsky added, "She'll be here in an hour to give us a detailed description of the guy."

"He went to chase him down," MacNeice said.

"To kill him for killing a dog?" Vertesi asked in disbelief.

"Why not?"

Williams shook his head in amazement. "Rocky, you've clearly never had a dog."

"They've pulled the file for me downstairs. It includes the guy's written description of Tundell. And guess what — there's a sketch on the back." Swetsky turned to leave. "I'll be right back. Oh, and Charlie Maracle? Get him in here. The guy's solid; he's seen stuff." He went thumping towards the stairwell. They could hear the metal structure groan as he descended.

Vertesi shrugged. *"I've* seen stuff."

[31]

THE DESCRIPTION WAS WRITTEN ENTIRELY IN CAPITAL LETTERS WITH a pencil. The forward-leaning and adjoined letters suggested that it had been done in a hurry. The drawing on the other side featured six women sitting at a picnic table with trees as a background. It looked like it had been rendered quickly. Some of the women were fairly detailed, others little more than shapes. Yet one could easily imagine the women's animated conversation, with hands gesticulating and heads tossed back in laughter. The trees behind them were simple and elegant, like silent sentinels.

"Ryan, make six copies of both sides."

"What are you going to do with them, boss?"

"Not entirely sure, but one set will go to Jeffery Ridout, that DAG curator. Depending on what he says, we'll visit every gallery and artist's studio in Dundurn. We may not find him, but someone might recognize his handwriting or drawing style."

Taping copies of the note and the drawing next to the mug shot of Tundell felt like progress. MacNeice stood back and eyed the board for several minutes. "I think we actually know a lot about this man. He's obviously studied art. And his description of Tundell tells us he's observant — it could have been written by one of us. Plus we know he's a strong man, strong enough to carry a corpse several hundred yards up to the Lower Falls of Devil's Punchbowl."

MacNeice studied the snapshots of Amelia Street and the Punchbowl again. "So far these scenes appear to be drawn from historical references or satirical takes on historical art. He's thorough, and when he's not — like leaving the boot prints and tire tracks — he doesn't mind giving up those details. I don't think he's too concerned about how this ends. He may think the ultimate sacrifice for art is to die with it."

Williams wasn't convinced. "I can't think of a motive that connects Tundell to Amelia Street. What did that old priest and his investor son do to deserve what happened to them?"

"That might be the point."

"I don't follow, sir."

"As I understand it, a great white shark may pass all kinds of fish, mammals, and surfboards without attacking them. But when the 'eat something now' urge is triggered, it's a killing machine for whatever's nearby." MacNeice tapped the photo of the young addict. "Tundell happened to be nearby. He stood out because of what he did to Wendy Allen and her dog."

"But a detailed note like that must have been done before

Tundell did the dog," Vertesi said. "Doesn't that suggest he was actually anticipating the attack?"

"Exactly." MacNeice wasn't finished with his analogy. "Before that, he was just an artist sketching people in the park. The trigger for the shark may be hunger, but the trigger for our man may be some sort of violation. It becomes the inspiration for another piece of art."

"You're making it sound like you think V's got a conscience." Once again, Swetsky wasn't convinced.

"Well, maybe a variation of a conscience," MacNeice said. "If he's our man and he pursued and killed Tundell, he might have been exacting justice . . . or consequences."

"I'll give you the dog-killer and a lawyer, but why an old priest?" Swetsky pressed.

"I can't answer that, John."

MACNEICE STUDIED THE note again. Absent of any flourishes, it was similar to field notes he had seen at the bird sanctuary in Suffolk. He'd spent days there with Kate's father, a field volunteer who had seen in MacNeice a willing student.

MacNeice loved everything about the place, including the address — Sheepwash Lane. The wind gusts skipped across the North Sea and tore through the marsh grasses there, sending a chill through him that would last the whole day. "The winds from Minsk," Kate's father would say as he buttoned his coat. The sea was usually slate grey, but occasionally when there was weak sunshine, the wind left a streak of gold on the water that seemed to delight the low-flying seabirds on their way to nest or feed. When his shift ended, Kate's father would hand MacNeice his notebook to read off the names while he committed them to the "Recent Sightings" board.

You know that he loved you, don't you.

MacNeice turned away from the whiteboard. He sat at his desk and continued to study a copy of the note.

He'd never say that, of course. But Mum told me once when we were at the farm picking up asparagus that you were the son he'd never had.

MacNeice swallowed hard and coughed unnecessarily to clear his throat. He was aware that Williams had turned his way. "I'm for a glass of water. Anyone need anything?" He smiled briefly and left the cubicle.

He also felt protective of you, because of your work. But then, we all worried about that.

MacNeice pressed the tap to draw cold water into a paper cup. "I know you did," he whispered.

Funny to think of it now. We're all gone and you're still there doing dangerous work.

MacNeice's eyes filled with tears. He coughed again and took a paper towel to wipe them away. "I loved your father."

I know. He knew . . . We all knew.

The phone was ringing in the cubicle. Ryan picked it up as MacNeice turned the corner. "It's Forensics, sir."

While it would take two weeks or more for absolute certainty, Rapid DNA analysis from the pickup truck corpses was in. Junior sounded serious — a modest breakthrough — as he delivered the news. "They're related to Kyros Galanis, sir, but they're not his sons. DNA, dental, and bone studies suggest they are men in their late forties, possibly early fifties. Best guess, they're first cousins."

MacNeice put down the phone with a sigh of relief. Her

sons might never forgive her for what had happened, but Mrs. Galanis would be relieved beyond measure that they were still alive. He picked up the phone and called McMillan.

"Good to hear from you, brother. You attending the press conference this morning?"

"No, Wallace has that covered."

McMillan erupted in a chest-rattling laugh that reflected forty years of nicotine and cynicism. "That's rich, Mac. I'll be there, and he's gonna feel my breath on his neck. Keep your back to the wall on this one, bud."

"A moment ago I decided not to worry," MacNeice said. "I've just heard from Richardson's assistant."

"We got that call too. Maracle's hopping around here, and he's already confirmed those boys were on an Olympic Airlines flight when Kyros was trading shots with you. After that little creep Junior called, Charlie spoke to the wife. When she stopped crying, she confirmed that the other two were his cousins, both Greek nationals here on temporary visas. Mrs. Galanis didn't trust them. Anyway, they hit Dundurn a couple of days before Palmer went missing."

"Thank you for offering Maracle. We can certainly use his help."

"It's just a loaner, Mac. He'll be there in a few hours. Remember, I want him back when Aziz is on her feet. Is she okay?"

"Yes."

[32]

"TELL ME, MacNEICE, WHY DID YOU BECOME A POLICE OFFICER?" Sumner crossed her hands over her notepad and smiled.

He returned the smile. It was a question he'd been asked many times, but one he'd never fully answered. Given who she was, he decided to tell her the whole story.

"When I was fourteen, my friend Peter invited me to his grandparents' farm out near Dunnville. We'd feed chickens, collect eggs, clean the barn — that kind of thing. I loved it. We'd also go down the road with fishing rods and sit on the bank of a river near a bridge. We never caught anything but a sunfish or two, and we'd toss those back. We'd talk about life, about the future, about what this bird might be saying to that one, about school and sports and girls."

He studied her face for a moment to see if that was the level of detail she wanted from him. She smiled and nodded for him to continue.

"Sometimes Peter's grandmother gave us sandwiches or homemade carrot cake wrapped in tinfoil. We'd eat it as the river flowed by. One day a loud car with a tin-throat muffler stopped on the bridge above us. A door opened and there was a sudden splash off to the right. Then the door slammed shut and the car rumbled away.

"It was a black garbage bag, and it floated for a moment before sinking. I stripped down to my shorts and dived into the water. I'm not a good swimmer, but I thrashed my way to the spot where it had disappeared.

"When I got there, I took a deep breath and went under, digging down through twelve feet or so of dark water. I touched the bag but ran out of breath. In a panic, I came up without it. Breaking the surface, I saw Peter treading water. I was coughing and couldn't speak, but I frantically pointed down below me. Peter took a deep breath and went down. When he came up, he was holding the bag.

"We collapsed on the bank and opened it. Inside were four tiny, wide-eyed black kittens and a brick. We got dressed, emptied our bait bucket into the river, and put the kittens inside. With our fishing poles in hand, we ran back to the farm and told the whole story to Peter's grandparents."

MacNeice remembered the sun in the kitchen, a huge pot of soup on the stove, and Peter's grandfather nursing a mug of coffee. A metal ashtray from the local feed store held two scrunched-up cigarette butts. MacNeice knew that two butts meant it was the end of the farmer's afternoon break.

"'They'll make fine barn cats,' the old man said. 'We'll

take care of them and keep one, then give the rest to friends
— unless you boys want them.' Peter was happy to imagine
them catching mice and voles on the farm, but I was just
angry. The old man asked what was bothering me. I said
whoever did it should be found and punished. His grandparents laughed — not in a mean-spirited way — but I was
insistent and said they needed to know they couldn't kill
kittens."

MacNeice looked for Sumner's reaction, some flicker in
her face, the slightest curl of her lips, her eyebrows heading
north, or a glaze of boredom that suggested he cut the story
short. He was relieved to see only a listener. He felt pleased
to be telling a story that even Kate knew only in part.

"The old man wanted to be reasonable. He pointed out
that we didn't know who'd done it. Death was a fact of life
for him, and while drowning kittens was unpleasant, he'd
probably known worse. He may have done worse.

"I surprised him by saying it was an orange 1972
Plymouth Barracuda. I had seen the rear end from where
we were sitting. It swept up like a boat." MacNeice drew
the soft curve with his hand. "I said there probably weren't
too many orange Barracudas around Dunnville, so this one
might be nearby. After all, they wouldn't drive all the way
from Dundurn just to drown kittens."

The memory of that statement still bothered MacNeice.
He was being rude to a couple who had been generous to
him, and it didn't matter that he was passionate and wound
up or even right. "It was a sarcastic comment, one that my
teenage brain thought suggested the obviousness of my
point." That day remained as clear to MacNeice as if it had
happened an hour before he arrived at her office. He flinched

a little at the thought of his youthful petulance. She noted that discomfort with a slight sharpening of her eyes.

"Anyway, I'd been watching Peter's grandfather. When I mentioned the Barracuda, the old man's eyebrows went up. Encouraged, I said that if we found the car, we'd find the mother of the kittens. But I was losing the old man. He sat back in his chair." MacNeice recalled him shoving his hat back with a thumb, revealing the white skin high on his forehead, the only real estate on his head not weathered and browned by the sun.

"I went too far. I said, 'If they're willing to do that to a bunch of kittens . . .'" MacNeice raised both hands like someone waiting for a Communion wafer. "I held up two air-pawing balls of fur and asked, 'What else might they be willing to kill?'" It sounded worse in the telling than he hoped it had been at the time.

"Up until that moment, Peter had been silent. He was happy just playing with the kittens. I guess he knew there was a line, a country code, that I'd crossed. For him the best strategy was to change the subject. He started talking about how we'd almost drowned diving for them. That was all it took. Suddenly the conversation was about whether we were okay. The river was deep under that bridge. His grandmother shook her head, said how awful it would be if anything happened, how would they ever tell our parents."

MacNeice took a deep breath and sat forward slightly. "That's when I knew I wanted to be a cop."

"Do you still feel that way?"

He didn't answer at first, and not because he didn't understand the question. "Well, there's been a lot of water under that bridge by now." He smiled, trying to pivot away from

the embarrassment. "I realized I wanted to keep people —
and kittens — safe. And yes, I still do."

"I sense a 'but' in that statement," Sumner said.

"Homicide's always called in after the fact. Someone's
been murdered. Our job — my job — is to bring the person
who did it to justice."

"Something was lost from that experience at the bridge,
then?"

"Something's always lost. In my work the kittens are
always murdered . . . a wife, a child, a husband, a cop, an
addict . . . a priest."

"Thank you for your story, Detective. The idealism of
youth is often the first casualty. While you've learned over
time how to manage your — let's call it 'enthusiasm,' I've
been aware of your idealism since our first session. It's a deep,
calm pool that defines who you are."

He wasn't sure about that. If he'd known then that there
was little he could do to eliminate murder, would he still
have wanted to be a cop?

Sumner may have read his mind. "Given what you know
now, if you had the opportunity to rethink the career path
your young self chose, would you take it?"

MacNeice turned away from her and looked through the
opening in the sheers, hoping something would land on the
sliver of silver birch outside. "I'm good at what I do. I've
accepted the idea that there's a cost to every job."

She smiled. "When our last session was terminated by
that call, I filled the hour by digging further into your record, Detective. It revealed that you are exceedingly good at
what you do."

He was still watching the narrow gap for signs of life.

He looked at her. "Is your question, Doctor, how long I can keep going?"

"No, not at all. I can easily imagine that you'll be in Homicide for a long time. And frankly, anyone looking at your record" — she opened her handwritten notes — "would be relieved to hear that."

"There's a 'but'?"

"Not a 'but.' More of an 'and.' Ten years ago I did a research paper on active-duty servicemen. Each member of my study group had had at least three tours of duty in Afghanistan, and all of them were going back again. It wasn't that they felt indispensable to the stated mission. They saw their value on a much more granular level. They were there for the local farmer and his family, there to protect the girls who wanted to go to school, the villagers who'd suffered at the hands of extremists. And of course they felt immense loyalty to their fellow soldiers. You have that same fundamental commitment to protect life while remaining loyal to your colleagues. The 'and' is that each of the soldiers felt certain that the moment they left the field for good, everything they had done to help would collapse. So they continued."

He nodded but said nothing.

"We have to ask, at what cost to the individual soldier, or to you? I am part of your support system, for one hour a week and for a limited time. You have no surviving family. You use alcohol to help you sleep. You are not delusional in the slightest, yet you have conversations with your late wife." She closed the file and put her notepad on top of it. "In short, my report to your superior will be that you are healthy, competent, and stable. Whatever methods you've devised to deal with your PTSD issues are yours alone. And they appear to be working."

"Are you firing me?"

Sumner laughed. "MacNeice, I left the curtains behind me slightly open for your benefit. I know you're looking and listening for birds through that narrow opening, not using it to escape from me or my questions, or my relentless gaze."

"You'd make a good cop, Doctor."

"I'm quite happy doing what I do, thank you. No, I'm not firing you. If you ever need a sounding board, call me. But we have fulfilled DC Wallace's request."

DRIVING AWAY, MACNEICE wondered where Sumner went to offload the horrors of her day. He made a mental note to ask the next time he visited.

[33]

MACNEICE PUSHED OPEN THE DOOR TO AZIZ'S ROOM AND FOUND the head nurse changing bandages. "Sorry. I'll wait outside."

"No, Mac, come in. You can be my patient advocate."

She was on her side, her arms above her head. The other intravenous tube was gone, and so too were the monitors. The nurse lowered Aziz's gown for modesty but kept working. The entry wound, a dark red pucker of flesh, was surrounded by a sloppy orange stain of surgical disinfectant. MacNeice couldn't help but notice the soft rise of Aziz's hip above the sheet. The nurse, who may have guessed where his eyes were focused, pulled up the sheet.

"How does it look?" Aziz asked.

"Like it's healing." He smiled. "How do you feel?"

"Much better. I walked the length of the corridor earlier, without any help."

"She did it with a walker, but you can tell where this is going." The nurse finished putting on the fresh bandage. "Lean forward now and we'll do the back."

MacNeice moved to the other side of the bed, and what he saw made his stomach tighten. The bandage came away with a large patch of dried blood. This was not a tight little pucker like the entry wound. Spidery lines of torn flesh surrounded a bloody crust the size of a quarter. The whole area looked angry, made more so by the black stitches crisscrossing the tears.

"How does it look?"

Aziz was so cheerful he wondered if it was the medication. "It looks fine, Fiza. Yes, I think it looks good. Nurse, do you agree?"

"That was pathetic, Mac." Aziz was straining to see the wound.

The nurse looked back at him, unimpressed by his attempt to sugar-coat the truth. "Well, Detective, the surgeon did a very good job." She wiped away the dried blood with disinfectant, which helped things. Turning to Aziz, she added, "Once this has healed, put vitamin E ointment on it every day and massage the scar tissue. In time it will settle down." She applied tape to a four-inch square of gauze and pulled the gown down and the sheet up. "I'm sure I don't need to tell you this could have been much worse."

Once the nurse had wheeled her supply trolley out of the room, Aziz rolled gingerly onto her back. "Tell me the truth."

"The truth? Well, you have a lovely hipbone. And you've

got a starburst scar that will fade with vitamin E. But right now, it does look pretty nasty." He pulled up a chair. "What did she mean by 'You can tell where this is going'?"

"I asked to be discharged today." Her eyes welled up and she turned away.

He laid a hand gently on her shoulder. "The hospital will arrange for a wound-care specialist every day, as well as someone to provide meals and bathe you. It's only for a week or so."

"I'm okay, Mac. Just feeling sorry for myself. And very, very tired." She turned and looked at him. "I do have a favour to ask, though. You can say no and I'll understand."

"Anything."

"Well, when I was a girl, my mother would run her hand through my hair to put me to sleep. I wish she was here . . . Will you stroke my hair, Mac, just for a while?" Her eyes focused on his. "And really, it's okay if you say no."

"I won't say no."

A FEW MINUTES later, MacNeice noticed that her breathing had slowed and she was asleep. When he'd begun stroking her hair, he'd noticed her brow furrowing and occasional twitches at the corners of her mouth, but now all was calm. Resisting the urge to kiss her forehead, he quietly left the room.

Walking past the lounge set aside for patients and their families, the flat-screen TV caught his eye. The sound had been muted, but looking at the press conference footage, he didn't need to hear it. Wallace's face gave it away. His mouth was closed and he was clenching his teeth as he fielded a question from a reporter. Judging by the flush on his neck, it wasn't the first question about what the local news had taken to calling the "Palmer-Galanis Affair." When Wallace spoke, his hands, holding onto the lectern, were white-knuckle tight. His eyes never wandered from his questioner. The screen was split: Wallace filled the left side and on the right were a photo of Palmer, smiling in his dress uniform, and a snapshot of Kyros Galanis in a T-shirt. He wasn't smiling.

"Chief's dancing. Covering for a bad cop," said an old man in a wheelchair, his voice barely above a raspy whisper. He was wearing a hospital gown open at the back, revealing the bony ridge of his spine.

His wife sat beside him, nodding, tapping the purse on her lap for emphasis. She added as she nodded, "You can tell he's lying. Look at that one next to him. They're all in on it."

DS McMillan was the one next to him, and it was true. He looked more wound-up than Wallace. Stone-faced, neither man gave an outward sign that they felt any empathy or responsibility for what had happened.

MacNeice's cellphone buzzed in his pocket. "Vertesi, boss. We've got two dead in an alley out on King West. Not far from the Golden Goose. And check this — there's a V, but this one's turned away from the action, not into it."

"I'll be right there."

[34]

THE ALLEY WAS USED MOSTLY FOR WASTE REMOVAL AND DELIVERIES to the neighbouring strip mall. Given the strong smell of urine, it was also the preferred toilet for the beer hall down the street. There were Dumpsters behind each business, with twenty- to thirty-foot gaps between.

As he approached from King Street, MacNeice saw Vertesi's unmarked car parked behind three cruisers and two EMS units. No emergency this; everyone appeared to be standing near their vehicles, drinking coffee, locked in animated conversation. The entrance to the alley was taped off behind three beefy uniforms, there to discourage onlookers. It struck MacNeice that the onlookers were being attracted by the flashing lights and the cops waving at pedestrians, kids on bikes, and passing cars. It wasn't the actual crime scene; that was hidden from the street by the Dumpsters.

Vertesi and Williams were standing between the third and fourth Dumpster. They turned as MacNeice approached. "It's Mister V, sir, but he's gone off script," Williams said, turning back to the gap.

"Give me a minute to absorb this." MacNeice moved past him.

One of the victims was wearing an iridescent green suit, an orange T-shirt, and black slip-on shoes. The other wore black zip-up ankle boots, white socks, a black suit, and a T-shirt that barely covered his stomach. The slim man in the green suit looked to be five foot six or so, while the other was six foot and heavy.

A chrome-plated pistol lay near the far bin, and a Glock a few feet from the man in black; his right knee and everything below it swung grotesquely at a right angle to his upper leg. He resembled a broken toy, if heavy boys in black were kids' toys. As MacNeice looked more closely, he saw that the man wasn't fat; he was what MacNeice's mother used to call "big-boned." His head was turned away and upward, as if he was desperate to see what was behind him without actually turning around.

"Neither weapon has been fired, boss," said Vertesi.

The man in the green suit was spread-eagled on his back as if he'd just passed out. But his nostrils were near his forehead and the length of his nose had apparently disappeared into his skull. That left behind his hideously exposed gums. Between his teeth was a tongue so swollen it looked like a gum bubble about to be popped.

The wrong-way V had been placed on the far side of the man in the green suit. MacNeice stood over it as he took in the scene. He scanned the buildings along the lane and counted two security cameras, the closest almost twenty feet from the bodies.

"Wallets?" he said, turning to his detectives.

"Mister Slick here is Paolo DeSouza, thirty-four, from Grey's Road in Secord, with six hundred bucks in his wallet." Vertesi waved the second of three evidence bags. "This guy is Gary Grant — no joke — registered at the same address. He's got fifty bucks and some change." He showed MacNeice a set of car keys in the third bag. "Brand-new Range Rover. It's parked in front of the convenience store on the other side of the block. It's clean, except for a small teddy bear in the back seat."

"Gary Grant." MacNeice shook his head. Judging by the look of him, he would have guessed he was a buddy or a butch — the kind of guy who if he had a real name, only his mom knew it. He had stubborn short-cropped hair that looked ready-made for a motorcycle helmet.

"Who was carrying the keys?" MacNeice asked.

"Grant. We figure Paolo's a pimp and Gary's his muscle."

Wrong again, MacNeice thought. Grant was driving a Range Rover. If he'd been a buddy, he'd be tooling around in a Mustang.

"We gave the names to Vice. Someone will be calling us back any minute," said Williams.

"And these security cameras?" MacNeice squatted over the V.

"That far one isn't working, but the closer one does." Williams pointed to the camera above the rear entrance to a drugstore. "The control unit's locked in a cabinet inside the pharmacy. The owner has the key and should be here soon."

"What do you make of it, Mac?"

"I think he's telling us that this isn't like the others, but he also wants us to know it's him. He doesn't want us to waste precious resources trying to find another suspect. Which is very thoughtful, if I'm right."

"We spend our lives hunting down killers and this guy leaves his calling card to tell us he did it?" Williams scratched his head. "Is he playing us?"

"It's possible, but I don't think so. Maybe he's concerned about his legacy. And for whatever reason, he doesn't want these two to be counted as part of that." MacNeice knew he was reading a lot into a V. "Or he was just distracted and overlooked this detail."

"No way. I like your first idea. This guy doesn't make mistakes," said Vertesi.

Williams's cellphone rang; he glanced at the call display and moved farther down the lane. In two minutes he was back. "We nailed it." Pointing at the bodies in turn, he said, "Pimp. Bodyguard. They've got a front called Exotic Escorts. Vice sergeant Meg Lundstrom says DeSouza's small-time." He closed his eyes to recall her exact words. "He runs four girls — quality product for hotel and home visits. Mostly deals with businessmen, academics, and women." Williams raised his eyebrows. "Gary's there for show."

Vertesi looked down at Gary Grant's twisted body. "Paolo shoulda paid for a bigger show."

"Two men, two weapons." MacNeice turned his attention to DeSouza. "This one's nose — cartilage and bone — was driven into his brainpan with no additional trauma to his face. That was probably hand-delivered with force and speed by someone who knew it would be fatal. And the bodyguard

Grant was crippled before that thick neck of his was broken. You don't break a man's neck before breaking his leg. Again, force and speed, and no rounds fired, even though we know our man favours well-placed chest shots."

Farther up the lane, a door swung open and a middle-aged man stepped out. "Sirs, I am Aarush Patel, owner and pharmacist of Patel Chemists. I have opened the security cupboard and you are welcome to review the recording now."

MacNeice's cellphone rang. "Get it set up; I'll be right there." He waited for them to go inside before answering the call. It was Wallace.

"Did you watch the press conference?"

"No, but I saw a muted recap of it at St. Joe's."

"How is she?"

"She'll be fine in time."

"Good, good. Glad to hear it." Wallace was distracted. "Look, Mac, this thing isn't going away." The media questions had been quite detailed. Why was Palmer being transferred back to First Division? What disciplinary actions were taken against him? Did they know of any more "illicit affairs"? When was Palmer's absence flagged and who was delegated to deal with that? Was lethal force necessary, and if so, why wasn't the Tactical Unit called in? How was Palmer killed? What did the police know about the Galanis family? They also inquired about Aziz's condition and asked if the case had anything to do with the other homicides.

"They've been busy." MacNeice was wading through the flood of words, searching for the point of the call.

"They've only just begun. Here's the thing: I'm going to be absolutely honest but I'm not going to lay it down in

front of them. So far I've answered all those questions truth-
fully. I've said that Palmer was disciplined once for his police
work, but what he did with another consenting adult on his
own time was his business alone, not the DPD's. I know the
union is with me on that point."

"Sir, I've got two men dead in a laneway. What would
you like me to do?" His impatience was showing.

"Shit. Right. Police work — that's what I want you to
do. Just know that you'll be contacted and I trust you to do
the right thing."

"I will." MacNeice tried to make that comment appear
less than obvious.

"Oh, and the two men found in the truck were Galanis's
cousins. According to the wife, both were shady. Her husband didn't own a gun. They might have put up Kyros to
upholstering Palmer." Wallace paused, then added, "You're
a good man, Mac. . . . That's all for now."

MacNeice called over one of the uniforms. "Get Forensics
and the coroner in here. Make sure all these shopkeepers
know not to open their laneway doors until we've cleared the
crime scene. Station two men here to ensure that happens."

THE SECURITY CLOSET was in a small storeroom that contained products from shampoo to toothpaste, sunblock to
tampons. With four men crowded around a small video
monitor, the room seemed even smaller.

Williams hit a key and the images began flickering backwards in their comical way. Cops ran back and forth to their
cars, stood around the bodies, spoke into shoulder mikes,
and squatted over DeSouza. A seagull landed on a garbage

bin and pecked at a plastic bag. Two pigeons arrived to inspect the bodies and, after deciding there was nothing to eat, walked like Charlie Chaplin down the lane. Williams allowed the footage to rewind to the point where the men first appeared. Then he pressed Play and sat back.

Three men entered from the street, an unknown man in front wearing a hoodie. The distance from the camera and the backlight from the sunlit street made it difficult to see any details. The third man walked casually, as if all three were close friends, and DeSouza and Grant followed closely behind.

"Our man's at least an inch or two taller than Grant."

"Pause it there," MacNeice said. "Look at Gary Grant's right hand."

Williams leaned closer to the screen. "He's drawn his weapon." Rewinding the footage back to the moment they entered the lane, he added, "Even though it's hard to pick out details against the glare, his right hand is inside his jacket." Williams let it play. "Now he produces the piece." The three men kept walking, and DeSouza checked to see if anyone was behind them. Seeing no one, he reached inside his suit jacket. "There, look. That shiny shooter just caught the light."

"What interests me is our guy," said Vertesi. "Cool as iced tea. He's about to get pistol-whipped or whacked and he still looks relaxed."

"I wish he'd lift his head," said Williams.

"He won't do that. He's already spotted the security cameras." MacNeice was impressed.

Williams pointed to the screen. "Now DeSouza's going in front. They're doing monkey in the middle."

"With the wrong monkey."

"DeSouza's reading the riot act, getting all agitated, waving that chrome piece in the air. And look, Grant's moving in behind our man."

What happened next was an elegant but lethal ballet that was over in seconds. They watched it several times before MacNeice asked, "Can you run it in slow motion?"

"No, but Ryan can."

"Then take it back to the beginning of the attack and do a stutter stop-and-start over and over."

DeSouza waved his weapon; he appeared to be yelling (he was a lousy actor). The hoodie man's head was down, as if he wasn't paying attention. A split second later, in one teeter-totter motion, he drove the pimp's nose up with the heel of his right hand and kicked back, separating Grant's lower right leg from the knee. The sight was sickening even with the low resolution of the security camera. DeSouza fell stiffly, like a tree. The bodyguard crumbled, his lower leg flopping independently, weirdly, as he screamed in pain.

"Jesus, what the hell was that?" Vertesi exclaimed.

"That's called 'I ain't lettin' this motherfucker get within ten feet of me.'" Williams wasn't joking.

DeSouza was probably brain-dead before he hit the ground. The man in the hoodie stood over him and patted the pimp's pockets. He wasn't interested in the wallet but took something from the inside jacket pocket and put it in the pouch of his hoodie.

"Cellphone?" Williams was guessing.

He stepped across the pimp to the bodyguard and said something. It seemed to calm down the injured man. In a tender gesture, he knelt on one knee and cradled Grant's

head. Then, with electric-shock speed, there was a snap —
and Gary Grant was dead.

"This is seriously sick." Vertesi turned away in disgust.

"But efficient."

"Look, here comes his signature move." Williams
pointed at the screen.

The man reached into the pocket of his jeans, turned
to the camera, and made a moment out of turning the
small object upside down before placing it on the pavement. He then turned, walked casually out to the street,
and disappeared.

"You're right, sir. V's telling us this isn't like the others."
Williams looked up at MacNeice, who was already at the
door.

"Take the tape, or whatever that is, back to Ryan. I want
the whole thing larger and sharper." He paused in the doorway. "Before you go, measure the heights of Grant and
DeSouza."

"Will you be in first thing tomorrow, boss?" asked Vertesi.

"No, I'm over to meet Mrs. Galanis."

WALKING UP THE STEPS OF THE MODEST APARTMENT BUILDING, MacNeice turned his thoughts to the woman he was about to meet. By now she'd been told how her husband died and that her sons were safe. She knew better than anyone what had led to his death. MacNeice had never imagined he'd be meeting someone who'd had an affair with Palmer. Nor could he believe that the man's shallowness wouldn't be obvious to any woman. And yet . . . and yet he'd seduced at least two women away from their husbands and families, leaving them to pick up the pieces of their lives.

MacNeice took a deep breath and stepped inside the dark lobby, where he paused, waiting for his eyes to adjust to the low light and listening for sounds of life. It was very quiet. He climbed the stairs and knocked twice at 2A. A slim woman in her late forties answered the door. She was wearing a black cardigan over a black dress, and a small silver cross hung from her neck. Another woman stood in the doorway to the kitchen, eyeing him with suspicion.

"Mrs. Galanis?"

"Yes."

"I'm Detective —"

"I know who you are."

He'd no reason to expect a warm welcome when he offered his hand. "Detective Superintendent MacNeice." She looked at his hand but didn't take it.

"May I come in?"

She hesitated before opening the door to him. To the left, a pale grey sofa was positioned in front of the window. Facing it were two high-back chairs clad in blue leather. In the space between was a large coffee table covered in embroidered linen. She motioned for him to sit down.

"Thank you. I won't take up much of your time." He made his way to the sofa.

Elene Galanis sat across from him in one of the chairs and poured two glasses of water from a pitcher sitting on the table. She handed one to MacNeice. "What can I do for you, Detective MacNeice?"

"Thanks. I thought that would be my question, Mrs. Galanis."

She sat with her knees together and her hands folded in her lap. Though she was petite, it seemed as if she were towering above him. Light from the windows lit her face, emphasizing her cheekbones. She had large, dark eyes that sheltered under thick black eyebrows, a long nose, and full lips. Her jaw was relaxed and there was no sign of tension in her face or neck. She carried her beating well; there was no indication of any attempt to cover the bruises with makeup.

She picked up her glass but didn't drink, holding it on her lap with both hands. Her eyes left him and scanned the windows. She wasn't looking at something; it was just the light she craved. He thought for a moment there might be a bird landing on the balcony outside, but realized that was just his fantasy.

The moments passed painfully. MacNeice put down his glass and started to get up. "I'm terribly sorry for your loss, Mrs. Galanis. I won't take up any more of your time."

"Did you have to kill him?"

MacNeice allowed himself to sink back into the sofa. When he was settled again, he spoke. "Yes, I did. Your husband had seriously wounded my partner. He refused to put down his weapon and he fired several rounds before DI Maracle and I returned fire."

"Did you know David Palmer?"

"I did."

"Did you . . . like him?"

"No."

"Why is that?"

"To be honest, I didn't trust him."

She turned her eyes to the window again. "Did he suffer?"

"He was brutally tortured, so yes, he did."

Her eyes filled with tears. They fell through the sunlight like crystals. He wasn't sure whether they were for Palmer or her husband. They sat in silence for another minute or so. She used the heel of her thumb to wipe away the tears and turned back to him. "My sons want to stay here, I hope with me. Kyros felt like he was losing his family. He was a proud man."

"And was he losing you?"

Her eyes sharpened and her mouth hardened. "I am a strong woman, Detective. My people come from the mountains of Crete. We have been goat herders and farmers for centuries. Both my grandfathers died fighting the Nazis. Kyros and his family were fishermen; his grandfathers fed seafood to the Nazis. I'm not afraid of hardship. Losing me? Yes and no. That all depended on him."

"Are you saying that your affair with DI Palmer was a message to your husband?"

"You are direct, Detective." She paused before continuing. "David flirted with several women, but he seemed most determined with me. He was like the boy who sees his own reflection in the pool. He wasn't serious about women . . . not really." She sighed. "Kyros was a strong man, but I never thought he could be violent. A smack in the face on occasion, yes, but I hit him too." She saw the surprise on MacNeice's face. "Oh yes. You don't believe me, but I also have a temper."

He reached for his water. "Did Palmer seduce you at work?"

She stifled a laugh. "Seduced? My god, such a word." She sighed again and returned his gaze. "He did his best, yes. I was angry with Kyros, and so I finally agreed. Perhaps that was the message. I wanted my husband to know that I would have my own life. I wouldn't go back to Greece, no matter what he did."

"What happened then?"

She nodded slowly, as if the image of what had happened was just coming into focus. "His cousins — they're dead now too — came here from Fort Erie. They were bad men. Either Kyros asked them to come or they came

because they heard what I had done to betray and dishon-
our my husband."

"Did you know what they were planning?"

"No, of course not. I didn't know they were still here."
Her eyes filled with tears that didn't fall. "I told David to
watch out for them. He didn't take me seriously. He said,
'I'm a cop. What can they do to me?'"

MacNeice had known the man was a fool, and now he
realized he was also delusional.

"Who sent the boys to Greece?"

"I did. But not because I thought this would happen — I
truly didn't. I sent them away because they saw Kyros beat
me. Sons should never see that."

MacNeice realized that what he was seeing in her eyes
were tears of rage.

"I should have tried harder to talk sense into Kyros. But I
would have killed him if he ever beat me again. I'm serious."

"I've no doubt you are." The bruise on her cheek seemed
brighter, and when she averted her gaze, he noticed a red
stain on the white of her blackened left eye. "Why did you
agree to meet with me?"

She sat back nodding, as if to say, *You've asked the right
question.* She moved her water glass away. "First, to tell you
things I haven't told the other officers. I wanted to tell the
man who killed my husband."

"Forgive me for asking, Mrs. Galanis —"

"Elene, please."

"Elene, who is it you mourn?"

She studied his face before speaking. "Honestly? I grieve
for my sons. I mourn the loss of their father . . . for their sake.
But I mourn even more the loss of their trust. And David

Palmer is dead because of me. I also mourn the senseless-ness and brutality of his death." She raised her hands and let them fall to her lap. "I know I caused this. I was seduced by loneliness and the chance for something new." Aware that MacNeice was watching her hands, she clasped them loosely together. "It was a mistake. I told my husband about David because I wanted us to try again; that too was a mistake." Her eyes caught the light streaming through the windows. They were as shiny as ink. "My sons will never forgive me. I know them."

WHEN HE WAS back in the car, MacNeice took out his cell-phone and dialled Wallace's private line. As soon as the dep-uty chief picked up, MacNeice said, "Sir, I've just come from an interview with Elene Galanis."

"Yeah?"

"I want to do right by her." He paused, but Wallace didn't respond. "I want you to reinstate her on a full-time basis, but move her to the accounting department of my division."

"Why? Because you feel sorry for her?"

MacNeice knew Wallace wasn't as hard-hearted as he pretended to be, so he didn't take the bait. "The woman has two sons. She lost her husband over an affair with one of our own. She did nothing wrong. We need to be on the right side of this and not victimize her further. If you let her go, you'll pile more shame on someone who is blameless. But if she comes back to work, you'll be sending a message of compassion to her, her sons, and the community. It will also go a long way towards mitigating the damage to the department's reputation."

Static on the line. "Okay, it's the high road. I'll see what I can do. For now, don't say anything to anyone, especially her."

"Thank you."

[36]

SWETSKY BARKED AT RYAN OVER THE OFFICE LANDSCAPING. "WHERE the hell is Mac?"

"He went to speak to Mrs. Galanis, the woman who —"

"I know who she is. When's he due back?"

"I'll try his cell again, sir." Ryan dialled and MacNeice picked up after the first ring. He had been about to turn the loaner car into his parking spot when he noticed it was occupied — by a new deep blue Chevy fleet car. The wheels were huge, as if they'd been lifted from a truck. He pulled into the next available spot.

"Ryan, did the motor pool drop off something big and blue for me?"

"Yes, sir. It's already in your parking space. All your gear's inside, and Sazabuchi gave you an upgrade on the CD player and speakers — top-of-the-line Japanese." Then Ryan realized the big man was hovering over him. "Sir, DS Swetsky would like to speak with you."

"Tell him I'll be right there."

WHEN SWETSKY HEARD MacNeice's familiar two-steps-at-a-time run up the stairwell, he made his way over to meet him. "Okay, you're gonna love this. I have a composite sketch of Mister V from Wendy Allen's description. But I wanted a comparison, so I called in the couple from the park. They did their own composite without seeing hers. And looky here . . ." He handed MacNeice a printout.

MacNeice studied the composite provided by Wendy Allen. Swetsky read from her description. "'He's got a wide face, strong cheekbones, and a wide, thin-lipped mouth.' Her take on his eyes: 'They were gentle and compassionate' — but that's probably because he came to her assistance. 'He has a thick, athletic neck and a bald head like a Brancusi sculpture.'" He glanced at MacNeice to see if that had registered. "I had to look that one up."

Swetsky handed him the second composite. "With these folks, I'm thinking they weren't as freaked out by a dead dog, so their description might be more accurate."

MacNeice looked at the sketch. The eyes, cheekbones, mouth, and bald head were all similar, but the chin featured a distinct cleft. And his nose, which was indistinct in Wendy's sketch, was stronger and appeared to have been broken. "Wendy didn't remember anything about his ears, so the artist put in as average-white-guy ears. But the couple said they were large and tucked in against his skull. They also said his skin tone was pale white and very smooth. The wife said he looked like a genuinely concerned young man, very compassionate. They never spoke to Wendy about him."

"Brilliant." MacNeice took off his jacket and draped it over a chair. "We are definitely getting to know him."

"Sir," Ryan said, "don't forget you've got an appointment with Jeffery Ridout, the curator, in ten minutes."

Moments later, Williams and Vertesi came striding around the corner of the cubicle. Behind them, on crutches, was Maracle, grinning from ear to ear. "We found buddy here just getting off the elevator," Vertesi said. Seeing the printouts in MacNeice's hand, he added, "They're good, and pretty close to each other."

Ryan had cleared Aziz's space for Maracle. He sat down, put his crutches within reach, and swung his chair around to face the whiteboard. Williams handed him copies of the sketches.

While Ryan was downloading the memory stick from the pharmacy security camera, Vertesi gave them an update. "There are four sign companies in Dundurn, but only two deal with metal signage; it's expensive and old-school compared to vinyl and plastic. Neither of them carry one-inch brass V's."

Williams added, "They said they'd never been asked for brass letters, but if they were, they'd both reach out to a large company in Toronto called Sylvester Signs."

"So we called them up and, yes, they have cartons of one-inch brass V's. But no one has purchased just V's in the last year. Robbie Sylvester, the owner, said in an English accent . . . take it, Montile —" Vertesi swung his chair around to face his partner.

"You see, mate" — Williams was enjoying the role — "usually a V is in a word, yeah, like *Sylvester* or *Divine* or *Vegemite* — ooh, 'orrible stuff that. Not many words begin and end with a V. 'Cause it's not a word, yeah; it's just a flippin' letter. And it ain't one of our more popular letters. I mean, it's not an A or an E, is it? It's just a bloody V."

MacNeice took the point and added one of his own. "I think, given what we know about our man, if he'd had an encounter with Mr. Sylvester, the police in Toronto would be investigating a murder at a sign shop." He picked up his jacket. "Keep looking. He got those brass V's from somewhere. Try Buffalo." He turned back to Swetsky. "Don't release those composites just yet. I want to show them and the killer's drawing to Jeffery Ridout."

"Right. I'll check in with police services in North America and Europe to see if anyone recognizes him," Swetsky said as MacNeice put on his jacket and slipped the photocopies into an envelope.

"We'll meet with Vice about the laneway killings," added Williams. "Look into Paolo DeSouza's women. Maybe one of them knows this guy."

"DeSouza . . . I know that name. He's a wannabe. Runs with a big guy," said Maracle. "I can help with that."

"Before you do, Charlie, there's a video you gotta see."

[37]

THE GALLERY'S OFFICES HAD THE SORT OF MODERN INTERIOR THAT made MacNeice uncomfortable — all chrome and black leather, sleek lines, and cool grey monotone walls. He felt out of place, clumsy, even before he sat down.

Moments later, Ridout swung the tall translucent door to the offices open and crossed the floor to greet him. He was a short, tidy man in a narrow-cut dark grey suit, yellow bowtie, and pointy brown suede shoes. His glasses were black-framed circles that made it difficult to focus on his eyes. They also contributed to a look of permanent surprise.

Ridout appeared to be sizing up MacNeice as they walked through to his small office where nothing appeared out of place. While there was little wall space, Ridout did have a narrow tilted bookcase that seemed to be standing on two points of black steel the width of pencils. MacNeice couldn't help himself. "How does that even work?"

"Gravity, Detective. If I were to take the large books off the bottom shelf, it would all come crashing down. But as it is, it's extremely stable. Here, look —." He shook the structure, and while the publications shuddered, nothing tumbled down.

"Well then, Detective, what can I do for you?"

MacNeice gave Ridout a brief recap of the killings and put the crime scene photos on his desk.

"Oh yes. Daumier and the Chapman brothers. Truly marvellous."

Surprised by his excitement, MacNeice shook off a desire to point out that the people really were dead. From the envelope, MacNeice took out the killer's sketch of Durand Park, the handwritten description of Tundell, and the two composites.

"Now, if you're saying this little sketch is by the same person who created these, I am surprised." Ridout took off his circular specs and used a small loupe to study the drawing. "Clearly classically trained, yet conceptually he's a very edgy modernist. And with these" — he pointed to the crime scene photos — "his intent seems very clear. They're obviously ghastly, but I'm grateful for having seen them."

MacNeice was speechless.

"But you're not here to hear me wax poetic on the beauty of these images, or their satirical commentary on man's endless capacity for slaughter."

"Correct."

"I thought not. You want to know if I've ever come across this artist. Sadly, I have not. Leaving aside the homicidal nature of his work, it is conceptually very sound. It's theatre, really. These two are crime scene photos, are they not?"

"Yes."

"It seems to me that he's creating these tableaus in order to render them in some other form. Perhaps he plans to draw or paint them from photographs he's taken." Ridout seemed to marvel at the snapshots. "How did you choose where to place your camera?"

"Actually, he told me. He placed a marker to indicate where to stand."

"Clever, though odd. It suggests in a way that you became his accomplice."

"Possibly." It was something MacNeice hadn't considered. "Where could he exhibit work like this?"

"From your question, I assume you're ruling out galleries in Canada or the U.S. — and you'd be right. But Paris, Berlin, Rotterdam, Brussels . . . There are collectors there with certain tastes."

"His sketch — does it look familiar?"

"In style, no. He's a draftsman and stylistically very clever. His strokes are quick and, I suspect, rendered from life."

"Durand Park."

"Ah. Well, in that case he's given it more energy than it deserves."

"Is there an arts organization or a neighbourhood where artists congregate in Dundurn?"

"Well, there is an established watercolour society. I mention that because of this sketch, though I can't imagine that the man who created these tableaus would be a member. Many of the younger artists here are economic migrants from Toronto, so they tend to be scattered throughout the city and surrounding communities."

"Do you keep a list?"

"Artists seek me out and I do conduct regular studio visits, but I've never seen this man's work. While it might be a waste of time, you're welcome to the list. You never know, one of them might know of him."

"Is there a bar where they gather?"

Ridout raised his eyebrows at that. "Yes. I think it's only been open a couple of years. Le Hibou — 'the owl.' As unlikely as this sounds, it's on the road to Ancaster. A French chef and his Canadian wife opened it as a truck stop." He clicked away on his laptop. "Here we are." Ridout turned over one of his business cards and wrote down the address and phone number. Handing it across the desk, he added, "I'll email you that list today."

As they stood to leave, Ridout did a quick head-to-toe study of MacNeice. "You'll stand out like a sore thumb at Le Hibou. I wasn't joking; it really is a truck stop. The artists who gather there are more or less indistinguishable from tradesmen."

"You're referring to these heavy black shoes with the comfortable soles and my dark but otherwise forgettable suit?"

"Why, yes, I couldn't have put it better myself." He nodded twice. That MacNeice could roll with such a critical assessment of his attire seemed to delight Ridout.

At the elevator, MacNeice asked, "How do *you* dress when you go to Le Hibou?"

"I go as I am; they expect no less. But were I to wear a torn T-shirt, paint-splattered coveralls, and worn-out penny loafers, no one would notice me. I'd be utterly invisible." His smile suggested that he didn't really believe it. "For the artists — and I know this is a stretch — Le Hibou is our Paris in the wilderness. Writers and philosophers, painters and sculptors — it's their Café de Flore. Some ride their bikes out from the city just for a coffee, a croissant, and the conversation."

The elevator doors opened and MacNeice stepped in.

Ridout wasn't finished, but his tone changed. Holding the door, he said, "Detective MacNeice, whatever else this man is, he has talent. Possibly an extraordinary talent. A diabolical villain without doubt, but a true artist today is rarer than hen's teeth."

[38]

INSTEAD OF GOING BACK TO DIVISION, MacNEICE WALKED AROUND the building to his new unmarked Chevy. Sitting inside, he scanned the interior before sliding a Roberto Occhipinti disc into the player. Driving slowly out of the parking lot onto Main, he headed south on James Street towards St. Joe's.

Aziz was sitting in a chair by the window. She smiled when he swung open the door, and with some effort stood to greet him. "Hi, Mac. I'm being discharged for home care today. I'm just waiting for the surgeon to sign my papers."

He closed the distance between them, gently wrapping his arms around her. "It's wonderful to see you on your feet." He stepped back to look at her. The colour had returned to her face but, though her eyes were brighter, he could see she was still running on empty. "I'll take you home and give you an update on the way."

"Please. I need to fill my head with something other than longing for a good meal" — she looked around the room — "and a different view."

OVER THE NEXT half-hour, Aziz became more alert. If MacNeice left out information she'd ask questions and he'd fill in the gaps. She was hungry for details and appeared more and more energetic as the conversation went on. Concerning Wallace's press conference, which she had watched from her bed, Aziz felt that saving Elene Galanis's job would go a long way towards saving Wallace's.

He told her about the police sketch composites of the suspect and the security footage of him killing an armed pimp and his bodyguard in a matter of seconds. "Charlie Maracle has taken up temporary residence at your desk. He's looking into the women who worked for DeSouza."

"Make sure he doesn't get too comfortable there." Fiza was smiling, but he took the point. She was determined not be written out of the script.

He spoke about his meeting with Jeffery Ridout and about Le Hibou, Dundurn's little Paris in Ancaster.

"Is it open for lunch?"

"Yes. I'm going to check it out after I drop you off at home."

"No, take me." Aziz saw his brow furrow and the muscles at the corners of his mouth tighten. "Look, Mac, I've only eaten white-sauce everything, and various colours of Jell-O since I've been here. I need something of quality. Take me to the Owl."

MacNeice wasn't persuaded, but reluctantly he agreed — if the surgeon approved it. "Ridout impressed me, Fiza. He didn't recognize our man from the composites or his sketch, but he saw the crime scene photos and immediately knew what the killer was up to. Ridout thinks he's a major talent."

"Too bad he's going to spend the rest of his life in prison." Aziz had heard enough about the murderous "major talent" and changed the subject. "A real French restaurant . . . on the road to Ancaster?" She shook her head impatiently. "Where's the surgeon?"

As if on cue, the door swung open and an entourage of clipboard-carrying young residents appeared, led by Aziz's surgeon. After a brief acknowledgement of MacNeice, he turned to his patient. Aziz knew the drill; she took off her jacket and sat on the bed. The clutch of residents and the duty nurse gathered around.

Since it was a teaching hospital, the surgeon's comments were directed to those around him, not to Aziz. "Looking good. The entry wound is healing very well. Here you see the exit wound — a more difficult fix, but also coming along nicely. Those stitches will come out in a few weeks. I've told Detective Aziz that I don't think plastic surgery is necessary, but let's wait and see. She's on ten days of antibiotics, but for the next week or so the best medicine is bed rest." As he resealed the bandages, he addressed Aziz. "We've set you up with a wound-care specialist. Once a day will be sufficient. They'll call you later today to set up a schedule."

"Thank you."

"Keep an eye out for any inflammation, swelling, or tenderness beyond what you have now, around either wound.

We'll call and book a follow-up for you here, but otherwise you're good to go home."

"Thank you, Doctor. And please, thank your team for me."

The surgeon took the discharge papers from the nurse and signed them. As he was about to leave, MacNeice coughed several times. The surgeon turned around and MacNeice coughed again.

"That's a dry cough, Detective. Shall I check your chest while I'm here?"

"He's fine, Doctor. He's giving me a not-so-subtle hint. There's a restaurant not far from here. MacNeice is going and I asked if he'd take me along."

Chuckles rippled among the young doctors. "I see." The surgeon drove his hands deep into his lab-coat pockets, considering the request. "I'm encouraged that you feel up to it, and your wounds are healing well. I approve, but with conditions. Don't have a heavy meal and don't stay out more than two hours."

Fiza got off the bed and picked up her jacket, trying to hide her pleasure in the victory.

"One last thing. If you have wine, only one glass. Remember, you're still taking pain medication."

LE HIBOU WAS nestled among the trees on Wilson Road on the outskirts of Ancaster. Mud-splattered suvs and pickup trucks shared the parking area with motorcycles, small cars, and a battered Volkswagen van. Scanning the door and panel signage on some of the vehicles, MacNeice noted electricians, drywallers, house painters, plumbers, general contractors, and a landscaping company. Several bikes were locked to a galvanized rack that looked vaguely like overgrown paper clips. Off to the side, three motorcycles leaned on their kickstands.

MacNeice pointed to the building's mansard roof, where a two-foot plastic owl stood watch. Judging from the birdsong in the surrounding trees, its use as a bird deterrent was limited.

The menu was beside the door. It promised *Nouvelle cuisine de France*. And below that, *Dishes prepared in the new French style*.

"In the remote chance that our man is here, I want you to leave immediately and call it in from the car. Understood?" Aziz nodded as he handed her the car keys.

The proprietors of Le Hibou were Agnes Gagnon and Chef Jean-Marc Gagnon. Agnes was the sommelier and manager, and she met them at the door. An attractive woman in her late thirties, she asked if they'd like a table or seats at the bar.

The zinc bar played a starring role, taking up half the length of the restaurant. Though guests sitting there had their backs to the room, they could see behind them thanks to a series of framed mirrors that were tilted down for better viewing.

"The bar's lovely, but I think that table in the corner would be perfect," said Aziz, looking to see if MacNeice agreed.

As Agnes led them to the corner table, MacNeice played the part of tourist, pretending to look at the art on the walls but really keeping his attention on the faces of the people in the booths and at the bar. No sign of the killer.

The lunch crowd was finishing up, and by the time Agnes arrived to take their order, the population of Le Hibou had been reduced to half of what it was when they'd walked in. MacNeice produced his badge and introduced himself and Aziz. Laying his hand on the envelope containing the police sketches, he asked, "Would you have time now to answer a few questions and look at an artist's rendering?"

Agnes looked at her customers, who were engaged in conversation or working through their slices of pie and coffees. "Yes, but I may have to cut it short. What's this about?"

MacNeice gave her a brief overview. "We're looking for a person of interest, an artist who may frequent Le Hibou."

"Shall I ask Jean-Marc to come out? He knows most of the artists who come here."

"If you wouldn't mind, yes."

Aziz coughed into her hand.

"Oh, and we will be ordering, if that's possible."

"Yes, of course. You can order directly from the chef." She smiled and disappeared into the kitchen.

A short, slender man appeared. He was handsome, exuding confidence and flair in his tight white double-breasted chef's jacket and houndstooth trousers. Gagnon wiped his hands on his *torchon*, picked up a chair from another table, and placed it next to Aziz. With a Gallic air, he took Fiza's hand and introduced himself in French as Chef Jean-Marc. She responded in French and introduced MacNeice, before asking him if they could continue in English.

"*Oui*, as you wish."

MacNeice gave the chef a brief overview. "Before I show you the sketch, can you tell me how you've attracted so many artists to Le Hibou?"

"*Ah oui*. And here, on the road to Ancaster. The simple answer is I do not exactly know. I meet Agnes in Toulouse; she comes to my restaurant and we fall in love. A year later we marry and Agnes convinces me to come to Canada. I agree, only if she agrees to return to France if it does not work out. But, as you can see, it did. Three years later I do not feel so much in the wilderness, though still a bit. As for the artists and workers, it is the same as in France — they find you. Remote does not matter to them. And there is so much construction here." His posture shifted. He sat close and tapped the envelope. "*Alors*, what do you have in there, Detective?"

"We're hoping you'll tell us. We believe he's an artist." MacNeice pulled out the composites and placed them before the chef and his wife. "Take your time. Like any rendering, they may be very close — or not."

Gagnon studied the sketches for several seconds before sliding them over to Agnes. She looked closely at the images before admitting that she didn't recognize the man. Gagnon tapped one of the drawings twice and abruptly walked off to the bar. A minute later, he was standing over their table sipping an espresso.

"Two years ago I cater a lunch for an arts group in Dundas. He was there, I am sure of it. He complimented my crème caramel." Gagnon finished his coffee, put the cup on the bar, and returned to look again. "It is a good likeness. I am sure it is him, but I have not seen him here at Le Hibou. I am sorry, I do not know his name or his work."

"Are there any customers here now that attended the Dundas event?"

Jean-Marc scanned the tables to focus his memory. "It

was not modern art. More watercolours and oil paintings of farms and barns and streams — very skilled. They do not come here. We attract younger artists and writers."

"That far table — are they artists?"

"*Oui*. Well, three are. The other two, one is a writer and the other, I think he is a musician." He put the chair back and said, "I have to continue with cooking. I do not know what you like, but I have made two different quiches for tonight. They are still warm. One vegetarian, the other with pulled duck. Both have wonderful local white asparagus."

"Pulled duck and asparagus, please," Aziz said, too quickly, she thought. Slowing it down, she added, "With a butter tart and crème fraîche to finish."

"I'll just have the vegetarian quiche," said MacNeice. "Thank you both for your time." As they shook hands, he added, "It will help our investigation if you consider this conversation confidential." He put the composites back in the envelope and moved it aside.

Agnes asked, "Can I offer you a complimentary glass of Burgundy?"

"That would be lovely, thank you." Powered only by anticipation and adrenaline, Aziz was alert, sitting up tall, and happy.

WHEN THEY'D FINISHED their meal, Jean-Marc met them at the cash desk. "Here's my card, Detective. On the back is the contact for that Dundas lunch, Jean Wishart. She is a fine painter and may know this person." He smiled before adding, "*Alors*, in English you might say she is a 'character.'"

Outside, as MacNeice dialled Jean Wishart's number on

his cell, Aziz looked for cardinals in the cedars. She'd never noticed birds before she met MacNeice. He'd taught her many things, but this was a gift of pure joy.

"Wishart's in. I'll take you home and loop back."

"I'd appreciate it. This was divine. The quiche was delicious, and I don't think it was just in comparison to St. Joe's white sauce."

As they were driving back to Dundurn, Aziz leaned against the door and fell asleep. MacNeice pulled over and lowered the backrest. She mumbled something but didn't open her eyes. As the seat descended, she smiled a smile better seen from the inside of a dream.

From then on MacNeice did his best to moderate his speed, avoiding rough patches on the road and anticipating stoplights. When they finally came to a stop at her apartment building, he turned off the engine and waited for the loud chatter of a nearby jay to fade before opening the door.

Aziz woke up as he unfastened her seatbelt. "Oh, my . . . I think I was fast asleep."

He lifted her legs out of the car and told her to put her arms around his neck. With her head resting on his chest, he lifted her out of the seat and closed the door. "Are you okay to walk, Fiza?"

"Oh . . . yes. Just give me a moment." She took a deep breath and stood upright for a second or so before she began to fall back towards the car.

Catching her, he said, "I'm going to carry you, Fiza. Just relax."

At the door, she punched in the entry code. Aziz had been in the same building for years and had managed to move to the top floor. At her door she asked to be put down. "It would be too much like carrying me over the threshold."

"Very funny," MacNeice said as they stepped inside. "You're all right getting into bed?"

"Yes."

MacNeice went into the kitchen, where days-old breakfast dishes were sitting in the sink. He put them in the dishwasher, where they joined breakfast dishes from several days before. From the cupboard he retrieved a water jug decorated with blue cornflowers. He filled it with water and squeezed in the juice of a lemon. Before going back to the bedroom, he picked up a glass from the drying rack.

"Are you decent?" He smiled, an acknowledgement that this was the first time in his life he'd ever asked that question.

He put the jug on the bedside table, noting a small stack of the *London Review of Books* on the lower shelf. Filling the glass, he asked, "What medications have they given you?"

"Just the antibiotics. They offered something for the pain, but I didn't take it. I'm fine with ibuprofen. It's in the medicine cabinet, but I don't need it now. I'll just sleep for a bit."

MacNeice opened the window to let in some fresh air and the certainty of birdsong. Then he closed the curtains, immediately plunging the room into a sleep-inducing blue dusk.

Aziz was struggling to keep her eyes open, making him appreciate how difficult it had been just for her to get in bed.

"Shall I do your hair before I leave?"

"Oh, how nicely put. You may, sir."

If closed eyes can smile, hers were beaming. He sat on the edge of the bed, consciously avoiding any contact that would put pressure on her lower back. MacNeice ran his fingers gently through her hair until all its resisting strands were free and aligned. He hadn't noticed the tension in her face, but after a few minutes he could see that, like a young girl, she'd fallen into a deep, worry-free sleep.

[39]

JEAN WISHART LIVED IN A SMALL 1880S HOME ON AUGUSTA, WHERE the living room doubled as her studio. A short and sturdy woman in her sixties, she was wearing a long, paint-stained smock when MacNeice knocked on the door.

"Come in, come in."

She directed him to sit on a sofa, sharing space on one side with several large books and on the other with a curled-up grey cat. The animal managed to open one eye in his direction, although its bisected yellow pupil didn't follow him. It simply registered that something had happened and then closed again.

"Don't bother petting Stein. She doesn't like it and you wouldn't enjoy the experience. I'll just be a moment."

MacNeice sat with his knees together, the envelope

containing the police sketches resting on his legs. He felt as if he were in someone's waiting room. Wishart was doing something with her painting kit, perhaps to keep it from drying out while they spoke. While she worked, MacNeice reassured her. "I won't take much of your time, Miss Wishart."

"Oh, I know you won't."

MacNeice's eyes were drawn to a cord tethered to the wall beside the window and coiled in a neat circle on the floor below. He followed the cord to the ceiling, where it dropped through a small galvanized pulley to a wooden chair that was rotating slowly. He looked up at the rest of the ceiling; six identical chairs were hanging like bats above his head and around the room.

"It's a modest solution to the need for space, Detective." Her head poked around the easel in his direction. "If I could manage it, I'd hoist up that sofa too. Mind you, it's been almost a century since that old thing has shown its bottom to the world."

He felt like Alice about to enter Wonderland. While there weren't any framed paintings, detailed studies of butterflies, flowers, and vines snaked up the walls. They were taped to the wall the way detectives tape up investigation photographs, though unlike those, the studies looked as if they should be framed. The easel was turned away from his view, and she wasn't inviting him to see what was on it.

MacNeice looked at her shoes and stockings, visible under the easel. The shoes were the type of lace-up oxfords that likely hadn't changed since the early 1900s, when nurses and teachers wore them. The stockings were thick support hose, vaguely pink, though probably beige. She wore a pleated grey skirt, the hem of which fell six inches below her knees.

"That should do it." She came towards him carrying the paint-stained stool from behind her easel. Sitting down in front of him, she said, "Your call seemed urgent, which suits the work I'm doing. Let's avoid unnecessary pleasantries and get down to it."

He watched as she picked up the composites and the Durand Park sketch. "Yes, I have met this man. Jean-Marc's memory impresses me." She put her hand on the composite's cheek. "He was there ostensibly to join our merry band of dinosaurs." She looked over her glasses at MacNeice. "He didn't, of course."

She held it at arm's length. "It's a fairly accurate rendering. Of course, you'll want to know his name, but alas, I cannot provide it. He called in and I never made a note. I suppose I thought he wouldn't appear. If it's helpful, I think he had an unusual name, said it was Spanish. I'm happy to ask the other members if they might recall."

"That'd be very helpful. Can we do it electronically?"

"By email? Yes. I will send you their contact information early this evening. You may introduce yourself using my name." She handed the composites back to MacNeice and picked up the Durand sketch. Moving the glasses to her forehead, she peered closely at the drawing. For the first time since he'd arrived, her face melted into a smile.

"This drawing . . . It's a mere wisp of a thing, isn't it. And yet so charming. It's the graphic equivalent of the smell of lilacs on the breeze. I can see why he came to us. He shares more with John Constable than he may feel comfortable acknowledging. These days it's flash and dash and the almighty 'concept.' This man has skill; he sees things most pups in the art racket would not. And yet, alas and alack, he never came back." Wishart slapped her thighs, either enjoying her rhyme or signalling it was the end of their meeting.

"How old do you think he is?"

"He'd lived a life, I do remember that. You could see it in his eyes, but you can also see it here." She pointed to the composite. "I'd say in his early to mid-forties."

MacNeice gave her his card, thanked her for her time, and walked out the door. Elapsed time since entry: twelve minutes.

As he approached the Chevy, his cellphone rang; it was Maracle. "Hold on, Charlie." He got inside and waited for the call to emerge through his car speakers. "What have you got?"

"I've been watching that alley footage in slow motion."

"And?"

"He's military, sir, most likely Special Forces. Rank-and-file foot soldiers don't learn those moves. And no one else trains for that — not cops, thugs, or security. I suppose it could be eastern training, some Bruce Lee black-belt move."

"Do you know any Special Forces personnel, by regiment or name?"

"They came from different regiments, but they never mingled with people like us. They all wore non-regulation gear. They'd chow down by themselves, hit the weights by themselves. They don't look up, not even if you walk by. And if you said, 'Hey, what's up?' you were greeted with silence. And then they'd be gone and no one — I mean no one — seemed to know where they went."

[40]

HE WASN'T SATISFIED WITH HER THIGH. IT NEEDED TO RISE SLIGHTLY, as in the first moment of defence, not enough to suggest that she was cowed by terror. While it was true she didn't know what was coming, she might have guessed it wasn't going to be the usual $500 slam-bam in the sack.

It took her a moment — less time than it took to remove her kimono — to recognize his face from the grocery store. The Kit Kat man. Still, money talks, and even an asshole needs to get laid. That he knew DeSouza and had called from his cellphone meant that Paolo had personally cleared him. But to further reassure her, he flashed the black Exotic Escorts business card from the pocket of his hoodie.

Her mother had taken the boy for the night to cover for her regular sitter. A movie and a pizza would do him right. As for her, she'd mastered the moans of ecstasy while dreaming about her real job, the one she hadn't attained: hairdresser for high-fashion models. Actually, that was her fallback dream career. In her early teens she'd really wanted to be a high-fashion model herself. But as her body developed, the only offers that came her way didn't require any clothes.

Kit Kat Man. What was it he'd whispered in her ear? No matter. A buck's a buck, a fuck's a . . . "So, you met with Paolo and Gary. I sent them looking for you."

"I did. He said you told him about the chocolate bar."

"Oh, yeah. Hey, that was nothing."

"I agree. Anyway, after we talked, he handed me his cellphone and you were on the other end. Consider this a makeup session, where we can both benefit."

"Yeah, but he'll take his cut from our pleasure."

"That's business. Anyway, my request is a little bit different."

There'd been many men, and even some women, who just wanted to look at her naked. But this time, hopefully, she wouldn't be asked to do the things no working girl wanted to do — like the woof-woof stuff.

Kit Kat Man said she just needed to undress, to let her chrysanthemum kimono slide down her breasts and stomach and over her thighs to the floor. "Do that over and over, while I watch."

His eyes didn't leave her for a second; he seemed to take in everything. He was studying her — not just her body, but also how she touched it. Her fingers undoing the silk sash, slipping the fabric from her shoulders, letting it slide over her breasts like a floral wave falling on a shore. After the third time, she was surprised to find that she was getting aroused.

Without fanfare, he removed a large sketchbook from his backpack and started drawing. In the beginning he didn't even look at what he was drawing, just at her. As he studied her, his drawing took shape on the paper like magic. He was right; this was different. Was she supposed to pose?

"Don't pose. Just stay natural. No one is in the room. You're moving to an internal fantasy." He could read minds.

Every time she tilted her neck the way strippers or models do, he'd correct her. "Natural. You're not auditioning. You've already won the part. You're perfect."

"I like it when you talk to me." She started touching herself. She cupped her breasts; her hands followed the soft curves to the nipples, which were already hard. How many times before had she needed to coax them to life?

She moved her right hand downward, but he told her to stop. "You're acting again. For now, just be."

But she was getting to the point where it wasn't acting; she was aroused. Maybe it was his voice — soothing, strong, calm. There'd been so many animal grunts in her working life, she'd forgotten that gentle voices existed. There was something about this man, about his roaming eyes and his pencil recording what was before him. Now he was looking from her to the drawing and back again, as if his previous approach had been a warm-up. He had large, fast hands but he was delicate with the drawing, emphasizing a curve here and the tender sweetness of a nipple there.

She could see her body slowly emerging on the page. She relaxed a leg, which cocked her hip, and a moment later it appeared on his drawing pad. This was thrilling. To look at it, he seemed to know what she loved about her figure. Could she make a living doing this? They were creating art together. She'd never imagined posing for a real artist, never imagined seeing her body framed and hanging in a gallery for other people to admire. Now she was imagining walking quietly through the gallery as people stared at the drawings. She'd listen, she'd smile, she'd be asked to meet them before they took the drawings home.

Her breathing was ragged and heavy when she asked, "Can I lie down? I'd like to, you know, lie down now."

"Yes."

On her back, she lifted her thighs and reached between them. That caused her back to arch and she turned her face away. And then, as if anticipating his correction, she let her legs slide down the sheets. Her tummy rose and fell more quickly now, and she began caressing her breasts again. Though she didn't realize it, she was biting her lower lip. For the first time in ages, she wasn't doing it because she thought it would look sexy.

He kept sketching. Sometimes he'd erase a detail and start over. That showed how much he cared about her, about the likeness of her. She'd catch his eyes — so intense — following her hands, surveying her breasts, her mouth, her belly, and below. He'd occasionally smile his approval, and when he did, she'd swallow hard, overwhelmed by how movie-romantic it was. But this wasn't a movie.

"Can I . . . do something for you?" Her voice was breathless, real.

"You're doing it. Stay focused. Just imagine you're all alone."

The moment was coming on fast, deep in her belly. She

closed her legs and slid her fingers downward. She was being swept forward, towards it. "Talk to me, Mister Kit Kat."

He kept sketching. "This is good. Keep going. Lose control of yourself."

"Am I beautiful?" she whispered, but he didn't answer.

She could hear his pencil scratching the surface, his fingers racing, smudging lines, giving her form — bringing her to life. Her hips began an old, familiar dance, one never seen by anyone. This was private; this was special. It always had been. She was groaning and whimpering and so happy that tears streamed from her eyes onto the pillow. What was happening felt epic and out of control. An artist was capturing it on paper, where this orgasm would live forever.

A whisper; the swift passing shadow of a hand; a thick, liquid gurgle; a brief dampness, then a flood. Orchestrated to her climax, it was a moment of exaltation — followed by a brief, unimaginable horror.

He wiped the razor clean on her chrysanthemum kimono, set the wooden chair in front of the bed, and arranged the camera several feet away. Then he sat down to wait for the shutter clicks.

[41]

CHARLIE MARACLE AND MEG LUNDSTROM MET IN THE INTERVIEW room. By the time she'd left he had the faces, names, and current addresses for all of Paolo DeSouza's known escorts.

"As word gets out about DeSouza," Lundstrom said, "these girls will be picked up by other pimps. That's how it works, so get to them fast." She looked at his crutches and added, "If you need help, Charlie, Vice can do a roundup."

"Okay, thanks. You check at your end and I'll check at mine, but assume for now that it's on."

After she left, Maracle hopped back to the cubicle with the file folder clenched in his teeth. On the whiteboard he taped the mug shots below the photo of DeSouza dead in the alleyway: Angel White, nineteen; Dolores Sanchez, twenty-one; Anna Kershawn, twenty-eight; Melody Mason, thirty-three.

"DeSouza's stable?" Williams asked, looking them over.

"Yeah. Last update was six months ago. His business could have expanded or shrunk, but this is a start." He turned to make his case to Swetsky. "Vice will round them up for us, if you're okay with that, sir."

"Do it."

Williams studied the headshots. "They're not exactly the girl next door, but these women look like people you'd meet anywhere."

"That's the point — they're not streetwalkers. These are 'by appointment only' escorts. They can probably walk into any hotel or club without anyone batting an eye."

Vertesi raised a hand from his keyboard. "I think I've got something." He'd been scanning local print and broadcast media for artists and art events. "Check this out." He moved out of the way of his monitor. "It's an annual art show called FotoBlast. These are from last year's opening night. Recognize anyone?"

Shot from a balcony, the photograph looked down on a gallery space packed with people. Most had a glass of wine in hand, and while there were several couples walking about, the majority had collected in groups of three or more, talking but not looking at the work. There was only one man who stood alone. He was turned toward the camera, making his way around a cluster of people who seemed unaware of his presence. His body was partially obscured, but his head and right shoulder emerged clearly. Vertesi held the composite drawing next to the screen and, to save time, pointed to the man in a baseball cap and hoodie. Though his eyes were hidden by the cap's peak, his jaw and mouth were visible.

"Maybe," Williams said.

"Yeah, could be him," Swetsky added, unconvinced.

"Ryan, can you sharpen and enlarge this guy?"

Ryan slid his chair over to Vertesi's computer. *Click-click-click* and the image filled the screen. It was blurred, but Ryan adjusted the focus and contrast. "I'll send it to my station and switch on the fabulizer. I'll need ten minutes; there's a bit more to do on the alley."

No one knew what a fabulizer was, but what he'd already done had made it possible to see the close resemblance to the composite.

"Okay," Swetsky said. "We need to track down the organizers of this event. Get a list of the artists and guests. Maybe we can put a name to that face."

"Do your magic, Ryan."

"I'm on it."

MACNEICE TOOK A deep breath before pushing open the cold stainless door. Its mechanical wheeze covered his uneasy exhale. Junior spotted the ruse and smiled. "Mary's taking one of the crispies back to the fridge. She'll be right back."

The second body from the Ram inferno was on Junior's table. Blacker than night, twisted and frozen in horror, it had lost all of its recognizable features. Where the joints had been broken — by emergency teams extracting it from the vehicle or by Junior's scalpel — the contrast between black and bright pink was dramatic.

For MacNeice it was nauseating. "I'll wait in her office, thanks."

He was about to sit down when he heard Mary approach.

"What an unexpected pleasure. With all the carnage of late, I didn't think you'd have time to visit."

MacNeice began to speak. "I have a few questions about the Palmer-Galanis case —"

"I thought you might. First, however, he died of asphyxiation, not from the shotgun blast. He'd been dead for hours when that happened. Whether he suffocated from the gag in his mouth, from the accumulation of blood and mucus in his air passages, or because he was encased in a chair — more likely a deadly combination of all three — it's impossible to tell."

MacNeice felt relieved but tried not to show it. Mary was waiting for him to say something, but he couldn't actually think of anything.

"Right. Well, on to Mr. Galanis and his cousins. What I found in the bloodstream of burn victim number one was a strong indication of methamphetamine. Suffice it to say, I believe Junior will very shortly discover the same with burn victim number two."

"And Galanis?"

"There we had more success. A very high dose of a methamphetamine — clearly it was shared among them. Mr. Galanis was wildly psychotic when you opened fire on him. Even with the gunshot wounds to his legs, he would have felt invincible. The kill shot entered his skull just above the left eye. It was catastrophic for the brain, of course, but I've sent off what remained of it for analysis. That may tell us how long he'd been on the drug and specifically which variety. But in the end, it won't change the outcome."

"That's it, then."

"Two remaining details. The man Junior's working on

was dead before the vehicle fire. And while the other one died in the fire, he would in all likelihood have succumbed to his gunshot wounds."

MacNeice was exhausted but suddenly aware of smells that could all too easily make him vomit. With some difficulty he pulled himself out of the chair.

"Mac, are you well?"

"I just need some fresh air, Mary. I'll be fine."

"It's the fluids. Junior's draining that cadaver. Let me walk you out."

With Richardson at his side, he managed to escape the lab without looking back at Junior and his "crispy." On the way down the tiled corridor, she spoke softly. "As for the other two, Grant, as you know, had a broken neck and a severed knee joint. DeSouza's fascinating, though. Blunt upward trauma applied to the nose, which sent bone and cartilage into the brainpan as if someone had swung at him with a cricket bat."

"Close. It was done by hand. We caught it on a security camera. Both were brandishing side arms when it happened."

"My, my. Well, he wouldn't have known what hit him." She shook her head slowly. "It says something, doesn't it, that the killer didn't use a weapon." She stopped for a moment and looked down at the floor. "This reminds me of my favourite uncle, who was a commando during the war. I vaguely recall him telling me about that method of killing. Presumably surprise and timing are critical."

"Meaning this isn't your average thug?"

"I'd say military." She fixed her gaze on MacNeice's eyes. She might have been looking for a speck of soot or rainbows in the iris, but he knew she wasn't. A few moments later she sighed; she had something to say. Her voice changed and she sounded almost motherly. "I think you're becoming a magnet for demented soldiers, Detective. Knowing how these men died, I feel certain that you're hunting another one. Take care, Mac." She rested a hand on his shoulder before turning away.

As he watched her return to the lab, Mary Richardson seemed energized. Without looking back at him, she waved, straight-armed the door, and disappeared inside.

MACNEICE APPROACHED HIS car, which was parked next to one of the concrete planters that defined the parking lot. He listened to the sound of house sparrows chatting up spring in the branches of a young gingko tree. As he got nearer, one bird in particular caught his attention. A female sparrow was squatting low and wiggling her behind so quickly it looked like an extreme jive. A male hopped from branch to branch above her, uncertain, it seemed, about the safest approach. When he fluttered down and came to light on her back, it looked tentative. After several attempts to hang on to her shimmying behind, he flew to another branch and waited.

MacNeice got into the car, certain that they'd work it out. As he slid the key into the ignition, the slender female landed on the hood and again began her furious dance. In seconds the male dropped down, his head tilting this way and that, and hopped onto her back again.

Were they aware of MacNeice smiling behind the windshield? He didn't know, but it was clear that the stability of the blue hood, possibly still warm from driving, was as good as a featherbed. When it was done, the male flew back to the higher branches and fluttered his feathers. The female appeared to be resting until MacNeice turned on the engine; then she stood up and flew off across the lot to the mature trees on the other side. The male's head swivelled back and forth before he followed.

MacNeice's radiophone rang. "MacNeice," he said.

"What are you up to, Mac?"

It was Deputy Chief Wallace, sounding bright, almost cheerful. MacNeice considered for a moment whether to tell him about sparrow mating rituals and how he'd watched one come to a climax on the hood of his Chevy, but decided against it. "I'm just leaving the chief pathologist's lab."

"Good. I've confirmed Elene Galanis's employment. There was a retirement in the department, and while that sounds convenient, it wasn't. To make their budget they weren't going to re-staff that position. I've promised to pick up the shortfall elsewhere."

"By not re-staffing Palmer's position?"

"Jesus, you can be a sonofabitch." Wallace sounded angry, but MacNeice could detect the relief in his voice. "Look, I've always felt we were top-heavy in Homicide — too many DIs. We'll bring up a constable to replace him. After all, Mac, it wasn't as if Palmer was doing a bang-up job."

Before he hung up, Wallace asked how it had gone at the morgue. MacNeice gave him a topline on the latest killings and reported that Galanis and his cousins had been cranked up on speed, possibly from the moment they'd snatched Palmer.

AS HE WAS nearing the division parking lot, MacNeice received another call, this time from Vertesi. "Glenn Grove Hotel in Westdale, boss. A body in one of their rooms with her throat slashed."

MacNeice told him they could go out together and pulled up at the division's rear entrance. In seconds, Vertesi and Williams came through the door.

"Shotgun," Vertesi said, reaching for the front passenger door.

"I'm used to it, Rocky. Folks will drive by thinking you're taking me in for questioning. They'd be so confused if they saw me sitting up front."

Once on King Street, MacNeice turned on the blue flashers and accelerated along the inside lane. He heard the click of seatbelts and realized Maracle must have mentioned his driving up on Paradise. Smiling into the mirror, he asked Williams, "You comfortable back there?"

"Peachy, sir. Just being cautious."

The Chevy tore past the basilica and the highway overpass, heading for Westdale. "Did a bit of research on the Glenn Grove," Vertesi continued. "Because it's near Brant University, the guests are mostly visiting professors, university delegations, and foreign students with heavy money from their parents. It also gets the families of patients at the BU Medical Centre."

"There's more to it, though . . ." MacNeice said, hitting his *woop-woop* siren to encourage an SUV to move over.

"Yeah. Charlie called his contact at Vice. The hotel's night manager is known for signing in prostitutes and their johns, provided they pay a premium."

"And our victim is one?"

Williams nodded. "It gets better. Lundstrom said the Glenn Grove — the 'GG,' as she calls it — is frequented by only two pimps. One of them was DeSouza. So this could be someone from his stable. Swetsky will let us know if one of Paolo's girls doesn't show up for her interview."

[42]

THEY WERE MET IN THE LOBBY BY TWO UNIFORMS, GIORDANO AND Tyler. Giordano pointed out the night manager, who was standing near the office door. He was just finishing his shift when an outside call had come in at 11:45 a.m. The caller, a man, said someone had died in Room 213. He told him not to open the door, just to call the police. MacNeice saw an employee in a blue blazer, so drained of colour that he looked like an upright, blinking cadaver. Clearly he had opened the door.

"The night manager, Brian Whitney, says she's an escort," Giordano said. "Her name's Melody Mason, thirty-three years old."

Vertesi and Williams exchanged glances, and Williams stepped aside to call Swetsky.

"Mason checked in alone late yesterday afternoon. There are no active video cameras in the hallways and none at the rear emergency exit. There's one in the corner here" — Giordano pointed to a camera looking down on the registration counter — "and another one at the elevator door in the underground parking garage. We haven't seen those."

"When's Whitney's shift?"

"Twelve a.m. to twelve p.m."

"So the day manager booked her in?"

"Yes, sir."

"Did they know Mason was an escort?"

"No. The pimps tell the escorts to say they're here for a medical conference at BU. And since they carry a small overnight bag, the day manager has no reason to think otherwise. She takes an imprint from a credit card and gets a fake address. It's only when Whitney checks them out that they pay the premium."

"Was he forthcoming with this information?"

"You bet, sir. He's scared shitless — of us, the pimps, or losing his job, we don't know. But he seems willing to talk."

"Did he touch anything in the room?"

"He says no, sir. Neither did we."

THERE ARE TWO carotid arteries, one on the left and one on the right side of the neck. Together they feed blood to the brain, neck, and face, and for thirty-three years Melody Mason had been unaware of their existence. When both arteries are severed, death is swift — certainly terrifying but possibly painless, if you disregard the slash of the razor. With more than a gallon of blood in the human body, cutting two major blood vessels while the heart continues to pump is, in a word, messy.

The wallpaper, a medley of mauve flowers and vertical aquamarine stripes, had been hit by a heavy spray as Mason's head turned. After that the blood had flowed over her upper chest, streamed under her torso, and spread over the bed and onto the carpet below. The greatest pooling, however, was under the body. Her arms lay relaxed and extended at her sides, the left hanging over the edge of the bed, suggesting someone in a deep sleep. Both hands had been covered in blood when she instinctively grasped at her neck.

"Jesus. First he does DeSouza and Grant, and now her." Williams shook his head.

"Look down, boss." Vertesi pointed to the carpet. Just beyond the swing of the door was a one-inch brass V.

Williams shook his head in disbelief. "We gotta get ahead of this fucker somehow. Man, he's seriously twisted."

"I want to keep this scene as clean as possible," MacNeice said from the threshold. He took out his point-and-shoot and framed the image above the letter. After he'd taken several photographs, he studied them on the screen. "The wooden chair is interesting." He toggled back and forth between the images. "Michael, go and sit there, facing the camera. Don't touch anything; just sit for a moment."

Vertesi walked across the carpet like a man in a minefield and sat down. He waited for MacNeice to compose the photo, then leaned over, elbows on thighs, head down, head up, hands on thighs, head turning to look at Melody's face. MacNeice kept shooting. When he was finished, he asked Vertesi to look around the room for anything that wasn't Glenn Grove property.

"There's a black leather bag open on the other side of the bed. Mason's clothes are piled neatly on the corner chair. Sequined black stilettos. That's a bloody kimono behind me, partially covering her legs." He turned his attention to the mirrored closet. "There's a hard-case carry-on in the closet and a makeup kit on the bathroom counter." He did one last scan. "That's it. No drinks, no paraphernalia. Do you want any of these things?"

"If you can get to her wallet. But other than that, no." MacNeice scrolled through the photographs. "I think our DAG curator needs to see this."

MacNeice squatted over the V and studied the carpet. There were two ancient stains — likely red wine — each the size of a nickel. The pale grey twill had been worn down in the high-traffic areas, but despite being brittle and crusty to the touch, the carpet looked clean. He got down on the floor and looked across its surface.

Near the wine stains were two tiny black splinters. MacNeice pulled his latex glove on tighter so he could pick one up. Holding it to the light, he smiled. "Graphite."

"What's that?" Williams leaned over, straining to see it.

"Pencil lead. The sharpened tip broke off. And here, look." He reached over and picked up something else, placing it in the palm of his hand, admiring it as one would a newly found jewel. "Eraser crumbs."

Williams shook his head, realizing he was missing the point. Vertesi also looked at it, shrugging his shoulders.

"He wasn't here to have sex," MacNeice said, accepting a plastic zipper bag from Williams. "He was drawing her."

"THERE'S FIVE HUNDRED dollars in fifties, a couple of credit cards, a health card, and a driver's licence. Nothing personal like a snapshot, just the cash." Vertesi closed the wallet and opened the bag. Inside he found lipstick, lip gloss, K-Y lubricant, a packet of condoms, and a brushed aluminum business-card holder with six black cards: EXOTIC ESCORTS was printed in hot pink, with no address, just a phone number.

There was a knock at the door. Giordano looked in to tell them the parking garage security camera was down. It had been disabled about the time Melody Mason checked in. The camera feed was on a computer in the office; while there was a lineup at the front desk, no one was in there, so it went unnoticed.

MacNeice wasn't surprised. He turned to Vertesi. "Find out where Mason lived, who she lived with, whatever family she may have had."

Montile leaned against the door. "I'll call Forensics and get a statement from the night manager." Looking back at the bed, he added, "I don't know why, but this one's more depressing than the priest, the lawyer, or Donkey-Head."

[43]

GALERIE WEITZMAN-BOURGET SPECIALIZED IN BOUNDARY-BREAKING international photography. Located on a narrow street in the Latin Quarter of Paris, the gallery was known as "*haute sleek*," a description it came by honestly. Carmen Weitzman and Chanel Bourget were partners both in life and in the gallery. For artists from such faraway places as Japan, China, Africa, South America, and also elsewhere in Europe, exhibiting at GWB was considered to be conquering the Mount Everest of contemporary photography.

The work shown at GWB was unquestionably edgy. Its openings featured gold-covered windows, with two men in black suits at the door. While they looked like elegant heavies, they wore white silk gloves and politely took the invitations from arriving guests. After one week of these private viewings, the gallery would drop the golden veil. There'd be an immediate reaction from passersby, and without fail there'd be some who'd ring the bell for entry, only to be ignored.

The very first exhibition at GWB, by a famous German photographer, had featured one-metre-square colour-saturated photographs of Weitzman and Bourget making love. The edition of ten prints per original image sold out, after which the negatives were destroyed at an invitation-only *brûlant* — a formal burning.

In their chic designer apparel, the partners were beautiful women of superb taste. Naked, however, they were stripped of any illusion of perfection. Carmen was zaftig, with large, sagging breasts, stretch marks on her stomach, and dimpled thighs. Chanel was thin and vaguely reminiscent of the actress Jean Seberg; there was a wasted quality to her, as if she suffered from terminal disinterest. It was strange how the voluptuous partner was light in spirit and ready to laugh, while the one with a real claim to beauty seemed heavy, burdened with hipbones that jutted out like dorsal fins.

Nonetheless, as a graphic exposé of lovemaking, the exhibition had been both exquisite and raw. The photographer (also a woman) revealed moments of passion, aggression, joy, submission. So intimate were the images that the sweat beading arms, breasts, and foreheads compelled some viewers to reach out and touch the glass, thinking perhaps it was just caused by moisture in the air from hyperventilation.

Each print was framed with wide panels of satin-lacquered wood in a colour Chanel dubbed *rose des lèvres* — "labia pink." Carmen felt that the frames sealed the deal in every case, and perhaps she was right. What they certainly sealed was the perception and future of GWB as too hot to ignore.

For the pair's bedroom, the photographer had printed two life-size images. Framed in labia pink, they faced each other from opposite sides of the bed. The artist's message was part gratitude, part tease: "Just in case you ever feel in need of inspiration," her note read, "*un petit soupçon.*"

INTO GWB'S WORLD of sophistication and decadence arrived an unsolicited portfolio from an unknown photographer. Accompanying the work was a two-page cover letter separated from the prints by a black card. Chanel began to read: "The intent of this series is to shine a light on history and the truth and lies of telling stories through images. There's a deep chasm between what is real and what is fiction. Each of us must explore this dichotomy, because what we see determines who we are and how we act."

While Chanel's English pronunciation was refined and her vocabulary sufficient to carry on a dialogue with the English-speaking clients who visited the gallery, she wasn't entirely sure that the author of this text was being serious. It sounded so pompous. She called in Jacqueline, her British assistant, for an opinion. As she stood watching the young woman read, she asked, "It is pompous, yes?"

"A little, but I think it makes sense. What are the images like?"

"I don't know. I wanted to read first, then look. Please use Google Earth" — she picked up the courier slip and handed it to her — "and find where is Dundurn, Ontario, Canada. Tell me what is there."

On the second page of the cover letter were images of the Daumier lithograph and the Goya/Chapman paintings. There were also six very fine photographs by an unnamed war photographer. Chanel sat down behind the long mahogany table that served as her desk. As she sipped her coffee, Jacqueline returned. Reading from her note, she said, "Madame, Dundurn is Canada's tenth-largest city. It's an hour's drive southwest of Toronto. It's known for industry and manufacturing, and it has one of the largest ports on the Great Lakes. With the collapse of some industries, the city has been changing. There's been a migration of artists from Toronto, where the cost of living is high. Dundurn has an abundance of nature —"

"*Merci*, Jacqueline. No more, please; it's too much." Chanel waved her hand dismissively and went back to the cover letter.

GWB —

This introductory portfolio contains four 12 x 12-inch sample prints of two subjects. A full exhibition will include twelve 24 x 24-inch signed and framed archival prints of similarly themed tableaus, with further editions of six photographs on request.

Regarding the artist's biography and exhibition history — nothing exists. Nor will it. The combat photographs by this artist were taken while serving in Afghanistan. They have never been shown and will not be included in the exhibition.

A METAPHOR OF INTENT

A farmer buys a farm from a farmer, just as that farmer bought the same farm from a farmer decades before, and before him, farmers had bought that farm from farmers ever since it first became a farm. Each might add a new crop or remove an old one, but essentially it remains the same farm. It just has a new name on the barn.

That's painting. Each painter is a farmer who adds a wrinkle. It may not be new and it's often not as good, but he claims it is — it's his wrinkle. And so it has been throughout the history of painting. The painter buys the same canvas, uses the same brushes, the same paints. He believes that his painting is a new crop from old soil.

Then came a revolutionary way to "farm" — photography. But, even after 150 years, it's just another way to farm the same soil. Only the tools are different.

This artist is determined to create something undeniably new. He wants to commit art.

COMPENSATION

For each photograph sold, after gallery fees have been deducted, cheques will be made payable to a Credit Suisse account under the name Romeo Charlie Victor (RCV). You will never meet the artist known as RCV. He will not appear in person, nor will he provide a portrait for marketing purposes. The point: that who he is, how tall he is, whether he has a nice smile — those and similar considerations — are unessential to the art. A manifesto will be provided to GWB for use as a title panel for the exhibition.

EXHIBITION TITLE
  Romeo Charlie Victor: With Respect

UNACCUSTOMED TO BEING preached to, Chanel stood up
quickly and considered returning the portfolio unopened.
But apart from the gall of its author, she couldn't argue the
point. For Bourget, the truth wasn't complicated: curios-
ity is a demon. Whatever she thought of the letter and its
presumption, she was curious to open the box. She wanted
the satisfaction of a laugh and of writing a short, vicious
response to an arrogant pretender.

Chanel opened a drawer in the desk and retrieved cotton
gloves and a large magnifying glass. She moved her empty
cup over to a credenza, put aside the black card, and carefully picked up the four prints. Removing the covering tissues, she placed them one by one in a row and stood back. In
a matter of minutes she was shaking her head in admiration.

Few things had the ability to shock her, but this work
did. Yes, they were small square horrors — they would be
even more powerful when blown up for exhibition — but
they were horrible in the tradition of Daumier and Goya.
The satirical trick of going further than the Chapman brothers also appealed to her. Whatever RCV had done to make
his tableaus appear so lifelike would possibly also remain a
mystery, but the re-creations had an unmistakable modern-
ity while respecting and paying homage to the originals.
The use of additional lighting, if it was present at all, was so
subtle that the images appeared to be lit by nature, by the
lamps in the bedroom or by moonlight. They were master-
fully long exposures.

Though Carmen was in Brussels concluding a lucrative contract, Chanel had an urge to call her and scream for joy. The thought of doing that made her laugh. It would be so out of character that Carmen might dismiss it as a crank call.

She picked up the magnifying glass and scanned the prints again for weaknesses or mistakes in the conceit. Was the blood lifelike? Was a chest or an eyelid blurred because the actor needed to breathe? Death is difficult to achieve when your face is full of life. Think of all the actors who died onstage or on camera. How many times did you wait for their chest to rise or their belly to quiver?

Chanel prided herself for spotting the tricks photographers used to achieve illusions. But she could find no evidence, no slip of a digital tool, no hard-edged cropping, cutting, or selective colour enhancing in these photographs. The work was seamless. She returned to the letter to read the remaining text.

POSTSCRIPT

Should GWB wish to proceed, simply send a text message to the number below, confirming same. Be specific with regards to the timing of the exhibition. RCV will deliver archival prints — excluding the additional edition of six — unframed, with specifications for the framer of your choice, one month prior to opening.

RCV has researched your gallery and feels that GWB is the right venue for this work. However, in the unlikely event that you're not interested, return the portfolio by FedEx to the post office box on the delivery slip.

"MAGNIFICENT BASTARD," CHANEL murmured as she returned the prints and the letter to the box. Laying her white gloves on top, she took her cigarette case and lighter from the drawer and walked outside. The sidewalk was narrow and busy, as always, with passing tourists, so she walked around the corner to stand facing the graffiti-crammed wall of Serge Gainsbourg's former home on rue de Verneuil. She inhaled long and deep, marvelling that her trick-monitor brain couldn't find a way to diminish her interest in the mysterious RCV.

Was he a charlatan? On some level, possibly, but the work resoundingly said no. Artists' pretentions weren't new to her. Chanel had spent two decades dealing with arrogance, insecurities, foibles, and kinks. She'd charmed, cajoled, and at times berated them into keeping their commitments. Of course, her own arrogance put most of her artists to shame, and of that she was exceedingly proud. Unstated, her message to each was clear: *You need me more than I need you.*

She leaned against the bollard, enjoying her cigarette and looking at but not seeing Gainsbourg's likeness staring back. Chanel was thinking about exhibition scheduling and which artist she could bump for RCV's work. Would June be too soon? She decided that was RCV's problem. Exhaling a narrow cloud of smoke, she said out loud, "June it is." Though it was one of her busiest months, she'd move the Italian photographer, because he'd originally changed his scheduled date from April.

She wondered what would happen if she insisted on a meeting before proceeding. No reasonable person would think that too much to ask, though she suspected RCV might be defiantly unreasonable. Nonetheless, a challenge trigger had been pulled for Chanel. It was the same one that had been pulled when she was a teenager attracted to her tennis coach, a woman fifteen years her senior. The same trigger her father had inadvertently pulled when he said she'd be wasting his money and her education by buying photographs for wealthy decadents. She smiled, recalling his exact words: "You'll never make your way doing this, *ma chérie*. I will always be your Bank of Papa."

Chanel dropped her cigarette butt on the ground, grinding out its fire and kicking it into the gutter, where it would be swept away the next morning.

[44]

JEFFERY RIDOUT WAS LEAVING FOR A STUDIO VISIT IN TORONTO when MacNeice arrived at the DAG. Standing near the entrance windows, MacNeice warned him that what he was about to see would be disturbing. Ridout smiled bravely.

He looked at the image and immediately turned away. "My lord in heaven." He took several deep breaths before returning to the photo. Then he flipped quickly through several others, including those with Vertesi in the chair. He slowed down, turning the photocopies until he stopped at one.

In the photo, Vertesi was looking down at the floor, elbows resting on his thighs. "It's this one, number six. The angle isn't right, but I know this one." Ridout shook his head in frustration that he couldn't put a name to it.

"I've got your card, Detective. Give me till morning. I might consult Nicole, but I do know this work." He folded it in half and put it in his jacket pocket. "He's referencing another artist. It's someone well known but perhaps second tier."

IT WAS 8:45 P.M. when MacNeice picked up his jacket, scanned the whiteboard one last time, and left the building. He left a photo of Melody Mason's body taped next to those from Amelia Street and the Punchbowl. Vice had no information about her home address or surviving family. But she had been caught in a sweep, fingerprinted and photographed, and released without charges. Her sheet cited lack of evidence. MacNeice had her mug shot posted on the department's online police alert page. In the morning she would appear in the media as a POI — a person of interest — in an ongoing investigation.

The composite of the suspected killer had already been released to local and regional news sources. While MacNeice was hopeful that the images from the alley or FotoBlast could be enhanced, there was little in them but the killer's chin and wide grin. They would refer to him as a POI in several recent homicides. The *Standard* had already begun describing him as a serial killer, and once Mason's photo appeared, he was certain every reporter would begin using the same language.

MacNeice was merging with the eastbound traffic on Main when his cellphone rang. "Detective MacNeice, I remembered where I'd seen that image." Jeffery Ridout was shouting to be heard over loud background noise. "I'm sorry for this — the artist here insists on playing this music — but it's even louder outside."

"I can hear you, Jeffery."

"It's Walter Sickert, a British artist who lived from 1860 to 1942. A young prostitute in London had her throat slashed on a bed in a dingy room. He called his painting *The Camden Town Murder* and then mysteriously provided an alternative title, *What Shall We Do about the Rent?* Sickert knew a lot about that killing, the crime scene details and such. Some thought he knew too much, and for a while he was considered a suspect. Though many were convinced that he'd killed her, it was never proven, and her killer was never found."

The background noise faded suddenly. "I've retreated to the toilet. I can't tell you what a chill it was when Sickert's paintings came onscreen." Ridout lowered his voice. "Honestly, I'm gutted. I don't know that I want you showing me any more of these . . . God, I hope it's helpful."

"It is, Jeffery. Thank you."

"Stay safe, MacNeice. I've never said that to anyone with more meaning."

SITTING AT THE kitchen table in his stone cottage, MacNeice pushed aside the remains of his hastily prepared pasta and opened his laptop. He typed *"Sickert what shall we do about the rent?"* and waited. What appeared was sanitized and bloodless compared to the scene at the hotel, but there was no question about the reference.

MacNeice's cellphone rang; it was Montile calling from Division. "Sir, I just got a call from the organizer of last year's FotoBlast. She said she knows the Dundurn photography scene really well but doesn't recognize our guy from the photo or the composite."

"Too bad, though I'm not surprised. He's an outlier by definition."

MACNEICE CLEARED THE dishes and poured a double grappa. He sat in the living room looking out at the forest, where dusk had already faded to night. The chatter of day birds had given way to bats and their reckless skimming flight. On the ground, the squirrels and lesser rodents had retreated to their nests to wait for morning. Soon, if he was lucky, a fox or coyote might amble by and glance his way. But for now — apart from the reflection of his hand lifting the glass — it was a still life outside and in.

You miss me still, don't you.

"More than words can say."

It's holding you back. I never wanted that for you.

"You're with me now. That's all that matters."

You think so, Mac, but you're a puppet master pulling invisible strings, providing words for an invisible puppet.

"Well put, Kate. . . . Through the window, among the trees, I know there's a fox peering back at me. I can feel him sniffing the air, waiting for me."

And if he isn't there? If he's like me, just something you imagine?

"Then I'm a lucky man to have you here and to have him there watching over me. As winter would miss the spring, I miss you."

I recall you once saying, "As the sea longs for the shore, I long for you."

"All true."

[45]

IT WAS 8:48 A.M. THE TELEPHONE RANG ONCE. RYAN ANSWERED IT and swivelled in his chair. "Sir, it's the managing editor of the *Standard* for you. Says it's important."

"Detective Superintendent, this is Charles Lowry. Your department published a composite of a person of interest in the *Standard* today."

"That's correct."

"I'm sitting with our photo editor, Dorothy Edwards. We're on speaker, so I'll let her take it from here."

"Hello, Detective MacNeice. Your composite looks very much like a stringer we've used from time to time to shoot football or hockey. His name is Patrick Manserra."

"Do you have an address for him?" MacNeice was rifling his desk for a pen.

"Not exactly. We send his fee to a PO box. We do have a phone number for him, but I've checked and it's no longer in service."

"I'll take it anyway." MacNeice wrote down the number. "What else can you tell me about him?"

"We haven't been using freelancers for a while, due to cutbacks, but he's very professional and a terrific action shooter. Typically he'd email ten to twenty shots from his assignment to keep his costs down."

"Do you have that email address?"

"Yes." Edwards gave him the address and added, "I tried reaching him a few weeks ago to tell him two of his shots had won national newspaper awards. But the email account, like the phone number, was down. I just assumed he'd moved on."

"How did you originally find him?"

"We didn't. He came by with some intense combat photography, stuff he'd never published. He offered to shoot free of charge. Basically, if we liked what he shot, he'd be paid like any professional. He didn't even ask about our rates."

"Can you describe him to me?"

"Well, he's handsome in a rugged-looking way — tall and wide, like a hockey player. Your composite captures him well, though it's a bit iffy around the eyes."

"How so?"

"Well, I know it's just recall, but I'd say his eyes reveal a very soulful man who's seen a lot of life, who's somewhat weary. He looks at you hard, as if any second he might lose sight of you forever. It's not creepy; it's very disarming, especially when he's smiling."

"Do you still have the combat photographs?"

"No. He didn't leave them."

"Do you recall anything about the uniforms, perhaps a shoulder patch or beret insignia, in those images?"

"I'm sorry, no. It's been a while. But I remember he didn't want to talk about them. It was seriously high-quality stuff. I thought that approach would be perfect for shooting sports, especially football."

"Anything else?"

"At the time we were forced to use supplementary images from other sources. So when Manserra showed up, a guy with an eye for the moment, and he was happy to work within our budget — it was a gift."

"What stories do you have coming up that might require a man of his talent?"

Sensing an opportunity, Charles Lowry broke in. "We don't have anything scheduled, Detective, but we could . . . in return for an exclusive."

MacNeice let the comment go unanswered. He understood the reason for it: times were tough. It'd be a fair trade in Lowry's mind, a serial killer for an exclusive story. Aware that his proposal had been left hanging, Lowry made a strategic withdrawal. "Of course, if we were able to ID him from this sketch, he may also have seen it. If so, it's unlikely he'd take the bait."

Edwards returned to the obvious. "And, as I said, we don't know how to reach him."

"What has he done, Detective?" Lowry asked. "You're the head of Homicide, so it must be bad."

WITHIN MINUTES THE team was hunting for Patrick Manserra. Williams was on the line with service providers to check the phone number and email address. Maracle was requesting a court order for more information about the post office box. Vertesi was checking social media and Swetsky was onto Veterans Affairs.

MacNeice studied the whiteboard. He had a nagging suspicion that the name would prove to be an alias. Why would someone so utterly thorough overlook such a dropped thread? On the other hand, this man was aware that several people in Durand Park had seen him and needed only the photo of Tundell to jog their memory. And while he hadn't had a choice about entering the strip-mall laneway, he didn't appear particularly concerned about the security cameras. It seemed that, with his hoodies and ball caps, the man spent his life looking elsewhere to avoid them.

Where did he live? MacNeice asked himself. He wouldn't live in the city, where he could be seen by many eyes. He'd live in the country, somewhere quiet on the concession roads that connected like latticework, in a house hidden among trees, not unlike MacNeice's stone cottage. A place where he could see everything coming and going long before it came or went. A place with an escape route if the police ever came knocking.

"Ryan, look up every rural house sale in the area over the past two years. Isolation is the key — a dormant farm with some land shielded from a road or highway, maybe a garage or barn. Start within a twenty-mile radius of Dundurn."

Like the pilot of a small Cessna, Ryan started flicking switches, pushing buttons, and manoeuvring his joystick. Before him three screens came to life, including the massive

Millennium Falcon, which produced a low but impressive hum even when it was sleeping.

"Timing, Ryan?"

"End of day, sir. But I'll try to do better than that."

"Give it to me in batches, then — say, five at a time — with the contact information for the buyer's real estate agent."

The telephone rang and Ryan answered. Listening to the caller, he swivelled around again. "Sir, there's a woman downstairs with the duty sergeant. Says she's Melody Mason's mother. She has a four-year-old boy with her — Melody's son."

THE RESEMBLANCE OF Melody to her mother was remarkable. They shared the same high cheekbones and narrow chin, the eyes hooded and dark. Melody's son Jamie, however, had fair hair, large brown eyes, and a buzz cut that emphasized his cowlick. Other than his pale skin, there was little of his mother or grandmother in evidence. By the look on his face, he had no idea why he was in a police station, but whatever the reason, he seemed delighted. Every time a uniform walked by, he'd turn and watch in apparent admiration, then glance wide-eyed up to his grandmother.

The desk sergeant, Leo "Moose" Stanitz, introduced Betty Mason and her grandson, then leaned over with his large hands clasped on his knees to speak directly to the boy. "I think you'd like a tour of this establishment, Jamie. It ends with ice cream in the cafeteria."

Jamie looked to his grandmother, who smiled. "Not too much, though. Remember, we're going out for lunch."

MacNeice offered Mrs. Mason tea or coffee. She declined both. Once she was in the interview room, he excused himself and went next door to study her from the observation room.

She wasn't fidgeting, but she looked worried. She glanced at the mirrored glass, clearly wondering if someone was looking back at her. She was smartly turned out, her hair brushed away from her face with a swoop on both sides that reminded him of Mary Tyler Moore. Her clothes were tastefully bright: a flocked red and orange military-cut top with a hip-hugging skirt. She was slim and probably in her mid-fifties. Her purse was dark grey patent leather, matching her shoes.

MacNeice re-entered the room, carrying two cups of tea. "I know you declined, but I thought you might enjoy this." Betty Mason thanked him and took the paper cup with both hands, though not for its warmth. She smiled briefly and apologized for being nervous; it was just because she didn't know what was happening.

MacNeice asked about her daughter.

"I know what she does for a living. She doesn't want to tell me, but I know." Betty sipped the tea. "What's happened to my daughter? She never came home last night. I don't know what to tell Jamie."

MacNeice's face softened. He looked down at her hands and noticed the wedding band. "I'm sorry, Mrs. Mason, but your daughter Melody was found murdered yesterday."

"Murdered . . . Why? How? Where? I don't understand. Are you sure it's her?" She left no time for answers as she processed the shock. He waited; he knew she didn't want to hear the answers, at least not yet. She was trying to steel herself for the grief that would follow once she had them.

She began sobbing, sending tracks of mascara down her cheeks, where they gathered before dropping to the table. Embarrassed, she tried to wipe them away. "I'm sorry. I'm so sorry."

MacNeice handed her several tissues. He waited patiently before asking, "I see that you're wearing a wedding band. Are you —?"

"Yes. Frank's an engineer. He works out west on the oil sands. What am I going to tell Jamie? Oh my God . . . I honestly don't know what to do."

"What about Jamie's father?"

"We don't know who he is . . . or was."

"In that case, you will tell Jamie his mother has died. But you'll have Social Services there when you do."

"Can it wait till Frank gets back?"

"Make it soon. You don't want Jamie's playmates or their parents confronting him with the news."

Whatever Betty's thoughts had been before coming to Division, nothing could have prepared her for this. But the shocks weren't over. "Mrs. Mason, I know this will be the hardest thing you've ever had to do, but I must ask you to identify your daughter's body."

"Jesus, Lord Jesus. What happened to her? How'd she die?"

"Her throat was slashed."

For a moment Betty didn't say a word. Her eyes were wide, her jaw quivering. Then she covered her face with her hands and began to shake violently. Her sobbing swept away any hope that the worst of it was over. MacNeice reached across the table and put a hand on her shoulder.

"Is there anyone we can call for you, Mrs. Mason? A family member or close friend who could stay with you and Jamie?"

It took some time for her to answer, and as she did she wiped her face dry. "No." She blew her nose. "Only Frank. I called him before I came and told him about Melody's picture being in the paper. He's flying home from Alberta today."

There was a knock on the door; it was Stanitz. MacNeice stepped outside and closed the door to shield Betty. Moose apologized for interrupting but said there was a young man at the desk with information about the Mason case. MacNeice glanced quickly up and down the corridor for Jamie.

"Not to worry. He's had his ice cream and I've set him up with a pad and pencil at my desk. Anyway, this fella comes in, looks at Jamie, and goes all bug-eyed. He's here to report a confrontation between Melody Mason and a man at a grocery store checkout."

"Thanks, Moose. Call my team and ask Vertesi or Williams to go and get him. They can interview him upstairs."

"Yes, sir. And the boy?"

"Keep him drawing."

"Yes, sir."

When MacNeice went back inside, Betty was dropping her soiled tissues in the waste bin. She appeared frail, but with her smudged makeup removed, she looked younger and even more like her daughter. Her breathing was steady but laboured, more like an ongoing cycle of sighs.

"Do you work, Mrs. Mason?"

"Yes, I'm a property manager for Hightower Incorporated.

It's a good job — they have five condominium buildings. Recently I've been working from home so I can be available to look after Jamie."

"Can you tell me about Melody?"

"Gosh. Well, she's our only child. She was wonderful . . . until she was almost fourteen. A boy she knew gave her drugs — cocaine, I think. I guess she liked it. Frank and I didn't know. Well, not at first. After that, things went downhill. She had been an A student but she started failing some of her classes. She went from wanting to be an engineer like her dad to wanting to be a model. She skipped school, but we didn't know. We knew she was having sex, because Frank went through her room and found things —"

"I don't need you to be more specific, Mrs. Mason."

"No . . . Okay, good. Anyway, we knew when she was arrested that Melody was a prostitute, even though she was released. Then along came Jamie." Her face softened.

"Was she a good mother to Jamie?"

Betty took her time answering. "I think she tried to be." She shook her head as if trying to erase a thought. "Melody was a very angry person. I don't think she was using anymore, but she had a terribly short fuse. And Jamie's a doll. He's so sweet." She took a deep breath and dabbed at her tears. "I think she frightens him. Of course, I tried to talk to her about it, but she responded by getting a babysitter. We only saw Jamie when the sitter wasn't available." Her eyes overflowed again, but this time she wiped away the tears with her hands. "Do you have children, Detective MacNeice?"

"No," he said softly.

"Well, there's no failure that hurts as much as failing your child. Frank and I failed Melody, and she was failing Jamie. And you see, that also becomes our failure."

"Do you have any questions for me?"

"Who did this to my daughter?"

"We don't know his name or much about him, but we're learning fast. We will find him."

"Do you know why he killed her?"

"We're working on a theory, but it's too soon to speak about that."

"What do we have to do to adopt Jamie?"

"Social Services will help you with that. Of course, you'll want to discuss it with your husband."

"Yes. But my lord, Frank loves Jamie as much as I do."

When they left the room, Jamie was standing in front of the duty sergeant's desk wearing a DPD cap. His face lit up when he saw his grandmother. He ran to her and they embraced, swaying back and forth, as reporting officers passed by to start their shift.

MacNeice watched them walk out together holding hands, and Jamie adding a skip to his step.

UPSTAIRS, WILLIAMS WAS waiting for MacNeice. "His name is David Parker. He's assistant to the assistant bank manager a block away from the alley where DeSouza and Grant were killed. He was grabbing lunch from the Golden Goose Family Market across the street. Melody Mason and her son were in the checkout line.

"In Parker's words, 'She was wound up tight and she freaked and started hitting her kid when he picked up a bag of chips. The man behind her in line gave the boy a chocolate bar to cheer him up. But she went nuts and started up on the guy.' Parker says he came in because of Melody's photo and the sketch of the man; he's pretty sure he was the guy in the Goose. He couldn't see much of his face, but there was something familiar about the sketch.

"There's more. As Melody was about to leave, the man whispered something in her ear. Parker says, 'She looked like she'd just seen the devil. She grabbed the kid and rushed out the door.'

"Parker described what Manserra was wearing, including the hoodie pulled over his head. He said that physically he looked like an athlete, possibly a weightlifter." Williams turned the page. "One last thing, sir. Parker said the guy was chilly. When I asked what that meant, he said, 'Cold. Like scary cold.'"

"Find out if there's a security camera on that Golden Goose checkout line, or outside in the parking area."

Ryan swung around. "Sir, I've got Mary Richardson for you."

MacNeice had been so focused on what Williams was saying that he hadn't even heard the phone ring. He dropped his jacket over the back of his chair and sat down. From experience, he knew it was advisable to take Richardson's calls sitting down. As soon as he put the phone to his ear, he could hear the cold echo of the lab. "MacNeice, I don't need you here for this, but I'm just finishing the preliminary autopsy on" — there was a pause while, he assumed, Mary reached for a file — "Melody Mason."

MacNeice said he'd just met with her mother, who would be coming by to identify the body.

"We'll need to make sure she's presentable. As you know, the bodies are piling up like cordwood —"

"What have you found, Mary?"

Richardson began a rapid-fire recitation. There were no drugs in the body. Some years before she'd had a tubal ligation, perhaps to eliminate the risk of unwanted pregnancy. Her breasts had been augmented — "a lovely job, authentic reproductions of 36D's." What little food was in her stomach was for the most part healthy. "And she didn't smoke. I suspect her lungs, heart, liver, kidneys, and eyes, if harvested, could have saved or improved the lives of . . . Well, enough of that."

MacNeice could feel his heart racing, partly because of the speed of the incoming information, partly because it made him feel slightly nauseated. He took a deep breath and waited for what was to follow.

"Interestingly, this lovely young woman doesn't appear to have been 'interfered with,' though presumably that's the reason why she was there. As she wasn't drugged, one has to ask if she simply fell asleep or was in a trance. You see, the question is, why didn't she scream or fight back?"

"I hope you have an answer."

"As it happens, I do. Though it will sound unbelievable and, but for the facts, I wouldn't believe it either. Melody's left hand was covered in blood, but her right had comparatively very little on it, and that was on the back of the hand, suggesting that she didn't use it to reach for her neck. You see, the moment her neck was slashed, she reached up with her left to staunch the flow."

"I don't know where you're going with this, Mary."

"Of course you don't. I believe Melody was in a state of heightened sexual arousal at the time of her death. She didn't see the blade coming because her eyes were closed."

"Something he was doing to her?"

"Far from it. Your assassin didn't touch her, at least not until afterwards, and then only to move her leg. No, this was digital self-stimulation — Melody was masturbating. There's residual evidence of that inside the vagina and on the fingers of her right hand."

MacNeice waited for Mary to continue.

"You're speechless. That's understandable, MacNeice. It's my first time as well. Simply put, I believe Mason's throat was slashed at the very moment of sexual climax. The carotid arteries were severed by a razor or scalpel, and it was done in a flash. This man knows his anatomy and his blades."

There was an inch of day-old water in the glass on MacNeice's desk. He drank it down — cool wet for a hot, dry throat. "Is there anything else, Mary?"

"Only this: I believe Melody was in the grips of an authentic and overwhelming euphoria when she died."

"And that was exactly the way her killer wanted it to be?"

"Correct."

"So we can add master seducer to his list of accomplishments."

"If a study were ever done, Mac, of the number of shattering climaxes a woman experiences in a lifetime, three-quarters of them would be self-induced."

"Thank you, Mary."

MacNeice picked up the empty glass and got out of his chair. In the canteen he added two ice cubes to a fresh glass of water.

As he was walking back, Swetsky's arm flew up. He was on the phone. "Yeah . . . Okay. Thank you, yeah . . . Very helpful." He put the receiver down gently and turned to

MacNeice. "Corporal Patrick Manserra, twenty-four years old, was killed in a firefight in Afghanistan in 2006." Swetsky studied MacNeice's face. "You don't seem surprised."

"I'm not. He's too smart to be discovered by a record check."

"Right. So it was too good to be true."

"Maybe, but it seems to confirm a connection to the military."

"Good point. I'll head over to the Armoury and show the composite to the commanding officer." The big man lurched forward. Though still favouring his hip, he was surprisingly graceful getting to his feet. "And then I'm off to the Department of National Defence office. A guy I know there offered to help."

"I'll walk you out."

"Where are you headed?"

"To check on Aziz. If she's willing and the doctor agrees, I'd like her in on this. Things are starting to move quickly, and while she and Maracle are both on 'injured reserve,' they can still make a contribution."

Swetsky walked ahead of him down the stairwell. "What's bugging you, Mac?" Big, physical men aren't supposed to be sensitive to the subtle changes in a voice, but John Swetsky was an exception.

"Maybe it's from coming up as a beat cop, but I've never felt comfortable doing police work from a command post. It's necessary and effective, but there are times when I need to be out smelling the ground, looking for boot marks in the sand."

"Following your gut."

"Exactly."

As Swetsky opened the door for MacNeice, he asked, "Is that all?"

MacNeice stopped to inhale the spring air. He listened to the chorus of house sparrows, the muffled sounds of traffic passing by on Main, and the single-engine plane overhead. "I need to think like this man thinks."

Swetsky nodded. Then he slapped MacNeice on the back and walked off to his car. Dodging an SUV as he was reversing, he powered out of the lot and onto Main.

MacNeice lowered the Chevy's windows to let the new car smell out and the birdcalls in. Hearing only sparrows, he slipped Bill Evans into the stereo and waited. When he heard "You Go to My Head" begin, he turned up the volume and began easing out of his spot. He wanted to follow the treeline at the back of the lot, where a pair of cardinals had made their nest.

[46]

HE DIDN'T SEE IT COMING. HURTLING DOWN THE LINE OF PARKED police vehicles was a grey Ford Explorer. It slammed into his passenger door, sending MacNeice hard into the console and the Chevy careening down the line. The airbag inflated, hitting him in the shoulder. His car smashed into a parked cruiser, spun around, and came to a lurching stop. Flashing lights and sirens were triggered in the damaged vehicle. But Bill Evans kept playing "You Go to My Head."

MacNeice pushed himself off the console. He had to see what he could do for the other driver. Clawing at the deflating airbag, he took hold of the steering wheel. When he lifted himself up to look out the windshield, the suv was speeding towards him again. Heavy smoke enveloped its hood, obscuring the driver's view. It rammed the Chevy's front end, pushing the car backwards. MacNeice struggled to find the brake pedal, and when he did, he hammered it down and the car shuddered to a stop.

The Explorer was surging again. It plowed into the Chevy's front end, slamming his body into the steering wheel and his foot off the pedal. Once again the car was driven backwards. He couldn't see the suv's windshield, but the smell of smoke coming from its tires indicated that the driver had pushed its accelerator to the floor.

On the impact, the Chevy's steering wheel whipped back and forth like an injured snake. The interior was filling with the combined smells of smoke, burning rubber, plastic, and paint. MacNeice's left hand was bleeding badly, but he hadn't noticed. He unfastened the seatbelt, retrieved his weapon, and released the safety. Holding it in both hands, he fired two rounds through his windshield and into that of the Ford Explorer locked onto his front end.

Suddenly the suv was screaming backwards, dragging its bumper and ploughing through its own smoke. It came to a stop at the end of the line, fifty yards away. MacNeice threw his weight against the door but it wouldn't open. At this point Bill Evans had given up.

The duty sergeant and several uniformed officers were rushing out of Division's back door. Some were drawing weapons, others moved tentatively towards the Explorer, and still others were clicking keys to shut down the onboard sirens triggered by the impact.

MACNEICE COULD HEAR the suv's engine revving again. His mind was racing. He threw his shoulder into the door while keeping his eyes on the Explorer. He considered climbing over the console or out through the smashed windshield, but he didn't want to get caught midway if it charged again. He glanced quickly at the passenger door, which by now occupied most of the passenger seat; there was no exit there. Again he threw his shoulder hard against the door. Through the smoke and steam escaping its buckled hood, he could see that the driver had dropped the Explorer into gear; its tires were squealing. As it closed the distance, shuddering and swerving all the way, he fired another shot into its windshield before bracing himself for the impact. Several officers fired their weapons, taking out the front and rear tires on both sides, but it wasn't enough to stop the Explorer's momentum. It slammed hard into the Chevy, and once again the driver was holding the accelerator to the floor. Amid the screaming of shredding metal, the hissing of red-hot breached radiators, and the popping and crackling of plastics and paint, the two vehicles were welded together.

Seconds later, the Explorer's engine exploded. Flames shot up where the grille would have been and its hood buckled enough to obscure the windshield altogether. Smoke filled the Chevy, and MacNeice realized it was also on fire. Two burly uniformed cops appeared and began pulling at his door. It still wouldn't budge. MacNeice struggled to get out of his seat. His legs were painful and unresponsive, but he managed to push himself straight back until his head was jammed against the ceiling. He was so disoriented he wasn't sure what to do next.

Someone patted him on the shoulder. "Sir, put your head through the window and we'll get under your arms. But do it fast."

All he could see of the man peering through the window were two rows of fantastically white teeth against brown skin. He grabbed MacNeice unceremoniously and pushed him into his seat. "Now stick your head through the window." MacNeice put his arms and head through the window, but when he realized he was facing the ground, he tried to drop back into his seat.

"Sir, don't go back. This is good. We've got you. Reggie, by the armpits — now!"

It wasn't as messy as childbirth. MacNeice squirted awkwardly out the window and with his next breath was standing, held upright by the two constables. With his arms around their shoulders, he was half-carried to Division's rear entrance, where they set him down on a bench. When he looked up to say thank you, they were already running towards the Explorer.

Vertesi and Williams had been on their way to get a sandwich when they heard shots being fired. They ran the distance between City Hall and Division and emerged from the back door with their weapons drawn, only to see MacNeice shaken and bleeding on the bench.

"I'm okay," he said. "Just a little fuzzy . . . a lot fuzzy." With that, Vertesi went off to check on the other driver.

A cop emerged with a first-aid kit. There was a perfectly semicircular puncture wound on the palm of MacNeice's left hand and it was oozing blood. She applied a wad of gauze and wrapped the hand tight with bandages and tape. "The medics will take this stuff off, but keep putting pressure on it till then."

"Thank you. Go and check on the driver of that vehicle."

"Will do, sir." She quickly packed up the kit and ran off.

MacNeice was still dazed. He kept shaking his head slowly, trying to sweep away the cobwebs. The Explorer and the Chevy were on fire, filling the air with acrid smoke and toxic fumes. Vertesi came back on the run, but before he could say anything, MacNeice asked, "Is he in one piece?"

"He is, boss." Vertesi noticed the growing red stain on MacNeice's bandaged hand. "He's over by the planters; Moose pulled him out. He took a round in the shoulder — yours, I understand — but he'll live. Ambulance and Fire will be here any second."

Another uniform came running from the direction of the burning vehicles. "We've got an ID, sir." He held up a brown leather wallet. "Musta fallen out of his jeans. Reggie spotted it on the seat."

"Who is he?"

"Yann Galanis. I think he's the son of the guy who did DI Palmer." He handed MacNeice the wallet before going back to help.

"Are we gonna wait for the other shoe to drop, sir?" Williams asked.

"Shoe?"

"Yann's twin brother."

"Right . . . I see." MacNeice got shakily to his feet. He took several deep breaths and made an attempt to walk, staggered, and reached for Williams's shoulder. "Let me get my bearings, Montile."

The cops standing over Galanis were obscuring his body. All MacNeice could see were the young man's legs thrashing about on the pavement.

With a loud burp of its siren, Dundurn Fire Department's big yellow pumper bounced over a speed bump into the parking lot. Behind it were two ambulances. Within seconds, firefighters were rolling out lengths of hose and two teams of paramedics were approaching quickly. MacNeice turned awkwardly and staggered back to the bench, with Vertesi and Williams under each arm.

The firefighters positioned their hoses to force the flames away from the parked cars, then opened them up on the buckled hoods, front ends, and wheel wells of both vehicles. Two of the paramedics started assessing and treating MacNeice. While one removed the makeshift dressing, the other shone a light into his eyes. "Just checking for concussion in case your head hit the window."

"The window was down. I was listening for birds."

Vertesi and Williams exchanged glances, both wondering how that would sound to the medics.

Moose emerged from the building carrying a small glass. "Here you are, sir." He handed the glass to MacNeice. "It's not water, but it's what you need."

The paramedic with the flashlight shot him a hard look. The desk sergeant's bushy eyebrows lowered and he smiled broadly, the tip of his nose nearly touching his upper lip. It was a smile that served two purposes: it was very friendly, but when aimed directly at the paramedic, it was also menacing. The paramedic got the message — as most people did — and focused on taking MacNeice's vital signs.

Within minutes the fires were out. A firefighter with an enormous crowbar pried the hoods and doors open so they could train the hoses on the insides. For a while the cars pinged and popped, and then they fell silent. A police photographer was already at work, recording the damage and the tire marks. The rage and determination reflected in those skid marks would remain long after the wrecked vehicles had been towed away.

The paramedic discovered a lump behind MacNeice's left ear. "I don't know what your head hit, sir, but I'm certain this is fresh. You may be feeling disoriented and fuzzy. I think you should get it checked out at Emerg. Get that hand stitched up while you're at it."

"I won't go with you now, but I'll go later. Where will they take that young man?"

"St. Joe's is the closest trauma centre."

His partner looked up. "I've cleaned the wound and applied sterile adhesive closures, but you will need sutures." The paramedics packed up their medical bag and wandered over to check on their colleagues.

"Michael, call the boy's mother and tell her what's happened. Then, assuming that your car isn't damaged, pick up her and the brother and take them to St. Joe's."

"Will do. My car's okay."

"Let me know when you're at the hospital. Perhaps I'll meet you there." With that, MacNeice raised the glass to his lips and sipped. The liquid was smooth, the way a knife is smooth. As it slid down his throat, he winced. He realized there was no way he could go on sipping, so he took it down in one shot. The heat was intense. He smiled up at Stanitz. "Thank you. That was . . . bracingly good."

"Instant courage. It's under lock and key in my desk, sir. But you know where to find me." Moose put the empty glass in his tunic pocket.

"Some of your CDs are fried," Williams said, carrying over a bag of MacNeice's belongings. "I counted seven

— five cruisers, two unmarked cars — hit. Some of them are done for."

"The pound's gonna have a meltdown," said Vertesi.

Moose leaned in. "Already been called, Detective. And it's eight vehicles, with your Chevrolet taking the worst of it."

[47]

MacNEICE'S CELLPHONE RANG; IT WAS AZIZ. "RYAN SAID YOU WERE attacked in the parking lot."

"I'm fine, Fiza. Really, I'm okay. It was one of the Galanis twins. He's wounded, but he'll make it." MacNeice was back at his desk and wanted her to know he wasn't being heroic. Yes, his head and neck ached and he needed a few stitches in his left hand. "I've arranged to get it done soon."

She was too smart to be easily persuaded, but his headache was too painful to discuss, so he tried changing the subject. "How are you doing?"

He heard line static and could imagine her face, her eyebrows dipping and her dark eyes piercing his ruse. "I'm fine. Mac. I'm only going to say this once: do what you would insist I do. Go to Emergency and let them decide how well you are."

"I will. I promise."

Circumstances had hijacked the reason for her call but not her commitment to say it. "Mac, I want to come back. You need me. I'm fine, and unlike you, I'll tell you when and if I'm not." She paused in case he wanted to protest the characterization. He didn't.

Her wound-care specialist would soon reduce their appointments to twice a week, and she could do them in Division's interview room if necessary. While she wasn't out of pain, she had begun taking walks in the ravine — albeit not far, but short and slow — and sitting at her desk reading and doing research on savage killings that had been captured in art.

"And?"

"Catholics have been particularly good at this kind of thing. I suppose Jesus on the cross is the first and best example. But so many of their saints in paintings and sculpture are depicted through the suffering that elevated them to sainthood."

"So you're saying he's a Catholic. Can you predict what he's going to do next?"

"Not necessarily Catholic. And no, I don't know."

"What does your surgeon say about starting work again?"

"Well, he'd prefer I wait till the wound-care specialist has finished poking silver nitrate sticks into my body. There's still a tiny opening in my back, but it's closing fast."

From the buffeting sounds, MacNeice knew Fiza was outside. She seemed unaware of the noise and continued. "When I pressed the doctor, he relented. I've got an appointment with him at midafternoon today. If he likes what he sees, he'll hold his nose and sign me off as fit for duty." She added the surgeon's proviso: "I must continue wound care until the specialist says I'm healed." She said that her walks, which had grown from five to fifteen minutes, had made her feel stronger. "Honestly, Mac, I'm ready."

"Are you sitting on the bench at the verge of the forest?"

"How the hell — ?"

"You're close enough to the road that you turned your head to see a car going by. Plus the breeze and the birdsong, the ambient sounds. It's different when you're deep in the forest, so I assume you're on the verge. You're also a bit breathless from the walk, which tells me you were marching rather than strolling." He was speculating, of course, but added one more thought. "You were returning to your apartment when you called in to speak to me. Ryan told you what's going on here, so you sat down on the bench — the one we sat on together a few years ago."

"When you do that booga-booga thing of yours, I really don't know what to say."

"Your appointment is at St. Joe's: three o'clock, sixth floor, west wing."

"How do you know?"

"Because I'll be there."

[48]

"**WALLACE WANTS YOU TO CALL HIM, SIR — IMMEDIATELY." RYAN** mimicked Wallace's tendency to elongate the word's first syllable. "He was in the mayor's office when, quote, 'the dust-up in the parking lot took place.'"

"Good. What else?"

"Detective Maracle left shortly after you, to go to the sports broadcaster. He's scanned all the televised home games from last season and isolated four sequences that he thinks show our photographer on the sidelines. They're going to clean up the file and put it on a USB stick. He'll be back in two hours."

"Good news. What else do you have?"

"I've got eight MLS listings for isolated suburban and country properties, sir. That covers the past two years in our target radius." Ryan set up MacNeice at the Millennium Falcon. He showed him what keys to push, how to bring up the aerial and ground photographs, and how to operate the zoom on both. Between his headache, sore neck, and throbbing hand, MacNeice wasn't sure anything had sunk in.

"Can you find a car for me, Ryan? I'll need to leave in a half-hour."

"Will do. Also, sir, coach me as you go through these listings — more of this, less of that — and I'll do another scan."

Sitting at Ryan's computer, MacNeice felt like he had the first time he got behind the wheel of his dad's car. His father had given him very little instruction: gas pedal, brake pedal, reverse, neutral, drive, and signal lights. The lesson didn't go well, but it was mercifully short. Eventually his uncle taught him how to drive, but by that time he'd saved enough money from his summer job to buy his own used car.

The first property to appear was well hidden from a rural four-lane, but its infrastructure was so extensive that it was clearly an agricultural enterprise. The price at time of sale reflected the health and scale of the operation. MacNeice couldn't imagine that their suspect might be a farmer who was also a freelance sports photographer and a murderer in his spare time. Did farmers even have spare time? If they did, it couldn't be in spring.

The next four were too close to either their neighbours or the road. MacNeice was beginning to think he might have to look farther afield. Perhaps Greater Dundurn had swallowed up any isolated marginal properties, and the legacy farms had all been sold to developers for more sprawl.

"Got you a loaner, sir. It's in your spot; keys are with Sergeant Stanitz."

"Thanks, Ryan. I'll try to bring it back in one piece."

MacNeice checked his watch and was about to break off when he decided to quickly scan the last two properties. Number seven would have ticked all the boxes, but for the fact that construction was underway on a major subdivision fifty yards to the east of its rundown farmhouse. Number eight sent a chill up MacNeice's spine.

Deciduous and coniferous trees lined a driveway that faded away to the left behind yet another cluster of trees. From the aerial view, he could see the house and garage, but both were hidden from the rural two-lane. In front of the house was a garden bordered by trees that acted as a windbreak. Behind it lay an open field of scrubland and bogs.

"Ryan, print out all you have on 2010 Valens Road. I want to know when it was sold and to whom, as well as the contact information for the selling agent. I'll make the calls; just get me the information."

GIVEN HIS ROLE in an ongoing murder investigation, MacNeice would have been put at the head of the queue for an MRI, but it wasn't necessary. The patient booked for 2:30 p.m. had had a cerebral hemorrhage and died in bed an hour before.

It wasn't the first time he'd slid into the cold and claustrophobic tube to await its mechanical wheeze and machine-gun banging. He recalled the deadpan voice instructions now being fed through massive headphones: "Breathe in . . . hold. Breathe normally. Breathe in . . . hold. Breathe normally."

When you go to your happy place, am I beside you?

"Beside, above, below, and in me." (Breathe in.)

You make our lovemaking sound epic. For me it was always gentle and sweet.

"And epic, at least once." (Hold.)

"That time up north on the bed of moss?" (Breathe normally.)

Yes, that was epic. Still, it was the gentleness of you . . . your hands, your eyes taking in every inch of me. (Breathe in.)

"I'm losing that, Kate. I know your voice, but it's getting harder to picture your face." (Hold.)

MACNEICE GOT DRESSED and walked through the maze of corridors to Emergency, where his hand would be treated. As he waited to be called, he studied the faces of those around him. He couldn't help but notice the resignation and boredom, the frustration, anxiety, and fear hanging over the room like a dark grey cloak.

Nothing surprised the medical staff. After a month or two in a trauma unit, they'd probably seen it all. And they knew there was more of everything to see with every shift. When someone got abusive — such as the loud inebriated woman in the terrycloth bathrobe holding a blood-soaked towel over her wrist — they did their best to calm her down. When that didn't work and her screaming outrage got the better of her, the nurse called Security and calmly went on to the next patient.

Within an hour, MacNeice's wound had been cleaned and stitched and a palm-sized bandage applied. He was taken to the neurologist, who said there was no indication of concussion on the MRI, but the lump behind his ear suggested a powerful blow that would have given his brain "a good shake." If he experienced dizziness, blurred vision, vomiting, a searing, unrelenting headache, or an inability to form coherent sentences, he was to come back.

MacNeice made his way to the sixth floor and walked towards the two cops guarding the door to Yann Galanis's room. They stood a little taller when they saw him coming. "At ease," he said and walked on to the nursing station, where he was told Galanis had just returned from surgery. The nurse said his mother had been with him; she had stepped out but the nurse assumed she'd be back.

He considered speaking to Elene Galanis but decided against it. That conversation would happen, as well as one with the other son, but not now. He made his way to the west wing, where a nurse directed him to a waiting room. Aziz was still with the wound-care specialist. It was 3:14 p.m.

He stood by the window, looking over the leafy neighbourhood to the grand sweep of the mountain. He expected to see turkey vultures riding the thermals but instead was rewarded with something completely unexpected. Two white swans were stretching their necks as they beat their way northwest, probably to the quiet waters of Cootes Paradise. Pumping gracefully and slowly, their wings provided only a power assist to the thermals. He turned, hoping someone was there to share the sighting, but he was alone. The swans were perhaps a hundred yards away, but he could see the elegant black tear shapes that dropped from their eyes and gathered around their orange beaks. Though he couldn't hear them, he could see that they were calling. What did they talk about, he wondered. Their bodies shimmered like snow in the sunlight, making the city below look dull. Before they disappeared from view, they banked to the right, their wings rising and falling more purposefully now, perhaps because they were leaving the escarpment behind or because Cootes was now in sight.

MacNeice took a deep breath, his heart racing. He turned away from the window and stood leaning against the cool metal of the radiator. When Aziz emerged moments later, she took one look at him and said, "You look like you've just seen God."

"I may have." He didn't elaborate. He didn't have the words to describe what he'd just seen. The strange thing was that the headache he'd been worried about from the moment he was pulled out of the Chevy was gone.

He helped Aziz into her jacket and they walked silently to the elevator. She kept glancing up at him. In the elevator, she turned and smiled. "I like it. That beatific face, so clear of worry and woe . . . it suits you."

"And the checkup?"

"Straight A's. She agrees that I'm almost done with the silver nitrate sticks. But it'll continue a bit longer." Aziz smiled as they stepped inside the elevator.

The elevator stopped at the fourth floor and three people boarded, each doing the duck walk to the rear and out of the way. It stopped again at the third. MacNeice was alert. He knew who was waiting even before the doors opened; he'd been expecting it each time the elevator stopped.

Elene Galanis was about to step in when she looked up and saw MacNeice smiling at her. He held the doors from closing. She stepped inside and turned to face the doors. "Thank you," she said softly.

Aziz nudged MacNeice; when he looked down at her,

she raised an eyebrow in Elene's direction. MacNeice nodded slowly. When the doors opened on the ground floor, Elene was first to exit. She stepped out of the way and then turned to face MacNeice, offering her hand. "Believe me when I tell you, Detective, that I am relieved to see you. I was going to call you."

"Detective Inspector Aziz, this is Elene Galanis."

Whatever mask Galanis had been wearing melted away as she recognized the face and the name. She took Aziz's hand and held on to it. "I'm so sorry, Detective. I hope you have recovered from your wounds."

"I'm on the way," Aziz said.

Elene smiled. "I told Detective Vertesi everything. Yanni is a good boy. But I know that's difficult to prove today."

"Let's not have this conversation here, Elene. But before we go, I'd like to know about his brother."

She shook her head. "Of course. Darius is without rage." Tears fell and she wiped her hand quickly across her face. "If you wish, you can see that my sons fought about this — Darius has a swollen lip and a black eye. He also loved his father, but he knows Kyros brought this on himself. Yanni is more like his father, but today that ended."

"I see." MacNeice knew he didn't sound convinced. "What were you doing on the third floor?"

"I met with the surgeon. . . . Darius didn't know about this." Her declaration was loud enough to attract the attention of a couple waiting at the elevator. She lowered her voice, stepped closer, and continued. "When Yanni left the shop, it was to pick up some supplies."

"I'm relieved to hear that his surgery was successful. For now, just be with your sons." He offered his hand.

"I'm so ashamed."

"No good can come of that." And with that, MacNeice said goodbye.

"TELL ME, FIZ, have I lost that beatific glow?"

Looking at him long and hard, she laughed. "I'm afraid God has moved on." She pulled the ready-for-duty papers from her bag and handed them to him. "Okay now, do we go straight to Division or do we have a coffee somewhere while I tell you my theory?"

"Take me to the bench where you were sitting earlier. We'll look for birds while I listen to your theory."

[49]

AMONG THE THINGS HE HATED DOING MOST, RETRIEVING MAIL FROM his post office box was close to the top of the list. Even with his ball cap pulled low, he never took his right hand off the grip of the pistol in the pocket of his hoodie. But there was another reason. The PO box was registered to David Allan Muller, a twenty-year-old reservist who'd volunteered for active duty in Afghanistan. Six weeks after arriving in Kandahar, Muller had flown home in a box.

Walking the two blocks from the post office to his van, he kept his head down while he flipped through his mail. One envelope stood out, postmarked Paris, France. That concerned him. He'd made it very clear that communication with the gallery would flow only one way after the initial text message of acceptance. He was tempted to drop it in one of the street bins, but he didn't.

Once he was in the van, he opened it. Galerie Weitzman-Bourget's logo topped the pale grey page. Written by hand in English, the letter was confident and cocky. The writer had used a broad-nibbed fountain pen and every word was a thing of calligraphic beauty. Designed to impress, he thought.

> My dear RCV,
>
> Galerie Weitzman-Bourget is very excited to present your work next month. So unusual was your submission that I must know more. I write to inform you of my arrival in Dundurn on 26 May. I will be in your city for four days only. My purpose is research — I must know more about where you are from, as clients always want to know. Of course, I would welcome the opportunity to meet with you, but that is not essential. The mystery is intriguing, and perhaps it should remain so. I leave that decision to you. I will take rooms in an Airbnb condominium of the Royal Connaught, Suite 400.
>
> I remain enthusiastically yours,
> Chanel Bourget
> Curator and Managing Partner
> Galerie Weitzman-Bourget, Paris

HER SIGNATURE WAS an elegant and swiftly rendered one-stroke *CB* that vaguely reminded him of the mark of Zorro. He folded the letter and tapped it twice on the steering wheel. If Chanel Bourget came to Dundurn with the images he'd provided, life could get complicated very quickly. It represented no greater threat to him than the police investigation, but it would put an end to the exhibition. He dropped the letter onto the passenger seat and pulled away from the curb.

Driving west on York Street, he ran through various scenarios, most of which had Bourget experiencing accidental encounters that would lead her to the police. But as she believed the works were art, staged or Photoshopped to appear authentic, it wouldn't occur to her to bring in the police. But she might visit the Dundurn Art Gallery to inquire — with his submission in hand.

From the media reports he was aware that Detective Superintendent MacNeice was leading the investigation. After researching the man's reputation, he was certain the detective was making progress. He felt like an animal before the arrival of a violent storm — all senses on high alert. Being apprehended wasn't the issue; that wasn't going to happen. His images would be seen— that was his only mission. They'd represent his testament, his homage to a brutality that spanned centuries. All but one of the series was ready, and it hadn't yet been created. Turning northward, it came to him. That final piece must complete and possibly define the entire exhibition.

He stopped the van next to the "No-Trespassing" sign before turning down the narrow-rutted road to the farm. He lifted a shoebox from under the passenger seat and set it on his lap. One by one he took out six garage-door openers, clicking them in turn as he proceeded along the lane. While there weren't any garage doors to open, he was meticulous and methodical about pointing, clicking, and returning each device to the cardboard section it had come from.

He parked the van beside the house, took out the last opener, and clicked it in the direction of the back door. A tiny red light, positioned above the W in an old "Welcome Home" sign, blinked twice before turning green. He put the last of the openers in the box, replaced the lid, and slid it under the passenger seat.

Once inside, he flicked the switch that rearmed what the door openers had disarmed from the lane. The only thing required now was to push a red light to green. He dropped the mail on the kitchen table and went to the fridge for a beer, glancing briefly at the Farmer's Co-operative calendar. May 26 was just a day away.

[50]

"I DIDN'T SEE IT FALL, BUT I HEARD AN AWFUL SMACK WHEN IT HIT the sidewalk." Aziz pointed to the spot where a grey squirrel had landed twenty feet or so from a telephone wire. "It twitched for a few seconds and then it was still." She looked over at MacNeice. "I immediately thought of you, as in: *What would Mac do?*"

She had walked towards the animal, thinking she'd stroke it back to life. As she got closer, it rolled onto its belly, one front paw outstretched, reaching for an invisible finish line. She couldn't tell if it had seen her or if that was just another phase of its dying. As she was retrieving her phone to call MacNeice, the squirrel stood up. Looking intoxicated, it stumbled towards the grass and into the flower garden bordering the trail.

"It was hard to believe it could survive that fall." She described squatting down and peering through the peony leaves to see the squirrel blinking back at her. "It was visceral, and I felt helpless." She cleared her throat. "Out of interest, what would you have done?"

"I don't know. Probably just as you did." He looked off towards the garden.

"I'm a realist, Mac. I know that every year cars hit hundreds, maybe thousands, of squirrels in this city alone. And I know many people think of them as pests."

"All true."

"You've done this to me, you know. Connecting me to birds, where they nest, wondering what they're calling, and why . . ."

"And now squirrels."

"Apparently." She laughed and asked what was becoming of her, though she didn't really want an answer.

"If you look up to the tree canopy behind me, you might see a red-tailed hawk."

Aziz swung her head around, looking at the trees to the right. It wasn't there; it was sitting on top of the hydro pole.

"I heard it call." He reached over and touched her arm. "Tell me about your theory."

Her demeanour changed, and with it her posture. She moved forward on the bench and turned his way. "This is about art, but not exclusively. I believe it's about sacrifice — not of the people he kills for his tableaus, but for individuals offstage."

"I'm listening."

Father and son, the drug addict and prostitute — it was Aziz's feeling that they were all symbolically innocent, no matter their circumstances or whatever crimes they may have committed. "DeSouza and his bodyguard were both guilty of crimes — likely much worse than anything the other victims may have done — but they weren't part of his plan. We know he has a better than average knowledge of art history." With her hands she created four rectangles in the air between them. "These were," she said, "works from the past and the present: Daumier, Goya, the Chapman brothers' irreverent take on Goya, Walter Sickert. He could continue mining art history, but we're overlooking the greatest trove of human-sacrifice art the world has ever known."

She looked up at him. "Like I said before, the Catholic faith. Any religion may experience or commit slaughter, but no other that I know of makes art out of it. And those examples have been depicted as religious art for more than two millennia." She nodded, seeing MacNeice's eyes widen. "The Renaissance lasted thirty-five years, but it produced Leonardo da Vinci, Michelangelo, and Raphael."

"Keep going."

"He could use artists' works depicting sacrifice from any time, so why choose such obscure references? Because he wants people to get it, or at least be intrigued enough to try. Like the donkey-head man." She sat up straight. "While all of this is conjecture, there's more. I do think he's a Catholic . . . or at the very least a lapsed Catholic. We all agree he's ex-military. I think these human sacrifices are saying something about the sacrifices he witnessed — or made — on the battlefield. His fury is all-consuming, but he's found a way to express it creatively." She stopped as MacNeice turned quickly towards her.

"We've discovered that the name he was using, Patrick Manserra, is that of a Canadian soldier killed in Afghanistan."

Aziz rocked back and forth, looking around for the hawk. When she couldn't find it, she returned to MacNeice with a sad smile. "He's paying homage. There may be more."

"More killings?"

"Well, yes, that. But more aliases as well. I think they were comrades. Let's find out how Manserra died and if there were other casualties. Most important, let's find out who survived."

[51]

CHARLIE MARACLE WAS FIRST IN LINE WHEN MacNEICE ARRIVED AT Division. He had ditched the crutches and was standing with a cane tucked into his pocket as he taped screen captures from televised football games onto a second and much smaller whiteboard. Shot at different games, they all featured a man in a sweatshirt, cargo pants, and a peaked ball cap. In one shot he was on his belly, legs spread, elbows planted in the fake turf, a long lens in front of his face. Seeing MacNeice studying the image, Maracle said, "Reminds you of something, right?"

"A rifleman."

"Exactly. This guy's going for a low-angle photograph, but he could just as easily be a sniper. He's selecting a target."

There were no clear images of the man's face. Between

plays the photographer was scanning the photographs he'd taken. Otherwise he focused on the game or had his head down changing a lens. He was a wide-shouldered, very fit-looking man. In one series of six stills, he was running down the sidelines as the play on the field unfolded beside him, shooting as he went. Maracle read aloud what a TV colour commentator had said: "Hey, that photographer should be signed up. He's as fast as the fastest man on Toronto's team."

Maracle was shaking his head. "This guy's hyper-focused. Look at the other shooters; they're focused too, but they'll turn around and look at the crowd, they'll talk to each other, check out the cheerleaders. Not this guy. As far as I can tell, sir, he's still on the battlefield. And he's carrying more gear than a receiver carrying a football."

Tapping that last image, Maracle said, "That, sir, is a battle-hardened soldier. I'd stake my other ankle on it." He took the cane out of his pocket and leaned into it to relieve the pain.

There was one more photograph. In it, their suspect was looking up, probably at the game clock. Most of his face was in shadow, but the wide jaw and mouth were clear. "Can that shadow be lightened up?" asked MacNeice.

"Not from what we have. But maybe if we got the original footage," Ryan said.

"I called another photographer, who was shooting for the *Toronto Star*; I described our guy and asked if he'd noticed him, maybe even spoken to him." Maracle opened his notebook. "He said, 'Oh yeah, I remember him. Everyone shooting that day would remember him. It wasn't just his shooting on the run. Whenever I looked up, he was lying on the ground shooting, or kneeling and resting the lens on a knee, shooting. He's unorthodox. Most of us use a mono-pod or tripod, or just steady hands and fast exposures. Not him.'" Maracle turned a page, looked briefly at MacNeice, then continued. "'I asked him about his shooting style at half-time. He said he'd been a combat photographer, and old habits die hard.'"

Maracle closed the notebook. "They didn't exchange names or business cards. As this guy explained, 'We sell what we shoot. If you're really good, it might take you to the NFL. It's a cut-throat game.'"

Williams shook his head. "Well, Manserra could teach him about cut-throat games."

Maracle nodded and made his way back to the desk. "My take? He's not a sniper and he's not a combat photographer. He's just a damn fine warrior. The pictures are just a hobby. A lot of guys carried point-and-shoot cameras; he's just good at it. Snipers don't get caught or even seen. They shoot from a distance and disappear. Hell, we've got Manserra on vid-eos." Maracle ran a hand through his hair. "This guy's Special Forces, or something weirder." Maracle shrugged his shoulders. "If I'm right, he's survived because of intense training and some serious skills. He'll know explosives, how to establish a defensive perimeter, how to use his enemy's force and skill to his advantage. He won't be the guy you nab with a knock on the door or in a traffic stop." He looked directly at MacNeice. "He'll make it messy, sir. Crazy messy. Whatever this is —" he pointed to the whiteboard, "it's his mission. And he's studying us as we study him."

MacNeice stood looking at the photos. Manserra had been talented enough to win assignments as a freelance photographer. He was meticulous in his restaging of major works of art, so much so that a cop could shoot from the V and his photo could be identified. He might even be convincing enough to have found a gallery to display them. MacNeice was sure Maracle was right; the bodies passing through Richardson's lab were testimony that his real talent was killing.

MacNeice wheeled back to his desk and dialled Aziz's number. "Question. What do you think triggered this for him?"

"That's a good question."

He could hear her sitting up in bed. When she spoke, she made it clear that drawing conclusions about state of mind was much hairier than connecting the dots on where the art might go next. "PTSD? Even if that's not the leading cause of his psychosis, it's likely a factor." She thought it was possible that something had gone sideways in his youth or lay in the failures and disappointments of adulthood — or even the successes. As a boy he might have really wanted to be an artist but something had kept him from becoming one.

Aziz had another theory too. "This one isn't without its flaws, but consider this. The druggie crushed the dog, the prostitute bullied her child, and the pimp and his bodyguard intimidated the wrong man. It's not that their sins were major or minor; it's just that, in an instant, he's capable of passing judgement and taking lives to serve his purpose. As for the priest and his son, I don't know. But if I had to guess, I'd say the priest was collateral damage. Our killer was there to mete out justice to the son . . . and there was an old man in the Daumier."

"It's hard to believe this is about art," said MacNeice.

"I think it's about power and sacrifice, and he knows that.

Art is about ideas — beauty, nature, spirituality, inspiration — but it's also about power and sacrifice. I think he knows that too."

"Last question. What do you think his next piece will be?" MacNeice was rubbing his forehead; his headache had returned and gotten worse since he'd arrived at the office.

"As I said, definitely something Catholic."

VERTESI WAS CALLING from his car and his windows were down, so he was almost shouting. "The name for the PO box is David Allan Muller. There was nothing in the box. The manager said that means Muller was likely there yesterday. I've called for Forensics to get someone over there to check for prints. Until they do, the manager's taped a panel over it."

"Did you ask to see the security camera footage?"

"I did. But just like the rest, he knows where the cameras are and never lifts his head. Same gear — this time a black hoodie, baseball cap, and shades."

"External cameras?"

"Yep. He comes out, turns left, away from the camera, and disappears around the corner of the building."

"Thank you, Michael." MacNeice hung up and dialled Swetsky's number. "Where are you, John?"

"Department of National Defence in Toronto. They were going to send me to Ottawa, but after some grovelling, they've patched me through."

"Good. Look up a David Allan Muller and get back to me." MacNeice spelled out the name. "See if Muller is connected to Manserra."

"So Muller's another alias?"

"Possibly . . . Probably."

MACNEICE STUDIED THE aerial photographs of 2010 Valens Road and the realtor's shots of the property. It had been purchased in October of the previous year by a James Wismer. Ryan looked but couldn't find anything on social media about him.

MacNeice considered a full-blown raid but ruled it out. Given what Maracle had said and what they already knew about him, the killer would expect it. He would have chosen a location he could defend and that provided a way to escape.

MacNeice asked himself what they could do to get up close to 2010 Valens Road, short of a raid. He suddenly recalled his father telling him about the aluminum-siding salesmen who had swept through Dundurn in the 1950s and '60s. They had defaced whole neighbourhoods by plastering "looks like wood, never have to paint it" aluminum siding over seven-decades-old brick.

What would a travelling salesman from the twenty-first century want to sell to James Wismer? Someone pulls off the highway into your driveway with a brochure for — what? He looked back at the real estate photos and the long shadows of trees, shot at the magic hour. MacNeice said aloud, "Solar energy."

Over the course of the next two hours, a plan was hatched. Ryan's brother was the sales manager at Sun Solar Systems. Ryan would get a nametag, some brochures, and even a magnetic door sign for his car. Not much of a plan, MacNeice was the first to admit. Williams and Maracle were skeptics. But it was so simple, he thought, it could work. No one shoots a travelling salesman.

Maracle would sit this one out. Vertesi, Williams, and Swetsky would be in the follow car and MacNeice would drive in alone. He'd wear a nametag identifying him as Sam Smith from Sun Solar Systems. They'd arrive at the farm at eight a.m. The follow car would stop short of the driveway, hidden by the trees and hedges. MacNeice would call in to their Chevy and leave his cellphone on in his jacket pocket. "If you hear me say 'wind power,' that's your cue to hit the driveway."

"Flaky. Man, it's flaky." Williams was shaking his head. "If Wismer is our man, do you really think he'll fall for this?"

"Yes, I do. For that reason alone — it's too flaky to be professional. And if he is our man, he's had salesmen show up uninvited before."

"Sounds nutty enough to work." Maracle shrugged. "Do you know anything about solar energy, sir?"

"No."

[52]

"**SERGEANT, IS THAT YOU?**"

He held the phone away from him to see a number he didn't recognize. "Who's calling?"

"Private Pete Napier, Sarge. We were in —"

"I remember. How'd you get this number?"

"Woz — Sorry, Steve Wozinsky gave it to me, sir. We boosted the phone, but it's almost outta juice."

Master Corporal Steven Wozinsky, nicknamed "Woz," had been in every respect a solid soldier. He'd take point on patrol without hesitation and was smart enough to be wary of everything. The younger soldiers respected him and never hesitated when he gave an order, though frequently the order was "Get the fuck down!"

"What's up, Nape?"

"Well, we were doing some crack. And Woz . . . well, he went first. Then he smiles — y'know, that crazy Woz smile — an' hands me the pipe. All of a sudden he falls back on the floor an' he's gone. Woz is gone, Sarge —"

"Resuscitation?"

"I tried. I did it all . . . but he's gone." Napier was sobbing.

"Where are you?"

"Yeah . . . uh . . . you know Lancaster, down near the waterfront? We're in an old building near there. It's got a rusty yellow Clark loader or some shit machine outside. There's two orange cones beside it."

"Stay where you are."

"Okay, Sarge. . . . I'm so sorry." Napier was crying.

"Napier, leave that pipe alone."

"Yup . . . yeah. I'm so sorry. We fucked up, Sarge."

THE LAST TIME he had seen Wozinsky was in Afghanistan. Like so many of his men, the muscles on his chest, back, and arms had been covered with tattoos. That had become a tradition among the Allied forces in Afghanistan — maybe for every warrior, going back to the Greeks. It was part male narcissism, part boredom and memories. His theory was that it fed a desire to be supermen, not fearful young men. Somehow the muscles and the tattoos would make them faster and stronger, able to terrorize the Taliban as fearless fighting machines, able to detect IEDs and dodge bullets, able to get home in one piece.

But they didn't guarantee a thing, though in some cases the tattoos helped Records identify their remains. Nothing was certain in Afghanistan save the climate and the terrain, the goat-like abilities of their enemy, the improvised explosive devices, the inability to distinguish friend from foe. When he'd left to be trained for Intelligence and black ops, it was Wozinsky he'd depended on to take his replacement from theory to the practice of asymmetric warfare. So many had died the previous year that it was hardly a send-off party. He was keenly aware that the action that had led to his promotion and transfer was one in which three of his men had died.

TURNING OFF LANCASTER, he eased the van up to the security hut. It was empty, and judging by the padlock on the door, it had been decommissioned and gutted a long time ago. It didn't take him long to find the rusting hulk of the Clark. He put on his ball cap and the same Oakley shades he'd worn in-country. He slipped his weapon into the waistband of his cargo pants and stepped out of the van.

He stood there, listening and looking. He didn't like it. There were too many sightlines, all converging on his back. His senses were twitching, so he gripped the weapon and released the safety. Sparrows called from the roof, but he was listening for something else.

Seconds later he heard a high-pitched whistle and could suddenly put a face to Napier's voice. In the field he'd hear him whistle like that to signal his position, that Taliban were approaching, or just to request a bottle of water. He had once asked him what bird he was imitating. "Yellow warbler, Sarge. They're thick as flies where I grew up."

He looked up. Napier's vaguely familiar head was peeking out of a partially boarded-up window. In a whisper loud enough to be heard fifty feet away, Napier said, "There's a ladder down the side in a metal cage thing. Come up."

Stepping inside, he was immediately hit by the smell of dead air and urine, of oil sludge buckets and ancient dust that would rise in clouds if you sneezed or stomped the floor too hard. There were two foam mattresses, yellowed by grime and sweat, surrounded by butts that looked like minnows trailing dinghies. Squashed up at the end of each mattress were rolls of toilet paper that doubled as pillows. The piss pot was a large plastic pail. There'd be a honey bucket somewhere, but mercifully it wasn't on this floor. *Say what you will about vets*, he thought, *they're professionally trained to live rough, like elite hobos.*

Wozinsky lay partially on his side, as if someone had just told him a joke and he'd fallen over laughing. He was wearing what looked to be the same fatigue pants he'd worn in Afghanistan. He had on a dirty white long-sleeved T-shirt and his jean jacket was folded neatly beside him. A folded bucket hat was on top of that. His boots — military-issue — now had strings for laces, but only enough to go through four eyelets. No socks. That was a very bad sign; every soldier knew the importance of clean, dry socks. His upper body was in shadow, but he looked like he'd barely break a hundred pounds.

He didn't need to feel for a pulse, but he squatted beside Wozinsky's head and felt for it anyway. Then he stepped over to the window where he'd first seen Napier. He scanned the ground below and the windows of the adjacent building. He took in a deep breath of fresh air and turned back to Wozinsky.

Napier stayed silent. He was pacing around at a distance,

like a worn-out lion in a bad zoo. With their scraggly hair and beards, both men looked like they belonged in this cold, abandoned shell. But once, and not long ago, they had been gods with bodies of steel, boasting hell-yeah tattoos guaranteed, they thought, to mess with Afghani heads.

"How'd you two connect when you got out?"

Fidgety, taking hiccup-steps towards him, Napier said, "Moss Park Armoury in Toronto." Napier was bobblehead-nodding in Wozinsky's direction. "I'm from Cornwall, Woz is from here. I tried goin' home but couldn't cut it. Woz wanted to come home, so we walked down the highway to Dundurn. We pan all day an' come here at night" — he looked around — "to our 'luxury loft.' That's what Woz called it. He was one funny fucker all right."

"Did you smoke that pipe after Wozinsky?"

"No, Sarge, I swear. I woulda, yeah, but it's killer."

"Who's your supplier?"

"Red Toque. That's all we know him as. A lanky redhead fucker with a topknot that makes his hair like a hat with a ball on top. He hangs around the bus station."

"Christ."

"The Terminal, man . . . That's the drain peeps like us fall through."

Wozinsky's wallet was worn thin by despair. It contained his health and social insurance cards, and a faded snapshot of a black Labrador rolling on its back in the grass. Tucked into the folding-money slot was a long-decommissioned one-dollar bill with a crude drawing of a bathing beauty that obscured the engraving of the Ottawa River and the Parliament Buildings. Under it he'd written *Jenna*. There was also a small piece of paper with a drawing of a cobra, its jaws open to reveal impossibly long fangs — some kind of giant sabretooth-tiger cobra.

Seeing it, Napier smiled and nodded several times. "Woz was gonna have that tattooed on his back if we ever got the scratch."

The sergeant considered whether to take Napier with him. But he couldn't think of a reason beyond pity, and that would be an insult. The man had walked to Dundurn from Toronto; he wasn't looking for a ride or a handout. Napier just wanted to help his brother.

The sergeant took the boosted phone and destroyed the SIM card. Napier didn't seem to mind.

"Let's get him down to the van."

As he pulled away, he looked in his side mirror to see Napier slamming his head with his fists. He thought about stopping, about taking him to a detox centre, but he knew better. Napier and Wozinsky were lost, doing the long dead-walk. And the short of it was, whether diagnosed or not, they had both drowned in PTSD.

His thoughts went to the first fish he'd ever caught, a pike. It did its flippy-floppy in the boat until it was still and gasping. Gasping for what? he'd thought at the time. As pike live in water, he decided it must be gasping for life submerged, so he dropped the anchor on its head. Judging by Wozinsky's emaciated frame, he'd been done with gasping long before he died.

Napier was faced with a choice: get clean or get dying. It might be that in his drugged-out, fuzzy squirrel brain, sucking a pipe and smiling before dying wasn't such a bad way to go. They'd both been on a first-name basis with violent death for years. They could tell who was going to make it and who wasn't, in spite of the heroics of the trauma unit. Wozinsky's exit had been peaceful.

Somewhere between Napier and York Street, he decided to leave Wozinsky at the entrance to Woodland Cemetery. He'd get there around midnight and turn on the van's flashing amber dome light, which would effectively render the van invisible. He'd lay Woz to rest where he'd be found the next morning. As he passed Woodland, he noticed the statuary, the angels with wings. That's when it struck him. He glanced behind him to Wozinsky on the van's floor. "Woz, I've just found Jesus." He smiled and headed for home, convinced that if Wozinsky were alive, he'd double over and bust a gut laughing.

He started calculating the logistics. Rigor mortis would set in within the next three or four hours. For his purposes, Woz needed to be limp, not stiff, but that would mean waiting another eighteen hours or so. He could make that work.

There was a lot to do in the meantime, but he felt energized to get on with it. "We could be heroes, Woz, just for one day."

[53]

TWO CHEVYS TURNED ONTO VALENS ROAD. IT WAS 8:07 A.M. ANYONE might wonder at two cars moving at moderate speed with barely a length between them. Though there wasn't a lot of traffic on Valens at any time, those that did pass were generally in a hurry to get somewhere else. The lives being lived in the modest farms along the way mattered as much as the clouds of road dust that trailed behind them.

MacNeice slowed to check the mailbox at the edge of the road. 2010 Valens Road. He spoke into the cellphone. "Here we are. Keep the phone on but stay out of sight." Swetsky laughed.

MacNeice felt certain that the bright yellow and red Sun Solar Systems sign would do the trick. He drove slowly down the treed lane, hoping that anyone looking out would think nothing of it beyond how to get rid of another salesman. As he swung around between the garage and the front door, he left enough room for a quick getaway. He shut down the engine and reached for his folder and tablet.

A screen door opened as he got out of the car. He turned to see a young couple standing on the stoop holding an infant and smiling back at him. "Good morning, folks. My name is Sam Smith," he said.

"Good morning, back atcha." The woman with the baby was smiling and squinting in his direction.

Her husband was looking at the sign on the side of the Chevy. "You here to sell us solar, Sam?"

"That's the idea. Why, have you considered it?"

"All the time," he said. "Not on the house though, but in that field to the east."

"Great idea. Have you decided?"

"James is dreaming, sir. We just bought this house. We don't have the money for solar." She wasn't peeved; it was just a fact — the sun may rise and set, but the money is gone.

"You know," MacNeice said, "you might be eligible to sell your solar power back to the provincial grid. And that means your farm would basically have solar power *and* a cheque from the province every month."

"Oh yeah. What are the chances of that?" James asked.

MacNeice walked up to them and shook their hands. They introduced themselves as Carol and James Wismer. He opened the brochure. "We'd have to do a study, starting with how many people live here."

"Just us, Sam, and Mabel. She's our ten-month-old," Carol said, still smiling.

MacNeice realized his intuition had led him to the

wrong place. He opted for another approach. "Do you know anything about your neighbours on either side? If they have solar or are planning it? That might affect your ability to get on the program. The government only lets so many in, you see."

The two of them looked at each other before answering. "Well," James said, "there's another farm just along the way you were heading. You can't miss it — it's identical to this one. Apparently, back in the early 1920s, two brothers bought these properties, and because they didn't want to pay double for design and construction, they put up identical buildings."

Carol added, "And the other way there's the park, the lake, and beyond that an industrial farm. Nobody we know of has solar round here."

"And is it a young family like yours at the other farm?"

"No, that one sold privately last year. As far as we can tell there's just one person. He keeps to himself."

"And that's just along the way, you say?"

"Yep, it's the next one over — 2020 Valens. Maybe five hundred yards or so along the road."

"We'd like to get solar if we can get on that plan," Carol said.

"Well then, thank you both." MacNeice closed the brochure. "I've been sent out to assess interest. And so, with your permission, I'll have one of the senior advisors make an appointment to walk you through it. Really, you won't be disappointed. Solar is the future."

"That'd be great," James said, nodding to his wife.

MacNeice shook their hands and turned to leave.

"Wait, don't you need our phone number?" Carol asked.

"Whoa, and don't I need another coffee. Yes, please."

He wrote down their phone number on the brochure, along with their names and address. He waved from the car before leaving.

"Is the phone still live?" he said, manoeuvring the car.

"Loud and clear," Montile responded.

"I'm going to turn right. Give it some time before you follow me. We're not going to stop at 2020 Valens. I want you to take photos of it from the moment it comes into view."

"Roger that," Montile said. "I'll take a video as we go by."

"Through the window — don't open it. Michael, do the same on the opposite side. I want to know what natural cover there is. Time your recording so that the images match up."

"Will do."

"Sounded like you were starting a second career there, Sam," Swetsky said.

"Well, maybe if this doesn't work out."

BY 10:30 MACNEICE had developed a police alert for the print, broadcast, and online media, as well as the department's website. In it were several photographs of "a person of interest in the murders of six people." He included the names Patrick Manserra and David Allan Muller as aliases and added two sentences in bold type at the end, just above the contact information: **This individual is considered armed and dangerous. If you see him or know his whereabouts, do not attempt to make contact — CALL 911.**

When he called the Deputy Chief to update him, Wallace asked if he needed a drone over the farm. "No. I believe this man is professionally trained to spot them. He'll know when he sees the alert that we're looking for him, but a drone might send him underground." He said they were going to review the footage from the drive-by and check the aerial photography. "If it's possible to remain undetected, we'll use a spotter. But knowing what we do about this man, he's capable of producing a high body count. We want to avoid adding to it."

"You've got decent photos of him?"

"No, but Swetsky's got a lead with the Department of National Defence that may provide better ones."

"How certain are you that he's in that farmhouse? Why there and not a factory or a shed in town?"

"It began as a hunch, but now it's quite a bit stronger. The man is a phantom. He's smart, never reveals his face. Coming and going from a factory or a shed in Dundurn would make that difficult. If I'm right and he's five hundred yards from his closest neighbours, it makes this an ideal location. The only way to find out, sir, is to pay a visit."

"Not without Tactical you won't."

"Can we discuss that?"

"We just did. They go in first. No offence, Mac, but I don't want another Paradise Road."

MacNeice hung up and turned around as Aziz walked in. They had a second to smile at each other before everyone else greeted her. MacNeice went to make coffee, and when he returned, Aziz was studying the whiteboards. He handed her a coffee and said, "I've got an idea. We're both convinced this man intends to exhibit his work, right?"

"Yes."

"And we're certain it won't be in North America."

"Correct."

"Where would it be?"

She took a moment to think about it. "A private gallery in Amsterdam, Berlin, or Paris. It would likely be viewed by appointment only and might not be shown publicly."

"Assuming that it will be open to the public," MacNeice said, "can you see if there are any exhibitions opening in the next few months by a Canadian artist or photographer? I don't know who to ask."

"I'll work that out." She looked around the room. Williams was sitting at her desk, shoulder to shoulder with Vertesi and Maracle. MacNeice's desk was in the corner, jammed against the filing cabinet.

"Welcome to the slums, sister," said Montile. "We can make room. Take my chair and I'll get one from Swetsky's." When he returned, he placed it between Aziz and Vertesi. "Cozy."

Ryan swung around in his chair. "I've split-screened those videos on the Falcon. They're synched to begin together, so you'll see what's on the left and right sides of Valens. In real time it runs forty-two seconds, but I slowed it down a bit."

They ran it several times, pausing at various points to study the cover. A tall cedar hedge hid more of the farm-house than its twin down the road. MacNeice was watching Maracle; his brow went from furrowed to something suggesting surprise.

"What are you seeing, Charlie?"

Maracle asked Ryan if he could take over the toggle. Moving the images forward and back, he settled on one that looked directly down the entrance lane. Trees stood like a colonnade leading from Valens. On the right, a large cedar hedge ran all the way from the road to the garage.

Taking a pencil, he made an air circle around the trees. "A couple of things, sir. If this guy's first-class — and I think he is – this road and the property are probably spooked."

"What's that?" Vertesi asked.

"Special Forces learned a lot from the Taliban. The best of them could build an IED faster than the insurgents." He looked up at MacNeice. "I think that lane is mined, booby-trapped, tripwired . . . If he's really good, he can make it blow with the flick of a switch inside the house." Maracle circled the infield to the left of the driveway. "And going through there might get really ugly too."

"Are you serious?" asked Montile.

"Affirmative. Manserra, or whoever he is, probably doesn't have an off switch. His on switch is on all the time."

"So you think we should go in heavy, with Tactical?"

"Heavy, light . . . That might not matter much to him." Maracle released the toggle. "In a way he's become the thing he hunted. He thinks like a Taliban."

"You mean he's not afraid of dying?" Williams asked.

Aziz looked up from her notebook. "Whatever his mission is, he believes it's glorious. And after he completes it, I think he expects a glorious death. Let that be a warning to cops who want to go home to their families at night."

"What are the chances of an airstrike?" It was hard to know if Williams was serious. A second later, the sound of a large hand hitting metal resounded through the cubicle, followed by Swetsky yelling, "Fuckin' A!" Arms spread wide, his jaw locked in triumphant determination, Swetsky pointed to the computer on Ryan's desk. "Get that thing ready, son. You've got mail." He crossed his arms and stood above Ryan as he opened the Falcon's email screen.

"Our ship is about to come in, and you won't want to miss it."

Click, click, click. Ryan tapped Enter and moved out of the way as best he could. An image began to appear from the top down. Hills, a sand-coloured Light Armoured Vehicle — "LAV III," Maracle said. There were four men, all with camouflaged helmets and beige scarves wrapped loosely around their necks. They wore packed-out tactical vests, bug-eyed sunglasses, camo gloves, and smiles.

Everyone in the cubicle recognized the wide mouth and tight smile. "That's V. That's him!" Williams shouted.

"Wait for it." Swetsky put his hand up as if he were stopping a kid from crossing the road.

Each man was carrying an assault rifle with a laser sight. They appeared to be going out on patrol, or possibly just returning. If it was the former, their smiles suggested they were keen to mix it up with the Taliban. And if they were returning, those might be smiles of relief, but MacNeice doubted that was true. They looked like men who enjoyed combat. Each had a side arm strapped low on the thigh. MacNeice leaned in to see if a name was stitched on the Kevlar vest.

"No need, Mac, we got a caption," Swetsky said. "Just wait, it gets better."

A second image followed, with a slow reveal of the Canadian flag. "Official portrait," said Maracle.

Head like a block, extremely close-cut hair, and a clean-shaven chin. No smile. He was gritting his teeth, forcing the tendons that supported his jaw to make a beeline for his cheekbones. "Richard Carlos Venganza, master sergeant, Princess Patricia's Canadian Light Infantry. Twenty-nine years old in 2010; that makes him thirty-seven now."

MacNeice looked more closely at the image. "Charlie, what are those decorations on his chest?"

Ryan enlarged the image for Maracle. "Campaign ribbons, sir. Every soldier who was in Afghanistan got one of those. But these three are the Medal of Bravery, the Star of Military Valour, and an oak leaf, which signifies 'mentioned in dispatches.' Those three are impressive. If this guy walked into a Legion Hall wearing these on his chest, people would either get out of his way or buy him a round."

"Ryan, amend that alert or send out an update with his portrait and name."

Swetsky glanced down at his notebook. "He enlisted in Montreal in January 2000 and was honourably discharged in October 2013 — not from the PPCLI but from CSIS." All heads turned his way. "Yep, the Canadian Security Intelligence Service. He was seconded to be an operative. My source says we won't get anything more than that, though he told me on the sly to approach with extreme caution."

"A spy and a super-killer. Can this guy get any scarier?" Williams asked.

Swetsky turned to Ryan and asked him to scroll back to the group photo. "Okay" — pointing with his ballpoint — "we've got Venganza here on the left. Next to him is Patrick Manserra, and next to him is David Muller. The guy on the right is Master Corporal Steven Wozinsky, a local boy from Dundurn. He left the service, and he's the only one in that photo other than Venganza who's still alive — but even that's a maybe. Veterans Affairs doesn't know where he is, and neither does his mother. Since 2015 his cheques have all been returned to sender. They're probably piling up in Ottawa somewhere waiting for him to surface. And he hasn't had a job or a visit to a doctor under his own name."

The phone rang. Ryan picked it up and looked over at MacNeice. "Sir, I've got an Audrey on the line. No last name."

"MacNeice."

"Your DC has asked me to check on you, MacNeice. If you're available now, come and see me."

"Sounds serious."

"It is to him."

"I'm very busy at the moment."

"Precisely why he wants us to meet. If you'd prefer, I'll tell him that —"

"I'll be there in fifteen minutes."

Ryan waited for him to hand back the phone. "Sir, before you go, here are the keys to your new car. I've loaded in all your gear. It's a light blue one this time. Sazabuchi says your radiophone will be installed tomorrow."

STEPPING OUT INTO the parking lot, MacNeice could feel his heart racing. His breathing was shallow and he had to force himself to inhale deeply. Pushing the button on the key fob, he listened for a responding beep. He found his new car parked along the treeline, but he was too distracted to look for the cardinals.

You're frightened, aren't you.

"A bit. More than a bit."

Why this time?

"I'm not sure. Too many loose ends? We're going on the offensive but it feels like defence."

That sounds like a smart strategy to me.

"It's not, my love. Montile is my best barometer. He's as courageous as any cop I've known. When his spider sense gets triggered, I need to pay attention."

But the others?

"We all have that sense. He's just the first to express it. Those twitches can save lives."

What makes this one different from the rest?

"The man we're hunting hunted and killed men as a profession. We're office detectives grinding through our days chasing leads, gathering evidence, conducting interviews. While we've been honing our intuition, he's been learning better ways to kill. It's something he does without hesitation."

It sounds like you're going to war.

"We're being drawn into one. The tactical team pretty much guarantees it. I just want to talk to the man."

THE SHEERS IN Dr. Sumner's office were billowing, lifted by a sighing breeze. Perhaps it was unintended, but the motion encouraged him to breathe gently. By the time she'd entered the room and handed him a glass of water, his jangly anxiety had subsided.

He drank and set the glass down on a coaster, aware that she was watching him, aware too of how calm she seemed.

"Do you know why DC Wallace wanted you to visit, MacNeice?"

Other than thinking he didn't have time to be sitting in her office, he was more relaxed than he'd been all day. He was enjoying the calm, knowing that an earth-eating storm was on the way. That was it. "Maybe he wanted to make sure my head was on straight."

She smiled but said nothing.

"The pace of events is being dictated by this suspect, and so far we've been several steps behind. It's moving exponentially now."

She might have asked what he most feared — losing Venganza or catching up to him. That would have been difficult to answer. For several cases now, it seemed to MacNeice that there was always a combat-seasoned suspect somewhere in the mix. With street thugs, even those who qualified as hitmen, there was an unwritten playbook shared by them and the cops. Stealth and sophistication in killing weren't the issue. It was hit-and-run, followed by the chase. In that scenario, the betting money favoured those who chased — that is, if time wasn't a factor.

"Well, for my part, Detective, I ask myself how I can help."

"I hope you have an answer."

"I think I might." She opened his file, which was thicker than the last time he'd seen it on her desk. "I've been reading through my session notes —" Sumner changed her mind and closed the file so suddenly it startled him. "I'm sorry, I didn't mean that to be so dramatic. What I'd like to know is, what does Kate say?"

MacNeice sat up in his chair. He struggled for a moment to remember what he'd told her about Kate. His conversations with her were private and personal, even sacred. Now he could feel the lump behind his ear throbbing.

She smiled. "In your own way you've been sharing this with her, consulting with her, no?"

"Yes. But Kate abhorred violence, so I spare her the details . . . to protect her."

"And does it?"

"What do you mean?"

"Kate's dead, MacNeice. Her death had nothing to do with your work. There's no earthly reason to shield her from it now."

The air suddenly left his body as if it had been punched out of him. He took several short breaths to get it back, but inside he was panicking.

"You see, though she's dead, Kate is still your intimate partner, someone with whom you can share everything."

He still couldn't speak, but he nodded like the toy beagle in the rear window of his father's car — slowly, continuously, pointlessly. He wanted to say that it would spoil their relationship, but he knew that would sound ridiculous.

"You still want to protect her . . ."

"Yes . . . yes, I do." He swallowed hard and choked back tears, worried that he was about to come unstuck.

"But you can't, you see. Kate died. She may be 'alive' and available to you now almost as a way of making up for that."

He pinched his eyes, wiping away the tears that were now falling on his pant leg. "I can't go there now, Doctor. Honestly, I can't talk about that."

"You don't have to, MacNeice. Just consider it. I think what troubles you about this man and the power he has over you is the need you have to protect your people, because you weren't able to protect her. You're terrified that this time you may not be able to."

A raw truth delivered like a weather report has the potential to open doors that may be impossible to close. MacNeice shook his head, not wanting to hear any more.

"And yet you continue to protect her from the truth, just as you would have when she was alive. Perhaps now, however, it's time to let her protect you. Tell her precisely what you're afraid of, and ask for her help."

It was clear that Sumner had reviewed the notes from their sessions and linked his relationship with Kate to his decisions as a detective. Events that had occurred or actions that were about to occur were filtered through his conversations with Kate. They allowed him to function. But in the absence of full disclosure, they couldn't be completely effective. It was perfect — and painful.

MacNeice's cellphone rang. He apologized but said he had to take the call. He quickly stepped out of the office. "MacNeice."

"Hello, Detective. It's Agnes Gagnon at Le Hibou. He's here now. They're just starting their boeuf bourguignon."

"They?"

"He's with a woman, a Parisienne. Jean-Marc spoke to her. Apparently she runs a gallery on the Left Bank. Jean-Marc knows it, and he said it's infamous. I asked if he meant famous, but he meant what he said."

"I'm on my way. If possible, find out the make and model and plate number of the vehicle he's driving. Where is he sitting in the restaurant?"

"They're in a booth at the end of the bar. He's wearing a

baseball cap and aviator glasses. We're quite busy, Detective. Promise me there won't be any violence."

"There won't be. Save me two seats at the bar, as far from him as possible. Out of interest, does he understand French?"

"He doesn't appear to, no."

"His back is to the wall?"

"Yes."

[54]

M<small>AcNEICE WAS IN THE DIVISION PARKING LOT, PUTTING ON HIS</small> clay-covered boots and stowing away his suit jacket and tie, when Aziz came out. He rolled up his sleeves, closed the trunk, and opened the door for her. "Hungry?"

"Yes, as always." She looked down at his boots, "You're dressing down a bit for lunch, Detective."

"I'm a contractor. You're my customer." He didn't say much more until they were on the 403 heading for Ancaster. "Venganza's at Le Hibou with a gallery owner from Paris."

"What are we doing?"

"We're going to have a meal. We won't confront him or even look at him. We'll order and leave after them. If possible, we'll follow him. If not" — he tapped his password into his phone and, when the screen lit up, handed it to her — "we'll have Michael and Montile follow him farther down the road."

"What do you want me to do?"

"Call Agnes at Le Hibou to see if she's got the licence-plate number and make of his vehicle. Give it to Michael. They're not to engage, just follow from a healthy distance. If he sees or even feels a threat, he'll take evasive action, whether that's a U-turn on the highway or tearing down some suburban street where kids are playing road hockey."

Aziz took out a notepad and pen before putting the phone to her ear. She looked sharply towards MacNeice and put the phone on speaker. Agnes said, "Sorry, he just left. They didn't finish their meal. I asked if there was a problem and he said, 'No, it's just time to go.' But — and this is weird — he left a note for you, Detective MacNeice."

MacNeice and Aziz exchanged glances. "What does it say?" MacNeice sped by a truck, forcing an oncoming driver to flash his lights and veer onto the shoulder.

"It's a folded piece of paper. On the outside it says 'MacNeice.'" He could hear Agnes say "wow" under her breath. "It just says, 'So sorry to disappoint you.'"

"Keep it. And his vehicle and plate number?"

"It's an old white Econoline van. It has Ontario plates that begin with BLXN, followed by numbers, but he left so fast I couldn't get them in time."

"Thank you, Agnes."

MacNeice switched on the flashing blue lights. Checking the rear-view mirror, he cranked the wheel and swung the Chevy into a U-turn.

"Where are we going?" Aziz was pushing against the console and bracing herself on the dash.

The sweet new-car smell gave way to a smell of burning rubber and the tinny complaint of a new engine as MacNeice pushed down hard on the accelerator. "To Valens Road. Hopefully we'll get there before he does."

"But we're still committed to no contact, right?"

"Correct. I noticed a narrow dirt road on the aerial photo, farther down on the other side of Valens. If I can get in there before he arrives, at least we'll be certain the property is his."

MACNEICE SWITCHED OFF the flashing lights when he left the regional road and turned onto Valens, slowing only to look for the white van. He couldn't see it, though Venganza might have already parked it in the garage.

He backed into the narrow lane across the street and farther down. The new wheels struggled to find the ruts, and when they did, tall weeds licked at the Chevy's underside and doors. When he felt that he had enough cover, MacNeice opened the windows and turned off the engine. The car filled with birdsong and metallic clicking from the car's overheated engine.

They put their cellphones on mute and waited. MacNeice opened the glove compartment and took out his folding binoculars, happy that Ryan hadn't missed a detail. He removed them from their case, which was badly scorched, and handed them to Aziz. "Focus on his licence plate."

"What do you think tipped him off?"

"I don't know. He may have overheard Agnes on the phone."

"But that phone is at the cash desk fifteen feet away, in a busy restaurant."

"Superior hearing?" MacNeice put up his hand. Through the fragments of brush and sapling leaves he could see the white van approaching. As it turned into the lane, it stopped. "BLXN 398. Has he made us?"

MacNeice released the safety on his weapon and held his breath. "Maybe." His heart was in his throat as he waited, considering whether to make a run for it. A moment later, the van moved slowly down the lane, stopping several times until it was out of sight.

MacNeice waited for several minutes, hoping that would give Venganza time to get inside before he started the engine. When he'd eased the Chevy back onto Valens Road, he continued slowly in the direction away from the farmhouse to avoid being seen. Until he left the side-road, MacNeice constantly checked his rear-view for a fast-approaching Econoline.

Once on the highway, he turned on the blue lights and increased his speed. "You're still hungry?"

"Famished, but now I'm also frightened."

He looked over at her to see if she was serious. "Venganza?"

"Only a fool wouldn't be afraid of that man, but I was referring to your driving."

He eased off the pedal and slowed to the speed limit. "Sorry, Fiza. Is your back giving you trouble?"

"No, that's not it. Just some leftover jitters from careering down the highway towards a psychopath."

MacNeice reduced his speed even further. "I see. Still, it was good for me to get a quick feel for this car, how it accelerates and handles."

"Because you wanted to know you could outrun him if necessary?"

He glanced over at her. "Something like that, yes."

MacNeice asked her to call Division and put it on speaker. When he heard Ryan's voice, he asked for Michael or Montile. It was Montile who picked up the phone. As Williams listened to the summary of their near encounter with Venganza, his eyebrows climbed ever higher on his forehead. Turning to Vertesi and Maracle, he mouthed the words *What the fuck?*

"Valens Lake is several hundred yards behind his house. If I'm right, there's a road back there that leads to the Valens Dam. There might be a hedge or some brush where we can drop a surveillance team to observe without being seen."

"Sir, you want us to go out there?"

"No. I'll ask Wallace for two members of the tactical team. Venganza has a woman with him, a French national. She owns a gallery in Paris and came out to meet him."

"Jesus H."

"I want you to set up a meeting at Division with Tactical. We'll be back in two hours."

AGNES MET THEM at the restaurant door and immediately handed Venganza's note to MacNeice. She seemed relieved to get rid of it. It was the tail end of Le Hibou's lunch rush, and Jean-Marc came out of the kitchen to take their orders. Both requested the boeuf bourguignon. When it arrived, Jean-Marc sawed off half a baguette for them to mop up the sauce and poured two glasses of red wine. He stepped back, crossed his arms, and waited for the first taste. Once he'd seen the smiles, he said, "I think maybe you want to know about the woman."

"Yes." MacNeice put down his cutlery and took out a pen and pad. "But this is delicious."

"Slow cooking, you call it here. Her name is Chanel Bourget. She and her partner own Galerie Weitzman-Bourget, not far from a restaurant where I was sous chef. The gallery is very forward, very . . . cutting-edge. *Très importante* and very successful, yes. I am surprised she comes to Dundurn, and so surprised to see her at Le Hibou. I never meet her before, but in Paris, when she came to our Michelin one-star, it was with her female partner. They never fail to float the energy."

"Lift the energy," Agnes said.

"*Oui*, lift."

Bourget had spoken very highly of Venganza, saying that he was a brilliant photographer with a unique perspective and approach to his work. She had told Jean-Marc the dates for his first exhibition at GWB, but he couldn't exactly remember them. "It is soon, though, maybe in June, before Paris surrenders to the tourists."

Filling their water glasses, Agnes said, "It was so strange. They had the same meal as you, and Madame Bourget seemed to love it. Then suddenly I look up and he's at the cash desk to pay the bill. They only had a few bites."

"*Oui, bizarre.* Madame was really looking forward to my *tarte au beurre.*"

MacNeice swivelled around. "You called me from the phone at that desk?"

"Yes, but I spoke softly. There was all the chatter and the music in the background. He couldn't have heard —"

"Ordinarily, I'd agree. But this man isn't ordinary."

"Did Bourget say where she was staying?" Aziz asked.

"*Oui.* She has rented a condominium in the Royal Connaught," said Jean-Marc. Watching them enjoy their meals, he asked, "Will you have dessert? Butter tarts — they are very special."

MacNeice watched Fiza's eyes dance before turning to Jean-Marc. "One please, *avec deux cafés noisettes. Merci.*"

Aziz used her napkin to hide a wide grin, then swung her bar stool around to face him and smiled without the napkin. As he studied her face, her eyes teared up and she turned away again.

"We'll get through this, Fiza, I promise." His statement was heartfelt but unclear. He thought about how to correct it, how to say what he really meant, but he didn't actually know.

When the coffee arrived, he turned his attention to the cup as if he found it deeply interesting. He realized he was still rattled from his session with Dr. Sumner. He trusted the psychiatrist's honesty and straight talk, but her comments about Kate had shaken him. Was that her strategy?

The tart came with a dollop of crème fraîche on the side and a drizzle of strawberry sauce. Jean-Marc put a knife, fork, and spoon beside the plate. "Though some people eat them like a cookie, it is not recommended. Enjoy. I must get back to preparing this evening's menu."

ON THE RETURN trip to Dundurn, Aziz closed her eyes and began to fall asleep. Back on the 403, MacNeice gently touched her arm. "Fiza, I'm going to take you home."

Aziz opened one eye and then the other. "That would be prudent, sir. Thank you." She sat up and shook off the fatigue as best she could. "Mac, I want to be part of this, whenever it happens."

"I know you do, but I can't allow it. And you know that."

"Then let me be in that rolling command post. I won't get in anyone's way and I may even be of some use."

MacNeice thought about it for some time before answering. "With one caveat: the tactical team leader has to approve."

"I accept." She smiled and closed her eyes again.

"What's that phrase you told me? 'If you have a hammer . . .'" His voice was soft enough that if she was asleep he wouldn't wake her.

Aziz didn't open her eyes but answered. "Abraham Maslow's hammer: 'If all you have is a hammer, everything looks like a nail.' Unless you're referring to the Peter, Paul, and Mary song." She opened one eye and smiled at him. "Why?"

"Why am I thinking about Maslow?"

"Mm-hmm?"

"It's a metaphor for Tactical. It's not that I don't understand or even appreciate the value of a tactical unit; I do. But I'm not entirely comfortable with a command mentality that depends on heavy weapons, menacing paramilitary machines, and men armed to the teeth. Besides, when compared to Venganza, our tactical team is outmatched. They're little more than show ponies, while Venganza is a warhorse. He can kill quickly and brutally without a weapon, all the while remaining calm. Tactical prefers killing from a distance. They adhere to command structures; he improvises. They train to fixed scenarios; he creates scenarios."

MacNeice didn't think he could talk Venganza out of his plan, whatever it was. But he wanted to try. He also wanted to save the life of the gallery owner, assuming that she wasn't already dead. He looked over at Aziz and asked, "Do you think Chanel Bourget is in immediate danger?"

"Most certainly. I think she's put her head in the lion's mouth, thinking it was a plush toy."

[55]

"**M**AGNIFIQUE. INCROYABLE.**" BOURGET TURNED AWAY FROM THE** exhibition prints stacked for her viewing on the kitchen table, and looked at him. "Where do you do your Photoshop work? It is extremely good."

"Actually, there's no Photoshopping in this work."

"You joke, yes? They look so real."

"Because they are real," Venganza said, his tone incredulous.

"But no. The blood is —"

"Blood."

"But look here, her throat is —"

"Cut." He drew his finger slowly across his neck.

"I do not understand." She was shaking her head,

convinced that her command of English wasn't as good as she'd thought.

"But you are beginning to. I can see it in your face, in the quiver of your jaw."

"I'm sorry . . . *Merde.*" Her voice turned sharp and clipped; she was angry. "These people appear dead. So you are doing it with either extraordinary makeup or Photoshop. There is no other way."

"Yes, there is — I kill them. And then I light them and take their portraits."

Venganza smiled broadly, sending chills down her spine. The colour drained from her face, taking with it her poise and elegance. She suddenly realized the peril she was in and the terrible folly of coming to Dundurn.

"You see, Chanel — May I call you Chanel?" She nodded weakly and tried to avoid his eyes.

He began putting the prints back in their hard case. "I made it clear that you shouldn't attempt to reach me, let alone try to find me." He put a large hand on her shoulder. "But then you're not accustomed to being told 'no,' are you."

"*Monsieur*, please . . . I will go back to Paris. I will not tell anyone — you have my word." She was shaking and digging her perfectly manicured nails into the palms of her hands. "I have done nothing to harm you. Please let me go . . ."

"But you have. You broke your word. Your acceptance of my work came with certain terms and conditions that you agreed to and then broke. And here you are asking me to trust your word again." He smiled warmly.

"My family can pay you . . . handsomely." She took out her cellphone and was ready to make a call when he gripped her wrist and flung the phone to the floor, where it shattered.

"I was only going to call my partner. She has money and will gladly pay you."

"You've heard the phrase 'A man's word is his bond'?"

"*Oui*, of course, but —"

"That also applies to women." Venganza took a work cloth from his pocket and knotted it. Her eyes were wide and filling with tears as he rammed the knot into her mouth and tied the cloth behind her head. She was so frozen with fear he had no difficulty putting her hands behind her back and binding them together with a zip tie. He lifted her up and carried her under his arm, like a small rolled-up carpet, to a metal chair. There he used a nylon rope to tie her legs to its frame. When he stood in front of her, she was frantically shaking her head.

"If you keep doing that, Chanel, you'll hyperventilate and pass out. You're going to be the main event, the climax of the exhibition. Given your aesthetic, I think you'll appreciate what I'm doing."

Bourget was doing her best to control her emotions, but every time it looked like she had calmed down, she started crying again, her chest heaving as she struggled for air.

"I've been where you are. The best strategy is to take yourself away . . . the Alps, the Riviera, in bed with your lover, or maybe to the opening of an exhibition." He placed a hand briefly on her shoulder and walked away. Panicking, she looked to see where he'd gone and then worried that he'd come back with a weapon. She listened for his footfalls, but realizing she hadn't actually heard him leave only worried her more.

Chanel took in her surroundings. It was an old kitchen,

with worn cupboards and a large pine table and four chairs. On the table were salt and pepper grinders, a bottle of Spanish extra-virgin olive oil, and another of sparkling water. They were neatly lined up like soldiers against the wall. Light streamed in through the small window over the sink; two tea towels were neatly folded on the cupboard handles below. There was a calendar but no art on the walls. On a nearby shelf sat a small colour photograph of a group of soldiers. She couldn't make out their faces from where she was sitting. Carving and paring knives were held by a magnetic strip near the window, and four jars of what looked like rice and grains stood against the wall on the other side of the sink — an opposing army.

As the sun shifted, it fell on her shoulder and, moments later, her face. She closed her eyes against the glare and listened hard for any movement behind her. In time, perhaps from exhaustion or jet lag, lack of oxygen, or the sun streaming through the window, she fell asleep.

CHANEL WOKE UP to find herself being carried into the next room. Venganza placed her in another chair and once again tied her legs. The windows had been painted over, and daylight could penetrate only as a soft glow. As her eyes adjusted to the darkness, the room gave up its secrets. The space had been crudely renovated and showed signs of recent work. Judging by the marks on the floor, he'd combined three original rooms to make one large studio. The vertical posts that supported the attic and roof joists were exposed; on these he'd pinned up a mix of sketches, postcards, and more snapshots of soldiers.

Only when he moved did she realize that Venganza was still in the room. He had his back to her and seemed to be working on something. When he stepped away, she was staring at an elevated platform. Pale grey drapery covered a series of wooden boxes of different sizes. Off to the right on a folding table, there appeared to be a body under a white sheet. She gasped at the sight of it, gasped till she choked.

He moved the cloth knot down to her chin. "Breathe normally . . . slowly." He placed his fingers on her neck, feeling for her pulse, until her heart rate returned to nearer normal. Then he put the knot back in her mouth and showed her a card. Kneeling before her, he smiled and his eyes softened. He held it in front of her face and watched as her eyes opened wide with awe.

"It's my final piece. It wouldn't have occurred to me if you hadn't disrespected my request to remain anonymous. But here you are. You're going to be my Virgin Mary. This piece, like the others, will have a twist . . . Actually, two twists."

Her breathing was heavy again and tears filled her eyes. He waited patiently for her to calm down, again feeling for the pulse in her neck.

"You've noticed there's a body on my worktable. That's Jesus. He's dead. He's been in my freezer but now he's good and flexible." Venganza pointed to the postcard of *La Pietà*, Michelangelo's masterpiece. "How he sculpted dead flesh and bone so accurately out of marble amazes me. Does it do that for you?"

The question astonished her, which didn't escape him. "I know, I'm a fool to think that you and I have anything in common, that we might have a conversation about Michelangelo's rendering of the sacrificed Christ." He stood up abruptly and walked away to a small drawing table to retrieve something. He turned and studied her for a moment.

She shook her head emphatically from side to side to suggest that it wasn't strange, that yes, she understood what he meant. But it was too late. He crossed the floor quietly and swiftly, with something clenched in his hand.

When he knelt before her again, she was shivering uncontrollably, trying to see what he was holding. He smacked her sharply across the cheek and the shivering stopped. Picking up the postcard of the *Pietà* again, he pointed to the Virgin Mary. "You can also see what makes Jesus so remarkable in death. It is the life that's so present in Mary. For this piece to work, she must be alive. Nod if you're following me, Chanel."

She nodded furiously. His hand darted to her chin to stop her. "Yes, exactly. I cannot do this piece if you're dead." He stood over her as if reconsidering her status. "It's clear now that my solo exhibition isn't going to happen. Nod if you agree." She did. "Right. Nonetheless, a beautiful and alive Mary you will be. What happens afterwards will be out of my control."

He opened his hand to reveal an alcohol swab and syringe. "This is for later. It's a sedative. It's not lethal. You'll go to sleep for a few hours and wake up feeling rested." He closed the hand again. "You won't be — what's that genteel phrase? — 'interfered with.' But I will take off some of your clothes. Nod if you understand." She nodded. Her mascara was a coal stream down her cheeks. "Don't worry. I'll clean your face, apply some powder, rouge, a touch of lipstick — not too bright, given the role you'll be playing — and you'll be ready."

He picked up the postcard again. "Another thing that's always struck me is the size of them. Jesus is large; he rests on Mary's knees like human drapery. But that meant Michelangelo had to make Mary large too, even larger than her son." He shook his head in amazement. "You know, if this had been attempted by anyone but Michelangelo, it would have been mocked and laughed at and destroyed by the Church. Don't you agree?"

It was hard to tell whether she did or not, as her brain was processing the insight in a moment of overwhelming terror. She nodded once and managed to make it not look frenzied.

"Exactly. I went back several times to look at *La Pietà*. That's what I saw, but when I listened to those around me, they were caught up in reverent awe at the art of it and what it meant to believers."

He placed the card on the floor in front of her. Like some bizarre form of method acting, she was to internalize the role and he'd capture it on camera. He walked back to the worktable and removed the sheet. He poked the body to check that it had thawed completely and lifted the arm to test that the rigor mortis had gone. The arm sagged and fell gracefully as he let it go.

"This is Master Corporal Steven Wozinsky." He turned to make sure she was paying attention. "Woz, to his men. He's the one subject I didn't kill. He was a brave man, a brother in arms . . . a leader." He turned again to look at her. She nodded. Venganza looked the way mourners do when viewing the body of a loved one. "He looks so deflated lying here on my table." He turned and pointed at the image of Christ reclining on Mary's lap. "But see for yourself: Jesus is also deflated. The spear thrust into his side, the nails through his hands and feet, the time on the cross in the sun — it all took a toll. Woz is a lot like that."

Venganza bowed his head. She couldn't tell if he was praying, weeping, or both. He stayed like that for several minutes before raising his arms to suggest the futility of the loss. "Woz is ripe, and he's going to get riper. You know, he's at least fifty pounds lighter than the last time I saw him. The man had a superhero's body — 'purpose-built,' with muscles, lots of them, to carry heavy weapons and wounded comrades. He could run for days, climb rocky inclines like a goat."

He turned around so quickly it startled her. His left hand was resting on the body's shoulder. "He's covered in tattoos. A lot of men in uniform do that, even a few of the women — though I can't speak to where they get them, except for their forearms." He meant that comment to be light or funny, but he could see it only made her more frightened. "Don't worry, Chanel, I'm not into tattoos — either getting them or inflicting them." He looked down at the ones on Wozinsky's chest; the grizzly bear standing defiantly on its hind legs took up one pectoral. It faced an equally terrifying cougar depicted in mid-leap towards its foe. Fangs, claws, speed. "There's a story behind them, of course, but now the stories are lost, and they look deflated too."

Below the animals was the PPCLI regimental insignia. On his lower ribcage, in black, was a Harley-Davidson logo, and next to it Smoke, his smiling black Lab, sat on its haunches above its name. Lower down, in beautiful calligraphy, was the name *Doreen*, surrounded by so many flourishes that it suggested a romantic swoon. Below them all, in Gothic script that spanned his abdomen, was Woz's personal credo:

Heaven is hell. War is hell. Heaven is war. Thank God for the Pats.

"Swagger dies with the man." While the ink remained vibrant, the tattoos looked as if they were printed on a worn-out T-shirt. Much sadder than death. "Tattoos lie. Woz wasn't invincible."

Shaking himself free of the moment, Venganza pointed to the platform with all its drapery. "That's where you'll be. It's on casters so I can move it around for lighting purposes. I've built up what looks like a grey rock and a seat that will take your weight and Wozinsky's. You'll be dressed more or less like Mary. And because you'll be asleep, I've got a frame that will keep your back, head, and neck where I want them — or, more precisely, where Michelangelo put them. There's another set of supports for Mary's right hand that takes the weight of Christ's upper body, while her left is raised slightly off his legs." He mimicked the position of Mary's hands. "It's either a gesture that expresses her agony or it's starting to point to heaven. I'm not sure if anyone knows for sure.

"Jesus will be wearing these worn-out fatigues but not the military-issue boots. They'll stand at the bottom of her cloak. Woz died of an overdose, but he really died in Afghanistan. By the end, he was *feeling as low as a snake in a tire track.*" He turned to see if she recognized the phrase, but she didn't. "The painter Philip Guston said that."

He took a moment to shake off his thoughts. "I've got a structure to support his upper body and head and props for his hips. They'll fall between your legs." Venganza leaned against the table and focused his attention on the mountains of grey cloth piled high on the plinth. "Funny thing, until I started building this, I never realized how big Mary's gown is. Sleight of hand, I guess." He believed it provided

Michelangelo with an opportunity to demonstrate how well he could create fabric from marble. But, more important, the crisp folds would contrast with and emphasize the soft, lyrical form of Christ's body lying limp on her lap.

"Michelangelo understood misdirection like a great magician. He wanted you to see what he saw. Even as your eyes wander, he keeps pulling you back to the faces of Christ and Mary. That was my epiphany."

[56]

TACTICAL SENT THREE MEN, TWO SERGEANTS AND A LIEUTENANT. They seemed to fill the interview room. They wore black caps with DPD/T embroidered in black above the peak, and loose-fitting black jumpsuits with zippered pockets, black holsters, and side arms. DPD TACTICAL was printed in white block letters across their backs. In MacNeice's opinion, the look was stylishly unsubtle, functionally dubious, and utterly un-Dundurn.

Ryan had loaded the Venganza files, including a Google Map aerial photo of the property, and stitched it together with videos from the Valens Road drive-by. It took the better part of an hour to review all the material. The three sat quietly, asking only a few questions for clarification. Their very presence seemed to whisper, *We'll take it from here.*

MacNeice and Swetsky sat across from them at the table. Maracle was at one end with his leg outstretched; Vertesi and Williams sat at the other, ready to take notes.

When MacNeice finished reviewing the digital file, he turned the meeting over to Lieutenant Sadler.

Sadler nodded before speaking. "Because this man is ex-military, you've assumed he's booby-trapped that property?"

"Obviously we don't know, but yes, that's our suspicion."

"No evidence?"

"Strictly instinct. Further to that, we assume he chose this property because there are ways to secure it. And while the woman may not be a hostage, we'd prefer to take them alive, even though we suspect he wants to end this with a loud bang."

"Have you had contact with him?"

"No. But as I was getting close, he left a written message for me." From his file folder MacNeice pulled out Venganza's note and handed it across the table.

"How'd it happen that he made you, Detective?" Sadler asked, handing the note back.

"I don't know exactly."

"How about Mac's arrest record? Maybe Venganza did his homework and figured out who was coming for him." Swetsky's face was flushed with anger.

MacNeice intervened. "What else do you need? What is the strategy, and what can we do to conclude this without violence or injury?" MacNeice put his palms down on the table and looked at Sadler.

For the next half-hour, Sadler and Sergeant Baker did the talking. The third man, Sergeant Washburn, took notes. Even though his eyes were gentle, MacNeice suspected

Washburn might be the toughest man in the room. His hands were massive; only the tip of his pen rose above the crotch of his thumb and forefinger. His knuckles were criss-crossed with old scars.

Sadler began a summary. "With regards to 'violence and injury,' that's entirely up to him. If he surrenders, he goes to jail and we all go home happy. If he doesn't, we will suppress and eliminate the threat by every means available. If he's ex-military, that's okay. Almost a third of my men, including myself, are ex-military."

Maracle, who'd been quiet throughout the briefing, felt compelled to respond. "With respect, sir, Venganza's not just ex-military, he's an alpha predator. And I promise you, that property is mined."

"I understand, Detective. I'll be in a command unit equipped with thermal detection drones. We'll have two armoured vehicles in front, as well as spotters and backup on Valens Dam Road. All in, we will deploy eighteen highly trained assets." Turning back to MacNeice, Sadler added, "And of course we'll have you and your men as additional backup."

"Thermal detection can be blocked by foil blankets, and he can get those in packs of ten at any surplus store," said Maracle.

"Thank you, Detective. Yes, I know." Sadler's voice betrayed him. From the sound of it, Maracle figured he'd been an officer at a desk.

MacNeice sensed that Sadler was digging in, so he said, "Returning to the possibility of mines and booby traps . . ."

"This isn't Afghanistan, Detective MacNeice," said Baker.

"It may still be Afghanistan for Venganza, though. And

Sergeant, it's Detective Superintendent MacNeice." He struggled to keep his tone collegial as he turned back to Sadler.
"Where will you deploy us?"

"On Valens. Hang back fifty yards from the driveway.
You'll be connected to our headsets. We'll call you in as
needed." He looked over at Maracle and added, "Through
our network, Detective, we would have heard about anyone
stockpiling explosives. They're highly controlled in Canada."

"With respect, sir, you don't understand IEDs. Venganza
knows how to build and disarm them."

"Thank you, Detective." Sadler turned quickly to
MacNeice. "Is there anything else?"

"Yes. Remember, my goal is to bring them in unharmed."

"We will accommodate him either way, DS MacNeice,"
Sergeant Baker said.

Washburn snapped a narrow-eyed look Baker's way,
clearly not a fan of his gung-ho banter. "We'll meet at the
depot on Burlington Street at 0430 and leave Dundurn at
0530. We'll roll down that driveway at 0600. Understood?"

Everyone but Maracle nodded. MacNeice handed Sadler
a memory stick of the entire file. Though they hadn't opened
the video of DeSouza and Grant being killed, he was hopeful that someone would, and take notice.

"Make sure you have EMS support, Lieutenant, both
ground and air."

"You seriously think he wants a bloodbath?"

"I think he won't hesitate to respond to a perceived
threat."

As the three men stood to leave, MacNeice gave Williams
and Vertesi a quick head-tilt. The two detectives intercepted
Sadler and Baker in the corridor to ask for some clarifications,

while MacNeice rounded the table to speak to Washburn, who was putting away his notebook and pen. "Sergeant Washburn, are you ex-military as well?"

"Military?" He chuckled at the thought. "No, sir. I'm ex-football, Michigan State." His voice was low and soft. He was at least two inches taller than MacNeice, tall enough that he was looking down at him.

"You're American?"

"Yes, sir. Detroit." Coming from him, it sounded like *Dee-troit*. "I fell for a Windsor girl and ended up in Canada."

"Where will you be tomorrow?"

"The first unit coming in off Valens, sir."

"I hope we stay in touch."

Washburn smiled and put a finger to his ear. "We'll be connected. Call me Wash."

They shook hands and MacNeice watched him leave, turning as he went through the door to avoid contact with his shoulders. For a man his size, he moved with ease.

[57]

MᴀcNEICE COULD HEAR WIND BUFFETING THE SPEAKER WHEN Wallace answered the call. After a few minutes of trying to hear and be heard, he asked the Deputy Chief if he could step indoors. A minute later, Wallace asked, "You're calling about the meeting with Tactical?"

"Yes, sir."

"Sadler just beat you to it. I didn't answer his call; I wanted to speak to you first. So tell me."

MacNeice gave what he thought was a measured account of the meeting, after which he spoke about his concerns. And because there were so many ways the operation could end badly, he took the time to elaborate each of them. At the end there was a long pause before Wallace responded. "I'm out at Chedoke doing eighteen holes with the mayor, trying to pry loose a few more shekels for our budget."

"Good luck."

"Yeah . . . Look, Mac, it's a tossup as to the best way to handle this, whether it's with desk cops or the jocks with big guns and body armour. But if you're right about this suspect, he has the ability to wipe out my entire homicide division."

"He could, but even if you throw eighteen men at him, the results might be the same."

"Point taken, though Tactical is at least an assault team with assault weapons. They have snipers where you have side arms and shotguns. They have virtual tanks and you have beefed-up Chevys. You follow?"

"I do."

"I'll speak to Sadler and reinforce that you are to be consulted every step of the way."

"Consulted but not considered?"

"He's in charge of the operation, Mac. What are the chances this can end peacefully?"

"Zero to none. But I'm concerned about the safety of the woman with Venganza. I don't think she knew what she was getting into."

"So you think he hasn't killed her already?"

"Aziz's theory is that she'll play a role in his next piece. He might want to keep her alive for that. Also, she apparently owns the gallery in Paris that's showing his work. That will change the moment those armoured units dust up the lane."

"Yeah, but where she's concerned, it might not matter whether it's three Chevys or two of those tanks, whether it's right now or at dawn tomorrow, when he's sleepy."

"If he sleeps at all."

Wallace was finished talking and asked if there was any-thing else before he hung up.

"Yes, sir. I'd like your permission to include Aziz in their mobile command unit. She could prove helpful if we do have the opportunity to talk to him."

"Agreed. I'll let Sadler know."

[58]

"**WHAT TIME IS IT?" CHANEL BOURGET HAD FALLEN ASLEEP. SHE** woke in a darkened studio with a dry throat and a terrible urge to pee. She could feel the knotted gag hanging around her neck.

"1600. I've made dinner for us. After that we'll get ready. I'm going to take the ties off your wrists so you can use the bathroom." He looked into her eyes. "I think you have enough sense not to try to escape."

She nodded and asked, "Do you have my purse? My makeup is in there."

"Yes, it's in a safe place. For now, just use water and soap. Remember, you're Mary, so no mascara." He tossed the plastic ties in the bin.

"Are you going to kill me?"

"Maybe."

"Please, don't make fun . . . Are you?"

"Actually, I haven't decided. Are you asking me to decide right now?" He smiled and turned back to the kitchen. "Well, as you'll be playing the mother of Christ, your prayers may be granted." Walking off, he said, "Dinner's in twelve minutes."

She shivered when she saw the gun in the beige nylon holster strapped to his thigh. Chanel stood up shakily and quickly made her way to the washroom. She closed the door behind her and looked in the mirror. Her face was twisted by fear and stained with mascara. She turned on the cold-water tap and wiped it several times, until it was clean. When she looked up again, a frightened young girl looked back. Burying her face in a towel, Chanel desperately tried to muffle her sobbing.

When her crying stopped, she took several deep breaths and started thinking about how she could escape. She'd offered money but he hadn't responded. She could offer sex, but she saw no sign that he was interested. Possibly, if she simply undressed as she would on the beach at St. Tropez, naturally carefree and confident, he might be tempted. But then what?

She realized that the only leverage she had with Venganza was his work. And as horrific as the reality of it was, the images were still very beautiful. She could tell him that the exhibition would still go ahead. That no one would be the wiser. They'd say, *It's such brilliant, edgy work. RCV is daring, a tremendous artist. Just look at that flawless execution.*

When she emerged from the toilet, Venganza was busy serving out two large portions of pasta. The table had been set. Cutlery, napkins, water glasses, water bottle, salt, pepper, grated Parmesan, and a large bowl of chopped basil leaves were all placed as if on a grid. The chairs too were centred and equidistant from the table. The hard case with the exhibition prints was nowhere in sight.

She stood with her arms crossed in front of her. "Shall I undress?"

He put the pot back on the stovetop and looked at her curiously. "No. Why?"

"I do not know why. . . . I thought you would want to see what Mary looks like."

"No, I don't. Sit down and eat your dinner."

As he pulled out her chair she asked, "Is this to be my last supper?"

"Cute. I take making pasta seriously, so don't let it get cold."

"No wine?"

"No wine. We've got work to do."

She wolfed down the meal, occasionally wiping tomato sauce from her mouth. Venganza was impressed. He ate at a slower pace, glancing her way as the bottom of her bowl emerged.

When she was finished and the bowl empty, she stood up and took off her dress, laying it over the back of the chair. Venganza looked her over, then turned away, slipping another forkful of pasta into his mouth. She couldn't tell if he was pleased or not, and found herself pulling in her tummy. Though he seemed to be looking down at his bowl, he said, "Your stomach's fine, Chanel." He put down his fork. "Your body's lovely. You'll be a great Mary."

"And the underwear, take it off?" She was reaching for the bra clasp behind her.

"No, that's not necessary." He took his bowl and the glasses to the sink before turning to her. "Now please, no more jokes. I'm Catholic. This work is reverent. So am I."

"*Je suis desolée.* I'm sorry, I am very anxious."

"I know. We'll fix that soon."

"When will I know if you are going to kill me?"

"When you don't wake up."

He led her over to inspect the grey mountain with its strange tubular framework going this way and that. He showed her Wozinsky, dead on the table. She was shaking before she got there, but he put a hand gently on her shoulder. "It's okay, Woz is gone. He's not in pain. He smells a bit, but just try to think about the man he was."

Venganza put his arm around her, the way a big brother would, and started telling her again about Wozinsky. About his tattoos, about the tremendous soldier and friend he'd been. He pulled a creased photograph from the pocket of Wozinsky's fatigues. "That's Woz on the right, me on the left. Manserra and Muller, the two in the middle, and Denis Charbonneau, who took the pic — they died together over there." He handed her the photo. "Woz has been carrying that around for years."

"*Triste.*"

"Hmm?"

"Sad. It is very sad." She studied the photograph. "This man, Woz, he was very handsome."

"Yeah, I've heard that before."

Every combat soldier he knew had understood there was a possibility that he or she might not come home in one piece, if at all. And even though they knew IEDs were the low-cost, high-return weapon of choice for the Taliban, they'd prepared their bodies as if they were about to engage in hand-to-hand combat and emerge triumphant. Bodybuilding was their naive attempt to tilt the odds. The theory was simple. If you could run longer, climb faster, and lift more weights than your enemy, if your equipment was better, your strategies and tactics professional, your air support lethal — you might survive. No one could argue against that logic, even if it was fatally flawed. The Americans and Soviets didn't argue, nor had the British long before them.

But no one, least of all the military, had told them how to survive in the event that they did make it home.

[59]

"T'S ME. I'M DOWNSTAIRS." STATIC ON THE LINE, HESITATION perhaps, but the door buzzed open and he went in. As he entered the corridor, she was standing on the threshold of her apartment in her pyjamas. Pale blue stripes on white, bare feet on dark hardwood.

"It's late."

"I know. I won't stay long."

There were things they needed to discuss. The operation would begin in just over five hours. Aziz asked him to sit down while she put on a dressing gown. He was tempted to say, *Please don't. Stay the way you are,* but he didn't. His heart was racing, and while he hadn't yet done anything other than showing up at eleven p.m., it was sufficient reason to feel guilty. He stood up quickly, as if he'd just sat down on a kitten. He went back to the door and waited.

When Fiza appeared, she was still wearing her pyjamas. "I decided I was decent enough. My robe's too warm." Seeing him where she had left him, Aziz looked confused. "I wasn't gone that long, was I?"

"No. I want to tell you about the operation tomorrow morning. I'll feel a lot better if I know you're in the command unit." He was aware that he was avoiding her eyes, and her pyjamas. He suspected that his face and neck were flushed and she'd notice.

She did. A look of concern came over her face. "What are you not telling me, Mac?"

He swallowed hard and then laughed, a short one, like a sneeze. He took a deep breath and told the truth about his concern for the operation. "We're backup to Tactical. They'll go in with two of their armoured units. Another will be on the road to the dam to cut off Venganza if he tries to make a run for it."

"He won't."

"No, he won't. I know that homicide detectives aren't up to a battle with this man. We're not warriors and we only have sufficient weapons to disable those who know less about how to use them than we do."

"I'm relieved to hear you say that, Mac."

"Tactical look like military, but they aren't. They go home as we do. They practise tactics and unleash hellfire consistent with that practice. I wasn't able to explain how different Venganza is from all of us." He was looking at the window across the room, at her reflection in it. "I wanted an opportunity to talk to him, to save his life and that of the woman."

"You can't, Mac. Short of dropping a fairy-dust bomb that puts them to sleep, Venganza's the one in charge of this operation." She reached out and touched his arm. "He wants to die, and he knows you'll be there when it happens."

[60]

NORMALLY COMFORTED BY A SLIVER OF LAMPLIGHT SPILLING IN from the road, MacNeice had overlapped the curtains to ensure he'd sleep. It didn't work. After dozing off briefly, he woke up at 2:14 a.m. to wait for the alarm. He drifted in and out of sleep, never certain whether his eyes were open or closed. He realized it didn't really matter, because anxiety made restorative sleep impossible.

Dear man, what are those thoughts, and where do they take you?

"I've seen too much, Kate. I feel like I'm on a parallel track, looking at the man I'm hunting as he looks back at me. We're separated now, but in the distance our tracks come together."

Do they, or is that just an optical illusion?

"I don't know. I woke up thinking it was a simple trick of the eye."

Do you like him?

"No, but I respect him. I'm attached to him on the same axle. He's a monster, but in some ways our lives aren't that different."

Except that he kills people while you try to save them.

"I'm lost, Kate."

Remember what you said when I told you I was through with performing?

"It was a quote from Yogi Berra. 'When you come to a fork in the road, take it.'"

Yes, and that was the best advice you ever gave me.

"Except you died. I couldn't save you."

But you tried, and oh, so mightily.

"People are likely to die this morning, no matter how mightily I try to stop it."

Follow Yogi's advice.

HE DIDN'T KNOW whether the puppet master had cut the strings and carried his waking conversations with Kate into his dreams, but when the alarm finally sounded, MacNeice woke up heavy with concern. Worse, he'd made a commitment to follow Yogi Berra's advice, though he had no idea what that meant.

A shower and a double espresso later, he was standing in the living room peering into the forest. Something flickered at the edge of his vision, an owl or a crow perhaps. MacNeice checked his watch: 3:19 a.m.

Crows like company as they search for carrion or steal

eggs from a nest. But to do that, they need light. In contrast, an owl hunts alone and often at night. It waits on branches, its head swivelling silently, looking for something to attack on the forest floor. Mice and voles and adolescent rabbits aren't nocturnal; they're just constantly hungry. Ever fearful, they move with caution and stealth. Lacking the night vision of an owl, they know they're at a terrible disadvantage. The owl flies swiftly and silently to its prey. The lives of small creatures end before their senses have time to twitch, before they know what hit them.

Venganza was an owl. A night raid, or one in the early hours of morning, wouldn't bother him. The stage had been set a long time before, and far, far away. MacNeice smiled ruefully. He'd already compared Venganza to a shark and now to an owl. But sharks and owls kill to feed their hunger; the only animals that don't are rabid. Venganza was many things, but he wasn't rabid.

Insights come in their own time, and while that wasn't much of an insight, MacNeice felt one coming into focus. He ran from the stone cottage to his car.

DUNDURN'S TWO TACTICAL tanks and the GMC Yukon that Montile referred to as the "Baptist van" were loaded and idling, their teams standing in clusters sipping coffee and taking final briefings from their senior officers. Behind them were Swetsky, Vertesi, Williams, and, standing on a hard cast, Maracle.

"Aziz is in the command unit, boss." Vertesi nodded towards the windowless black bus with the satellite dishes and loudspeakers on top. As he saw for the first time the never-used acquisition that had cost more than the salaries of the entire homicide division put together, MacNeice's jaw dropped.

Williams couldn't resist. "It's Dundurn's state-of-the-art war on wheels, sir — wow for short."

MacNeice nodded and made his way over. On closer inspection it looked like a slick makeover of a Dundurn Street Railway bus. He stepped inside, where the lighting was blue. Along the far wall were four men and two women sitting at large computer screens, all wearing Kevlar vests in the team colour — black.

Sadler was at the end of the bus with his headset around his neck, talking on a cellphone. Aziz stood nearby, looking a bit like a student who'd been called to the principal's office. Seeing MacNeice, she raised her eyebrows and smiled.

"What's going on?" he asked.

"Lieutenant Sadler just woke up the DC to ask for my removal."

MacNeice smiled. "It won't happen." He led her away from Sadler. "I've had an idea. Maybe not much of one, but an idea nonetheless."

"A bit late, now that we're on the magic bus. The show's about to begin." She cast a look around. "The tension's building by the second in here —"

MacNeice interrupted her. "Venganza didn't come this far to engage in a slaughter. He's been hunting prey with precision, killing for his art. Correct?" He waited for her to respond. When she agreed, he added, "DeSouza and Gary Grant provoked him, left him with no choice. The others, as far as we know, committed some transgression; it amounted to some form of natural selection."

"Okay?"

"This . . . all of this" — he waved a hand at the computer screens — "the tanks outside and the men with assault weapons, stun grenades, smoke bombs, and God only knows what —"

"God and Venganza know what."

"Exactly. This is provocation. I'm now convinced that Venganza is prepared to deal with whatever it is."

"And your idea?"

"Like I said, it's not much. But I think if I walk unarmed down that road to the house —"

"Absolutely not, Mac. Sorry, but no. This man is everything you say, but he's also a bona fide psychopath with a twisted sense of honour — and, for that matter, of art."

"I'm not saying he's not. But all his victims have played a role in becoming his art."

"Father Terry?"

"Right . . . that's a problem. But what if he knew the old man was dying of cancer, that his eventual death would be extremely long and painful."

"An act of compassion?"

"Well, yes."

"Leaving conjecture aside, Mac, you'd walk up that road to do what, exactly?"

Sadler came up behind them. "Wallace says he approved Detective Aziz being here." He was addressing MacNeice as if Aziz wasn't standing next to him. Turning to her, he said, "You'll be behind me, over there." He pointed to the upholstered bench that ran the length of the bus, like a bleacher seat for watching the big game. "One of my men will hook you up to a headset. You'll be in touch with MacNeice and the rest of the team."

"Thank you, sir." Aziz was at her most polite.

"Your set is listen-only, so if you want to say something, tap me on the shoulder. Understood?"

Aziz considered asking how she would be in touch if she couldn't speak, but she realized there was no point. "Yes, sir."

"Lieutenant, I have an idea I want to run by you."

Sadler checked his big-faced watch. "Not now, MacNeice. We roll in ninety seconds."

"It won't take long."

"Detective Superintendent, I request that you return to your men immediately. Run your idea past me over the intercom."

"One on one, Lieutenant, if you don't mind."

Sadler gave him a cell number to call, then nodded crisply and walked away.

MacNeice turned to Aziz, hoping that all he wanted to say would travel silently between them. She was shaking her head. He put a hand on her shoulder, smiled, and left the bus.

He hadn't made it to the Chevy before the bus, two tanks, and the Baptist van were on the move. They began with such precision you'd be forgiven for thinking they shared the same chassis. Swetsky and Vertesi stood waiting, hands in pockets, watching the Black Marias motor out of the depot. MacNeice looked back to Williams and Maracle, who were standing next to the second car. He waved his hand in the direction of the exit and tossed the car keys to Williams. "You drive. I'll sit in the back."

WHILE IT WAS clear that Wallace had set Sadler straight about roles and expectations, his message clearly hadn't been well received. And that, MacNeice felt certain, would come into play the moment he revealed his idea.

He was right. While Sadler did answer the cell, he listened with considerable distraction until MacNeice had finished explaining his plan. He hadn't had time to take a breath before Sadler said flatly, "Negative, DS. You are not authorized to do so." And with that, the call ended.

MacNeice looked up to see Williams staring at him through the rear-view mirror, jaw-dropped and speechless. In the passenger seat, Maracle was shaking his head slowly and looking out at the predawn landscape. In less than a minute MacNeice's cellphone rang; it was Wallace.

"No, Detective. Better still, now that I'm truly fucking awake, no goddamn way. Do I make myself clear?"

"I think you're making a mistake, sir."

"I don't doubt that you do." Wallace slammed down the phone.

The radiophone connected to the tactical team and the command bus was quiet for some time, after which there were brief communications between them.

"EMS following, sir. One mile behind."

"Roger that."

"Tactical Three, turning off to the dam road in ten seconds."

"Roger, carry on. Keep your eyes peeled."

"Will do, sir. Good hunting, One and Two."

MacNeice looked out at the passing homes, a few with porch lights on, still waiting, perhaps, for someone to come home. Dew-covered cars and pickup trucks sat in driveways, and every once in a while he'd see someone jogging along the road wearing fluorescent gear that lit up in the headlights or someone walking a dog. Dog and owner would turn to watch as the mysterious convoy passed by.

Long, ropy clouds were collecting in folds along the horizon, waiting for the sky to warm up. It was still clinging to night, more turquoise than the red-orange of morning. It was the sign of a reluctant sun. MacNeice let his head fall back on the headrest and closed his eyes. He didn't know how long he slept, but when he woke up, he saw Montile looking at him through the rear-view mirror.

"Sir, were you seriously going to walk up that road alone and unarmed?" Williams turned his eyes back to the road.

"Yes."

The silence that followed left no doubt as to the opinions in the front seat. As they made their turn onto Valens Road, a great blue heron lifted off from the drainage ditch. It flew beside them for several seconds before peeling off and returning to the ditch. MacNeice watched it, and so did Maracle.

"Beautiful, isn't it," MacNeice said. "A wingspan of six feet. It always seems like they're lifting a massive weight." He recalled that when he'd shared that thought with Kate's father, the old man said. "Hmm, so it seems. And yet they weigh only five or six pounds." MacNeice smiled at the memory. Everything he knew about birds, he'd learned from him.

Maracle said softly, "It's a good sign, sir."

"A good sign, Charlie."

[61]

TACTICAL'S PLAN WAS TO BLOCK TRAFFIC FROM CROSSING VALENS Road by parking the command vehicle two hundred metres north of the driveway, roughly fifty metres from the entrance, obscured by the trees and cedar bushes lining the lane. At that point, like flight crews getting ready for takeoff, the tactical team would be taken through a final checklist, during which two drones would be launched to observe the farmhouse and its surrounding grounds.

As the Chevy came to a stop, MacNeice slowly removed his headset and laid it on the floor under the front seat. Leaning forward, he said, "I'm leaving the car. Follow Tactical's instructions and stay here until you're called for."

Williams snapped his head around. "Sir, don't do this."

Maracle had his hand on MacNeice's forearm. "You were

given a direct order not to interfere with this operation, sir. If you're wrong, there's a lot more than your life at stake."

"And if I'm right, Charlie?" He removed Maracle's hand.

MacNeice stepped out of the car, took off his jacket, and threw it on the seat. Williams rolled down the window. "Sir, this is insane."

MacNeice tapped the roof and walked slowly towards the tanks. To anyone observing, he was going forward to ask a question. But he was fairly certain they were checking switches and gear and watching what the drones were watching.

He pulled the holster off his belt and carried it at his side. As he passed T-2, the driver simply nodded at him, as if it was natural to see him walking along the road minutes before an operation began. Someone must have radioed Command, however, because the door of the first tank flung open. Washburn was waiting for him.

"What are you up to, DS?" He towered over MacNeice. Behind him, inside the vehicle, several men were trying to see what was going on.

"Following a hunch, Wash. If I'm wrong, I'll pay for it. Stay inside and follow Sadler's commands."

"I am. Sadler told me to stop you, to cuff you if necessary."

"You could, but I hope you won't. I've been told those headsets are frequently affected by static." MacNeice smiled and kept walking.

"With all due respect, sir, you are one crazy mother-fucker." Washburn closed the door.

MacNeice stood for a moment at the driveway's entrance. He bent down and slowly placed his service weapon on the road. The sun was inching skyward, laying warm bands of light onto his back. As he stood there, he could see the shadows of his lanky legs stretching farther down the driveway.

He took his first step towards the farmhouse and felt warm for the first time that morning. Somewhere behind him, a blue jay called.

"WHAT THE FUCK is your commanding officer doing to my operation?" Sadler's voice came over the headsets. Williams and Maracle weren't sure if he was speaking to anyone specific. A second voice came online: "That's one grandstanding cop."

Someone else was yelling at Washburn. "Wash . . . Wash . . . Respond, goddammit!"

It wasn't Sadler or Washburn that answered. "Sir, Wash's headset is on the fritz. I'm going to give him mine."

"Roger. We move in two minutes."

"Copy that."

Someone spoke up. "Lieutenant Sadler, what do we do about Detective Superintendent MacNeice?"

"Run the fucker down if he doesn't get off that road. Tactical One and Two, the operation goes ahead as planned," said Sadler.

"Ninety seconds."

"Copy that."

Washburn came on the line, his voice loud and clear. "Lieutenant Sadler. Couldn't hear you, sir. Assumed DS MacNeice was here on your instructions. Over."

"Where is he now?"

"Laid his weapon on the ground. He's walking towards the farmhouse, sir. Over."

More confusion on the line, people talking over each other. "One at a time. Keep this line clear." That sounded like Baker.

"Wash, stand down. We go in sixty seconds. Drone has MacNeice proceeding slowly to the house." Sadler was angry, but more than that, he was disappointed.

Maracle looked at Montile. Williams whispered, "What . . . the . . . fuck?"

"It's called military precision," Maracle replied, and shrugged.

"T-1, T-2. Go, go, go!"

[62]

MAcNEICE WAS STILL SOME DISTANCE FROM THE HOUSE, AND EVEN though the windows were painted over, he felt certain he was being watched. He was tempted to check the garage in case Venganza was lying in wait, but it didn't matter — he was committed to moving forward. In any event, he knew there was very little he could do to defend himself. In spite of the warm sun, his legs were trembling beneath him and he was embarrassed by his fear.

Behind him, the heavy engines of the tanks were moving them forward at a walking pace. MacNeice resisted the urge to turn around. He listened for the moment when they turned into the driveway, closing on him slowly over the hard dirt and rocks. Stealth, he realized, wasn't the point of these behemoths. They were designed to intimidate.

The undercarriage of T-1's belly dropped into a gap left by a storm sewer. It landed with a heavy *wumph*, followed by another when the rear wheels followed. In an attempt to avoid the sewer, the driver of T-2 eased over to the cedar hedge on the right. The manoeuvre kept the right wheel from dropping but sent the left lurching deeper into the gap. Inside, heavily armed men were thrown off their seats as they reached for something to hold on to. MacNeice thought he could hear them swearing, but their shouts were drowned out by the dozens of cedar branches raking the length of the tank's black siding.

Ten yards from the house, MacNeice was startled by a series of small explosions behind him. They were followed instantly by sighs, snaps, and creaks that may not have been heard inside the heavy vehicles. He turned to see the tall maples that lined both sides of the lane topple onto the front and rear of both tanks. The charges had been set eight feet off the ground to ensure that whatever came down fell fast and heavy. As a maple pancaked onto the hood of the second tank, it sent ice-cube-sized chunks of windshield splashing everywhere. The tank's engine raced, whined, and rattled before it fell silent. Within seconds, black smoke started pouring through the gaps in the hood.

Both tanks were left without room to manoeuvre forward or back. Looking through the mesh of leafy branches, MacNeice could see Washburn behind the windshield. The engine of his vehicle shut down and he moved out of sight. Other than the hissing and popping from T-2, the assault had fallen silent.

MacNeice took a deep breath and turned back to the farmhouse.

WHEN SHE HEARD that MacNeice had left his vehicle, Aziz leapt off the bench and stood at Sadler's shoulder. As panic set in and the expletives went from occasional to constant, she shouldered her way in front of him.

Sadler's cheeks were purple with rage. He covered the mike of his headset and shouted, "Get back on the bench, Detective!"

"Sir, I can help," said Aziz.

"You can't do shit! Sit the fuck down or I'll have you removed."

"He knows what he's doing, sir. He's studied Venganza. He knows who he is."

Sadler ripped off his headset and, with his face inches from hers, screamed, "I don't give a shit if your boss is suicidal, Detective! I will not have this operation jeopardized because of him — or you. Sit down or you will be cuffed to that bench."

Aziz tightened her jaw and walked back to the bench. She slid sideways to get a better view of the drone images.

"Give me a report on thermal. Where's Venganza? What's he up to?" Sadler was pointing furiously at the video feed.

The first drone operator said briskly, "Negative, Lieutenant. He's either not there or he has some kind of infrared shield."

The second drone operator shook her head. "Same here, sir. I can't detect a heat source." Sadler dialled Wallace on his cellphone. He talked tough while relating the current events but fell silent when the DC responded. There was too much noise on the bus for Aziz to hear the sounds spilling from the phone, but they were sufficient to register that Wallace was furious. The veins in Sadler's temples were swollen as his heart pushed blood to counter the career-ending stress. "Yes, sir . . . no . . . MacNeice left his headset in the vehicle . . . Sir, I'm told his weapon is on the road in front of the driveway . . . Yes, he's approaching, very close to the house."

The call ended and Sadler put on his headset. He turned to look at Aziz. "Wallace will be here in five minutes —" He was going to say more, but one of the drone operators grabbed his arm.

"Sorry, sir. You've gotta see this."

Aziz stood up but stayed near the bench. Along the row of heads beside her and over her headset, people seemed to be freaking out. The aerial view showed little of the reason why — just drifting puffs of smoke. But a second later, like falling dominoes, the treetops shivered and fell onto the vehicles.

Aziz could see MacNeice, unharmed, turn to look at the tanks before resuming his walk towards the house. She removed her headset and laid it on the bench. In the chaos of the control room, no one noticed as she made her way to the shallow steps and out the door. Setting her sights on the Chevy, Aziz began walking, slowly at first and then as quickly as she could, ignoring the pain in her back. She listened hard for Sadler's men rushing to retrieve her and put her in cuffs. But the farther away she got from the command bus, it was only the sound of her own footfalls and breathing that she heard. Her heart was beating faster and faster. As Aziz drew closer to the unmarked cars, she feared that MacNeice might already be injured or dead.

She willed herself to think about something else. She took several deep breaths and looked about. The sun was rising, the birds were calling; she wondered if MacNeice could hear them. He'd identify what they were and tell her stories about their lives, stories that were always true but heavily anthropomorphic. For him they were little people. He said they had personalities and character traits, that some were thugs but most were saints. She smiled and quickened her pace.

Through clenched teeth, she spoke aloud. "You risk your life, waste your life, without care. If you're dead, Mac . . . If you're dead, I will be so fucking angry with you." Tears were streaming down her face and her nose was running, but she kept swallowing to keep from sobbing, to keep from collapsing from the searing pain in her back. When she'd left the bus, MacNeice had been close to the door of the house. Where was he now?

Aziz cleared her throat several times, coughing up something. She spat it out, then spat again. Vertesi was out of his car and running towards her. She stopped on the road. She put her hands on her hips and spat again, this time with a low, loud growl. Vertesi wrapped his arms around her. "Fiza, Fiza, trust him. Trust him, Fiz."

She tore herself angrily away from him, her arms outstretched, her fists clenched. Bending over, she panted until her breathing returned to normal. "I don't know, Michael. Honestly, I tried to pray. It doesn't fucking work." She wiped the tears from her eyes in disgust.

"The rest of this is bullshit, Fiz. You know that. Boss is trying to make sense of it."

She stood upright, groaning from the pain in her back, and shook her head. She turned back to look at the bus, then took a deep breath and sighed. "I know that. I do . . ." Seeing the concern on his face, she added, "I couldn't pray, but" — she put a hand on his shoulder — "I learned what it means to be so angry I could spit."

[63]

FIVE FEET FROM THE DOOR, MacNEICE LOOKED BACK AT THE TANKS.
He realized that the only doors left to open would expose
them to withering fire from the farmhouse. He looked for
any sign of Venganza but saw nothing. He began to second-
guess the spotters' report that no one had left the house during the night. Yet the Econoline was in the garage.

He heard one of the tank doors open and turned to see
Baker and six armed men jump clear of its smoke-filled interior, coughing and swearing. Two scrambled under the trees
behind the vehicle to establish defensive positions. Baker and
the other three took off at a run across the infield to flank
the building. They didn't get far. The first to fall was the fastest. He went down screaming, disappearing beneath weeds,
leaves, and ancient fallen branches. As the other two ran to

his aid, one tripped over a fallen branch and landed with a loud, guttural wail. Realizing there was a hidden threat, the last one stopped and looked back at Baker, who signalled for him to return to the driveway. He hesitated, then turned and had taken two steps before MacNeice heard the snap of metal jaws on flesh and bone. The man's head snapped back and his assault rifle flew in an arc before sinking into the brush. He screamed, struggling for a moment to stay upright, then fell with a shriek into the brush.

Baker was frantic as he called for medics over his headset and requested further orders from Sadler. Then, realizing he was exposed, he turned slowly and tried to retrace his steps back to the lane. The brush was so thick he might as well have been looking for footprints in the ocean. Baker was two feet short of the driveway when something hit. He went down hard, howling in pain.

Washburn was standing in the open door of the first tank when Sadler's voice broke through the screams of the four men. "What the hell is going on, Wash?"

"Check the drones, sir. We've been treed from both sides. Came down like scissors. T-2's out of commission and on fire, and we're blocked front and back by trunks. He detonated both rows of trees, all except the two near DS MacNeice."

"Who's screaming? What's happened to the men?"

"That's Baker's team, sir. He and three of his team just went down. Not sure from what. We need medics now, sir. The other two are behind the vehicle, taking cover under the trees."

"Can you move the injured men to safety?"

"Negative, sir. That field is booby-trapped. And we don't know by what."

"Can you storm the farmhouse?"

"Sir, we're gonna be exposed the moment we step out of this vehicle. The rear door's blocked. We only have one way out."

"Hang on, Wash. We've got a drone overhead; I'm waiting for a zoom. Tell the injured to cut their headset feeds. You're the only one I want to hear from."

Washburn gave the command. Baker was reluctant but discarded his headset. The screaming from the infield continued, but now it was a mix of pain, fear, and rage. Baker had had enough. "What's happening, Wash? Get us the fuck out of here!"

"What hit you, Sergeant?"

"Looks like wooden stakes . . . four of 'em. Thick, like sharpened axe handles. Trip-wired. Came from both sides . . . took out my leg."

Washburn called to the men on the ground. "Report. What hit you?"

Amid groans, someone called, "Looks like a beartrap."

"Mine too . . . caught my arm when I fell. It's bleeding something fierce."

After a stream of expletives, the third man yelled, "Don't know, Sarge. Both legs gone . . . Get a medic here, fast!"

"Listen, hang tough. Put on tourniquets above those wounds. Do 'em tight." Washburn went back inside and called Sadler. "You heard that, Lieutenant?"

"Yeah. Not a shot fired and we've got two tanks disabled and four men down. Tell them the EMS teams are on the way."

"Roger that, sir. But there's no way EMS will go in there."

"What do you suggest, Wash?"

"I'm saying the more men we throw at this, the more men we're gonna lose. And given what he did to the trees, the guy knows how to blow things up. He's going all hunter-gatherer on us."

"Make your point."

"He doesn't want to kill us . . . at least not yet. Sure as shit, if we open an assault on that house, he'll change his mind. So far it's been about disabling."

"Gimme something, Wash. We can't just sit here."

"All we got now is some heavy fire. We unleash that, there's no telling what'll happen. Sure as shit it's gonna get ugly . . . But we do have MacNeice, sir."

"Explain yourself."

"Let MacNeice talk. He may be crazier than a shithouse rat, but unlike Baker's men, he's still standing." Washburn looked through the branches on the hood. "Correction. He's making his way to the door of the house."

WILLIAMS AND THE rest of MacNeice's team were still wearing their headsets and had been listening to the exchange, trading glances and shaking their heads. Williams decided to interrupt the tactical team's communication. "Sergeant Washburn's nailed it, sir."

"Who the fuck is speaking?"

"Montile Williams, DI, Homicide."

"What are you saying, Detective?" Sadler couldn't hide the disdain in his voice for the breach of protocol.

Williams disliked being lorded over by anyone, but given the lenth of time he'd known Sadler, his back was up. He laid on a heavy helping of sass. "Brother Wash is on that road, not in my car or in your fancy black bus. He knows Venganza could have blown up both tanks and taken out MacNeice, who is unarmed." And in case his point would be missed, he added, "He could just as easily nuke your boys with all their toys. But he fucking didn't. Why?"

"Your insubordination, Detective, is duly noted and recorded —"

"Sir, I trust my boss. You're a boss, but you're not *my* boss. His ass is on the line. This guy will either kill him or not. But four of your men are cut up and losing blood. So far, sir, this thing's going precisely the way Venganza planned it."

"Thank you, Detective," Washburn said. "I think we get the point. Right, sir?"

"We need to get those wounded men out of there."

"You'll either need a map of the traps or get a sweeping unit in there before EMS will touch it," Swetsky said, barely keeping his temper under control.

"Okay, okay. We give MacNeice ten minutes. If he hasn't come out by then, we can assume he won't be coming out at all."

The line went dead and the homicide detectives began to process the cold truth of Sadler's statement. If MacNeice was still standing, he would be negotiating. That could take longer than ten minutes. If he was dead, why wait at all?

Swetsky was fed up with thinking. He took off his headset, opened the door, and got out. A moment later Williams stepped out of the car, laying his headset on the roof. Vertesi, Maracle, and Aziz didn't ask where they were going — they knew. Without exchanging a word, they made their way towards the lane.

In minutes they were all lined up across the end of the driveway. They could hear the groans, cries, and swearing from the infield, but they couldn't see anyone but Baker. His back was propped up on the shoulder of the driveway. He looked their way but said nothing, as if he had half expected to see them standing there. He stared for a minute or so before turning his attention back to his leg.

Swetsky said softly, "You boys realize this may cost you your jobs? Sorry — you too, Aziz."

"She's one of the boys, Swets."

"Indeed I am. I even said 'fuck' today, so I certainly qualify."

"No problem, Swets. I'll go back to stand-up. After this shit, I could use a good laugh," said Williams.

They didn't know where MacNeice had gone but assumed he'd entered the house. Swetsky watched the windows for signs of movement, a muzzle flash or any other signal that they should dive for cover.

"Remember when someone said MacNeice was grand-standing? What do you think they'll make of this?" Maracle asked, shifting his weight off the ankle cast and chuckling.

"That MacNeice is diseased and it's contagious," answered Williams.

"Yeah, well, maybe it is," Maracle said. "But for the record, I've seen grandstanders. I've listened to 'em carry on, putting shine on deeds that don't deserve it. This isn't grandstanding."

Williams considered it for a moment before answering. "Yeah, but pretty crazy all the same."

"Check yourself, brother. We're not crazy and we're standing here," said Maracle.

"That's us — a band of brothers, like that television series," added Vertesi.

In a low voice full of gravitas, Aziz began to speak. "This story shall the good man teach his son; and Crispin Crispian shall ne'er go by, from this day to the ending of the world, but we in it shall be remember'd; we few, we happy few . . . we band of brothers."

For some time no one spoke. The sound of groaning men had slipped behind the calls of birds in the fallen trees and the gentle rustle of dying leaves. Up ahead, black smoke continued to spiral skyward from the hood of T-2.

"That was beautiful, Fiza," Williams said. "I'm serious — really beautiful. Where'd that come from?"

"Shakespeare. *Henry the Fifth*."

They were quiet again until Swetsky asked, "So who's Crispin Crispian?"

"Saints," Maracle answered, to the amazement of everyone. When he noticed the side glances, he added, "What, because I'm Native I can't know my Christian saints? Crispin and Crispian were Romans. They became saints."

"Do you think Mac's still alive?" Vertesi asked.

Swetsky cleared his throat. "Brothers and sister, what you have in MacNeice is someone with a kinda other level of understanding. I don't know exactly what that is, but I wish I did. Maybe someday he'll pay the price for it, but in my heart, I don't believe that day is today."

[64]

MacNEICE WAS REACHING FOR THE SCREEN DOOR WHEN HE CAUGHT sight of Venganza — not much more than a large shadow. He should have expected it but hadn't. It stopped him in his tracks. He withdrew his hand as if the door handle were hot. He inhaled deeply and waited. Venganza raised his right hand and, with a cupping motion, signalled for him to enter. MacNeice swallowed hard and took hold of the handle.

As MacNeice stepped inside, the screen door slapped against his back. For a moment he felt ridiculous, and that seemed to amuse Venganza, who was already studying him. There was a trace of a smile on his face, and though his hand rested on the weapon strapped to his thigh, he gave no indication that he felt concerned enough to remove it from the holster.

"You're not with the wannabes, MacNeice. And I assume that's your ragtag bunch out by the road." Venganza cocked his head to one side. "Let me guess . . . You've gone rogue and they're just following your lead." He focused on him the way scientists do when they come across a new species of dragonfly or tree frog.

"Something like that, though I didn't know they were there."

"What about the wannabes?"

"In what sense?"

Venganza stepped closer. "It's going to get a lot hairier. So, if they wanna be heroes, they've come to the right place. Though I believe you're the one who found me."

"Do you want it to get hairier?"

"Not my call, sir. But I'm sure the genius who commands them is feeling humiliated right now. He might want to even the score. So far they've just messed up their nifty uniforms and snapped a few bones. Didn't you try to stop this?"

"I did."

Venganza nodded. He understood how command structures worked — and how, somewhere down Valens Road, the guy running the show was wondering what to do with his failing plan. "You want a coffee?"

MacNeice's jaw dropped. "You're not concerned about what's unfolding outside?"

"Not in the slightest. Everything's wired, set to blow — including this place, with you and me in it. That team out by the dam? You know, where you had a spotter camped last night."

"You noticed."

Venganza cocked an eyebrow. "They'd best stay where

they are. The distance between there and here is . . . very unfriendly. But then, you don't actually have any sway with them, do you."

"No."

"So, coffee? If we're going to talk, I'd like a coffee."

"Black. A single or double shot."

Venganza smiled and led him into the kitchen. He went over to the counter and picked up something that looked like a large cellphone, pushed a button, and set it down. Immediately Sadler's voice came on; he was speaking to Washburn.

"Wash, any sign of MacNeice or the perp?"

"No, sir. It's quiet."

"What's his team up to?"

"They're just standing at the end of the road like they're waiting for a bus — or for MacNeice to come out. Maybe they got weapons, maybe they don't. I can't tell."

"Roger that. DC Wallace just arrived. I'll get back to you."

Venganza smiled, poured the coffee into mugs, and handed one to MacNeice. "Wallace is the head boss?"

"He's their commander and mine." The coffee was brewed and very strong.

"Smart?"

"You mean Wallace?"

"Yeah. Is he smart?"

"I think so . . . but we'll see."

"You mean he's got office smarts but you're not sure he's got field smarts."

"Accurate."

"Why are you here, MacNeice?"

MacNeice looked hard at him. "On my way down your

lane, I honestly didn't know. When you started popping the trees, I was even less certain. And when those men got torn up out there, I was convinced I'd misjudged you."

"And now that you're in front of me?" He put the carafe back on the stove.

"Now I'm climbing back to hopeful." MacNeice needed time to think; he wasn't sure where the conversation was going. He picked up the mug again. "In spite of the considerable evidence to the contrary, I think you are an honourable man, Venganza. I don't think you kill for sport."

"You're thinking I'm not going to kill you, is that it?"

"I said 'hopeful' . . . and that's one of the things I'm hopeful about."

Venganza laughed and raised his mug as if to say *cheers*. The radio beeped to life again; this time it was Sadler. Venganza appeared relaxed. He drank his coffee just as he might on any other day.

"T-3, can you cross the distance to that house from where you are?"

"Negative, Lieutenant. We'd need an ATV for that, and we've got a loaded Yukon."

"Then double-back to the command unit. Pronto."

"Roger that."

Venganza finished his coffee, washed the mug, and dried it. Putting it back on the shelf, he turned to MacNeice. "Looks like we're opting for hairy."

"Is your radio one-way or can you communicate through it?"

"That's not going to happen, Detective. I'll let you leave right now or you can stay and watch the show. I'm not gonna get all cozy with the wannabes."

"No one else needs to get hurt here. Just tell me what you want."

"Too late. Besides, I don't want anything . . . Actually, I do. I want to finish my last piece — and I will." He reached into the pantry and pulled out an assault rifle. "But just so you know, it was never about running. I'll admit, I didn't think you'd work it out as fast as you did, but this last piece is my most ambitious."

"Show me." MacNeice put the mug on the counter and followed Venganza into a darkened room.

"There you go." He stood aside and waited as MacNeice's eyes adjusted to the lack of light and he took in the bizarre tableau. After a few seconds, the detective turned to him. It was the form of it that spoke to him. Even in the gloom, he recognized it at once. "*La Pietà.*"

Venganza broke into a wide grin and shook his head with delight. "You've got some serious chops, MacNeice. I am impressed."

"It's not me alone. DI Fiza Aziz — that's her on the road — she worked out that you were going to mine Catholicism."

Venganza went to the laptop in the corner and zoomed in on an image. "That her?"

"Yes. That's the homicide team."

"Good-looking woman." He looked up at MacNeice. "These people obviously love you. Why don't you go back to them before it's too late."

"I'm not leaving."

"Actually, chief, I wasn't asking." Venganza levelled the rifle at MacNeice's chest.

"Let me leave with the woman." MacNeice nodded towards Mary.

The device came to life again. "Washburn, this is Deputy Chief Wallace."

"Washburn, sir."

"We haven't met, Sergeant, but I understand you're closest to that farmhouse."

"Roger that. Thirty yards or so. Stuck behind some trees."

"I'm going to ask you a question and I don't want you to give me the party line. You know what I mean by that?"

"I think so, sir. You want me to speak the truth as freely as I see it."

"Exactly. What's the truth as you see it?"

Everyone who still had headsets — plus Venganza and MacNeice in the farmhouse — waited for Washburn's answer.

"Sir, this man's a professional. I believe whatever aggression we bring to the situation will be met by overwhelming aggression in return. Look at us. We arrived here not long ago and we've got four men down and two tanks that ain't goin' nowhere. Hell, one of 'em is all smoked up." He left some time for that to sink in before continuing. "Venganza's had months to plan how to defend this place. I honestly believe we've seen just the tip of this fucker's iceberg. Pardon my French, sir."

"Thank you, Sergeant."

"I like that sergeant." Venganza was cradling the rifle in his arm. "So Wallace is smart. A commander who listens to a sergeant . . . as I live and breathe —"

"Ah, T-3 here. Do we stay in our vehicle or come over to you, sir?"

"Come to Command. A new strategy's in the works."

"Oops," Venganza said. "I spoke too soon. I knew it was too good to be true."

"The woman, please?" MacNeice knew Sadler wouldn't give up on the operation.

"No. But I have an idea about what to do with you."

Venganza took MacNeice by the arm and led him to a barstool. He told him to sit down and then went off to close the kitchen door, throwing the room further into darkness.

MacNeice's ears popped as he listened for Venganza's movements. He strained to see him but couldn't make out anything in the darkness. He heard footfalls to the left and his heart began to race. He had an urge to run for the door, but he'd seen how quickly Venganza could move and decided to stay put. He was clinging to the theory that Venganza could have killed him at any time, even before he reached the screen door, and didn't. That he might not was hope on a tightrope. In that awful void, a thought slipped through his neural circuitry: sharks don't kill for pleasure.

With a pop, a powerful light came on, momentarily blinding him. It was on a high tripod, focused on the pyramidal form. As his eyes adjusted, he could see Mary and Jesus. He held his breath.

Venganza walked past him and lit another tower. MacNeice could see that Jesus was wearing camouflage pants but nothing else. Venganza watched his reactions and smiled as he walked over to the third tower. This light revealed *La Pietà* in three dimensions. MacNeice kept blinking, trying to remove the three bright dots from his vision. He wasn't aware of it, but his jaw had dropped.

At the bottom of the piece, where the cloak draped beneath Jesus, was a worn-out pair of boots. Seeing him looking at them, Venganza said, "Standard issue for service in Afghanistan. You can get up now, MacNeice."

He walked over to examine the tableau. Specifically, he wanted to see if Mary was still alive.

"She's not dead, if that's what you're thinking. She's only sleeping." Venganza was placing one-inch brass V's on the floor beside each lamp stand.

He approached and put a hand on Jesus's shoulder. "Master Corporal Steven Wozinsky." He turned to MacNeice. "I didn't kill him. Drugs did that. After four tours, he came home for good. He was fried and he knew it." Venganza's eyes were filled with rage and sorrow. "There's a tall red-head, wears his hair in a bun and hangs out at the bus terminal. He took this fine man's life."

The radio came to life; Venganza walked over and picked it up. He handed it to MacNeice. "Hang on to that; I've got work to do. Go back to the stool."

Venganza picked up a large, box-like camera mounted on a tripod. He placed it directly over the small V on the left, and within minutes he was taking light readings from Mary and Jesus's faces, each time popping the three flashes that once again blinded MacNeice. He went back to the camera and made several adjustments to the aperture and checked the focus through the lens. After shooting several frames he went over to a small desk, where the images slowly appeared on a computer screen. When he had finished studying them, he returned to the camera and pressed the shutter ten or twelve times, occasionally making subtle changes to the focus. MacNeice closed his eyes to the flashes.

Venganza picked up the camera and tripod and repeated this process twice again, aligning the tripod directly above the other two V's. He was focused, absolutely calm and

unhurried in his work. He'd hum to himself or say something — a correction or an observation — that would lead
to a tiny adjustment of the camera or tripod.

Midway through the third position, the radio barked.
Venganza didn't divert his attention from what was in front
of him, but MacNeice was certain he was listening.

"Washburn, we're bringing the team from T-3 through
the hedge on your right, exactly ten minutes from now. Get
your team out of T-1. The two standing members of Baker's
team will provide cover. Your men will get behind the
tank. Meet up with T-3 coming on foot through that hedge.
Together you'll make your way towards the house, using the
tank for cover. Split your assets into three assault groups.
Fire smoke and stun grenades through those windows. Six
will storm the front and four will hit the back door."

"Roger." Washburn sounded resigned.

"T-2, copy that," said someone from Baker's team.

"Set time: ten minutes from now."

"Copy set."

Venganza was still shooting, but he turned to MacNeice.
"Sounds like the wannabes have abandoned you, Detective."

Washburn came back on the line. "Lieutenant, advise.
We still have MacNeice and a woman in there."

"Understood, Wash. They may be casualties by now.
Your assets are to use precision targeting."

Venganza was finished. "*Assets* . . . oh my. Only an officer
who's never been in combat would refer to combat soldiers
as assets." He moved the camera and tripod to the side and
walked back to the computer, where he began loading the
files. "Sadler hasn't considered how his team can use precision firing when they've just filled the house with smoke.

It's more likely that they'll fire at each other through the fog and confusion. Either way, he hasn't considered you."

"Or he has and doesn't care. Maybe he thinks that if the Virgin Mary and I were smart we wouldn't be here in the first place."

Venganza laughed. "Yeah, well, put that way, he would have a point." He checked his watch. "Nine minutes." He walked over to *La Pietà*, lifted Jesus. In the light, the sad arc of his emaciated rib cage fanned upward. Venganza returned him reverently to the table and set the worn-out boots at Wozinsky's feet, *ready for inspection.*

He lifted the grey cloak off the framing and rigging that had supported Jesus on Mary's lap. It was an ingenious rig that had taken Wozinsky's weight off the slender legs of a still-sleeping Chanel. When he removed the cloak from her body, MacNeice was surprised to see she was wearing only bra and panties. Venganza folded the heavy cloak. "The underwear was her idea. She didn't want to get overheated and sweat up Mary's face. She was certain that Mary didn't sweat."

"What's going to happen to those men advancing through the hedge?"

"They'll experience the true intimacy of pain, but they'll survive. However, their careers in Tactical will be over."

With the exception of a static buzz, the listening device was silent. Venganza clicked the laptop mouse several times until, one by one, a quartet of active surveillance video feeds came to life. After a moment, he clicked the mouse and the photographs reappeared.

"Venganza —"

"Call me Vennie."

"Vennie, let me try to stop this."

Venganza's head snapped around. He was angry, but said nothing. Seconds later, his mouth relaxed and he smiled. "They call you Mac. Correct?"

"Yes."

"Well, Mac, you're probably wondering why I let you in, or for that matter why I haven't unleashed a Taliban party trick on your five colleagues out there."

"I have wondered about that."

"I didn't know either, until a few minutes ago. He tilted his head towards the computer. "I'm doing the final selects of *La Pietà*. I am going to add these to the rest of the exhibition pieces and give all of them to you on a high-res memory stick. You're going to be the official keeper of my work."

He glanced back at Mary. "Her name is Chanel Bourget. Up until the moment she arrived in Dundurn, she was a Parisian gallery owner keen to exhibit my images. She was convinced they were faked and said they were 'the finest depictions of man's inhumanity to man.'" Venganza seemed to enjoy the irony of that comment but kept on working. "She'll wake up in roughly thirty minutes. You'll be her keeper as well. Her clothes are in the bathroom; her purse is in the pantry."

"And you?"

"Don't worry about me. What's left of your tactical team will rush the doors. I'll deal with them. But you and Bourget need to get into the cellar. There's an airtight safe room; it's got lighting, water, and some munchies. The air will last for six hours. Take her down and stay there till this is over." He looked over at MacNeice. "There's a hard case in there with my exhibition prints inside, except for this one."

"What about you?"

"Determination is an asset in your line of work and in mine, Mac. But insistent determination in your present circumstances is risky."

"I can stop this."

Vennie screamed, "I don't want you to stop it! Now, have I made myself clear, Detective?"

"Very clear."

And as quickly as it had come to life, his fury subsided. "I'm sorry, Mac, that was out of line. Now you're thinking I'm a psychopath. I am, of course, but I've never killed anyone when I'm angry."

"I believe you. At the risk of breaking your tradition, I have to ask again. Let me try to call this off." He looked at his watch. "We've only got six minutes. I promise you, Vennie, I can talk Wallace down."

Venganza's chair went skidding away and he moved swiftly across the floor. MacNeice stood up, bracing himself for whatever was coming and sliding his hand under the seat, thinking he'd use the stool to defend himself. It was a desperate and ludicrous idea. Venganza snapped the receiver away from him and then shoved it back — hard — into MacNeice's chest. The impact knocked the wind out of him. He fell back against the wall, coughing. Venganza waited for him to stop and then smiled. "Make your call, Detective. By my watch, you've got four minutes, thirty-one seconds."

[65]

MARACLE WAS THE FIRST TO NOTICE THE SIX MEN SETTING OUT from the command bus on the run. "Sadler's rolled the dice." The others craned their necks to see the heavily armed men sprinting single-file along Valens Road towards them.

Vertesi tapped Swetsky's shoulder. "Washburn's out of his tank."

Washburn jumped first, followed by his team. They ran back towards the road, hurtling, climbing, and falling over trunks and branches until they were in front of the burnt-out tank. From there, they scrambled along the same tree, trying to avoid contact with the blistering hood of the T-2. When they were finally on the safe side, they stood with their backs against the tank, trying to catch their breath.

"DC WALLACE. THIS is MacNeice. DC Wallace, come in."

Over the airwaves, someone yelled, "Sir, that set isn't one of ours! It's coming from inside the farmhouse."

Sadler responded. "You're saying the perp hacked into our communication network? It isn't fucking secure?"

"Yes, sir."

"Yes, sir, he did or yes, sir, it's secure?"

"Well . . . both, sir. It's supposed to be secure but he's definitely on our channel."

Suddenly people were speaking over each other to such an extent that it was impossible to make sense of anything. Someone — MacNeice thought it might be Wallace — barked, "Everyone down the line, shut up. This isn't the time for forensics. We've got two squads of men closing on that house, for fuck's sake."

"DC Wallace . . . Come in, please."

"MacNeice, talk fast. There's a situation developing here." Wallace sounded distracted.

"I'm well aware of that, sir. Venganza has been listening in from the start."

"Mac, you have one minute, forty-nine seconds." Vennie's voice was calm and measured.

"Who the fuck was that?" Wallace shouted.

MacNeice shook his head. "That's Venganza, sir. Tactical's heading for a booby-trapped hedgerow. The field and house are also rigged. You've got to call this off, sir."

In the static that followed, Venganza said, "I didn't say you had permission to tell them that." But he was smiling as he turned back to his downloading. "You have roughly forty seconds to get down to the basement, Mac."

Washburn's voice came online. "Lieutenant Sadler, we

have eyes on those men approaching. They'll hit that hedge in twenty seconds. I respectfully request, sir, that you shut down this assault immediately."

"Understood, Washburn," More chatter and crosstalk.

At the computer, Venganza laughed and shook his head.

"DC Wallace! Call this off!" MacNeice raised his voice above the din.

"And what, just let that man escape?" Sadler yelled.

"They'll hit that hedge in ten seconds," Venganza said.

Wallace cut in. "Okay, call it off . . . CALL IT OFF!"

Washburn screamed, "T-3, stand down! Stand down!" And in case the men on the other side of the hedge weren't listening to headsets, he barked the order as loudly as he could. "T-3, stop where you are. Stand down. Do not approach. The hedge and the house are booby-trapped."

"Mac, come over here." Venganza had finished downloading his images and was now looking at the surveillance video of six men standing around in the field beside the hedge. Some were looking back towards the command unit, while others were speaking to Washburn and his men through the hedge. He glanced at MacNeice and said mournfully, "There's nothing sadder than warriors without a war."

"I wouldn't know, Vennie. For me, this is a good day."

"Tell Washburn he'll find three rakes in the garage. Before they go in for those injured men, they need to use the rakes to trigger the traps. Allow four feet around each man. And do not go any farther."

"Will do."

MacNeice gave Washburn the instructions and told him to have EMS standing by. He hadn't even finished when Venganza pointed to the computer screen, which showed three men running to the garage and emerging with the rakes.

Wallace broke in on the line. "MacNeice, what now? Please tell me that man is going to surrender."

Venganza took the receiver. "With respect, sir, I believe you've just surrendered to me."

"MacNeice!"

Venganza handed the set back to him with a smile.

"MacNeice here. I don't believe Venganza will be surrendering, sir. Nor, as I understand it, will he attempt to escape." He turned to see Vennie nodding slowly. "I understand that Chanel Bourget and I will be allowed to leave." Again Venganza nodded. "Any further attempts on this house will be explosive, sir."

"Affirmative," Venganza said, reaching for the handset. "This is 'the perp.' What I need from you, sir, is one hour to prepare."

"Prepare for what?"

Venganza shook his head at Wallace's pretence of control. He smiled. "I need one hour to prepare, after which it'll be safe for your men to enter. Once inside, no one will come to any harm. You have my word."

"Jesus Christ. Your word? Why should I trust you?"

"Don't trust me. Trust Detective MacNeice."

Venganza handed the receiver back to MacNeice. "Carry her into the bathroom and put a cold towel on her face. She'll wake up. Get her dressed, then both of you leave. Do not come back."

"Understood." MacNeice spoke for the last time into the handset. "Sir, I trust him. I'll be out with the woman shortly."

Venganza handed him the memory stick and offered his hand. At first MacNeice hesitated, but then he took it. "Vennie, why all of this? What was worth the lives of all those people? What can I learn from what you've done?"

Vennie chuckled and looked over at Mary in her underwear. He shook his head and smiled. "I've nothing to teach you, Mac. If I have to explain art, I'm doomed, and it wouldn't be art."

MacNeice put the listening device on the stool and said, "Thank you for letting it end this way, Vennie."

Venganza nodded but didn't reply. The conversation was over.

MACNEICE LIFTED CHANEL off the stand and carried her over his shoulder. As he approached the door, Venganza was making final adjustments to the three small brass V's on the floor. They formed a precise equilateral triangle, roughly ten feet between the points. At its centre was the stool.

MacNeice sat Chanel on the toilet and, as instructed, covered her forehead with a cold, wet face cloth. When that didn't work, he smacked her cheeks several times. He was worried that whatever Venganza had given her had been too strong. He was tempted to go back and ask but realized that would be tempting fate, so he smacked her cheek again.

Seconds later, her right arm lifted from her thigh and waved drunkenly about before falling limp at her side. He smacked her again and her eyes flickered open. She looked at MacNeice but didn't see him. He said her name several times, until her forehead creased, her eyes opened, and she focused on him. "I'm Detective Superintendent MacNeice from Dundurn Homicide. You're safe, Ms. Bourget. Nod if you understand . . . you are safe."

She nodded once, but her head didn't look like it was tethered to her body; it fell sideways with a dull thud against the wall. Her eyes opened wide as she made an effort to focus on him. It took time for her to work out why he was sideways, but when she did, she pushed against the wall and sat upright.

MacNeice smiled. Her dress was neatly folded next to her shoes on the counter. "I'll help you get dressed. Then we'll leave. Can you stand up?"

She appeared to be deciphering the question. When she did, she shook her head.

"That's not a problem." MacNeice helped her with the dress and, with some difficulty, her shoes. He swung her around on the toilet so she was propped up between the sink and the corner of the wall. When he was certain she wouldn't fall, he went into the pantry to retrieve her purse.

Switching on the light, he was confronted by an arsenal of weapons and ammunition. He picked up the purse, turned off the light, and closed the door. Only then did he realize his breathing had returned to normal.

He returned to the bathroom, where Bourget was on her feet, hanging on to the sink. Though her legs threatened to buckle, she didn't fall.

"Put your arm around my shoulders. I've got your bag. We'll walk out together."

"Where is Venganza? What has happened to him?"

[66]

STANDING ON THE STOOP, CHANEL WAS BLINDED BY THE DAYLIGHT. In an attempt to shield her eyes, she lost her balance and fell against MacNeice, mumbling something in French. Once she was stable, MacNeice lifted her gently down to the stone walkway and together they staggered towards the laneway.

Though he'd seen the downed trees when it happened, he could now appreciate the brilliance of Venganza's battle plan. Both tanks were rendered useless, one crippled and smoking, and four men lay scattered and wounded — all without firing a shot. It was elegant and efficient. Sadler's attack had been doomed before it began.

Through the maze of trees and men and smoke, MacNeice could just make out the ambulances and fire trucks, but only because their lights were still flashing. Washburn's men were closest to the house. They were crouched down with their assault weapons trained on the door and windows, expecting that any second Venganza would burst through the door with guns blazing. Washburn wheeled about and told them to lower their weapons until MacNeice and the woman had passed.

MacNeice walked her a few steps more before realizing there was nowhere to go. The path was blocked and the hedge and field still booby-trapped. In the field were four EMS teams in fluorescent green jackets. MacNeice noticed that the medics, firefighters, tactical team, and city cops were all wearing gloves, and certainly not because it was cold. He asked Washburn, who smiled ruefully. "Someone found a small sign Venganza'd placed against the ditch on Valens. In big, bold letters it said: 'Warning. Poison ivy field. Enter at your own risk.'" Watching MacNeice's face while he processed the information, he added, "Seriously, sir, you can't make up this shit. Goddamn, it's humiliating."

"It could have been worse, Sergeant. Much worse."

"True." When he stopped smiling, Washburn asked, "You think this man is done?"

"I do. By his choice."

One of Washburn's men arrived with two folding lawn chairs from the garage. He set them behind the line of men with weapons, looking towards Valens Road.

Washburn nodded to MacNeice. "Ringside seats, sir."

Two tactical team members stood near the triage teams, holding rakes at the ready. "Turning weapons into plough-shares," MacNeice said quietly. And, while they were difficult to see through all the foliage, medics were portaging old-style canvas stretchers over and through the downed maples.

Four firefighters with chainsaws were getting into position to deal with the trunks, while others were dousing the burning tank with foam retardant. Luckily, or perhaps by design, the fire was contained to the engine compartment. MacNeice watched as the black column of smoke danced elegantly upward.

As one of the chainsaws came growling to life, the noise startled Chanel. Her body stiffened and she opened her eyes. MacNeice put a hand reassuringly on her forearm. In quick succession the other saws kicked in, and soon plumes of wood chips were flying from the branches. Once sawn off, they were thrown into the field, where they triggered more traps.

MacNeice turned to Washburn, shouting over the noise, "Where's my team?" Wash frowned and shook his head. He pointed in the direction of the road but shrugged to indicate that he really didn't know. That left MacNeice wondering if the entire First Division homicide team had been dismissed on the spot. He was fairly certain he'd be suspended, possibly even demoted to DI. But the funny thing was, he didn't care.

He glanced at the woman beside him. She was staring at the smoke column as it gradually changed from black to grey to white. Soon she'd be examined by medics, questioned extensively by the police, and later interviewed by French consular staff, but Chanel Bourget would likely be back in Paris within a week or two. He wondered what she was thinking. He assumed she was reflecting on her choices, her acumen as a curator, her brief appearance as the Virgin Mary with a dead soldier Jesus on her lap.

MACNEICE LOOKED AT his watch. Twenty-three minutes until the end of Venganza's hour. He was concerned about what was going to happen. While he thought he could take Venganza at his word, the man was a serial killer. Who in his right mind trusts a serial killer?

One by one the chainsaws fell silent. The tree canopies and trunks had been reduced to firewood in a minefield. A three-foot path had been cleared from where he sat to the road, where a large and ever-changing cast of uniforms stood milling about.

MacNeice stood up to get a better view, and that's when he saw them. Vertesi was the first to wave. MacNeice waved back and looked for Aziz. Swetsky came into view, pulling Williams, Aziz, and Maracle to the front of the cluster so MacNeice could see them all standing side by side. Swetsky made a fist, pounded his left chest, and pointed at MacNeice. Aziz had her hands in front of her mouth; she looked like she might be praying. MacNeice nodded slowly, hoping she'd know he was nodding at her.

Minutes later, Sadler, Wallace, and a black-clad entourage walked in front of them. Sadler still had his headset on and was communicating to someone, but it wasn't Washburn, who was silent, his attention remained on the farmhouse. Wallace led the way, his hands driven deep into his pockets. Chin down, he was focused on the path. He looked grim.

As they approached, MacNeice noticed that both men were determined to avoid eye contact with him. He stepped out of their way and looked beyond them to find the homicide team. With the mass of black uniforms blocking his view, the only face he could identify now was Swetsky's.

Without warning, Sadler turned on MacNeice. "You were

out to sabotage my operation from the start. Are you happy with what you've done?" He gestured vaguely to the men in the infield but he was looking at the smashed tanks. He pushed a clenched fist hard into MacNeice's chest. "You're lucky I don't —"

MacNeice quickly stepped back from the fist and, planting his left foot, pitched his body forward, landing a hard right to Sadler's jaw. It sent the lieutenant's black cap and headset flying into the brush. The furious Sadler lunged for MacNeice. Members of the tactical team grappled with their commanding officer to hold him back.

Wallace screamed, "Stand down! Christ almighty, Sadler, if MacNeice hadn't gone in there, your whole team might have ended up like those men over there" — he pointed in Baker's direction — "torn up for good." His face was purple with rage. Then he lowered his voice, aware of the many eyes watching him, and pointed at Sadler and MacNeice. "Aw, fuck it. You're both up on charges."

Around them, the tactical team exchanged glances but remained silent. MacNeice's hand throbbed with pain, but he was breathing normally. Washburn broke the uncomfortable silence to say there were six minutes left before they entered the farmhouse.

Behind them, Baker and two of the wounded were being carried out to the ambulances. The one with the injured arm walked slowly behind them, wrapped tightly with bandages and accompanied by a medic to keep him from falling.

One of the medics came over to check on Chanel Bourget. He shone a flashlight in her eyes and asked her to follow his finger as he moved it from side to side. He took her blood pressure and heart rate before turning to MacNeice. "She seems okay, sir. It looks like she's coming off something, but whatever it is, it must've left her system. Her vitals are fine. If you want to have her checked out at Emerg, we'll take her."

"I do, but not now. Please stand by."

Everyone seemed to be looking at their watches. There was one minute to go, give or take a few seconds. Washburn made it clear that he'd give it a few more seconds after that before going inside.

Sadler and Wallace and several members of the tactical team made their way towards Washburn's men, with Swetsky and the homicide team close behind. MacNeice suddenly realized how vulnerable they all were, walking in single file towards the farmhouse. Venganza could easily wipe out the whole lot.

Wallace's face was still flushed. He glanced briefly at MacNeice and Chanel before turning his attention to Washburn. With his team behind him, Sadler stood angrily at the side of the house as Washburn and his men approached the door. On the hour — plus thirty seconds, as a margin of error — the screen door was propped open with a sandbag. One by one they filed through and were swallowed by the darkness inside.

No one outside said a word. MacNeice was dreading the sound of heavy gunfire, fearful that a devastating explosion would end it all. He wanted to believe that Vennie could be trusted, but still . . .

FIVE MINUTES FELT like an hour before Washburn's large frame filled the doorway. "It's over, sir. Best you see for yourselves, though." He stepped aside as his men came out and walked back towards the tank to rack their weapons. No one said anything about what they'd seen, but several of them looked ashen.

Turning to MacNeice and the homicide team, Sadler said, "Give us time to secure the site, MacNeice. Stand down for now."

MacNeice wasn't surprised, but before he could respond, Wallace spun around on Sadler. "Absolutely not, Lieutenant. MacNeice and his team will enter with me. You and your team will enter once we've exited the building."

As Wallace passed Washburn at the door, the sergeant's eyes opened wide. Under his breath he whispered to MacNeice, "That's gotta sting — that and the haymaker you landed on his chin." Before they moved on, he looked at the homicide team. "Brace yourselves, folks. It ain't pretty."

[67]

EVEN WITH THE SOUNDS OF FOOTSTEPS, RUSTLING CLOTHES, AND heaving breathing, the farmhouse felt eerily quiet and empty. MacNeice and his team walked solemnly and hesitantly forward, knowing that whatever they were about to see, they wouldn't soon forget it.

On they went through the kitchen, passing the open pantry that contained more firepower than what came with the tanks, until they stepped into a large room. Wallace froze in his tracks and was bumped by Vertesi, who in turn was bumped by Maracle. "Sorry" rippled comically down the line. Wallace chose to step aside rather than continue. Aziz, who was directly behind MacNeice, also hesitated.

In the dimly lit room, a light stand appeared to be positioned on a dark mirror. As he approached, MacNeice realized the mirror was a large and creeping pool of blood. A red light was blinking on the back of a video camera mounted on the tripod. It was positioned at one corner of the triangle. The stool MacNeice had been sitting on earlier was flipped on its side, its legs lying in the blood. High above and rotating lazily were the remains of Venganza.

He was naked but for his boxer shorts that were drenched with blood and gore. Above the waistband, Venganza had made a large incision that opened his abdomen. His entrails spilled out and down from a sagging flap of flesh that ran from hipbone to hipbone. His hands were locked on the handle of the sword driven deep into his stomach. Above, his head was forced violently to the side by a noose. His face was deep purple, in sharp contrast to his white teeth, which were bared in a grotesque open-mouthed grin.

Vennie had planned it so well that the viewer had to look up, just as Christ looked up to heaven. The rope was tethered to a tie beam supporting the roof; its length — three feet or so — was so short that Venganza could easily have saved himself if he'd wanted to.

MacNeice could hear the others gasping and swearing. He took a deep breath and turned to look for Aziz. She was standing directly behind him, horrified. He touched her arm and said softly, "Go. I'll be right there."

"No. I'm staying with you."

Williams walked over to the camera, carefully avoiding the blood around the legs of the tripod. He rewound the footage. Turning to MacNeice and Wallace, he said, "Sirs, you should watch this."

Wallace had been looking across the room at Wozinsky's corpse. He glanced at Williams and shook his head. "I'm okay, son. I've seen enough." He cleared his throat, turned, and left the room.

MacNeice and Aziz, Maracle, Vertesi, and Swetsky stood behind the camera as Williams pressed Play.

[EPILOGUE]

NO ONE IN THAT ROOM EVER SPOKE ABOUT THE VIDEO, TO EACH other or to anyone else. As with the generations of veterans unable to talk about their combat experiences, it would remain unspeakable. But occasionally, MacNeice suspected, just as it was for him, that small blinking red light would return to terrify them while they slept.

The video was entered as evidence, and, for all MacNeice knew, it would never be seen again. It was stored in the vault several floors below Homicide, where it shared a shelf with the portfolio of exhibition prints, police photographs, forensic and pathology reports, and the memory stick Venganza had entrusted to MacNeice.

Two weeks after they left the farmhouse, the homicide team was called before Deputy Chief Wallace and the head of the Police Union. Swetsky, Vertesi, Aziz, Williams, and Maracle were given official reprimands and three-day suspensions for insubordination. Considering the nature of the insubordination, Wallace said, it deserved to be longer, but doing so would greatly diminish the department's readiness.

MacNeice was also reprimanded — for disobeying an order and for striking a fellow officer. His suspension was for a month. Upon his return, he was ordered to attend bimonthly sessions with Dr. Sumner.

With his suspension papers in hand, MacNeice returned to Division and the cubicle, where the only person waiting for him was Aziz. Ryan looked like an abandoned puppy, dreading perhaps that at any moment someone would walk in and tell him his services were no longer needed.

As they left the building together, Aziz said, "What now, Mac?"

"Now . . . Well, it's a beautiful midweek morning with very little traffic. I'm going up to Kate's hill, and I'd welcome your company."

"Are you sure you don't want to be alone?"

"I'm sure. I want you to join me. There's country apple crumble and ice cream in it for you."

"Am I that easy, Detective, to be wooed by sweets like a little girl?"

"You're my hero, Aziz. I consider you one of the finest, most intelligent, most compassionate women I've ever met — but you do have a serious sweet tooth."

"Tricky syntax, that. I'll assume its most flattering interpretation."

"Every word is true."

As they were driving west on King Street, Aziz asked, "What will you do for your suspension month, Mac?"

Charles Mingus's languid and sensual "Goodbye Pork Pie Hat" played through the speakers. He let the main phrase slide by before answering. "I'm thinking about going to Paris."

"Where you met Kate."

"Yes, but that's not why. I need to wander streets both familiar and unknown. I want to stay in jazz clubs till late at night and not think about murder all day. I want to sip hot chocolate in paper espresso cups, walk along the Seine, watch the change of light. I want to breathe foreign air. And I want to see Chanel Bourget's gallery."

"Sounds lovely, except for that last bit."

"Not to worry; I won't let it take over. I just have this nagging feeling that the images Venganza sent her to secure his exhibition are still there."

"Did she see *La Pietà*?"

"Yes, I showed her earlier this morning. She wept but said nothing. That was an hour before someone from the French consulate arrived to take her to the airport."

"Someday I'd like to see Paris."

"Well, here we are heading north to visit a hill. Paris isn't that much farther." He glanced over at her as she turned sideways in her seat. "And I'm going to be there for a month."

"You're teasing me."

"No, Fiza, I don't think I am."

[ACKNOWLEDGEMENTS]

FIRST OF ALL, I want to thank Shirley Blumberg Thornley, my partner for the last thirty years. She is my first reader and has known MacNeice from the beginning. I am deeply grateful to Scott Griffin for believing in these novels, and for his unwavering commitment to storytelling and poetry. Thank you, Krystyne Griffin, for believing in MacNeice, and me. Thank you, Sarah MacLachlan, president and publisher of House of Anansi, for recognizing the potential of these books and putting the firm's resources behind them.

I especially want to acknowledge my editor, Douglas Richmond, for his wisdom, support, and patience during the creation of this novel. I also extend my gratitude to copy editor Gillian Watts, for her contribution to *Vantage Point*. I congratulate Anansi's designer, Alysia Shewchuk,

for bringing consistency to the covers of all four books. I'm grateful to managing editor Maria Golikova and senior publicist Cindy Ma for their support and enthusiasm.

I am fortunate on this journey to be represented by Bruce Westwood, Chris Casuccio, and Michael Levine of Westwood Creative Artists — champions from the start.

Some subjects are never done, while others are left undone. I have long been fascinated by the subject of post-traumatic stress syndrome, especially as it applies to returning warriors or to the police and first responders on our streets. While *Vantage Point* is a work of fiction, PTSD is not. I am indebted to psychiatrist Dr. Dody Bienenstock for her reality check of the manuscript. Thank you to Drs. John Bienenstock, Gerry O'Leary, and Rae Lake for taking my many and likely strange questions seriously. Thank you to Roberto Occhipinti and Steve Wilson for sharing my enthusiasm for the music that we, and MacNeice, listen to. Thank you, John Michaluk, for keeping me in touch with the North End of our youth — you have the heart of a cat and the constitution of a bull. Thank you, Malcolm "Lew" Lewis, for taking my portrait

I am grateful for the support and understanding of our family — Marsh and Andrea, Daniella and Lucas, Ian and Tyler, and Sophia, Charles, and Kathryn — and Murphy.

© 2013 Marcia Leeder

Murphy the Wonder Dog

SCOTT THORNLEY grew up in Hamilton, Ontario, which inspired his fictional Dundurn. He is the author of four novels in the critically acclaimed MacNeice Mysteries series: *Erasing Memory*, *The Ambitious City*, *Raw Bone*, and *Vantage Point*. He was appointed to the Royal Canadian Academy of the Arts in 1990. In 2018, he was named a Member of the Order of Canada. Thornley divides his time between Toronto and the southwest of France.